THE RIGHTEOUS

&

THE REST

THE RIGHTEOUS

&

THE REST

A Tall Tale of The Weird West

by

Keith Edwards

SIGIL PRESS

Copyright © Keith Edward Kisser 2025
All Rights Reserved.

This is a work of fiction. Names, characters, places, and incidents either are the product of the author's imagination or are used fictitiously, and any resemblance to actual persons living or dead, business establishments, events, or locals is purely coincidental. No part of this publication may be reproduced in any form, converted to any other medium, or used in the training of Language Learning Models without the permission of the author. No Artificial Intelligence or algorithmically generated material was used in the production of this work.

Cover art by Tithi Luadthong/Grandfailure

ISBN: 979-8276825441

Fiction—Historical Fiction
Fiction—Westerns Stories, American
Fiction—Horror Tales, American

SIGIL PRESS | Poteet, TX

For Ed and Ben
&
For Snake Eyes
See you in dreams, old friend

Contents

1.	Silver Linings	3
2.	Seeing The Elephant	17
3.	The Hour Of Need	36
4.	As The Crow Fly	49
5.	A Solomon Of Sorts	64
6.	It Means "White Flower"	83
7.	Unmarked Graves	99
8.	Moonshine & Magnolias	118
9.	The Bells Of San Catrina	142
10.	Southern Volunteers	160
11.	A Dollop Of Thunder	178
12.	Down To The River	197
13.	A Refuge For Scoundrels	216
14.	The Blue Ribbon	231
15.	The Firefly Path	246
16.	The Last Hootenanny	260
17.	Tell Old Pharaoh	273
18.	Where All Roads Lead	293

THE RIGHTEOUS
&
THE REST

1
Silver Linings

Jim Hawkins had been lulled by the gentle rocking of the train car as it ambled down the track, through the night, and into the morning, until the train's last lurch into the station nudged him awake. He sat up. And in his dream-dazed state, Jim looked out the window and saw a vast blueness of sky punctured by a blaring May sun over an ocean of prairie grass. And not much else.

"Where am I?" he said, more to himself than anyone else.

In answer, the Pullman Porter in his tidy blue uniform of the Atlantic and Pacific Railroad Company called, "Vinita! Last call for Vinita!"

Jim stood and wobbled to the front of the car. In short order he found his legs, the bottom step onto the platform, and his carpetbag sitting on the deck. The train hissed and exhaled a great plume of steam, then chugged its way down the track and out of sight.

He looked around. There was a small clapboard shack beside the platform that served as a station house, with a large moonfaced clock on the wall and that was about it. The town of Vinita, Oklahoma was a smudge of indistinct civilization across a vast field of sun-baked grass.

Jim checked his pocket watch against the clock. He was an hour slow. Or maybe the clock was fast? Time had always been a vexing concept for Jim, but half-asleep in the middle of nowhere, it took on a metaphysical quality that was near inscrutable. How did one go about determining the correct time? It had been evening when he had boarded the train Back East. Of that he was certain because the enormous clock at Grand Central Station and his watch had been within a second's agreement of one another. Assuming this state had persisted during the trip, why now was the clock in Vinita off by an hour?

The instructor of his science course at the University had discussed this matter at great length, and Jim and his fellow students had debated long into the night the proper mechanism for determining time's acuity. They devised at least five methods of divining the true and correct hour, all of which proved meaningless when they all overslept, and arrived late to class the following morning.

As Jim stood on the station platform, trying to sort out time and space, he heard a familiar voice shout from a great distance, "James! James Galahad Hawkins!"

Jim looked up to find his brothers Edmond and Travis trudging through the tall grass to meet him.

Travis was the oldest. Tall and broad-shouldered, with his dark hair down to his shoulders and the first wrinkles of thirty crimping his eyes into a soft wink of oncoming middle age. He wore the fanciest boots Jim had ever seen. They were green and black snakeskin, with silver spurs and toes. Save the boots, Travis was the spitting image of their Pa from the old tintype that sat on the mantle back home, the one that Jim had looked at so many times, studying his mother and father on their wedding day, looking for some sign of things to come.

Edmond was the middle son, and a bit rounder, looking more like their mother with his perpetual baby cheeks, even if his roundness was flattened out by the dark preacher's suit he wore these days.

Travis climbed onto the platform, ignoring the steps. Edmond trudged up the steps one at a time. Both arrived at Jim's side at the same moment.

"Jim, good to see ya," Travis clapped him on the back and shook his hand. "You look good. You put on some weight?"

Jim looked down at his loose waistcoat and skinny frame. It took him a moment to realize his brother was joking, but it always had taken him a moment.

"How was your trip?" Edmond asked. The sour look on his face suggested he wasn't so much concerned with Jim's answer, as he was impatient to get on to the reason for their impromptu reunion.

"It was fine. I came quick as I could. Soon as I got the telegram, I went straight to my room and packed a bag."

The telegram was a shock. Jim had read it over and over again on the train ride:

LIZZY HAS GONE.
MEET IN VINITA POST HASTE.
—Father
Texarkana, US

What did it mean? A thousand notions crowded for attention in Jim's mind, and he'd run through every conceivable and inconceivable scenario before the train had even reached Baltimore.

"What's it all about?" Jim asked.

He looked from one brother to the next. Travis avoided making eye contact. Which was when Jim knew it was serious. It fell to Edmond to make the necessary explanations, as usual.

"Lizzy has gone."

"That much I'd gathered from the telegram. But where to? With whom? And when?"

"Our dear sister's ultimate fate is as yet undetermined at this time, but the wherefores and with whom, well that is the conundrum."

"Edmond ol' boy, you're making even less sense now that you've become a preaching man," Jim smiled, trying to play it off. "Leave the fancy diction to King James and speak plain to your dim little brother, would ya?"

"I see our father's money has been ill-spent in educating you, James, so to put it bluntly: our dear sister Elizabeth has been absconded with."

"Absconded with?" Jim looked at Edmond, then Travis, then back at Edmond.

Travis picked up Jim's carpet bag and handed it to him. "I'm afraid so." He stalked off into the grass, cutting a rut, into which Edmond nudged Jim.

"Seems she was getting a bit friendly with one of the hands Father hired to mind the cattle in your absence, and well, he got the wrong idea about our sister's virtue," Travis said.

"I have told the girl a hundred times that her cheerfulness would one day be mistaken for something far more nefarious," said Edmond.

"I'm going to ignore that little slight, implying that this turn of events is somehow my fault for not being there," Jim said. "Instead I'd like to focus on the more pertinent details. Who is this nabob and where do we find him?"

"He goes by the name Francis Shonka," said Edmond. "Rumor has it he is from Osage territory. Who knows what his true Christian name is, if he even has one. He stole an Appaloosa that he had been breaking for Father and abducted Lizzy sometime before dawn on Monday."

Jim counted on his fingers. "That gives him a two day head start, assuming it's still Wednesday… How will we even know where to begin searching for them?"

"They were seen heading into Osage Territory this morning," Travis said. "An acquaintance of mine saw them enter the Res, and as of his last telegram, hasn't seen them leave. So that's where we're headed first. Any questions?"

"Only a million. Not to question the veracity of one of your fellow cardsharps, but how reliable is this information? And how are we to get to Indian—"

Jim's question was cut short, or rather, answered itself as they exited the field onto a dirt road that led to a small two-story house. On the street stood three horses, tied to a post and kitted out for the range.

"—Territory. Oh. I'm not quite dressed for it."

"I wasn't going to comment on your duds there, but now that you mention it," Travis looked him up and down. "You do look quite spiffing."

Since starting college the previous autumn, Jim had exchanged the drab brown and blue farm hand look for a more dapper city attire that was, if not fashionable, at least more in line with what the other students were wearing. This included a three-piece suit with a cutaway sack coat. His watch chain was tucked into his waistcoat pocket and he wore a bowler perched atop his head. Not exactly horse riding attire.

Travis took a bedroll from one of the horses and thrust it into Jim's arms. Tucked inside was one of his old shirts, a pair of denim trousers, and Jim's old boots tied up with twine.

"Figured you'd turn dandy on us," Travis grinned.

"What exactly will be my role in this expedition?" Jim asked.

"We shall explain all over a good luncheon," Edmond clapped his hands as he stomped up the steps.

The Boarding house was a stately piece of civilization, one Jim had not expected to find out here on the edge of Indian Territory. There were hooks for coats and hats, which Travis and Edmond availed themselves of, as did James. An antique mirror hung over a vase of dried flowers and an Oriental rug, worn a bit bare in the middle, padded the floor. A cut-glass chandelier hung in the foyer, where it cast a dazzle of sparks around the room, and gave the parlor a homely feel.

The proprietor was one Theresa Cassop, a matronly woman in a starched collar and ankle-length dress who appeared at the door to the parlor and welcomed them with a smile.

"Ah, there are the Misters Hawkins," she beamed. "And I take it this is your wayward younger brother?"

"James, ma'am," Jim nodded.

"Welcome, James. Luncheon is already on the table, help yourselves."

They hung their hats on hooks and Jim set the bedroll Travis gave him on the floor beneath his hat.

The three brothers made their way through the parlor, past the crushed velvet settee, to find a wide oaken table in the dining room, on which was laid out the sort of lunch Jim had only ever seen before on holidays. There was ham, rolls, potatoes, corn on the cob, plus a selection of jellies, mint, fruit, and otherwise.

Seeing as how all he'd had to eat since the night before was a cold sandwich from a street vendor on the way to the station, Jim was famished. He'd already piled a mess of food onto his plate before he even noticed there were two other guests.

"Afternoon," said a sprightly older gentleman with a bushy mustache. He was introduced to Jim as Judge Rogers.

"Afternoon, your honor, Sir." Jim nodded and heaped another slice of ham onto his plate.

Opposite sat a fussy little man with thick spectacles named Abbott. He nodded and smiled at the brothers, "Travis, Edmond, well met my boys! And this must be your brother, James. I have heard tell of you, son, and I must say, your brother's effusive descriptions do you no compliment."

"Uh, thank you, Mr. Abott."

Travis and Edmond took their seats. Edmond bowed his head and muttered Grace. Everyone paused to listen. Jim held his plate mid-air, waiting for his brother to finish. Then they all ate heartily.

"So, I take it to you boys are headed out to Indian Country then?" asked Judge Rogers.

"Yes'r," said Travis between bites of ham. "Right after this fine luncheon is through, we'll be saddlin' up. I reckon we can make it to the edge of Indian Territory by nightfall."

"Oh. We're leaving that soon?" Jim asked.

"Of course," Edmond dabbed at his chin with a crisp white cloth napkin. "Lizzy waits to be rescued. Do you not think we should oblige her?"

Mr. Abbott nodded solemnly.

"That poor dear," Mrs. Cassop shook her head as she drifted in from the kitchen with more biscuits.

"I mean, it's a travesty and all, but," Jim hesitated. He looked around the table. "Well, I've no knack with a firearm."

This was true. The few times their father had tried to teach him to shoot, he'd managed to spook every tin can put to a post, and miss the chickens in their roost by mere feathers' breadth.

"Are you turning yella on us, Jim boy?" Travis shot him a hard stare over the ham bone.

"No! I want to help. But shouldn't one of us stay behind, to coordinate with the appropriate law enforcement? I could go to Kansas City and hire a Pinkerton while you two proceed to the Res to observe the situation. Reconnoiter, I believe, is the term."

"God in Heaven and all his angels!" hissed Edmond. "A year in that Babylon of a college town and you have turned as yella as the daisies!"

"I have not turned any shade of yella!" Jim protested. "I know my own self and that I have not a lick of sense riding a horse to no Res, nor shooting any person with a gun. Even if said blaggard deserves it, as you say."

"Ah, here we go, the college man, come to tell us, yokels, what's what," Travis huffed.

"Judge Rogers, would you have a word with my brothers?" Jim asked. "Do you not think it a wise course of action to include the law in this venture?"

"Well, there's the law and there's the Law, ain't there?" Judge

Rogers offered a wry smile from beneath his bushy mustache. "Your brothers have filled me in on the particulars of the situation, and I don't mind saying, their course of action strikes me as not just legally sound but morally so as well. Family is what matters, son. Besides, this is Indian Territory we're talking about and well sir, the laws of man are a bit fuzzy where those pesky natives are concerned. And what you young men might find it in your necessity to do while in said nebulous territory, well that's between you and God Almighty."

"Amen to that," Edmond interjected.

"Well ain't this the height of civilized discourse," Jim stared at the meat rendered on his plate in stark daylight from the bay window. "Here we are eating lunch while talking about hunting a man down like some rogue steer."

"Where, dear James, is your sense of honor?" said Travis.

"He has turned yella at that," Edmond grumbled.

"Tell me, Padre Ed, what business a preacher such as yourself has on this venture? Don't think I didn't notice that old hunting rifle, tucked under your saddle."

Edmond had carried the infernal gun around with him everywhere from the time he was fourteen until three years ago, when he had decided to take up the Book and become a man of the cloth. He'd made a show of handing that rifle to their father and asking that it be put away in the case in his office. That it had made an appearance here and now, in these circumstances told Jim right away that the matter was something serious.

"The Lord is my shepherd, and I shall not want," Edmond said. "Not for the wisdom of the Good Book, nor for the necessary tools to carry out His justice."

"Here here!" Mr. Abbott tapped his glass with his fork.

"Would you be available to help, then, Mr. Abbott?" Jim asked. "To avail us of your experience in these matters of blood and cunning?"

"I would, dear boy, if not for certain issues of ill health, mount one of those fine ponies outside and lead the charge. But alas, I have a condition," he patted his stomach gingerly. "You understand."

"Oh, I understand." Jim looked at the Judge, who was pushing seventy if he was a day.

As if reading his thoughts, the Judge said, "I've spoken in confidence with Travis on this matter. Your course of action is clear."

"Seems it is." Jim looked down at his plate to find that he'd suddenly lost his appetite.

After the plates were cleared away, Jim retired to the room Travis and Edmond had shared the night before to change his clothes for the road. He laid out the bedroll Travis had given him and unfolded a rumpled blue shirt. When he put on the denim trousers, he found a silver dollar in his left pocket. He'd forgotten all about it the last time he wore those trousers and remembered that day.

Jim had spent the morning mending a fence with Old Luke. Jim would wrap the barbed wire tight around the post while the farmhand nailed the wire taught. They were finishing one last post before breaking for lunch when Lizzy came to fetch him. She was dressed in a summer frock, her dark hair tied up in a bow, ready for an outing.

"I'm heading into town to fetch some supplies. Pa said for you to hitch up the surrey."

"Can't you hitch it yourself?" Jim said.

"Sure. But Pa said for you to come with."

Jim grunted and pulled the barbed wire taught. "Kinda in the middle of something here."

"Shoot, ain't nothin' I can't handle," Old Luke patted Jim on the shoulder and took over. "Go on."

So Jim hitched the surrey and rode into town with Lizzy, talking about nothing in particular. He wandered around after her in the general store as she selected some cotton fabric, flour, and a few sundries. Then he loaded the whole mess into the surrey. The change was an even silver dollar.

"Here," Lizzy handed Jim the coin. "You'll need this."

"Pa's already set me up. I don't need your charity," Jim handed it back.

"It's not charity, you mule. Buy one of those fancy hats the college boys are wearing. I won't have my little brother lack for fashion."

Lizzy put the coin in his hand and folded his fingers around it. Then she hugged him tight. Jim had felt embarrassed, as he couldn't remember her hugging him like that since he was small.

"What's that for?"

"Told you. It's for a hat."

There came a knock at the door, pulling Jim out of his reverie. Travis opened it and stuck his head in.

"We're all saddled up and ready to go." He nodded to the coin in Jim's hand. "Where'd you get that?"

"Lizzy gave it to me. Must've left it in my pocket, last time I wore these trousers."

"So what you're saying is, it's not your money then?"

"Is now," Jim pocketed the coin.

Travis grinned. "Come on. Let's go save her."

Jim nodded and headed for the door. Travis wrapped an arm around his shoulder as they headed out.

Jim joined his brothers outside and checked the saddle, and their supplies. He once again noted the old rifle tucked under Edmond's saddle. He didn't ask, not then anyway, if the rifle's presence had some larger theological implications, but he would think on it the whole way to Osage Territory.

Mrs. Cassop, Mr. Abbott, and Judge Rogers joined them on the porch to say farewell.

Mrs. Cassop handed Edmond a pack of rolls, wrapped in a kitchen cloth and said, "Bring her back by here, if you can."

"We will," said Edmond. "And thank you all for everything."

Edmond and Travis mounted their horses. As Jim climbed onto his horse, Judge Rogers nodded to get his attention.

"I know you'll do what's right when the time comes, James."

Jim nodded in farewell. He reared his horse and headed out after his brothers.

They rode on in companionable silence, until the sun set, painting the landscape in purples and blues. By the time they reached the Eastern border of Indian Territory, evening had fallen. Travis found a spot beside a brook with a brace of elm trees and decided this was as good a place as any to camp for the night.

"I do not see why we cannot continue on," Edmond said. "It is but another hour to Bon-Ton."

"Don't want to be caught In Territory after dark," Travis said.

"More like you are looking for an excuse to sleep on the spur," Edmond sulked.

"You still spooked sleeping out under the night?" asked Jim.

"I do not care to have all those stars looking down upon me."

"You gonna get the night terrors again?" said Travis.

He and Jim both laughed.

"I was twelve! And Pa put too much cayenne in the beans."

It didn't take long for Jim to recall how to tend a campfire and set up camp. He'd done it enough with Travis, Edmond, and their Pa, for as long as he could remember that the skill came back to him at once. More so: he realized he'd been setting camp in his room at college for a year without consciously realizing it.

"I would like to take this moment to appreciate the event," aid Jim. "Even if it is under dire circumstances."

"What event is that?" asked Travis.

"Us. The three Hawkins brothers, together again, camping under the sheltering sky."

Neither Travis nor Edmond was much impressed by this.

Another moment of silence stretched over the crackling campfire between them. Jim decided on another tack.

"So, Travis, Ma's last letter said something about you courting Meredith Henderson, and that you were making headway with her father, clerking at his law firm."

"Yeah, well, Ma is prone to exaggerating ain't she?" Travis spat into the fire. He avoided catching Jim's eye as he fished through his saddlebags in search of some other topic of discussion.

"Travis has once again taken the coward's route and run away from the oncoming hoof beats of responsibility and adulthood," Edmond said.

"That is a bald-faced lie!"

"So what happened?" Jim asked.

"Nothing happened." Travis found the biscuits Mrs. Cossop had given them. He broke one off and tossed one to Jim and another to Edmond. He chewed on his biscuit for a moment.

"Opportunities come and go," he said after a moment staring into the fire. "The coming is always more widely discussed than the going, which gives everyone the impression that the former is better than the latter. But sometimes, there's no escaping an ending."

"My," said Edmond, "that is a fancy way of saying you are a failure at making love to a girl!"

He and Jim laughed.

"Yeah, well, that's beside the point right at this moment, ain't it?" Travis said around a mouthful of biscuit.

"So where are we headed?" Jim asked. "I mean, after the Res. If they light out, how will we track them?"

"They'll be wanting to steer clear of civilized places, which means there's but one place for them to go, and that's into the Switch."

"Oh, now here we go again..." Edmond shook his head and bit into his biscuit.

"For a man of the cloth you sure do lack faith," Travis winked at his brother.

"It is a fairy story! The land beyond the border of all civilized countries, where the animals talk, and the wind roars, and everything is out to eat you. Hogswallop!"

"I don't know," said Jim. "Maybe there is something to it. You remember when I was nine and that hired man was digging a well? He found a giant's skull down in the mud. It had teeth as wide and sharp as a knife blade."

"Yeah, whatever happened to that old skull?" asked Travis.

"Father buried it again," said Edmond. "I know not where. And here you are, James, a supposedly educated young man, talking about giant's skulls!"

"Well, I have come to find out that there are such things, though they aren't the fabulous giants from the Switch."

"Oh, do tell," said Edmond.

"Back in college, we learned that there were these great lizard creatures that lived around these parts, long ago. Who knows what's out there?"

"I met a fella, been there," Travis said. "Told me all about it."

"There is nothing beyond the Res, save desert, and maybe a few of those Red Skins the Army has not yet smoked out," Edmond declared. "And that is all."

Travis leaned over the fire, shadows dancing on his face. Jim leaned in to listen.

"The Switch is real. Ain't quite as fanciful as the stories say. There's no Bigfoots, nor lost tribes of wandering Jewfolk, but there's danger to be had. The creatures what live there are all poisonous. And the folk that lives there, deadlier still. We best hope to find dear Lizzy on the Res, for I fear what fate might befall her, should her captor light out for that dreaded land."

"That sort of talk is likely to send us off hunting clouds when our sister's life is at stake." Edmond shook his head and laid back on his bedroll. "That will be enough of such talk. Goodnight to you both."

Travis and Jim settled in as well, exchanging pleasant goodnights around the fire. Still, Jim would lay awake until the coals were nothing but cinders, his mind engaged in a fierce wonder.

2
Seeing the Elephant

The Hawkins boys reached the Osage Reservation late the next afternoon. Jim wasn't sure exactly what he expected the Reservation to be, but it wasn't this. The first sign was an actual one, big and wooden, on the road into town and it read, *Welcome to Pawhuska*.

Beyond that, they found a tidy frontier town, with a packed dirt road lined with shops and people going about their business, heedless of the newcomers. Jim had heard tales of the Reservation life, of squalor, disease, and depredations beyond count. And while some of the buildings needed a lick of paint, the place looked like any other frontier town he'd visited. Judging by the number of well-fed horses out front of the dry goods store, it gave Texarkana a run for its money.

What marked Pawhuska as unique though was that most everyone was Indian, and not all were Osage either. There were Cherokee, Choctaw, Chickasaw, Creek, and Seminole—all the civilized tribes—all going about their business. This was expected of course, as it was an Indian town, on a Reservation. But seeing tall, dark-skinned men in bowler hats and native women in dresses with shawls gave Jim a sight. They had every other vestige of the sort of civilized culture he knew from Back East. Jim wasn't the only one flabbergasted.

Travis tipped his hat further back on his head. "Well, knock me down with a feather."

Edmond scoffed. "Were you expecting teepees and camp fires?"

"Naw," Travis scratched the three days of stubble. "Guess I don't know what I was expecting..."

They found the stable at the end of the street. After settling their horses into adjacent stalls, the brothers headed out.

"Right," Travis surveyed the street. His face lit up with a smile as he saw the painted sign advertising a saloon named *Hattie's Place*. "I'm off to, what was it, Jim? Reconnoiter?"

He slapped Jim on the shoulder and headed straight for the saloon.

"What are you doing, Travis? How is this helping Lizzy?" Edmond shouted down the street after him. He sighed. "Jim, never follow that man's advice."

"I said as much back in Vinita."

Edmond gave him a stern look. "Jim, there are times in a man's life when he must do what must be done."

Jim looked him square in the eye. "Edmond, there are times when you are downright incomprehensible."

Edmond waved away his concern. "I am off to the local mission. I have contacts there that may help us in our search."

"Now that makes about as much sense as having a drink at the saloon!"

Edmond stalked over to him and laid a hand on his brother's shoulder. "There is help, even in the humblest of places. Now be a good lad and see to the supplies and find us suitable lodgings for tonight." And with that, Edmond stalked off.

"Okay, but how?" Jim stood there on the dusty boards in front of the shops, trying to look like he knew what he was doing.

He was so bad at it, that after only two minutes, the Sheriff walked up to him.

"Hawé," he said, and touched the brim of his hat. He wore a brown suit, and an embroidered vest, lined with yellow and purple designs. A silver-plated six-shooter hung on his hip and a tin star on his lapel. "Sheriff John Two Wolves. You here to see the elephant?"

Jim looked around as if a circus was about to march down the street. He saw nothing but folk going about their business. "Beg pardon?"

"Are you out and about, looking to see the world?" the Sheriff clarified. "If so, it'll cost you."

"Uh. No. I mean, hello, Mr., I mean, Sheriff Two Wolves, Sir." Jim took a breath. "My name is James Hawkins and my brothers and I are looking for someone."

Sheriff Two Wolves looked around. "Brothers?"

"Yes'r, they... took off. I mean, went to take in the scenery. I mean... they're reconnoitering."

Sheriff Two Wolves chuckled. "You look a bit worse for the wear, son. How about a cup of tea?"

"Thank you, much obliged."

Sheriff John Two Wolves led Jim down the street, to a small inn, called Mary's Place. Aunt Mary was a jolly woman who chatted with the Sheriff in their native tongue. She seated them at a small table by the window. A few minutes later, she delivered a pot of tea and two cups, along with some molasses cookies. Soon Jim had ordered his thoughts enough to explain himself to the Sheriff.

"...Now I don't know all the particulars of the situation, but she has been taken from our family homestead. And well, you see, we're real anxious to find her and bring her home."

Jim sipped his tea.

Sheriff Two Wolves nodded. "I've not heard of this Shonka fella before, but we do get folk now and then passing through. Far as I know, no one's come by the last day or two with anyone fitting your sister's description. But I'll keep an eye out for them, and should I see anything, you'll be the first to know."

"Thank you, Sheriff Two Wolves, sir."

"Call me John."

"Yes sir."

"Now, let's get you and your brothers situated, shall we?"

Aunt Mary drifted in with a warm smile. Jim wasn't sure if she was John's real Aunt, or if that was a moniker. Everyone called her Ihcímį, which Jim supposed meant the same thing as Auntie. She had that way about her some women have; don't matter if you're Osage or Chinese, slave or free, they are willing and able to offer advice and the sort of support a young person might need, and are thus everyone's Auntie.

"This here is James Hawkins, Ihcímį. He's from Back East," Sheriff Two Wolves said.

"Oh is he now?" said Aunt Mary. "I had a pillow from there. You remember, Johnny? The one with the lace embroidered on it. Wonder where it got to?"

"Ihcímį, James here is in search of lodging, for him and his two brothers."

"I got a room free up. Only got two beds, but one's big enough to share."

"That'll be fine, Ma'am," said Jim.

Aunt Mary and Sheriff John Two Wolves took Jim up to see the room. It was a tidy little chamber, with a washbasin on the table, and two beds. The nightly rate wasn't too expensive, but neither was it cheap. Still, Jim accepted the room with a smile. He had no idea how many nights they would be here in Pawhuska, but at least for tonight, they would sleep in comfort.

"Rooms are nightly or weekly," Aunt Mary said. "Breakfast is at seven, Luncheon at noon, supper at five."

"Thank you, Ma'am this will do nicely."

"Oh call me Auntie, dear."

"Yes Ma'am."

"Ihcímį will see you settled. I'll make my goodbyes," Sheriff John Two Wolves shook Jim's hand. To Aunt Mary, he said in Osage, *"Don't fleece him too bad."*

"Oh you're no fun!" Aunt Mary swatted his shoulder.

John Two Wolves tipped his hat to Jim and left. Aunt Mary

lingered another minute and then left Jim sitting alone on the edge of the bed.

That night, Jim woke to the sound of thunder rumbling in the distance. He climbed form bed and looked out the window. Below and saw a familiar figure running down the moonlit street.

"Lizzy..." Jim whispered her name. She looked over her shoulder as if she could hear him, then broke into a run.

Jim climbing from bed and ran down the steps, into the street. He saw but a single pair of footprints in the dirt and followed them out of the reservation and into the desert. He climbed up a steep bluff. At the top, he found a ring of gnarled, old trees, their bare limbs scratching at the darkening sky. In the middle of the ring stood a woman with her back to him. Above, clouds billowed. Thunder and lightning rolled in. The flashes of lightning illuminated something in the cloud bank: a giant bird, its massive wings unfurling, crackling lightning as it swooped out of the sky. Jim approached the woman who was at the edge of the bluff. Her long dark hair streamed behind her. She wore a gray ragged dress, torn to shreds.

"Lizzy, it's me!"

When Lizzy turned around, Jim found that her face was a skull stripped of flesh, but her eyes remained.

"Do not follow!"

Jim sat up in bed.

He was still dream-drunk for a moment, but soon it all came back to him. This room, this town, and everything else. It was morning and the sunlight streamed through the curtains. The other bed was empty and had not been slept in all night.

When Jim came down to breakfast he found Sheriff John Two Wolves waiting for him at the dining table with a cup of black coffee. Most of the other lodgers had already eaten but there was still a plate of cold eggs and biscuits.

"Morning, Mr. Hawkins," The Sheriff sipped his coffee.

"Morning Sheriff. Do you take all your breakfasts here, or am I honored with your presence for another reason?"

The Sheriff smiled. "I did some checking. Seems a man by the name of Francis Shonka has been seen around town. Thought I'd help you with your search this morning."

"That's mighty kind of you, Sheriff, you have my thanks. And my brothers. Though alas, they are not here to give you it themselves."

"I noticed their absence but was not going to mention it."

"I suspect their reconnoitering took them further afield than they had anticipated. They will most likely drag their sorry carcasses back here shortly and spend most of the day abed, leaving me to procure our provisions on my own."

"Well I can help you with that as well. In fact, we might well be able to kill two birds, as they say. The dry goods store is the local hotbed of pertinent information. Everyone who comes into town ends up there, one way or the other."

"And don't worry about your two brothers," Aunt Mary drifted in from the kitchen to clear the table. "I'll see to them if they drop in."

"Much obliged, Aunt Mary," Jim grabbed a biscuit from the pile on the table, made a sandwich of it with some bacon, then followed the Sheriff into the morning.

The town of Pawhuska was already up and at it. There were no late sleepers on the Res, much to Jim's surprise. The Chinese Laundry was already doing a brisk boil of linens from the Mission, as attested to by the scrupulous woman in a dark habit who was loitering about watching the process. The chicken man was about, delivering a cart full of wooden cages, between the slats of which issued squawks and cockadoodles aplenty. The shops were open, and a small boy, barely older than Jim felt deep down, swept the sidewalk boards clean.

Since going away to college, he'd felt like a child playing dress-up in his father's clothes, and at any moment someone would find out. This trip into the Res and wherever it was bound to take him and his brothers, only enhanced that feeling ten-fold. The Sheriff and his Aunt were nice folk, but Jim suspected his luck wouldn't hold.

He was lost in thought, licking the bacon grease from his fingers when he heard someone calling out, "Hawkins! Telegram for James Hawkins!"

He turned to find a young Osage boy, half a minute older than him, wearing the uniform of the Western Union Telegraph Office. He was waving a telegram, searching the street for its owner.

"That'd be me," James said. He fished a penny out of his waistcoat and exchanged it for the telegram.

Jim opened the telegram and read it quickly:

> ACCEPT NO HELP FROM STRANGERS.
> BRING OUR LIZZY HOME.
> WALK THE RIGHTEOUS PATH.
> —Father
> Texarkana, US

"Good news, I hope?" the Sheriff asked.

"Hmm? Oh, more cryptic than good. But that's our father. He never was one for effusive praise. All my life, I can't recall more than ten words he ever said to us, and those were commandments to be followed."

John Two Wolves nodded. "Fathers can be like that. Do you and your brothers have any idea as to how long you will be in town?"

"I don't plan to overstay our welcome, Sheriff. As soon as we hear word of Lizzy's whereabouts, we'll be out of your hair."

"I didn't mean to imply that you weren't welcome, son. Only that we get more than our fair share of treasure hunters, bandits, and all manner of unsavory folk passing through, and I wouldn't want you to get caught up with them. You seem a respectable young man and I think you'll do right by your sister. It's other folk, I'm not so sure about. They might try to take advantage of a trio of brothers in need."

"I appreciate the advice, Sheriff, but my mother raised no fools. Then again, my absentee siblings are making a strong effort to prove me wrong. I swear they are real, and not figments of my imagination."

"Of that I am aware." The Sheriff said. "I met your brother Travis at the saloon last night."

"Ah," was all Jim could say.

"He was deep into a bout of reconnoitering, I believe is what you called it. Didn't cause any harm, so I left him to it."

"Travis does have a high estimation of his own abilities when it comes to both drinking and playing cards. But when the chips are down, he comes through."

Jim stepped around a pothole filled with mud. "But while we're on the subject. Travis seems to think this Francis Shonka fellow might light out for uncharted territory. Were this the case, would you be able to recommend a reputable tracker, someone familiar with points beyond who could lead us after our query?"

"Where exactly does your brother think this Shonka fella is headed?"

"Travis is under the impression he'll head into the switch to avoid capture."

The Sheriff nodded. "If he's as much a bandit as you say, he may disappear down some hole, never to be seen again."

Jim stopped short of a puddle. He diverted a step to the left and hustled to catch up to the Sheriff. "Which is why we're keen to find them here. If they are here."

They had turned a corner and were passing the stables. There they found a young woman with dark skin and long locks tied behind her left shoulder. She looked to be all business, dressed in leather jerkin and checking her saddle for the road. On her thigh she kept strapped a Colt Navy revolver with a pearl handle and an old cavalry saber on her saddle alongside a jug of liquor.

Sheriff Two Wolves nodded to the young woman. "Mercy. Lovely morning for it."

"Sheriff," she nodded back, combing the tangles out of the mane of her big gray stallion. The horse grumbled a bit and Jim felt like the animal was sizing him up.

"And who's the tenderfoot?" Mercy Nightingale smiled at Jim in a way that made Jim's stomach feel funny.

"This here is young James Hawkins," said the Sheriff. "He comes from Back East. He and his brothers are here on business."

"Mercy Nightingale," she swung one leg over her saddle.

"Ma'am," Jim squeaked. "Ahem. That's a fine quantity of liquor you're hauling. What's a lady like yourself need with all them spirits?"

Mercy smiled. "The spirits ain't in the bottle, James Hawkins, but that's what I feed 'em, should I come across any. And the reasons being are mine, and mine alone."

"I meant no offense, ma'am."

"None taken. And no man's called me ma'am before, certainly not twice," she said. "You keep charming like that, and you'll be in a heap of trouble. Nice to meet you, Young James Hawkins. Sheriff," she nodded once more and headed out at a steady trot.

Once she was gone, Jim said, "Who was that?"

"Mercy Nightingale is a tracker. One of the finest, this side of the Divide."

"Really? She knows the area around these parts, then?"

"She does indeed. Suspect she's heading out and about on some mission now. Usually leaves this time of the month." The Sheriff looked up at the morning sky, blue as could be, as if checking the time on some celestial clock, looking for a millennium hand made of clouds.

Jim followed his gaze for a moment. Then a thought occurred to him. "Do you think Ms. Nightingale would be back in time, should we need to hire a tracker?"

John Two Wolves shook his head. "I know you value your sister's life, but if this Shonka person does head into the Switch, I'd advise you against going after them. That Miss Nightingale has been there and back again is not a testament to her fortitude but to her mania. She is driven by a force you do not want to tangle with."

"I understand, Sheriff, But I—"

"Take my advice, Mr. Hawkins. You want nothing to do with Mercy Nightingale, lest you yearn for a short, interesting life." John clapped his hands. His face brightened with a smile. "So. To the dry goods store, shall we?"

The dry goods store was clearly the social center of the town. It was also quite a bit larger than the one they had back in Texarkana, with a few more amenities specific to the locals' needs. There wasn't much call for skinning and butchering deer back home, but they had a full-service butcher and tanner on the premises. Lucky for Jim he did have the Sheriff riding around in his back pocket, as the shelves were arranged in such a way that he had no idea what was supposed to be where, and how to find it.

John Two Wolves helped him navigate the nooks and crannies, loading his arms up with supplies. Jim wasn't sure what he would do with twenty pounds of venison jerky but John assured him, should they need to pursue their quarry out of town, it would become a welcome addition to their campfire.

"...We've got venison jerky, cartridges of 40 aught for the repeater, and I noticed you were short a skillet."

"Yes, but—"

"Right. They're in the back, I'll go get one." The Sheriff left Jim standing, arms full, in a corner, watching the patrons haggle with the clerk, or size up various goods on the shelves. He happened to turn around and nearly knocked over a slender young woman with dark hair, and a gently swelling belly.

"Oh, beg pardon, ma'am, I—" Jim's words caught in his throat as he saw the woman's narrow face and blue eyes. "Lizzy?"

"Jim!" His sister threw her arms around his neck. Jim dropped his gear with a clatter. She held him at arm's length and smiled. Jim nearly cried.

"Let me look at you. My you're skinny! They don't feed you in the school of yours?"

"Lizzy... I..." He looked her up and down. "You're..." Jim pointed at her belly.

"Oh. Right. I'm starting to show, I'm afraid. You see now why I had to run off, don't you?"

"Yes. I mean, no... but... how? I mean I know how but... where's the..?" Jim looked around, saw Lizzy glance to her right. Jim turned to find a tall dark-skinned fellow with long jet black hair down to the middle of his back. He was dressed neatly, in a tailored suit of blue with an embroidered vest and holding a hat with an eagle feather tucked in the band.

Lizzy said, "Jim, this is Francis. My Husband."

"..." Jim said.

"James, it's a pleasure," Francis offered a hand.

Jim stared at it.

"I've heard great things about you from Elizabeth."

"And I've heard nothing good about you at all," Jim scowled.

"Now, Jim, that's no way to speak to your new brother," Lizzy chided him. She smiled and swatted his lapel.

"That's alright, given the circumstances, I suspect you've heard a great many things about me," Francis did not smile but looked at Jim hard. Jim tried to look away but found the man's gaze magnetic. "I am not the villain you imagine me to be."

"Prove it," Jim demanded.

"Francis," Lizzy tugged on his arm and nodded. Jim looked away, feeling a little dizzy from the sway of his glare.

Jim looked where Lizzy had and saw the Sheriff approaching with a cast iron skillet.

Frances took Lizzy's hand and they headed for the door. Several customers turned to watch them go, but no one stopped them.

Sheriff John found Jim, still reeling a bit.

"Was that your sister?"

"Yes."

"And that was Francis Shonka?"

"Yes."

"Forget your sister then, and go home," he dropped the goods and walked away.

Jim scooped up the goods and threw a handful of paper money at the clerk as he ran into the street. He nearly collided with Edmond, but instead, dropped their supplies.

"Was that..?" Edmond said.

Jim grabbed the saddled bags and hastily stuffed their supplies inside, "Yes it was! Come on!"

Jim tossed the saddlebags with the ammunition and venison jerky over one shoulder, and handed the skillet and a bag of assorted odds and ends to Edmond. "Here, take this."

"This is no time for sundries, James!" Edmond shoved the bag back into Jim's arms.

They ran down the road after Lizzy and Francis, dodging mud puddles, people, and a stray dog, but no matter how fast the two brothers ran, their query kept ahead of them. They lost them altogether around a corner in the west end of town, near the stables.

"Where did they go?" Edmond demanded. "They were right here! Why did you not stop them?"

"What?" Jim dropped the bag of sundries. "And where have you been, Preacher, out all night? Why didn't you stop them?"

A thunder of hooves stopped their bickering.

Edmond turned in time to see the horse rushing headlong down the road. The beast was bereft of a saddle, with nothing but a blanket on which sat Francis with Lizzy clinging to him.

Edmond drew his bible from his jacket and held it aloft. "I command thee, stop in the name of the Lord!"

Francis did not stop or even slow the horse one step.

Jim threw himself at Edmond, toppling along with the rolly polly minister into the dusty street. The horse clipped Jim's shoulder but they were otherwise unharmed.

By the time the two brothers pulled themselves out of the dirt, Francis and Lizzy were at the end of the street, heading past the sign that said, *Welcome to Pawhuska*.

Edmond and Jim burst through the swinging saloon doors to find Travis seated at a table, staring down a pair of Queens.

"...This here is what they call a winning hand!" called an older gentleman in a white hat with an alligator skin band. He had a bushy white mustache, a terrible gleam in his eye, and a pile of chips nearly up to his chin.

"Dang it!" Travis threw his worthless hand on the table.

The rest of the players folded as well, though most kept their poker faces in place. Except for one, a sturdy woodsman draped in a bear hide, who stood and grumbled, "fils de pute!" as he wandered away from the table, leaving an empty chair in his wake.

"Adieu, Trapper Jean," said the gambler who'd laid down the pair of Queens, "Parting is such sweet sorrow."

"Travis! We found her! She's here!" Jim shouted, out of breath. Edmond ran up, two paces behind him, huffing like a steam locomotive.

"Ah there they are. Edmond, James. This is Diamond Joe. He's a good-for-nothing card sharp."

Diamond Joe laughed. "Awe, he's sore because that's the third hand in a row he's lost to me!"

"Third hand in a row?" Jim looked at Travis, and his minuscule pile of chips. "Is that all you have left?"

"Not if you float me a few dollars, Jim," Travis whispered. "I've got him where I want him. Few more hands, and we'll be set."

"Didn't you hear what I said?" Jim landed the bag of sundries he'd hauled all the way here into Travis' lap. "Lizzy is here. We saw her!"

Travis nodded, barely listening. He pushed the bag of supplies to the floor. "That is a fortunate turn of events."

Edmond, finally having caught his breath, flicked Travis's left ear. "Have you not heard a word Jim has said, you miserable wretch?"

"Ow! I have, but I'm in the middle of something here."

"They are lighting out for the trail, you addlepated fool!"

"That is a predicament, I agree," Travis said. "My turn to deal?"

He picked up the cards Diamond Joe had shuffled.

"Travis, we need to go, now," Jim said.

"I'm afraid that's not possible. I owe Mr. Diamond here a considerable sum of money. I'm on the hook as it were."

Sheriff John Two Wolves entered. He pulled out the seat vacated by the trapper and sat. "There a problem here, fellas."

"Sheriff, this swindler is holding my brother hostage under some odd rule of the table," said Jim, "thus preventing our pursuit of Francis Shonka and our sister."

"Oh, we finally meet the brothers," the Sheriff smiled. "Travis, I've encountered before but you must be Edmond. Hawé." He shook hands.

"I take umbrage at being called a swindler there, son." Diamond Joe tipped the brim of his hat back and smiled at Jim. But it was a mirthless, dry smile. His eyes were cold and stared through him. "I ain't never counted a card, nor hornswoggled a man in my life. I'm an honest gambler."

"An honest gambler," Edmond scoffed. "I suppose next you will lay claim to the title of most faithful fornicator in these parts!"

"Who's this moralizing bumpkin?" Diamond Joe looked at Travis for an answer.

"I, sir, am the Reverend Edmond Israel Hawkins."

"You've wandered into the wrong establishment, Preacher. Church is down the road. Adios. Now who's ready to play some cards?"

"We are indeed," Travis said. "You playin', Sheriff?"

"Not much of a card player. And your brothers here have some concerns about your prowess at the table. Luck seems not to be in your favor this afternoon."

"Luck never counted into it," Travis looked at his cards.

"To be sure. But your sister and her abductor absconded from the premises. One would think that might take precedence over a friendly game, yes?"

"He's not her abductor," said Jim. "Lizzy said he's her husband."

"That so?" Sheriff John raised an eyebrow.

"Indeed," Jim said. "And there's more, but I don't like to air our family's business in public."

"This is foolishness," said Edmond. "The girl has obviously been bamboozled by some native sorcery."

The saloon grew quiet. Jim had never known what it was like to have an entire room full of eyes upon him. Even at school, standing before the classroom for a presentation, attention would wander. Now, there were ninety-nine eyes drilling holes in his backside and the sensation was not a comfortable one.

"You'll have to excuse my brother," Jim said in a shaking voice. "Recent events have unnerved him and his wits are scattered." To Edmond he whispered, "Now let us not have such talk."

"I will be muzzled by no man, and especially not by my younger sibling." Edmond stared definitely around the saloon.

Several grog-sozzled eyes returned to the bottom of their cups. But a number of patrons, most of them native, continued to eyeball the three Hawkins boys.

"Travis, will you come with us?" Jim pleaded.

"Go prepare our horses," Travis said, "I'll be along by and by."

"We insist you come with us now," said Edmond.

"Well now let's hold on a moment, shall we?" said Sheriff Two Wolves. "I've been eyeballing the situation here, and it has been made apparent to me that Travis here does in fact owe a debt to Mr. Joseph. Until that debt is squared, I'm afraid I can't give your brother leave to go."

"Are you sure, Sheriff?" Jim asked.

"Lest you want to spend the night in my jail, yes I am."

"Let it not be said the Hawkins men are a raggedy bunch," Edmond sighed and took a seat at the bar.

"Diamond Joe, sir," Jim said, "would there be a manner in which we could expedite the squaring of this particular circle?"

"I play cards, son," Diamond Joe said, tossing a ten-dollar chip into the pot. "And the Lady of Spades works on her own schedule."

"Jim, I have this particular situation well in hand," Travis whispered.

"I see that, brother, and it hinders us at every turn."

"You placing your bet, Hawkins?" asked Diamond Joe. "If so, who's staking? Cause the way I count, you don't got enough even for the blind."

Travis looked at his chips with suspicion bordering on paranoia, as if in their lack, they had conspired against him.

"Come, Jim, let's collect our supplies and ready the horses," Edmond said.

"Supplies you say?" For the first time since they arrived in the saloon, Travis looked at his brothers. Jim saw the shadows under his eyes. Had he been here drinking and gambling since their arrival?

Jim picked the bag of sundries up off the floor and dropped it in Travis' lap again. He tossed the saddlebags that had been weighing on his shoulders atop them.

"Well there ya go!" Travis turned back to Diamond Joe. He

dropped the saddlebag and sundries onto the table. "There's my stake. Plus three horses. That ought to be more than enough to see me through this hand."

At that Diamond Joe smiled and locked eyes with Travis. "I've seen neither hide nor hair of these horses or supplies," he said.

"I can vouch for their existence and condition," said the Sheriff.

"Well. That's good enough for me. Not being one to rob a man of his only transport, I'll leave you two of them horses, save whichever one carries those supplies. Place your bet, young feller. Let the Lady of Spades judge your worthiness."

The hand passed quickly, as bets were placed and cards dealt. Jim, never much a student of the art, couldn't tell what was what until Travis hissed, "damn it all!" and threw his cards on the table. He had a pair of threes.

Diamond Joe threw down his hand. Three Jacks—hearts, diamonds, and clubs, with the Ace of Spades and the Eight of Spades beside them.

"Is that... bad?" Jim asked.

"Quite," Edmond sighed.

"Looks like the Lady is trying to tell you something, though whether or not you wanna hear it's another story, ain't it?" Diamond Joe smiled and raked in the pot. He tossed the bag of sundries and the saddlebags onto the floor at his feet. "Leave my new horse tied up out front as you go. And thanks for playing, son. You're welcome at my table any time there's an open seat."

Travis stood and buttoned his jacket. He drained his mug of beer and sauntered towards the door. Jim and Edmond each grabbed an arm and lifted Travis, carrying him through the swinging saloon doors and halfway down the street.

They shoved Francis through the barn door of the stable with a bit more force than was physically necessary, but enough to convey their feelings on the matter. Francis wheeled, managing to spare his boots a fresh polishing with dung.

"You damn fool!" Edmond said. "Lizzy is probably halfway to the Gates of Hell by now and all because you could not control yourself! Why, if Pa could see you now..."

"Pa? Pa never cared a damn about me, or Lizzy. Or any of us!" Travis swayed a little as he stood. He was exhausted, and drunk, and the thrill of the table had left him. He shivered visibly.

Edmond shook his head. "Ungrateful wretch!"

"You're awfully rambunctious for a preacher," Travis narrows his eyes. "A bit judgmental, to boot."

"Travis, you can't see the hole in a ladder," Jim said. "Maybe we should rest a spell."

"I'm as fit as can be," Travis staggered backward and caught himself on the post hitch between two horses.

"You are surely made of God's own gully fluff and I shall give you the anointing you well deserve!" Edmond lunged for Travis.

Jim, ever the cooler head of the three of them, stood between the brothers. "We have to go. Now."

"Mount up, Travis, you apple-faced buffoon," Edmond said.

Travis made to mount his horse, but couldn't quite find the stirrup and ended up sitting on the floor.

"Let me relieve you of that particular burden."

They turned to find Sheriff John Two Wolves standing in the doorway. The sun was setting behind him. He walked up and petted the horse, who nuzzled his hand. "I'll see him delivered to Diamond Joe. Now, if I was you, I'd turn around and ride off home, beg your father's forgiveness, and mourn your sister."

"You speak as if she were already dead," said Edmond.

"Far as you're concerned, she might as well be. You'll never see her again, and giving chase after her and that particular fella will only see you likewise into a shallow grave."

"Your attitude changed in stark contrast once you saw the man Lizzy called Francis," Jim said. "Who is he to you?"

"Not a person to be trifled with is who he is. And where they're headed is a place none of you will return from."

"I think you'll find we are made of sterner stuff than that," Edmond said. "Our resolve is set, and our mission just."

"They were headed into the Switch and no manner of resolve, no matter the righteousness of the cause, can stand up to the Powers who reside there."

But Edmond would hear no more. He pushed Travis onto his horse and then climbed up behind him. He took the reins and nudged the reluctant creature towards the door.

"I'm sorry for all our hassle," said Jim. "I wish circumstances were different. But I have to see this through, for their sake as much as Lizzy's."

Sheriff Two Wolves nodded. "I understand, James Hawkins. And I hope one day those brothers of yours deserve the amount of love and devotion you show them. All I can say to you is to be quick and be honest. Trespass lightly, for where you are going, you must always respect the Powers, or you shall never return."

Jim nodded goodbye.

And the three Hawkins brothers set out, despite the lateness of the hour, and unsure of their destination, riding after Lizzy and Francis, into the setting sun.

3
The Hour Of Need

The road out of Pawhuska came to an abrupt fork not more than a mile from the edge of town. The road bending to the right led on into the hill country, and a sign said that El Paso was a mere 900 miles away. The left-hand path dipped down into a rough patch crossed by a dry creek bed before disappearing into a piney wood.

"Which way did they go?" Edmond demanded.

"Now how the heck should I know?" Jim said. "They've got the better part of an hour on us. They could be anywhere by now."

"Naw," Travis drawled. "They'd avoid the straight and narrow road. Take yonder left turn up ahead."

"Now that there is some terrible advice," said Edmond. "Why in the name of the ever-living word would they do that?"

"To avoid bein' followed, of course!" Travis spat.

"But it makes no sense. They would've gone—"

Jim's eye caught a wayward movement.

He turned to find a horse with two riders picking through the underbrush.

"There! I see them!" Jim spurred his horse on. Edmond shook the reins limp-fisted but the horse got the idea and followed Jim's horse into the piney wood.

They passed beneath the bough of a large and gnarled oak tree, forming a sort of archway in the settling dusk. Jim had recalled seeing such a tree back home on the ranch. Old Luke called it Lonesome Oak. He would tell stories about such meetings of tree limbs; how, on certain nights when the moon was high, you could see other lands through that wooden gate.

Jim had paid those stories no mind, once he'd turned twelve and a half. But now on the edge of the piney wood, chasing after Lizzy and Francis, he felt the old chill up his spine. Just like when Old Luke would go on about the wandering Willer Trees and Old Man Oak who made a door for the Devil.

Once they passed through that oaken gate, it did seem to Jim that the world changed. No longer was there a road behind them, but an old game path. And up ahead, shadows swam in the distance. He doubted his own eyes. Had he seen Lizzy and her abductor? Or had it been wishful thinking and a trick of the light?

Before long, it grew too dark to see, yet still the Hawkins boys kept on. A wind came up, the likes of which they had never felt. It rattled their bones and distracted the horses, howling black and empty.

Jim had a compass of course, but there was no light to check it by. When the clouds finally did break and the howling wind died down, the moon came out, fat and silver. Jim fished the compass from his pack and watched as the needle spun in search of true North.

Any sign of Lizzy and Francis was gone. Jim had but a vague sort of flutter in his belly to tell them they were heading in the right direction, but he dismissed this as mere hope; as much that they might find her but also that the venison bacon he'd had for breakfast wasn't coming back to haunt him.

Their two horses trotted onto a flat plain. Dry grass hissed as they trod some path invisible to human senses. Before long, the horses found hard scrabble earth under their hooves. This seemed to calm them after the wind died down.

Jim had been an avid, if amateur, astronomer from a young age and attempted to gauge their location by the position of the stars. When they'd gone camping with Pa, he'd always delighted in charting the constellations. This practice proved fruitless however; when the stars finally came out, Jim couldn't identify any of the constellations. Instead, unknown stars wheel overhead in silence.

Travis, meanwhile, was still drunk. Edmond had to lash him to the saddle with his belt to keep him from sliding off to the left. He would fall asleep, only to startle awake and yell into the night. When he finally did come around, it was worse. Now he took every rustle and twig breaking in the woods around them for a sign some fiend had come to take their horses.

After another hour of wandering through the piney wood, they stopped to water the horses and relieve themselves. That was when Travis availed himself of the rifle once more. He took to shooting at some hoot owl in the trees to their right, pausing every few shots to listen.

"Did ya hear it?" he said, cocking the rifle and firing another volley at a tree.

"That ain't nothing but a Barn Owl," Jim hissed. "And here you are, spending our ammunition, firing at whiskey phantoms!"

"Now exactly what do you propose we use to defend ourselves with when we catch up to them?" Edmond scolded Travis. He'd always been the judge. Even as a boy, he presided over their play, offering rulings even when it was only cloud talk or horse play.

A whisper came rustling out of the woods, like some great beast had exhaled and rattled the trees.

Travis grabbed the rifle back from Jim, cocked and fired a volley into the face of the wind. Nothing. A cloud passed in front of the moon and all grew dark once more.

Instead of a howling mad wind, what emerged out of the woods this time was a cold and haunted laughter. It gripped their spines and shook hard.

"That were no Barn Owl," whispered Edmond.

"It was just the wind," Jim said.

"The wind don't laugh," Travis raised the rifle and took aim at the nearest shadow-cloaked tree. "Alright! Show yourself!"

A clap of thunder rang out. A storm of time-black shadows followed as a great column of spotted moths poured out of the piney wood. There must have been a million of them, Jim reckoned. Their velvety wings kissed them on the cheeks and brushed against their foreheads. The moths knocked Travis's hat and sent him, in his stupor, flailing to the ground. He and Edmond wrestled for the rifle. Jim was too stupefied to notice until Travis came up, chambered the gun and fired right into his belly.

Nothing but a click of the hammer on an empty chamber.

The moths fluttered away into the night. The silver moon came out from behind the clouds. And all was silence once more.

"Hey!" Jim yelled. "You dang near shot me!"

"Luckily for us, Travis exhausted our ammunition on that last volley." Edmond sighed and hoisted himself off the ground.

"Well isn't that a fine turn of events," Jim huffed. "Lost in the woods with two dullards, no food, no ammunition, and no way home!"

Travis and Edmond both turned the brunt of their ire on him. But came up short by another sound: the clop of hooves and rustle of high grass through the trees.

"What fresh hell is this?" Edmond said.

Out of the trees came a woman on horseback, her dark skin shining like the moon. Mercy Nightingale stopped short and brought her horse to a standstill right in front of Jim.

"Well now, if it isn't Young James Hawkins," she said. "I take it these two noisy cats are your brothers?"

"They are at that, Ma'am," Jim said.

"And here he goes with the Ma'am again." Mercy smiled and shook her head.

"Who is this... person?" Edmond said, looking Mercy up and down.

"Mercy Nightingale." She touched the brim of her hat. "Tracker, poet, and seeker after treasures the likes of which you sir, have never imagined." She looked down her nose at Edmond, parrying his disdain.

"You'll have to Excuse Edmond," said Jim. "He's a bit much."

"That he is. Edmond, thou art excused." Mercy flicked her hand in his general direction and turned her eye on Travis. "And who might you be?"

"Travis Enoch Hawkins Jr, at your service," He bowed and kissed Mercy's hand, as gallant as he'd never been in his life.

"Careful, you don't know where that hand's been. This here is Abraham Lincoln, the one and only." She stroked her horse's mane.

"That is a horse," Edmond said. "I take it you named him after the one and only. You do not expect us to believe this beast is the former and deceased President of these here United States?"

"These here states ain't as united as all that, so get off your high horse. As for this one, he is one and the same, the former man, come back to us by the principle of transmigration of souls." She scratched behind his ear.

The horse whinnied and said clearly, "...and how was the theater, Mr. President..."

"What sort of heathen nonsense is all this?" Edmond said.

Jim cut him off by stepping between him and Mercy. "We are grateful that you came along. Another minute, and I'm afraid we'd have resorted to cannibalism."

Mercy looked around the woods, at their exhausted horses. "There's three of you and only two horses. I'm 'fraid to ask what became of your steed, Young James Hawkins."

"Oh, not mine. It'd be Travis's horse offered up on the altar of the Lady of Spades, back in Pawhuska."

"Had a run in with Diamond Joe, did you?"

"And how would a fine lady such as yourself acquaint that no-good, scoundrel of a card sharp?" Travis asked.

"Well first, because I ain't no lady, and second because I shack up in Pawhuska, same as him. Though home to mighty fine and friendly folk, it's not the biggest berg in the world, now is it? Then again, you weren't the first hayseed dumb enough to wander into Hattie's Saloon and to play cards with the chosen consort of Our Lady of Spades!" Mercy shook her head. "Seems the place is big enough to draw in its share of suckers after all."

"Well that is uncalled for rudeness, Ma… Ms… er, Mercy," Edmond said.

"Sho'nuff," Mercy agreed. "Take it your fellas need escortin' back to town then?"

"No, actually we're hunting down a quarry of our own." Travis lowered his voice a measure, trying to sound swell.

"And where, pray tell, has this query gone?"

"Into the Switch, or so these two lunkheads claim," Travis smiled.

"Well, then you won't be needing my services, since you're already there. Toodles then."

Travis's smile fell off his face and landed in the tall grass.

Jim said, "So it's true then, what they say about this place?"

"True enough," Mercy said.

"But we need to find our sister and the uh fella who's absconded with her," Jim said. "They came this way not too long ago and we'd like to bring her home."

Mercy shook her head. "Well that's a mighty big ask. What sort of payment, or goods in lieu of payment, would you have on hand to compensate for services rendered? I have no debts, but expenses are another matter."

Jim looked at Edmond and Travis, who both frowned.

"I don't have time nor inclination for a charity mission," Mercy said. "I'll need some sort of down payment."

The three of them made a show of having not a thing on offer that Mercy found appealing.

"Sorry Ma'am, but we seem to be short on funds at the moment," Travis offered a smile.

"I can offer naught but my most fervent prayers on your behalf," Edmond waved his Bible.

Mercy made a face.

Jim remembered the silver dollar he'd left in his pocket by accident. The one Lizzy had left him the previous year on their shopping excursion. He found it in his pocket, right where he'd left it.

"This is my last silver dollar," Jim held it up. "It kinda has sentimental value and I wasn't gonna part with it. But, well, it's all we have against losing our sister."

"Well now Young James Hawkins, you're a rich man indeed! Or desperate in a true and familiar way." Mercy held out her hand.

Jim deposited the coin onto her palm.

Mercy pocketed it and swung a leg over Abraham Lincoln's saddle.

"…four score and seven years…" the horse muttered.

"We have an accord then?" Edmond said.

"On the condition that you each swear to me that you will follow my orders and do as told, yes?"

Jim nodded, "I swear."

"I'm serious now, no fooling around. You ignore me once, it could cost us our lives and I'm too pretty to die for the likes of you three."

"You have our oath," Travis said.

"I don't know," Mercy said. " This is serious business, out here in the Switch. We need to rely on one another, not go running off on a whim, and whims will come to call, mark my words."

Edmond took out his Bible and laid a hand on the top. "You have my assurance, as a man of the cloth. I and my brothers will behave like perfect gentlemen, and follow you to our last recourse. Do we have an accord?"

"Humph. We have an accord," Mercy Nightingale said. "Right

then. You three figure out how to ride two horses, and we'll be in business."

At Mercy's suggestion, they set camp on the other side of the piney wood. Mercy found a small stream for washing up and watering the horses, with a copse of trees acting as a curtain. They soon had a tidy little camp set up, with a low burning fire in a ring of stones. It wasn't much but it set a mood, casting a low glow for about a dozen feet in all directions.

By this time, Travis was finally sober enough to make a nuisance of himself. Mercy set Edmond to prepping the meal while she tended the horses. Jim and Travis took their canteens to collect water from the stream.

"So, what do ya think about this here, Mercy Nightingale?" Travis asked in a low, conspiratorial whisper. He took a swig from the canteen Jim had filled.

"She seems honorable enough," Jim said. "You getting ideas there, Travis?"

"I always got ideas," Travis patted his shoulder.

Jim knelt to fill the second canteen.

"Where'd you come across this here lady tracker, Jimmy boy?"

"Met her in Pawhuska, while you were off squandering our funds at the gambling table," he said.

Travis's smile faltered a second.

"Now I said I was sorry for that."

"No you didn't."

"Well I am!"

"Means nothing, seeing as we're miles from the nearest gambling establishment," Jim said. "Easy enough to promise not to dance in the rain on a sunny afternoon."

"Now Jim, I do wish you'd go easy on me. It's been tough, this last year with you away. Pa... well, he ain't been all too well these past few months. I wasn't going to mention it. Didn't want to worry you on top of everything else, but he's not long for this world."

"And that's got what exactly to do with you swindling our only means of defending ourselves you haven't yet wasted?"

"Jim, I'm trying to have a serious talk with you about our father's health and well-being and you aren't making it any easier on me. Is that what you've learned from all your schooling Back East? They've 'bout turnt you into a faithless cynic."

"If anyone has set my faith to wobble in the direction of cynicism, it's my slothful and arrogant brothers."

Jim walked away. Stopped. Turned back to Travis and marched back, leveling a finger at his chest.

"And furthermore, I dislike the implication that this situation is somehow my fault for being away. You and Edmond were both at the homestead. What, too busy gazing into your own navels to notice our sister was fixin' to run off?"

"She didn't run off, she was abducted!"

"That's not the way she told it." Jim took the canteens from Travis and headed up the gentle slope of the creek bank, towards the camp.

"Ah what do you know? Struttin' around with your fancy book Learnin'!" Travis stumbled over a large rock at the top of the incline. He caught himself on a tree limb.

"I leave the struttin' to your own self," Jim said.

He set the canteens down beside the fire. Edmond was stirring a pot of beans and looked up as his brothers returned. Mercy, who was busy combing out Abraham Lincoln's mane, watched and listened.

"Edmond, will you talk some sense into this young 'en?" Travis stared at his brother.

Edmond stood, wiped his hands on his trousers and sighed. "I have given up that cause," he said. "Seems education has had the opposite effect on young Jim here, rendering him impervious to reason and sense."

That brought an end to the matter, at least enough for Mercy to find a cue for her own exit.

"Right, that fire's looking feeble," Mercy said. "You three stay here while I fetch some wood. Mind the horses, and one another, and don't set foot outside the ring of the firelight. Ya'll don't want to tangle with what might be out and about."

"I think we can handle ourselves," said Edmond.

Mrcy raised a skeptical eyebrow. "With what weapons? An empty rifle and a bunch of pretty words?"

"I have the only weapon I need, and it is The Word," Edmond held up his Bible. "First and Last, on every subject."

"Weren't the rifle yours, too?" Jim asked.

Travis guffawed. "He's got you there, Rev."

"You swore to mind me," Mercy said. "If'n you a preacher man, that oath ought to be true enough."

"You have our word, Ma'am," Edmond bowed his head. "I shall tend our tiny flock till you return."

"And what about you?" Jim asked. "Won't you be in danger?"

Mercy smiled. "I like that you're kind, Young James Hawkins. Try and stay that way." Then she trudged into the darkness.

"Woo wee!" Travis chuckled. "She's a firecracker ain't she?"

"That is no way to talk about a lady or our guide," said Edmond.

Travis bit his thumb at Edmond.

Jim took over preparing supper. All they had left from when they'd set out from Vinita was cold beans and stale biscuits. Jim stirred the pot and set it to simmer over the fire and hoped it would do.

Edmond meanwhile, set about reading his Bible and muttering. Travis paced around the edge of the firelight.

"What, do you reckon she meant by what's out and about?" Travis said after a bit. "Can't be nothing worse than some coyotes, or a few wild hogs?"

"If we are in the Switch, there might be all manner of hoodoo-derived beasts on the loose," Edmond chuckled.

"Stay put, Travis," said Jim. "Don't make any more mischief."

Travis pointed to himself and smirked. "I would never. But if we're to face down some mad beast in the middle of the night, I'll want more'n a rifle butt and some lady rover's pea shooter."

"She also had a saber," Jim added.

"Handy for when we're fencing some ne'er-do-wells, I'm sure."

"Stay put," Jim said curtly.

"Oh look who's the boss of us," Travis hefted Edmond's rifle. "I'm gonna have a look-see. No harm in that."

And he stepped out of the ring of fire light. Though he'd not put any stock in her warnings, he still made a show of his departure. "Lookit me! I'm in the darkness, Woo-oo-oo…" he laughed at his own joke until he was out of earshot.

With nothing much else to do, Jim sat by the fire and tended to the coals, trying to breathe some more red into their glow. Edmond settled into his bedroll, hat over his face, pretending to sleep. Jim knew he was pretending, as he never slept well out of doors.

A twig cracked in the dark. There was a rustling sound, from outside the ring of light.

Edmond sat up, clutching his Bible. "Travis? That you?"

No answer but the wind.

"Mercy?" Jim whispered.

A rustle of leaves.

"…Be sure you put your feet in the right place, then stand firm…" said the horse.

"Good advice. Thank you, Mr. President." Jim stood and straightened his back and in a loud clear voice called out into the darkness, "Hark! Who goes there?"

A moment's waiting brought nothing but the sound of the wind through the trees.

About then, Mercy came upon the camp, with an armload of kindling.

"I see two brothers. Where'd that other fool get to?"

Travis ran out of the shadows, close enough for them to make

THE RIGHTEOUS AND THE REST 47

out his wild-eyed, half-drunk features.

"This way!" he said, before disappearing into the gloom once more.

"Where are you going, Travis?" Jim called after.

"Over here!" he hissed.

Mercy looked to Jim and Edmond but finding blank stares and shrugged shoulders in place of sound advice, decided to see for herself what was amiss. Mercy was sure she would regret it.

They followed Travis into the line of cedar trees beside the creek. Edmond hadn't been paying mind to his footfalls and stumbled into a shallow gully. At least, that's what he thought it to be at first. But upon inspection, he found himself standing in an open grave, one that was already occupied by the desiccated corpse of a soldier.

Travis, Jim, and Mercy had seen the body before him and stopped at the side of the shallow grave. Edmond came to, only to find himself nose to noseless face with the dead man. He jumped out of that grave and cowered beside the others.

The soldier was clad in calvary blues, which clung to his gray bones. The old flesh, dried like some jerky, pulled taught across the frame, like a drumhead. In his hands, he still clutched a saber.

"I'll have that then," Travis knelt to pluck the saber from the dead soldier's hand, like picking a daisy from a field.

The soldier's corpse recoiled, clutching the sword tight to his chest.

Travis jumped up, ran in a circle and stood behind Jim. Edmond held his breath and crossed himself. Jim didn't move at all, just observed.

"Hang on a moment," Mercy said, trudging back to the camp. Over her shoulder she yelled, "Don't you fools touch nothin'!"

The three fools obeyed, for once.

Mercy returned a moment later, carrying the jug of spirits Jim had seen her pack on her saddle back in Pawhuska.

"Damn fools, withering the dead... Swear to Montezuma, you'll doom us all," Mercy muttered as she knelt.

She uncorked the bottle, and tilted it back, wetting the dead soldier's lips.

"Sip o'the spirit, for the spirit of this one," she said, intoning low. "Speak now, when spoken to."

Mercy stood and corked her jug. "Soldier, we have a powerful need for your sword. What is the price you ask for its loan?"

A dry wind rustled through the trees.

"Bury me pretty..." came a voice. It came neither from the lips of the dead man nor from anywhere else Jim or his brothers could identify.

"Fair enough," Mercy said.

Travis knelt down and tugged at the sword, but the soldier's grip would not relent.

"...him..." whispered the dead man. He offered the sword to Jim.

"Me?" Jim said.

Mercy and Travis looked at him. Mercy pointed to the dead man. "Ain't got all night."

Jim knelt and took the saber in one hand.

"Thank you, soldier," he said. The soldier relented at last and as Jim came up with the sword in hand, the dead man lay back and breathed no more.

Edmond found some wits and went to fetch a shovel. The brothers took turns digging a grave proper and deep for the soldier and then Jim and Travis laid him in it. Mercy tied a wildflower in his hair while Edmond muttered a prayer over his bones.

Afterward, they returned to the camp in silence.

4
As The Crow Fly

That night, Jim saw the Thunderbird again. That rough beast flew through the night. The movement of her mighty wings was enough to turn sweet summer breezes into hurricanes. Lightning leaped from her beak, striking the mountains, and the trees. A bolt smacked the desert sand, right where Jim was about to set foot. When the shadow of the Thunderbird passed, Jim looked at the spot where its lightning had left a mark in the sand. There was now a mirror of the darkest glass, reflecting his face. But it was not the youthful face that greeted him in the shaving mirror or shop windows in the waking world. This was a face worn down by age and wind and life to a web of creases and lines. His lips were dry from the desert and one eye was covered by a black patch, lost in the ache of long ago. In the dark reflection of the glass, Jim saw the map of his life laid out before him in all its tragic beauty…

Jim startled awake to find Travis kneeling beside him.

"Come on, Jimmy boy, it's time for breakfast."

Jim sat up, bleary-eyed. It was not yet light, and the fire had gone down to coals. Mercy was still abed, wrapped in a horse blanket, back to the fire, hand on her pistol. Edmond lay stretched out beside the cold fire, snoring into his hat.

"What do you mean, breakfast?" Jim croaked. "We ain't got breakfast."

It was true. They'd about run out of rations at last night's supper. Mercy had told them that the first task of the morning would be procuring supplies.

"I aim to fix that," Travis whispered. "Come on lazy bones!"

Jim grabbed his boots and sword and staggered still half asleep after his brother. He hadn't managed to get more than twenty steps before doubling back to find his hat.

"So what's on the menu this morning, chef?" Jim yawned.

"Thought I'd rustle us up some eggs and bacon, mess a flapjacks. You know, get a good feed on before we hit the trail."

"Mmm hmm," was all Jim could say to that.

It sounded good, but there didn't look like much of any of that from what Jim could tell. All that was around them was scrub brush and the occasional mesquite. There were a few old oaks in a staggered line on a hill east of the camp, and it was towards these that they headed.

Jim was uncertain that they'd find what Travis was looking for there. The last chicken he'd seen had been back on Pawhuska. As for bacon, there was something like a pig lurking outside the ring of their campfire last night. Where it'd gone to now was anyone's guess. Either way, the prospect of spending the day prepping a fresh kill for the trail was enough to turn Jim's stomach.

The sun came up at their backs as they wandered into the grove of oak trees.

"We should wait for Edmond and Mercy," he said.

"Ah, you big baby," Travis punched him on the shoulder.

His whole demeanor had shifted. Now, in the morning light, he was gregarious where he'd been sullen the night before, still in his cups. The passing of the sweet summer rain of his brother's intemperance had left the world glittering and clean in its wake, and clarified his brother's mind. How long this state would last, one could never guess.

It occurred to Jim that this version was the brother he'd liked most growing up. Often when describing his eldest sibling to others, it was this impression on his mind. He now found this man was nothing but the after-effects of too much drink from the night before. This realization threw a stark and somewhat somber light on more than a few of his childhood memories.

The grove of old oak trees sat on a low rise, overlooking the creek. They could make out the embers of their cook fire, in the distance. Either Edmond or more likely, Mercy was awake now, tending to the fire.

"So what exactly are we looking for?" Jim asked.

"Vitals, son, vitals!" Travis stalked about like he was after a hare, and was sneaking up on it. Then he stopped and took off his hat and looked around because there weren't nothin' there.

"I think there are some biscuits still left in the pack," Jim offered. "Maybe we should settle for these until—"

The sound of a branch creaking overhead drew their attention. There, they found a small brown-skinned man clinging to one of the larger branches. He wore old buckskin, his white hair tied in a braid down his back, and a necklace of animal bones and beads.

"Morning!" The old man smiled and scooted a little more along the branch.

Jim and Travis exchanged a look. Then they turned their attention back toward the feller in the tree.

"Old man, what you doin' up there?" Travis said.

"Getting breakfast," he said, keeping all his attention on the small nest perched in the crook of the branch. They'd have missed it if he wasn't on top of it.

"That there's a nest," Travis said. He looked at Jim.

"Eggs?" Jim asked.

"Eggs!" said Travis.

Travis handed Jim his hat and scampered up the tree. He'd always been a climber and was the one they'd send up the old dead mesquite back on the homestead, to fetch the kite. This old knack was turning out to be handy for more than fetching mislaid toys this morning.

Travis managed to clamber up into the bough opposite the old man. Leaning around, he hung off a high branch to survey the nest. There were three eggs inside and not a momma bird in sight.

"Well. Ain't this fortuitous," Travis said. He grunted as he adjusted his grip on the tree limb. "One fer you and two for us!"

The old man shook his head.

"Take no more than you need, young'en."

"Nuts to that. I'll have the whole clutch if you don't mind." Travis reached out for the eggs only to feel a sting on the back of his hand.

The old man had grabbed a switch from the tree and stripped the leaves quicker than Travis could tell.

"Leave two," the old man swatted at him. "I'll share one with you."

"But there's four of us," Travis said. "Three if you don't count our guide."

"And why would I do that? Besides, there's another hereabouts who'll miss those eggs. Don't be a travesty."

"Sorry, sir, he's a walking one of those," Jim said, feet on the ground.

"Enough of this," Travis reached for the eggs only for the sting of the switch to cause him to recoil. "Now stop that, old-timer!"

Travis made a quick grab for the eggs only for each finger to receive its own quick swat from the old man's branch.

"I told you to stop now, young feller," said the old man.

Travis was sucking on his stinging fingers when Mercy and Edmond found them.

"Charlie Snow Owl, is that you?" asked Mercy, grinning.

"Siyo, Mercy! How you do?"

"Little harried, keeping track of these three."

"Siyo, fellers! Who might y'all be?"

Travis made to grab the eggs only to lose his balance. He almost fell out of the tree but caught himself in time.

"These here are the Hawkins boys. James, Travis, and Edmond,"

Mercy made introductions in turn.

"Oh, well, if you boys are kin to the hawk, then you're friends of mine. Let's go sit a spell and see if we can't find us some breakfast."

Charlie lifted one of the eggs out of the nest and tucked it under his chin. Travis tried to snatch the other two but a stern eye from Charlie stayed his hand.

Once back on the ground, Charlie Snow Owl led them in a roundabout way through the oak grove, talking all the while with Mercy. Seems they were old friends and had much to catch each other up on.

"...Do you still hear from Old George?" asked Charlie.

"Not as much since he passed on, but I run into him in dreams," she said.

Charlie nodded as if it were the right and proper way to hear from folk.

Though only two years older than Jim, Mercy had lived a storied life. Seems she learned the fine art of tracking from her father at age twelve, going on her own by sixteen. Charlie, near as Jim could fathom, was an old family friend.

How old was up for debate, as he seemed to have stopped counting birthdays some time ago, but he had known Mercy's grandfather, plus assorted cousins, and other relations. Though perhaps his mind had begun to wander, as he made a passing remark about serving as a scout during Lord Dunmore's War, which was more than a hundred years ago.

Despite these flights of fancy (and in part because of them), Jim got the distinct impression Charlie was a trustworthy sort. He felt at ease with him and didn't balk at some of his odder habits, like the fact that he lived in an oak tree.

Said tree was a grand old specimen, big as a house, with boughs stretching out over a carpet of moss and stones. Charlie had set up a right little homestead under the tree's shade. The low branches he used to hang jugs and assorted chimes and other dangling decorations. Around the trunk, there sat a rug woven from grass and a cot hung from two of the larger limbs, facing East, which offered him a gentle breeze as he slept.

There was even a ring of old stones forming a hearth, arched in the old tree's roots. Charlie had strung up an old tin flue and chimney, which ran along one of the limbs and up to the top of the tree, to move the smoke out of the way.

An old flat stone served as a table. Around it sat enough smaller rocks polished by the behinds of many a guest into smooth flat chairs. Mercy set her things down and took up on one of these stones as if making herself at home. The brothers did the same, though a little less at ease. Travis had to stoop to avoid having his hat knocked off by the branches. And Edmond was at first reluctant to sit on the ground.

"I am a civilized man and do not need to wallow in the dirt like some bird," he said.

Charlie shrugged. "Suit yourself."

Jim found the low stone chair comfortable, which was a pleasant surprise.

Charlie hummed as he puttered around the hearth. There were a few hollows in the tree, which he used as his cupboard, stashing herbs and spices in clay pots.

To Jim's astonishment, he drew an old cast iron pan from out of the tree and slapped it onto the fire.

While it warmed, he fetched some wild thyme and cilantro growing at the foot of the stone table. He plucked some mushrooms from the side of the tree. These he broke apart with his nimble fingers and dropped them into the pan, searing them good. Then he cracked the egg he'd procured on the side of the pan.

In short order, he had breakfast cooked and served on a wooden plank in front of them. Edmond of course turned up his nose at the fair. But Travis, being a slave to his stomach, couldn't resist, even if

THE RIGHTEOUS AND THE REST

there wasn't a slice of bacon or ham in sight.

Jim savored the food, enjoying it as much as the conversation.

"...I haven't been Back East in many years," said Charlie, when he learned of Jim's studies. "But there was this great place in Savannah, Georgia that made their own sausage. Some of the best I've ever had."

Eventually, the conversation turned to their quest.

"So, what brings you out and about this season, Mercy?" Charlie asked between mouthfuls of egg.

"These here miscreants," Mercy wiped her hands on her trousers. "Seems they've misplaced their sister, who may or may not have run off with a feller."

"Our dear sister, Elizabeth has been absconded with," said Edmond. "That is the Lord's truth of the matter. And we wish to find her and her abductor and bring justice to the situation."

"Well, that is a mighty tall order. What sort of justice you got planned there, Reverend?"

"Our Lord's own," Edmond said. "In point of fact."

"Seems I recall from the Bible that the Lord himself is the only one capable of meting out said Justice. So, I don't see what the fuss is all about."

"I hardly think you a qualified expert on the subject, Mr. Snow Owl," Edmond sniffed.

"Well sir, I helped translate the Good Book into Cherokee. But that was some years ago, so maybe I am forgettin' a verse or two."

"There's some dispute between my brothers as to the exact nature of the relationship between Lizzy and her companion," said Jim.

"There ain't no such dispute!" Travis slammed his hand on the rock.

"You see what I have to work with here?" Mercy sighed. "Don't suppose you might ask the wind, give us a helping hand?"

"Happy to," Charlie said. "What do these young folk look like?"

"Lizzy is fair and charming, so I'm told, while her abductor is an Osage feller named Shonka," Mercy said. "Goes by the name Francis."

Charlie nodded. He selected a green leaf from the nearest tree limb, which he twisted off and placed between his teeth. He blew loud and long. It sounded like a giant bumble bee trying to sing Yankee Doodle.

After a moment of performing on his leaf harmonica, Charlie returned to the table. Not a minute passed before half a dozen crows, a family of squirrels, plus two armadillos joined them.

"Well hello there!" Charlie said, greeting each of the animals in turn. They, like Mercy, seemed to be old friends of his.

After a few minutes of chitchat, Charlie described Elizabeth and Francis to the animals. They set off forthwith. All except one crow, who lingered a moment, eyeing a scrap of egg yolk clinging to the serving plank.

"You finished with that?" The crow asked.

"Oh sure, all yours, Cori." Charlie stroked the young crow's iridescent feathers and then shooed him away, with the egg in his beak.

"Talking horses, talking corpses, now talking birds," Edmond muttered. "Every blessed thing has a voice out here in the wild…"

Charlie heard him and smiled. "Now you're gettin' it!"

With breakfast over and help rendered, Travis and Edmond were grumbling about getting back on the trail.

"We do need to be going, alas," Mercy said.

"Well thank you for giving an old man some company for the morning, I do appreciate it," Charlie said. "To show my thanks, can I interest anyone in a reading of their fortune? Not you Mercy, you already know your fate," he laughed.

Edmond muttered something about blasphemy while Travis huffed and kicked a rock.

"You can read mine, Charlie," said Jim.

"Now there we go!" Charlie grinned wide and ran over to the tree. He fished around in a hollow for a moment, producing a deck of cards.

Charlie returned to the stone table and shuffled the deck. He laid it in front of Jim and asked him to cut it. Jim took a little more than half off the top and set those cards aside.

"Again, please."

Jim obliged, leaving about a dozen cards in front of him.

Charlie turned them over one at a time. He scratched his chin a moment as he looked over Jim's cards.

"Hmm. We have the Queen of Hearts next to the King of Aces, that's lucky in love. Only seen that particular pairing once before," he winked at Mercy. She rolled her eyes.

"And here's the Nine of Diamonds. Interesting..."

"Is that good interesting or bad interesting?" Jim asked.

Edmond and Travis, their curiosity piqued, looked over Jim's shoulders at the cards.

"Says here you're touched by the Thunderbird."

"Is that good?" Jim asked.

"No," said Charlie. "But it's not bad neither. Means you'll have an interesting life."

"Well, that ain't nothin'," Travis grinned. "Already this morning's been a lot of interest."

"But there is one thing you should be aware of," Charlie said, tapping the Jack of Spades. "Evil Men are afoot."

Mercy chuckled and swatted his shoulder, "You old charlatan! That's vague and eternally true."

"Yes. But it's worth remembering all the same."

He looked Jim in the eye. He could see the old man, even though he was smiling, there was a seriousness in those dark eyes. Charlie glanced to Jim's left, where Travis was studying the cards.

"Bet you could make a tidy sum turning these cards for folks," said Travis. "You wouldn't want to teach the art, would ya?"

"I thought we was in a hurry, Mr. Hawkins?" Mercy nudged Travis's boot.

They waved their goodbyes to Charlie and headed out.

They returned to camp and packed their gear, then set out on the road once more. By then, the sun had cleared the ridge, affording Jim his first good look at this strange new territory.

Where they had camped the night before was a narrow spit of dry bush land between a shallow ridge to the north and a river to the south. In between, rolling hills, still green from the Spring rain, and dotted by mesquite and oak, stretched as far as the eye could see. Off to the West—where they were headed—lay a thick wood, the likes of which Jim had only ever heard tell of Back East. Still, this was a ways off. Between them and the forest lay a great swath of dry brush and little else.

"Where are we headed then, Miss Mercy?" Edmond asked, mopping his brow. He and Travis were taking turns on the horse they shared, Edmond walking the first leg, while Travis still hung over, teetered and lolled on the back of the mare.

"West, round those woods, towards open county. And no need to stand on formalities. Just Mercy'll do me fine."

"Will they not head into the woods, to try and lose us?" Edmond asked.

"They don't know we're tracking them, and if your feller knows this land like you suggest, he'll avoid those woods on any account."

"Still, wouldn't traversing them put us ahead of them? Give us the element of surprise?"

"There ain't no more likely a surprise than anything else out here," said Mercy. "And there's really only one way to go, if they are indeed headed away from any civilized place, it means they are going to lead us into the pass at Thunder Rock, 'less they cut through the swamp. And no creature is that foolish. Thus, there is but one way to go."

"Still, I think—"

"Enough of your thinking', Reverend!" Mercy was curt. "You agreed to listen to me and follow my lead, did you not?"

"My apologies, Mercy," Edmond wanted to say a whole lot more, Jim could tell, but he bit his tongue.

"Is Thunder Rock far?" Jim asked.

"Far away enough that getting there is more than a little effort, but close enough, depending on the way you walk."

"What nonsense," said Edmond, "Man hath but two legs, what other way to walk is there?"

"Man ain't the only creature that walks, Padre," said Mercy. "The Switch has a way of changing you. Stay out here long enough, you become the true thing you always were, underneath. And deep down, some men are the worst kind of animals. Which is why we have need to tread lightly."

This did not satisfy Edmond, but it gave him something to chew on intellectually for a while. Which was good enough for Jim, who remembered how obnoxious his brother could be when it came to the sport of talking.

Jim wasn't sure if it was the heat of the road or the light breakfast they'd had, but it didn't take long before Travis found his old sullen self again. They'd packed up their gear and headed out on the trail right after leaving Charlie's tree, and it wasn't an hour later before Travis became fixated again on Jim's sword.

"Now look here Jim," Travis turned as stern an eye as he could muster on his brother, "I intend to hang onto that sword for the duration. Now give it over."

"I won't," Jim adjusted the sword, which he kept tucked in its scabbard beside his saddle.

"Give it over!" demanded Travis. He was riding behind Edmond and nearly fell off the back of their horse, reaching for the sword. Mercy swatted his hand.

"Not his to give," said Mercy. "Excuse me for buttin' into family affairs, but that there sword? Our soldier gave it to Jim to hold. And it is his until such time as said owner comes to reclaim it. Therefore, it is not his to give over, to you nor anyone."

"And what sort of poppycock is this?" Travis said, straightening himself on the back of the horse.

"We find ourselves in the midst of heathen and superstition in this benighted land," Edmond shook his head. "There is no sense to be had from it at all."

"...When you reach the end of your rope, tie a knot and hang on..." said Abraham Lincoln.

"I rest my case," said Edmond.

"Fine then," Travis huffed. "Keep yer dang sword. All the good it'll do ya. We catch up to Francis and Lizzy, that ol' pig sticker ain't gonna do you a lick of good." Travis teetered a moment on the back of the horse, righting himself by nearly pulling Edmond over with him. They soon got situated on the horse's back once more. Though it did nothing to silence Travis's muttering.

"...Find myself a proper gun..."

"You do that," Mercy said.

They rode on in blessed silence after that.

By the tilt of the sun, Jim reckoned it was late in the afternoon when Mercy led them off the road, onto a game trail that led into a darkening wood.

"We have need to traverse this here forest," Mercy said. "Mind your footing."

"Would not the trail be easier if we went around?" Edmond pointed out the well-tread forest road.

"We'd never reach anything like a suitable campsite before dark headed that way," said Mercy. "And you don't want to be out here after the sun sets."

"I fail to see why. We camped last night in the open, did we not?"

"We did no such thing," Mercy checked her side arm. "And again, I remind you, preacher, you agreed to follow my lead."

"I say we put it to a vote," Travis, attempted to thread the needle and strike a chivalrous pose at the same time.

"This here ain't a democracy," said Mercy.

"Mind your oath, Travis," Jim chided.

While they were busy discussing the matter, a shadow swooped across their path, as if some great flying cross had come between them and the sun.

Travis looked up, squinting into the sun. "What kind of bird is that?" he asked.

"Crow," said Mercy.

"Too big for a crow," said Edmond. "It must be a sort of eagle, or perhaps a condor..."

"Nope. Crow," said Mercy.

"Is it friendly?" Jim shaded his eyes to get a better look.

"Course it ain't friendly," scoffed Travis. "It's a crow."

"Mightn't a crow be friendly?" Jim asked.

"Of course. Crows, like any people, come in all kinds," Mercy said. "My cousin is a crow, on my mother's side."

"Poppycock," Edmond said. "Crows are but rude animals. They lack an immortal soul."

"You can tell my cousin that," said Mercy.

The great dark bird glided over the treetops and alighted on Mercy's saddle horn. He squawked and shook his feathered head.

"Well, now, we was just talkin' about you, cuz. How you be?"

"Better than I deserve. And you?" asked the crow.

"Well, they ain't buried me yet," said Mercy. "Any word on our query?"

"That's why I stopped by. Two riders fittin' their description passed over the ridge, into the edge of the woods. But take warning, Mercy dear, they're pursued by dark riders."

And with that, the crow flew off.

"Right, then," Mercy's entire demeanor tightened as she checked her rifle.

"If I am to believe this bird, our sister is down in yonder holler?" Edmond said.

"Looks like it. So, we got us a change of plans. Now. This situation might get hairy. You three keep your heads or I swear to Montezuma, I will shoot each one of you myself. Comprende?"

They each nodded. Then the brothers set their two horses after Abraham Lincoln, who led the way.

They'd only rounded the bend and were still well above the tree line when Mercy paused and produced a spyglass from her pack.

After a long gander she said, "As I thought. The road leading through yonder wood is a path to a distinct unkindness."

"What sort of unkindness?" Jim asked.

Mercy handed him the spyglass. He'd never handled one before, but in a moment sorted out the simple trick of the thing. Through the glass, the smudge on the horizon became more distinct: it was a company of soldiers on the march, and though he was unable to make out their faces, their banner was a surprise.

James handed Mercy her spyglass.

"Soldiers, it looks like, but if I'm not mistaken, they're flying a rebel banner."

"Indeed," Mercy said. "They are revenants of the Confederacy, and they're nothing but trouble."

"You've had run-ins, I take it?" asked Travis.

"One or two," Mercy said. By her look, Jim thought it a wise idea not to press the matter. His brother was not wise.

Pshaw," Edmond scoffed. "There are not any Rebels still about!"

"Fine, you go ask them, Preacher," Mercy said. "See what that gets you. Meanwhile, we'll trot on up this here pass, and meet you in Hell."

Edmond had nothing more to say on the matter and let the sleight go unremarked upon.

Mercy checked her spyglass again. "They've picked up their pace. Looks like they've spotted someone... there!" She handed Jim the spyglass.

He took a looksee. "It's Lizzy!" He said, following the action as best he could from such a distance.

A rider in a gray hat raced ahead of the Confederate troops, raised his rifle, and squeezed off a shot. It took a moment, but the echo of the rifle's voice found them in the pass.

"They're taking fire! We have to help!" Jim returned the glass to Mercy.

"Let's hold on a sec there," said Mercy.

"But we must away!" Edmond reared his horse, sending Travis spilling first to the left, then the right, and having to grab onto Edmond just to stay on.

"Now Edmond, be sensible," said Jim. "Let's listen to Mercy."

"Only a fool rushes into a situation with Johnny Rev," she said.

"But it is Lizzy! Have we not paid you to find her for us?" demanded Travis.

"And I have at that. And yet to hear a thank you for it, but never-you-mind. We will follow, and see what we can see from a distance. Now. Be quiet, if you can."

Mercy set Abraham Lincoln onto the path to intercept the horse and its two passengers. She hoped they got there ahead of the Confederates.

5
A Solomon Of Sorts

In a holler, beside an old oak, Lizzy and Francis stopped to catch their breath and assess their situation. Shadow stood guard outside the ring of firelight cast by the hasty campfire Lizzy had assembled. Lizzy was more interested in tending to Francis's wounded shoulder than constructing a proper cook fire but it cast enough light to get the job done. The job being a bit of minor surgery, gave Lizzy a moment's pause. With a needle and thread to sew up his bloody wound and a bit of whiskey to clean it by the light of a thin fire, she managed, but only just.

Francis took a swig of whiskey and grunted as she slid the needle into the meat of his shoulder.

"Oh, hush, you big baby," Lizzy said, cutting the thread with her teeth. "You caterwaul more'n my brothers."

"Your brothers shoot each other a lot?" he said, wincing as she pulled the thread taught.

"Depends. You mean with guns or with their mouths?"

"In my experience—uh!—talking never led to this much pain."

"You are an only child, aren't you?"

Shadow whinnied to get their attention.

Lizzy put away the needle and thread. Out of the pack, she pulled a pistol. She opened the chamber, checked that it was loaded, and slapped it shut.

Francis stood and closed his eyes a moment, listening.

"They're coming," he said. "No matter what happens, I want you to remember one thing: I will always protect you."

Lizzy kissed him. "You're sweet." She raised her pistol and cocked it.

Out of the gloaming dusk and into the ring of firelight stepped Jim. Edmond and Travis were right behind him. Mercy led Abraham Lincoln out of the trees and into the camp.

"Jim!" Lizzy lowered her pistol and ran to hug her brother.

"Edmond, Travis, what are you three doing here?" She said, looking them over.

"We've come to fetch you home," said Edmond.

"Fetch me home?" Lizzy looked at her oldest brother. "Travis, did you not tell them?"

The whole party turned as if they shared a pair of eyeballs.

"Travis," Jim looked at his brother hard. "Have you been withholding on us?"

"It weren't me! Pa sent us to bring you home. Now come along."

"I'm not going home. There's nothing for me there. Not anymore." Lizzy returned to Francis's side and took his hand.

"Jim said you had spun some tale of illicit matrimony to this nabob," said Edmond. "Is this true?"

"It is," Lizzy said. "And Travis knew before we left."

"Travis?" Edmond stared down his older brother. "Is this true?"

Travis let out a short, sharp laugh. "We're getting off topic here."

"I hate to break up the family reunion," Mercy said, "But we're about to have visitors. I suggest we all mount up and skedaddle, maybe pick this up down the road a bit? I'm Mercy by the way," she offered a hand to Lizzy and then to Francis.

"Pleasure. You a friend of my brothers?"

"No ma'am, our arrangement is strictly professional, which is why I'm in kind of a hurry to get out of here before Johnny Rev shows up."

They all made to leave, only to find that outside the ring of the meager firelight stood a wall of shadows bristling with rifles and malicious intent.

Into the ring of firelight stepped a tall man wearing a much-repaired Confederate uniform, embellished with a necklace of animal bones and feathers. Perched on his shoulder sat the largest crow any of them had ever seen. Jim at first thought it was stuffed, until it stretched out a giant wing and preened its feathers.

"My, my, my, what noisy cats are we!" said the Captain.

Jim could see his eyes had been replaced with black glass beads that glinted in the meager firelight. Still, he looked over the Hawkins brothers, Lizzy, and Francis, coming at last to Mercy.

She did not look away nor flinch even a little.

"They do not concern you, Talbott Swann," said Francis. "Let them pass."

"We'll deal with you momentarily," Travis said. He turned to the Confederate officer, offering a genial smile and a hand to shake. "Travis Hawkins, sir. This man does not speak for me and mine. Who might you be?"

"Captain Talbot Swann," he touched the brim of his hat.

"Captain?" Edmond scoffed. "In what army, sir?"

"Why, the Army of the Confederate States of America, 3rd Texas Cavalry."

"I do not believe there is such a thing," said Edmond.

"The official status of my regiment has, alas, succumbed to the degenerate motion of all things wrapped in red tape," Swann smiled. "However, I assure you, we are in fact a real fighting organization." He raised a hand and a dozen men stepped forward, rifles tipped with bayonets. In the gloom of the low firelight, their raggedy uniforms hung lank on their skinny frames, but the steel of their bayonets was real enough.

This served as proof enough of his credentials to Edmond and he shrank back beside Travis.

Swann grinned and held out his hands in an expansive gesture. "Tezu, my old friend."

"That name is not yours to speak," said Francis. "And you were never a friend, Talbot Swann."

Swann shrugged. "True. Finch! Hoots!" he bellowed.

Two raggedy men caught up with Captain Swann. Dagobert Finch was of a portly middle age, with an unkempt beard. He wore filthy long johns and boots half obliterated by years of wear. His companion, Hoots was even worse for wear, a skinny and cadaverous creature of indeterminate age, and dressed in rags that were once a confederate uniform, his lank hair dangling about his shoulders.

It took Finch several moments to catch his breath. Hoots did not appear to be burdened with the need for such things as breath.

"Cap'n Swann, sir?" asked Finch, wheezing.

"Mr. Finch, would you and Mr. Hoots be so kind as to relieve Ms. Hawkins—or should I say, Mrs. Shonka—of her shootin' iron?"

"Yes'r," said Finch. Both he and Hoots stepped forward.

Lizzy squeezed the trigger.

Hoots took a bullet to the chest and staggered back a foot, groaning.

"Now, Mrs. Shonka, that was unkind of you," said Captain Swann. "Especially seeing as how you're a guest here."

"This is not your land, Talbot Swann," Francis said. "And it never will be."

"The particulars of ownership of this here piece of real estate is a matter I leave to lawyers and other theologians."

Lizzy raised her pistol again.

"Once is happenstance, little missy. Shoot me or my own twice, I might start to think you don't like me."

"Why doesn't the gun work?" Lizzy whispered to Francis.

"Can't shoot a man who's already dead," he said.

"That right?" Lizz cocked her pistol. "Let's find out."

"It's true enough, you can't kill a dead man twice but you can hurt him plenty." Swann nodded and Finch and Hoots moved towards them.

Before Lizzy could fire again, Finch yanked the hot pistol from her hands and threw it into the dusk.

"Stop," Francis said. "We will go with you. Please don't hurt her."

"I'd never dream of it, Tezu," said Swann. "The General would like a word."

A short trek along a narrow rocky path delivered them to a military camp fallen to seed. Tents were moldy and in need of a wash, and the soldiers were likewise filthy and ragged, barely identifiable as remnants of the Confederacy. Swann led them to an improvised coral, where Shadow, Abraham Lincoln, and the rest of their horses were tied up alongside Swann's horse, Sebastian.

Swann led everyone to a large tent. Inside was a table set up on one side, a bed on the other. At the back of the tent, sitting in a wooden chair like some feudal lord, was the man Francis has run all this way from.

General Elkanah Greer wore his gray confederate uniform with pride. Unlike the soldiers he commanded, he had not let his uniform become stained by their time in the Switch. His only affectation was a necklace with snake teeth strung on it and a ring with a curious glinting shard of a gem set in it. This he wore on his right pinky and fiddle with habitually.

As they entered Greer smiled and spread his arms as if to embrace them all in an enormous hug.

"Welcome back, Tezu. Or is it Francis, now?"

"Francis, who is this low down, filthy so-and-so?" asked Lizzy.

General Greer stood and doffed his hat. "Forgive me, Ma'am. Being on the spur for this many a year has whittled my manners down to the nub. I am General Elkanah Greer, at your service." He bowed. "Swann, be a lamb and fetch the lady a chair."

Swann nodded and stepped outside.

"I'm afraid we're a bit short of comforts at the moment, so the rest of you gentlemen will need to sit as you can."

"What do you want with us?" Lizzy stared at him hard.

"With you, nothing," General Greer said. "We do not often receive visitors here, let alone of the fairer sex. But it is your beau here that demands my attention. I can have Swann show you the sights, such as they are."

Francis glared at Greer. "She stays with me."

"Have it your way," Greer said.

Swann returned with a chair. Greer led them over to the table, where two other chairs were already in place. There was a rude bench off to one side. Edmond and Jim hauled it over. In short order, they were all situated around the table, like some wayward family sitting down to a meal together.

"I have introduced myself, but I do not believe I've had the pleasure of your names. The Messrs. Hawkins, was it?"

"Yes, sir. I'm James, this here is our oldest brother, Travis. And the unusually quiet one there is the Reverend Edmond Hawkins. Elizabeth, you've met. We're out of Texarkana."

"Lovely territory," Greer said. He turned to Mercy, eying her with suspicion. "And who might you be, Miss?"

"Name's Mercy Nightingale. Tracker in the employ of these three," she said. "And there ain't no miss, nor madam, nor any other how-ya-dos before my name. It's Mercy, plain and simple."

"A pleasure," Greer said in a way that made it clear that it was anything but.

A large man in filthy overalls entered followed by two revenants in worse shape than Hoots. They lurched to the table and deposited a large platter, then loped out of the tent. The chef stayed a moment to observe.

"I hope you don't mind, I had Cookie whip up something to eat while we chat. Thank you, Cookie. Smells divine!"

Cookie grunted and left.

Lizzy looked at the food with apprehension. It did not resemble any animal she could identify.

Francis ignored the food and everything else, staring at the General. "What do you want with me, Greer?"

"General Greer, if you please. You know how I am, a stickler for the formalities. For what are we without them but animals wallowing in our own filth?"

"What do you want with us, General?" Francis scowled at him.

Lizzy had never seen him this tense before.

"Now that is no way to talk to an old friend. I want to simply chat. We have much to catch up on, you and I."

"You have no right to keep us," Francis said. "By the Powers, I am no longer bound to you."

"That is a matter of some dispute," Greer said, tucking a napkin into his collar. "The circumstances of your departure from my company seem to be shrouded in a bit of mystery. We are, admittedly, a bit lax in the recordkeeping department, my clerk having succumbed to the way of all things some time ago."

Greer ripped a hunk of meat from the carcass on the platter. He flopped into his chair. After a long thorough bout of chewing, he dabbed his lips with the corner of his napkin.

Greer continued, "Since you insist on getting directly to the topic at hand then let's have at it. You have dishonored me. You have betrayed my confidence, and furthermore, you have abandoned your post. You, sir, are a deserter, in a time of war, no less! And for that I will see you hanged. Pass the gravy, if you would please."

This last was directed at Edmond who dutifully handed him the gravy boat. "What war, pray tell, is he a deserter from?" Edmond asked.

Travis shot him a hard stare. "That's besides the point, Edmond, He's a blaggard who's abused our sister's honor!" Travis turned to the general. "Sir, I applaud your upholding of justice. However, my brothers and I have a matter of our own honor to discuss with this feller, namely, the abduction of our sister."

"He didn't abduct me, Travis and you know it!"

Edmond shook his head. "You must understand, General, that this union was not sanctioned by our father."

"I was not aware, Reverend, thank you for the clarification." Greer sat back and chewed his meat for a moment. "I see why this matter perplexes you all so. Now, I'm not one to pry into a family's business. I will say that striking a balance between familial duty and the motives of the heart is a challenge that has bested greater men than I. However, I propose a solution that might satisfy all parties here today, save of course, our Mrs. Shonka. My condolences. You make a handsome bride but alas, your poor choice of groom has left us in a tricky spot, hospitality-wise. I do hope you will not hold it against me."

"You intend to hang my husband," Lizzy said. "I most certainly will hold that against you till the day of my last breath!"

"You see now this is why I dislike inviting womenfolk to camp," Greer chuckled. "They simply do not grasp the intricacies of martial affairs."

"And what solution might that be?" Jim asked. "The one you propose?"

"You have a directness about you, son, and I like that!" Greer paused to scratch his chin then continued. "The solution I propose is one that unties every Gordian Knot. As stated, I intend to hang Francis here, which will see him punished for all his many crimes against man and God. But to you Hawkins men, I can offer some restitution."

"Restitution?" Travis said, his smile perking up for the first time since they'd arrived in this infernal camp. "What we talking about here, General? Money?"

"Alas, Mr. Hawkins, I am but a simple soldier. I know only my orders and my cause, which is a righteousness that fuels me, ever onward. I have little in the way of funds, but what I do have is opportunity. Opportunity for you and your brothers to contribute to a righteous cause. I see in this place the chance for greatness—a greatness in potential, if you will. But it needs a strong hand, someone who can bring it to flower, as it were. Pardon the botanical metaphors, a healthy repast does tend to make me ramble on so. But I hope I have made my point. Greatness compels me to perform heroic deeds."

"I don't follow, General," said Jim. "Are you recruiting us?"

"That I am, young James, that I am!"

The three brothers passed a look around their side of the table. Jim was of a mind to walk out then and there but noticed the armed guards at the tent's entrance.

Greer stood and paced the tent. He rubbed his pinky ring absently as he spoke.

"To you brothers, I offer positions among the ranks as befit your talents and station. Field commissions, of course. Alas, Miss Mercy, we have no need of a tracker, I'm afraid."

Jim looked at Mery and noticed that she had been sitting in silent contemplation the entire time they'd been here. She had known ever since they arrived what fate awaited her. It was, Jim then realized in that moment, the fate that ultimately awaited them all.

"And what about me?" Lizzy asked.

"Directness, I see, is a family trait," Greer offered a sly smile. "I see why you admire her so, Tezu. Alas, Mrs. Elizabeth, you must remain under my protection."

"Now hold up here, General," Travis said.

"That is completely unacceptable," Edmond crossed his arms. "Lizzy must be allowed to journey home to our parents, for her own safety, if nothing else."

"This is a non-negotiable addendum," Greer said.

He nodded to Swann, who had been loitering by the tent opening. The Captain drew a revolver, which he cocked and placed at Lizzy's head.

Lizzy bit her lip and straightened her back. She looked at Francis. They shared the same bond, the same soul, and could communicate entire monologues with a glance. This one, however, was universal.

"Am I to have no say in my own fate?" Lizzy looked at Greer, then to Travis, Edmond, and Jim.

"Understand this, Mrs. Elizabeth: The road will not be easy, but we will shortly be putting into a more comfortable abode. There you will be treated as the fair angel you truly deserve to be. You will be cared for, attended to, and want for nothing. More than that, even—you will serve as the embodiment of the noble family for which all true men of valor will gladly lay down their lives to protect. You must admit, that is far better than death by the noose or the slow depredations of life as the paramour to mischief."

"I object to this whole affair," Edmond said. "I, sir, am a Reverend of the Good Book, not some thief in the night. I will have no part in this."

"Well now see you are in fact vital to the endeavor," said Greer. "I need you to serve as the Hand of the Lord in these matters. We've been in want of a new chaplain, ever since our last one, well, met an untimely end. And I'm gonna need an unimpeachable soul to mind the men at their task, make sure they stay on the straight and narrow, you understand."

"And if we still refuse?" Jim asked.

Greer held his hands out, palms up, as if in supplication. "I could do with you as I like. This here is an Army camp, one I command to the man. And you all have been found in defiance of the laws of man and God alike, aiding this here treasonous so-and-so. I am perfectly within my right, and bound by martial law to dispose of traitors and those who abet them with the direst of punishments. If'n you would rather we dispense with the pleasantries, I can of course move on to the sentencing."

They all grew quiet once more. All except Lizzy.

"Just like a Confederate. Why, I bet you'd snatch the wind from its moorings if you found some profit in it! You… You… no account, pie eating, son of a poltroon!"

"Sticks and stones, my dear, sticks and stones. But you'll have a place when the South rises again." Greer raised his glass and sipped some wine.

Travis looked at his brothers. Edmond's perplexed scowl was hard to read. He was either deep in thought or about to pass gass. Jim, however, sat stone-faced. He'd made up his mind. Travis could tell, which left him but a narrow window to speak before his youngest brother cocked up the whole situation.

"You drive a hard bargain there General, but I think I speak for my brothers when I say that I look forward to the coming challenges."

Greer smiled. "I am sure that you will not be disappointed, Master Hawkins!"

Both men stood and shook firm hands.

"Wait," Jim said.

"Jim, don't," Mercy whispered and shook her head.

Francis sat stoically. Lizzy held his hand.

Travis leaned in to whisper in Jim's ear.

"I don't know what angle you're playing, little brother, but now ain't the time to show off your book learning."

Jim looked at his brother and for the first time, saw the horror behind his eyes. The grasping vanity, the dissolute aspirations to become... what? Whatever he could, as long as it gave him prestige over another.

General Elkanah Greer clapped his hands. "Well, now that we've settled the business, let us celebrate our new venture with a toast." Greer stood, glass in hand. Edmond and Travis did likewise, though Edmond stood on shaking legs.

"I am sorry," Jim said, remaining seated. "But I cannot be part of this farce."

"Jim, let us pray on the matter some," Edmond said. "I think with reflection, you and I may find some common ground with the General."

"Common ground?" Jim glared at Greer. "With this traitor to God and Country? Never."

"Humph," Greer's smile faltered. "And here I thought we were beginning to get along."

The General nodded to Swann. "Captain. If you would be so kind as to escort them three to the brig," he nodded to Jim, Mercy, and Francis. "And then fetch three lengths of rope."

Swann rocked Francis forward in his chair, nearly drawing it out from under him. Francis caught his feet however and stood. He looked to Lizzy, stoic as ever, then turned and led the way. Jim and Mercy followed without another word.

"Now that we've dealt with that unpleasantness," Greer sat in his chair. He looked at Travis, Edmond, and Lizzy. "Let us tuck into this feast Cookie has left us, shall we?"

Greer ate with gusto and no lack of decorum. Travis, Edmond, and Lizzy took not a single bite between them.

Once Greer finished his meal, he gave the order to strike camp. Swann gathered up Jim, Mercy, and Francis and they set out ahead of the regiment on horseback.

It was dusk by the time they reached the hanging tree. That's what everyone called it, and Jim could immediately see why: this old gray oak, dried under uncounted years of sun and wind and rain, stuck out of the earth like some beckoning finger of a buried giant. A single sturdy limb stuck out over the place where two roads met.

It was here that Jim, Mercy, and Francis were set to the grim task of digging their own graves. Swann tossed them each a shovel and pointed to a bare spot beside the left hand road.

"Dig," he said. Then he wandered off to yell at Finch and Hoots, who were busy fumbling with the ropes they would use to tie their nooses.

So they dug.

By the time the sun had set, Jim and them had found the rhythm of it, a grim drumbeat of their shovels hitting dirt, a grunt of effort, then dirt flinging to the ground.

Jim took a breather to wipe the sweat and grime from his brow. Francis and Mercy did the same.

"I'm sorry to you both for getting you into this," Francis said in a low voice.

"A tracker's life ain't nothing but a high steppin' dance to avoid this fate," said Mercy. "Bound to fill my dance card eventually."

"You two seem awfully resigned to our fate," Jim said.

Mercy and Francis shared a quick look that spoke volumes.

"What was that?" Jim asked.

"Don't worry, James," Francis laid a hand on his shoulder and gave him a friendly squeeze. "Stay close. When the time comes, you'll know what to do."

"Stay close?" Jim shook his head. "Now what the heck does that mean?"

"Back to digging!" Swann grumbled.

The great bird that normally sat on his shoulder had taken up a roost on the hanging tree, directly above them, watching their every shovelful.

"Shirkin'!" squawked the bird. "They's shirkin'!"

"Indeed, Mr. Daw." Captain Swann made a show of examining their work. "Shoddy digging, if I do say so. But it's your grave!" He slapped Francis on the back, hard. Then he wandered off, laughing at his joke.

A short while later, General Greer arrived to survey the scene. By then, the camp had been struck, the wagons loaded, and the revenants had been regimented in their ranks, lined up to march.

"It is a shame to see a stalwart figure such as yourself resigned to his fate," Greer said, looking down at Jim. he stood at the edge of his grave, hand on his saber, smiling.

"You can go to Hell, sir," Jim spat in the dirt and kept digging.

Swann raised a hand to strike him but Greer caught it.

"He's a free soul now," Greer said. "Let him empty his bile at me. Soon he will lie in that ground till Judgment Day comes."

Swann pouted at being denied his petty cruelty but complied.

Greer waved his hand and Swann led Francis, Jim, and Mercy out of the dirt to stand before him. Lizzy, Travis, and Edmond arrived then and once they were all gathered 'round, Greer said, "You may now say your goodbyes. But be quick. A Maudlin scene is an ill omen." Then he turned and left.

Now, Francis and Lizzy, having carried out a clandestine love affair under the noses of their family and community, had developed a sort of code that they used to pass information to one another that, to the outside observer would seem like innocuous chit-chat, but had, upon deciphering with the key of their hearts, another meaning entirely.

Thus, when Lizzy said, "It's a shame about the weather," Francis knew she was really asking, *where shall we meet, if we can?*

Francis nodded and said, "Yes. These clouds will make for some poor road conditions, should it rain." This translated as, *I'm sure that escape will be difficult to impossible, best not chance it.*

Hoots and Finch looked at the dark sky, devoid of clouds, and showing a waxing gibbous moon. They looked at one another for an explanation and shrugged.

"Clouds are clouds, sure enough," said Lizzy. This meant, *I'm aware of the difficulties that lay ahead, but should an opportunity for escape arise, I will take that chance.*

"Whether it rains or not, only time will tell," Francis said, which also meant, *I will come for you no matter what.*

Francis and Lizzy kissed.

"Ah, young love," said Finch. "Ain't it sweet?"

Swann spit in the dirt.

Next, it was the brother's turn to say farewell.

"Jim. It's not too late for you to come to your senses. Join us,"

Travis said. He leaned in close to whisper, "We can turn the tables on this here fool. You and me and Edmond can make a go of it on our own! Come on What do you say?"

"What do I say?" Jim stared at him hard. "I say that you've always been a no-account so-and-so, a puffed up bag of nothin', and a poor older brother. That's what I say."

Travis shrugged and moved on.

Edmond hugged Jim tight and then held him at arm's length. He looked him square in the eyes and said, "Though I may walk through the valley of the shadow of Death, I fear no—"

"If it's all the same to you, Reverend," Jim said, "I'd as soon as you don't."

"I will pray for your immortal soul, James, know this," Edmond nodded and climbed onto the fresh horse Greer had provided. "At least I am no longer tethered to my brother like Able to Cain."

Even Hoots rolled his eyes at this.

Lizzy turned to Mercy.

"I'm sorry about all this," Mercy said.

"Ain't nothin to apologize for," Lizzy said. She gave Mercy a hug, which she wasn't expecting. It left her flustered in a way she would not be able to put into words, never having had siblings herself.

Lizzy whispered something in Mercy's ear, but no one heard what it was.

Jim, she hugged last and longest.

"Seems I'm always saying goodbye to you, little brother," she sniffed back a tear.

"I… I'm sorry, Lizzy. I tried…"

She whispered in his ear, "Stay close to Francis. He'll bring you back to me."

She pushed him away then.

"What sweet sentiments," Swann said.

"Do you have any family, Mr. Swann?" asked Lizzy.

"Cannot claim that I have. And it's Captain Swann."

"Your loss," she said. "And speaking of loss, your side was roundly defeated in the recent war, so your rank and titles are as hollow as your heart."

Lizzy joined Travis, Edmond, and the rest of the soldiers on the road out of the camp. Greer was the last to leave, surveying the scene of their impending hanging once more. To Swann, he gave one final order.

"Be quick about it, then rendezvous with the regiment. We have much work to do before the party."

Swann saluted. Greer rode on. Jim, Francis, and Mercy watched as they all rode off into the darkness, and stayed even after there was no sight of them.

"Well now," Swann said. "Let's get on with it then, shall we?"

Finch and Hoots led Abraham Lincoln, Shadow, and Jim's horse, whose name Jim had forgotten. They were set on their respective horses and then their hands tied behind their backs. The horses were lined up next to one another, Mercy on the outside, Francis inside, and Jim in the middle, beneath the hanging tree. Hoots and Finch tossed the nooses over the tree limb and then tightened them around their necks. The brigade then gathered around, led by Swann on his own horse, Sebastian.

"Y'all have been found guilty of desertion, aiding and abettin', blah blah blah." From his perch on Sebastian's back, Captain Swann could look each of them in the eye as he grinned. "Frankly, none that matters. Y'all were born to hang, and that's a fact."

Swann waved his hand and Hoots walked behind the horses, swatting each on their flank. Abraham Lincoln and Shadow both held their footing.

But Jim's horse bolted.

He ran straight towards the brigade of soldiers who had been meat-starved for weeks to make them compliant. The horse stood no chance against a dozen revenants, who dragged it down gnashing it to bits with their blunted teeth. The sound of the horse screaming to death was a haunting one that none present would soon forget.

"Dang it! His neck didn't snap," Finch pouted. "I like it when their neck snaps. Sounds like a bundle of twigs breaking…"

It was true, though the horse bolted as planned the drop did not break Jim's neck. Instead, he dangled from the end of the noose, kicking, his hands bound, trying to find the ground, but it was two feet below the heel of his boot.

Shadow and Abraham Lincoln, being far more reliable steeds, remained where they were, keeping Travis and Mercy upright and with enough slack that their nooses were of little concern.

"Corporal Finch, your knotsmanship leaves something to be desired," bellowed Swann from his own saddle. "Shew them horses. I want a show, Got dang it!"

Finch and Hoots stepped to the horses, only for them both to rear up and kick. Finch took a hoof from Shadow to the stomach, which sent him reeling back. Abraham Lincoln planted a solid hoof print on Hoots' forehead, and it was lucky for him that he was no longer counted among the living, for such a blow would otherwise mean instant death. It did send him tumbling to the ground, however.

Swann dismounted to better berate his men.

"On your feet, soldier!" he yelled at Hoots, whose neck was broken in three places. "I want those three dead!"

Mercy had clung to her saddle, feet in the stirrups, and though her hands were bound behind her back, she had a small knife concealed under Abraham Lincoln's saddle. With this, she quickly cut her bonds.

Jim was struggling to breathe now; his face had turned a terrible shade of red.

Francis, who knew a thing or two about knots and the tying thereof, had freed his hands and lept from Shadow's back. He tucked his knees together and landed atop the nearest revenant soldier, snapping his neck. It did in fact sound like a bundle of dried twigs breaking.

"Brigade!" hollered Swann, "bring me his head!"

A dozen revenant soldiers moved towards Francis and Mercy. Abraham Lincoln kept them at bay with a volley of bucking, and kicking, though this did hinder Mercy's ability to free her hands.

Francis kicked Hoots in the behind, sending the struggling cadaver tumbling over onto his face. There in the soldier's pack was his bayonet. Francis grabbed this and rushed for the nearest soldier.

The six soldiers who advanced on him were a raggedy bunch. With his bayonet in hand, Francis proceeded to stab the first soldier within reach. He plunged the rusty length of steel once into his stomach, once in the eye, and once through the ear. As the dead man tumbled to the ground, Francis plucked the bayonet from his pack. Doubly armed, he leapt on the remaining soldiers, stabbing at every soft spot he could find.

Mercy, meanwhile, had freed her hands.

With all haste, Abraham Lincoln moved beneath Jim, who was dangling still, his face a pale shade of deathly white she was all too familiar with. Mercy caught him and hauled him bodily over Abe's bridle and sawed away at the rope around his neck.

Once the rope was free, Jim's body slumped to the ground.

Francis came up covered in blood.

"Talbot Swann! You and I have old grudges." He pointed both bayonets at Swann. "What's say we settle them tonight?"

Swann black glass eyes twinkled in the firelight. Then he turned and ran, stumbling through a thorn bush, calling, "regroup!" as he sprinted into the night.

Finch and the remaining revenants who could find their feet staggered after their captain.

"Yella bastard," Francis hissed.

He dropped the bayonets and ran to Mercy's side.

She had rolled Jim over and pulled the rope from his neck. She gave Francis a grave look.

"He ain't breathing," she said.

6
It Means "White Flower"

On the morning of the first day of her captivity, Lizzy awoke, nauseous but also resolved. She allowed herself a moment's indulgence, naming all the other places she wished she would wake up to find herself (in Tezu's arms, back in her bed alone in Texarkana, in the abandoned outhouse Travis locked her in when she was seven). But no. She awoke in some mildewed tent, gripped by the same stomach-churning queasiness that was as much a result of her situation as it was her morning sickness.

After vomiting into the bucket she kept beside her cot, she decided it was time to stop feeling sorry for herself and sort out the situation. She dressed, brushed her hair, found her boots, and went to greet the morning.

The camp was already up and about. Lizzy's tent was adjacent to Greer's beside the campfire, next to the tent shared by her brothers. She eased herself onto the small wooden stool with a threadbare pillow and stretched to put on her boots. She found her feet ever so slightly more out of reach than the day before. This was due to her belly, which was growing daily. Still, she managed to put her boots on with some creative negotiation involving a rock and her own stubbornness.

As she leaned back and caught her breath, one of the greasy little scullery boys approached with her breakfast. This was a tray of hard biscuits, warmed-over beans, and a flagon of weak tea. As she ate, she studied her predicament, weighing the facts and sussing out the boundaries.

During the War, a regular, on-the-march living and breathing Brigade of Confederates would have comprised some 12,000 men, with attendant privates, corporals, captains, majors, lieutenant colonels, colonels, brigadier generals, surgeons, cooks, adjutants, chaplains, and the like. However, Greer's party was a threadbare affair and might have mustered one complete regiment of approximately one thousand bodies. There were but nine companies of soldiers, and these made up what Greer referred to as the corps, though he liked to pronounce the word with a hard lisp, so it sounded very much like he was saying, "corpse," on account of them being, to a man, already dead.

How this state of affairs came to be was a matter that seemed perfectly natural to Greer and his officers, but struck Lizzy as unnatural a predicament as could be imagined.

Their present encampment was set on a somewhat level spit of dirt between a grove of trees, which allowed the corralling of the soldiers. There they could mill about groaning and shuffling as they wanted. The goal was to keep them from wandering off and spooking the locals until such a time as spooking was called for.

The officers, who were, near as Lizzy could figure it, still breathing folk, would set their tents in a square around the central fire pit. This served as a primary lighting source, counsel place for Greer, and cookfire. Cookie, the burly fellow Lizzy had met upon arrival, would haul his wagon up to the south face of the fire and unload pots and pans all in a clatter, while his scullery crew set about boiling and skinning whatever was to serve as that night's repast.

Despite his appearance and neglectful hygiene, Cookie did set a decent table for Greer, one to which Lizzy was made a guest. It took some getting used to but the meat she had been served was usually fresh chicken or rabbit, the latter a tad greasy but well-seasoned. It came with a side of boiled vegetables, usually root veg such as carrots or, on occasion, corn, but mostly it was whatever had been pilfered from some field encountered during that day's march.

This seemed to be much of the purpose of their progress, simply foraging for enough comestibles to support the two dozen breathing bodies that comprised the Council of the Confederate Army in Exile, which is how Greer referred to them.

Lizzy chewed on her biscuit, sipped her tea, and came to a realization: if there were other souls here—living souls that is—then perhaps one or maybe even two of them might be serving under duress. Perhaps not quite a hostage to the degree she was, but wrangled, shanghaied, or otherwise conscripted into Greer's service through duplicity. If such was the case, all she needed to do to make her escape was win over one of these men; to find her own confederate among the Confederates. As Lizzy finished her meager breakfast, she spied the first soul she might be able to sway back toward the light of reason.

Marmaduke Hatch was the Company surgeon, but everyone called him Doc Hatchet. Lizzy found the sobriquet a bit off-putting, even though he was one of the more reasonable of Greer's officers.

Doc Hatchet was a genial man in his fifties with a weathered face and sober hand. He wore a tweed suit and pocket watch, which he checked on the regular, though it appeared to have stopped counting hours sometime in the distant past. Despite this eccentricity, he was one of the few who gave Lizzy any respect at all.

"Well good morning, Mrs. Lizzy," he doffed his hat like he was some neighbor come to chat about the weather and share the local gossip. "And how are we feeling this morning?"

"I'm tacking into the wind, as my grandpa used to say."

Doc Hatchet made himself at home atop a barrel.

"Now I haven't heard that old saying in a coon's age! You're from Texarkana way, so I hear, is that right?"

"That is correct, sir."

"Oh, none of that sir nonsense! I work for a living—sometimes they even stay that way!"

He laughed. Lizzy did not.

"If you don't mind me saying, Doc, I find that joke a bit macabre, considering the nature of some of those under your care."

"Oh, you are referring to the uh…" Doc Hatchet glanced around, noting the squad of loping cadavers shambling in something like a line as they marched off to the morning patrol. "Ahem yes, well… gallows humor, as it were."

His smile faltered a little. This was the opening Lizzy had been hoping for.

"And how did a scholar of the human condition such as yourself come to find himself in service to such a villain as the General?" she asked.

Doc Hatchet grew silent as if he'd not given the matter any real thought before.

"The General is a conundrum, to be sure," he said at last. "But the opportunity I have is immeasurable. Do you know I learned more about the healing arts in my first six months out here in the Switch than in all of my two years of medical training Back East? Look here…"

He took out the battered leather journal he carried with him and showed it to Lizzy. Its pages were filled with diagrams, anatomical sketches, charts, and cramped handwritten notes.

"Few more years out here, I'll be able to go Back East with a cure for the common cold!"

"That is a noble goal, to be sure," Lizzy said. "But is there perhaps too high a cost to that knowledge? The General surely is in league with forces that mean him—and by extension, you and me—no good turn, correct?"

Doc Hatchet shrugged. "The General's methods and aims may strike the uneducated as unorthodox, I agree—but as a man of science, I would not pass up the opportunity he has afforded me for all the tea in China, as they say."

"Of course," Lizzy said.

"Now, unless you have any medical ailments I need to check on, I'll return to my morning perambulations. Good morning, Mrs. Lizzy." The Doctor donned his hat once more and set off to make his rounds.

Lizzy sighed to herself. The Doctor was no use, as in thrall to Greer as the rest of these nincompoops. And what an assortment they were. Whereas Doc Hatchet's pleasant continence belied a simpleton's grasp of the politics of her situation, he was preferable to any of the other officers who were, to a man, a loathsome assortment of scalawags with names like Palmaroy, Smails, Dillford, Grimly, and Chance. Though sounding like the vilest Law Firm this side of Perdition, there was not a scholar between them of anything but torment.

And then there was the matter of Travis.

He emerged from his tent, dressed in his new uniform. New, here meaning new to him, as it looked to have moldered in the bottom of some half-forgotten footlocker for most of a decade. The former owner's rank and medals were still attached, and Travis polished his buttons as Lizzy marched up to him.

"What do you think?" he puffed out his chest.

"Why, if Uncle Marcus could see you now," she spat.

Their uncle Marcus had fought in the war for the Union. He'd spent time in a Confederate prisoner-of-war camp, catching pneumonia and subsisting on moldy bread until he and a handful of fellow prisoners managed to escape. He spent the rest of his days down a whiskey bottle, looking to forget the life (and three fingers on his right hand) that the war had cost him.

Travis's smile deflated as he caught the gist of Lizzy's comment.

"Now that ain't the right way to talk to your eldest brother now is it?" he said. "Why can't you be happy for me? I'm making something of myself!"

"You're making a fool is what you're making!"

Travis dismissed her anger and frustration with a wry smile.

"The General is right about one thing," he said, "Womenfolk ain't got the metal for noble deeds."

"And what the hell does that mean?" Lizzy said.

"It means you got no idea what I've got planned. You oughta watch yerself, so as not to get in my way."

"You mean, like Jim did?" Lizzy stared at him hard.

"Forget about Jim! I'm going to be part of something grand!" Travis sputtered. "Something historical! And you're just going to be a bystander to it all."

He turned and stalked off into the camp.

Lizzy spent most of the next two days in the back of the provisions wagon. The road was long, winding, hot, and dusty; there was but little to see but dry ground, baked and blistering under the summer sun.

The provisions wagon and mule team was tended by the Quartermaster, a spindly feller named Willhelm Gates. He was a pleasant enough chap, for a conniving tramp who had consigned himself to oblivion and ignominy as one of Greer's lackeys. He spent the better part of the first day rhapsodizing about a sweetheart back in San Antonio, whom he hoped would wait for him, "Until the war's agreeable end," as he put it.

Lizzy had not the heart to tell him that most likely his sweetheart was now either an old maid or had found herself a more respectable beau than some pining traitor to God and Country.

Having exhausted all avenues of conversation with Quartermaster Gates on the first day, Lizzy spent much of the second day laying in the back of the provisions wagon, cradling a bucket while using a sack of flower as a pillow. To ease the nausea of the road, Lizzy instead focused on other matters. Mostly, she dreamed up elaborate and foolhardy escape plots, but also fantasies of bloody revenge executed upon her brothers, and acts of shocking violence against Greer and his men.

Lizzy was startled to find how easily she could imagine throttling them all with her bare hands or stabbing their fleshy parts with whatever metal implements were to hand (she wasn't certain as to the cutting efficacy of a serving spoon against a man's carotid artery, but was willing to give it a try).

As these thoughts were neither pleasant nor practical, she prayed to the Four Winds to carry them away, for they would do her only harm to linger on them. So preoccupied was Lizzy with her sorry situation, that she didn't even realize they had stopped until the bugle announced Recall.

Lizzy stuck her head out the back of the wagon. When last she had looked, they were drawing alongside a dry creek bed, with nothing but the blaring blue sky and the desert earth as far as she could see. But now, they had turned up a lane and were marching down a wide boulevard lined with huge oak trees, moss hanging from their limbs.

To either side were wide green fields surrounded by rolling hills. In the fields, dozens of workers toiled away. They paused to mop their dark brows and take in the sight of the army marching home. A young boy was sent ahead to inform one and all, which he did by yelling, "They home! They home!"

Samuel was working in the blacksmith's shack, sweat dripping down his forehead and staining his shirt. He was so lost in the rhythm of the hammer banging on the anvil that he didn't even hear the news until Tandy was standing right in front of him.

"You hear, Samuel?" the little boy grinned, "They back!"

It took Samuel a moment to understand what the boy was saying and another for it to register completely.

"We heard ya, Tandy," Ben said. Ben was older by a few years, graying at the temples but he still could swing a hammer. He pulled the horseshoe he was quenching out of the steaming bucket and dropped it onto the workbench.

Ben wiped his brow. "Now go make yourself useful, and tell Miss Rachel."

Tandy grinned and ran off.

Ben threw a towel at Samuel, who caught it and wiped his face.

"Best quench that," said Ben, not even looking.

Samuel nodded and put down the hammer. Using a pair of tongs, took the wedge of red hot steel he'd been shaping over to the bucket and dropped it in. Out of the bucket of steaming water he pulled a new arm for the old padlock he'd been fixing.

Ben looked over the half a loop of molded steel approvingly.

"Looks good," he said. "Best get that lock finished, now that they back."

Samuel nodded.

By then, the Revenants were filing along the narrow lane that led into a wooded area. Samuel and Ben stood in the door of the blacksmith's shack and watched them lope down the lane.

"S'pose they won?" Samuel asked.

He and Ben shared a look. And laughed.

"Best not ask that up at the house," Ben said.

Samuel was young and couldn't recall much from before the war. He'd only been three or four when it began, and as far as he was concerned, it was simply another part of life on the plantation. Still, he had questions.

"You think it'll ever end?" Samuel asked, more serious.

Ben shrugged. "Not for me to say."

"But you remember before. What was it like?"

"Same as now," he said. "Some are righteous born, destined to conquer and fight, and the rest of us, well we make horseshoes and don't ask too many questions. Ya hear?"

"Yes'r," Samuel said, and returned to the anvil and hammer. Soon the rhythm took all the questions he had and flattened them into sparks until nothing was left of them but an ache in his shoulder.

* * *

Tandy ran on, telling everyone the news. By the time he'd made a complete circuit around the plantation and returned to the front porch, he was out of breath.

"General… Greer… Sir…!" Tandy called breathless. "Welcome back…!"

The General had dismounted and stood watching Tandy as he ran up to him smiled wide.

"My, my, is that Tandy? Gracious, son, you're shootin' up!" General Greer offered the boy a hand. He took it, and gave it a firm pump. "And a strong hand, too! Well now, we'll have to see you apprenticed soon, put all those grand muscles to work!"

"Yes'r, Little Tom's got me helpin' out the Cooper, pickin' scrap wood off the ground. Says I'm doin' good, sir!"

"And I am glad to hear it, Tandy," Greer smiled.

The caravan stopped at the front steps of an enormous plantation house. It was big and white, and in need of a lick of paint, but imposing still, with columns lining the font and grove of magnolias surrounding the West Wing, the pungent scent of the flowers in bloom wafting on a gentle breeze.

"Well, I'll be snookered," Travis said. He dismounted and straightened the buttons on his new uniform.

"Is this your home, General?" Asked Edmond. He likewise wore a gray coat retrieved from the bottom of someone else's footlocker. It was a size too big but Quartermaster Gates assured him they'd have it tailored, and chaplain's epaulets applied and everything.

"It is indeed, Reverend Hawkins. Welcome to Blanchefleur, my ancestral manse."

Greer headed to the back of the wagon and offered a gloved hand to Lizzy. She took it, but only out of necessity; she needed to steady herself as she climbed down from the cart full of barrels and half-empty crates.

"Come, Miss Hawkins, let me show you to your new home," Greer offered an arm.

"My name is Mrs. Shonka, thank you very much." Disdaining his gallantry, she marched up to the front where her brothers stood with the other officers, basking in the radiance, as it were.

The front door opened wide and a dark skinned feller with curly hair emerged. He wore a fine suit with a silk cravat and spectacles. Beside him stood a tall woman in a dress with a starched white collar. Her black skin appeared dark blue in the light filtering through the trees. He bowed and she curtsied to the General and his men.

Several house servants followed behind her, attired in finery, their dark complexions equally regal in the afternoon light. Greer marched up to them, removing his gloves and looking them over, each in turn as if reviewing a menu.

"Welcome home, General Greer, officers, gentlemen, and lady," said the man. He nodded to the officers and bowed to Lizzy but never took his attention off the General for more than a moment. "I trust the campaign was a success?"

"As well as can be expected, Robbe, thank you." Greer handed the butler his gloves. Robbe handed them in turn to one of the valets.

"Everything in order here?" Greer asked.

"Of course, General Greer, sir," said the woman. "We maintain."

She had a lovely Creole accent that reminded Lizzy of the trip her family had taken to New Orleans the summer when she turned twelve. Lizzy had been mesmerized by the perfume of the city; its regal dilapidation and heady intermingling of passion and commerce. Lizzy had been transfixed, almost as much then as she was by this curious woman now.

"Very good. Miss Rachel, we have some new members of the coterie, see that they are welcomed in an appropriate fashion."

"Thy will, General," Miss Rachel nodded.

With a snap of her fingers, several servants unloaded the officer's belongings and hauled them into the house.

"This way, gentleman," Robbe smiled. "Refreshments have been laid out in the parlor."

Lizzy followed the officers into the house.

"See Lizzy, this is not so bad." Edmond took her arm, as much for his own sake as hers. They moved into the foyer, all mahogany and polished teakwood, with a crystal chandelier and a staircase winding to a landing. "I could find a place like this quite homey. Lovely, even. Look at those doilies! Are they not something? I've always admired a well-made piece of lace."

Lizzy pulled her arm out of his grasp and shot him a look.

"Jim is dead," she said. "As is my husband. And you wanna talk about lace doilies?"

Edmond didn't know what to say to that. He had been wrestling with the knowledge that he had a hand in Jim's fate, even though Travis had dismissed his concerns. And here came Travis, to add fuel to the fire.

"What are you two on about now?" he hissed.

Lizzy offered him a hard stare then stomped off into the parlor.

"It is Jim's fate that has her... upset," Edmond said.

"Jim made his own bed," Travis said. "And Lizzy too. They don't share our vision."

"And what, pray tell, is our vision?" asked Edmond.

Travis slapped Edmond on the shoulder. "Well let's go find out, shall we?" He grinned and stomped off into the parlor with the rest.

Edmond and Travis found Lizzy already seated in a high-backed chair beside an empty hearth. As it was late spring with the summer fast approaching, there was no need to warm the room. A large pair of windows stood open, lacy curtains wafting in a gentle warm breeze.

The officers were, to a man, markedly changed: whereas they had been stern and worn down by months on the spur, they now stood around relaxed, hands fiddling with their buttons as they spoke in convivial tones about the weather, the fine decor, and the pretty serving girls.

These were a trio of young black women, ranging in age from fifteen to twenty, who smiled as they emerged from a servant's entrance bearing silver trays with tall glasses. They were followed at a pace by Miss Rachel carrying a carafe of golden brown liquid, a sprig of flowering herb swirling inside. As they passed, Lizzy smelled the unmistakable scent of summer lawns, sun-warmed horse flesh, and peppermint.

General Greer entered last from the opposite side by the main door. He made a sweeping gesture and wore a wide grin.

"My, it does my heart a glad turn to see such fine men and women in their roles. At ease by the way."

A round of chuckles circled the room.

The girls delivered a glass each to Edmond and Travis and one for Lizzy as well, though she set hers on the table, pointedly avoiding the doilies and letting the sweating glass drip onto the table. Edmond had already downed his Julep before the General raised his glass in a toast.

"Welcome one and all to Blanchefleur! Salud!"

"Salud!" the officers called and drank their juleps.

"We stand here on the eve of greatness, gentleman," the General went on. "Soon we shall have our day. And on that day, each and every one of you will be called upon to do your duty. Only then can we restore the old order and begin a new in the story of this great nation. But until then, we must buttress our reserves. To that end, I enjoin you all to make yourselves home here. Quartermaster Gates will post what light duties are required of you, but your time will be mostly your own. Consider this R and R. Again, I welcome you all, and especially our new guest, Miss Lizzy. By the way, Rachel, have a room ready for the Widow Shonka, if you will."

Rachel nodded and drifted out of the room along with her three shadows.

"Now Miss Lizzy, I see you have not partaken of your refreshments," Greer stalked over, his boots ringing hollow on the oaken beams. "Are you at all well?"

"Ain't thirsty," said Lizzy.

The truth was she had a powerful thirst, agitated by the dust of the road and made all the more acute by the arrival of the julep. But she would be a got-danged fool if she gave Greer a moment's satisfaction, in this or anything he would bid of her.

"I offer a toast and you do not drink?" Greer clucked his tongue. "That's poor manners."

"Drink up, Lizzy," Travis said. He handed her the glass.

She set it down again.

"Juleps turn my stomach," she said.

"Now I know for a fact you once drank all the julep at one Fourth of July party," Edmond said. He chuckled meekly.

"I was twelve," Lizzy gritted her teeth. "And it's on account of that party I don't care for the beverage no more, Edmond."

Greer sighed. "I can see you intend to make yourself as cheerful as a thorn bush."

Lizzy could see a coldness behind his smile. He was a sly one, the General, but it was a lonely and cold wind that filled his heart. Such a coldness turns all it touches brittle. And brittle things, Lizzy well knew, were easy to break.

"You are of course free to do as you please, Miss Lizzy," Greer said. "This place can be your refuge from a world of hardship and torment or it can be a prison of your own making. The choice is yours."

He turned to the group, raised his glass, and prepared to make another toast.

Lizzy heard not a word of it, as Travis leaned in and hissed in her ear, "Don't ruin this for me!"

He turned back to the crowd and clapped along with the rest at Greer's words.

Lizzy looked at the julep sweating on the table. She left it there, untouched.

After the speechifying was through, the officers retired to their rooms. Lizzy was shown to hers by a friendly young girl named Haney who was fifteen if she was a day, and a chatterbox to boot.

"...This one time we had fireworks! Now Miss Coffie—she's the Cook and makes the best apple pies!—Miss Coffie said she ain't never seen fireworks like that before, all bright and red and yellow, like diamonds in the night sky. I think it was to commemorate the Siege of Vicksburg, whatever that was..."

The train of this conversation had begun, as near as Lizzy could recollect, at her commenting on Edmond's slight about the Fourth of July under her breath. How they had ended up at the Siege of Vicksburg, Lizzy couldn't say. Fireworks may have been involved.

"...And now here we are, Mistress Lizzy."

They reached a door about midway down the hall.

"You can call me Lizzy, dear, I ain't no one's mistress."

They entered the room to find it small but well-appointed and clean. There was a bed, a dressing table, and a large wardrobe in the corner, with a window looking out on the fields. Below, a dozen workers were toiling away.

"Oh, no Ma'am, that's not how things are done here at Blanchenflour, I mean, Blanche flower, I mean... dagnabbit!" Haney said, then looked at Lizzy, eyes wide. "I'm sorry! Don't tell Master!"

"I wouldn't tell that scoundrel the time of day if my mouth were a church bell." Lizzy squeezed the girl's hand. "You're fine."

"Thank you, Miss," Haney sniffed back a tear. "I'm sorry I never could get that silly name right. It means white flower in French. Why can't they say 'white flower' and be done with it?"

"It is a silly name, to be sure," said Lizzy. "It comes from the tales of King Arthur. Blanchefleur was his sister, and mother of Sir Galahad, who was one of the truest, bravest knights of the round table."

"Hoowee! You sure know your stuff!"

"Ma liked to read. In fact, she called my younger brother Galahad," Lizzy drifted away in thought but found herself after a moment. "Don't suppose you have much time for that sort of thing though."

"No, Ma'am. None of us here read, exceptin' Miss Rachel, and Little Tom, and he but a little bit. Master says it's above our station and'd give us notions."

"There are worse things than having notions," Lizzy took a turn around the room.

"Oh no, ma'am! My older brother Jonah, God rest him, he had the notions somethin' bad. It was his undoing."

Lizzy chuckled. Haney did not.

"Oh, you're serious… Oh. What happened to him, if I may ask?"

"He got the notions bad, as I say. Drove him to try and escape Blanchenfl—leave here. Master done him in with the whip."

"Greer whipped your brother to death? And did nobody tell the authorities or no one about this?"

Haney shrugged. "Don't know about no authorities. But Master Greer says that's the fate of a runaway slave—the lash or the noose."

"Slave?" Lizzy fell off the edge of the bed.

Haney helped steady her.

"There you go, Misses. Can't have you fallin' like that!"

"When you say, slave you mean—" and the words left her. Lizzy found a humming sound where her thoughts should be, and the more she tried to force her tongue to form the shape of the word she couldn't say, the more her head ached.

There was a silver tray on the dressing table Lizzy had not noticed when they came in. A mint julep sat on it. Haney brought the glass to Lizzy's lips and helped her sip. Once the heavy mint and smoky bourbon hit her tongue, she felt refreshed. Lizzy took another sip, eventually draining the glass.

The ache in her forehead was gone in an instant and with it vanished the thought she had been trying to form.

Lizzy found herself all of a sudden sleepy, and a bit dizzy.

"Oh. I need to lie down…"

"No wonder, the day you've had, Misses."

Haney helped Lizzy undress and then bathe in a basin of warm water. From the wardrobe, Haney pulled a shift and helped her into it. Lizzy wanted to say something to the girl, something important. But the dizziness of sleep had crept up on her and Lizzy found she could think of nothing more. Before long, she found herself laying in the big bed, a comfy blanket tucked under her chin.

"G'night, Miss Lizzy," Haney whispered as she crept from the room.

7
Unmarked Graves

Jim awoke in utter darkness. He was in some narrow passage, barely wider than his shoulders. He couldn't even move his hands, at first. But eventually he pushed and wiggled until he had turned himself over and began moving first one shoulder, then another to move himself forward. By and by he found the passage had grown so narrow that he needed to dig out the way in front of him. This proved a challenge, as his arms were pinned at his side. With some deft turning in a corkscrew fashion, he managed to free first a few fingers, then a hand in front of him and began clawing at the dark soil.

Soon, he was shoveling fistfuls of dirt and tossing them over his shoulders, worming his way through the dirt until his fingernails scraped against something hard. It was wood. He cleared enough of a space behind the wooden wall to get himself into a standing position and pushed with all his might. The planks gave way and Jim burst forth into the air once more.

He spat the dirt from his mouth and looked around. Four steep walls of soil surrounded him, but above was a wide opening through which he could see the night sky wheeling, all full of stars.

Jim clambered out of the hole, and back to the surface. There he found torches lit at the four points of the compass. The hole in which he'd found himself, he realized with some astonishment, was a grave. The large stone above the opening attested to this fact.

Jim stood and dusted himself off as best he could, shaking the grave dirt from his hat and shirt. The sound of something moving in the dark, outside the ring of firelight reached his ears.

Out of the darkness and into the gloaming light of the torches came a rider dressed all in black. He wore all black, including his hat and a fringed mask over his face. Even his steed looked like it was cut from shadows on the dark side of the moon. The only thing that wasn't was the horse's eyes, which glowed red, and the silver star upon the rider's chest, which had seven points and bore the name upon it older than the hills, but which Jim could not read.

"James Galahad Hopkins," said the Black Rider in a voice slick as rain and deep as thunder. "I have come to fetch you to your judgment."

"I don't have time for all that," Jim said. "I've got to go rescue my sister and have words with my two no-account brothers."

The rider smiled beneath the fringe of his mask. And in his grim visage, Jim saw the glee of eternity. "You don't argue with The Law, boy!"

"You a lawman?" Jim asked. "What jurisdiction you got here?" Jim looked around at the bare trees scrabbling against the sky.

"I have jurisdiction everywhere, for I am Death's own Sheriff! I collect them who have escaped justice in life and deliver them to be judged by Death himself."

"But I ain't done nothin' wrong!" said Jim, "Save trust my dang fool brothers. That one's on me, I admit."

"So you admit that you have sinned?" asked the Sheriff with glee.

"Ain't we all sinners? That's what they told me in Sunday school at any rate. But if it's justice you're serving, then it ain't me you're after."

"Is you is, or is you ain't the one they hanged?" The Sheriff asked.

"Hanged?" Jim scratched his neck. It was tender. "Suppose I was. Though it ain't for what I done, but what I didn't do, if you follow."

"I do not follow," said the Sheriff. "You have died a criminal's death, and therefore, are a criminal."

"Ah," said Jim. "I can see how circumstantial evidence being what it is, how you might make a mistake, Sheriff Death, sir."

"There is no mistake," said the Sheriff. "I say what is and what will never be in these parts!"

"Oh yeah?" Jim looked around, making a big show of being unimpressed. "Well sir, you can keep these here parts."

Jim turned and grabbed the nearest torch. He then ran out of the ring of firelight into the darkness.

He had no mind as to where he was headed, exactly. But his feet seemed to know the landscape of this place well, what little of it he could make out from the light of the torch he waved before him. After a while, the terrain did seem familiar. A thin gray light shone behind those black mountains, while above, tattered clouds scudded across the lightning sky.

Jim had a notion that he'd walked these trails a thousand times, crossed the lanes of night between lives, and found pathways between the stars. Maybe he could find another now, a way back to the world...

The sound of the Black Rider chased after him, the hoofbeats of his terrible stallion pounding like a heartbeat through dust and bones, which cracked under its weight.

Jim had his doubts that he could outrun this rider, but you never know what you're capable of until you give it a try.

So, he ran.

He ran until his lungs burned.

Then he ran some more.

He stumbled amidst scattered bones and skulls of every type of creature. But he picked himself up and ran further. He ran until his lungs ached. And still the hoof beats of that terrible rider and his fearsome stead chased after. That Black Rider would never cease his persuit. Would never waver, would forever follow, his horse stomping out a drum beat of a gallop that would ring in Jim's ears til Judgement Day.

The torch began to sputter and dim. Jim knew he needed that light to direct his way and grabbed the sizzling ember and swallowed it in a gulp.

His throat burned and his side felt like a knife had been driven into his flesh. Still, he ran until he was lost to the darkness, stumbling blindly over rocks and skulls, unable to remember where he was trying to get to in such a hurry.

Out of that velvet night came the rustling of wind. Feathers kissed his cheek and Jim turned and saw in the darkness, glittering like a star, the whitest snow owl he'd ever seen. It wheeled overhead, and once it was sure Jim had seen it, the bird flew on, heading towards what Jim could now see was the horizon. The sun's first rays lit the peaks of a mountain range that lay beyond. The owl was heading straight towards the sunrise.

Jim ran after the owl until his eyes felt like they might explode till the thought of drawing a breath made him choke for longing…

Jim gasped and sat upright. He was sure he was lost in a dark desert, but now here he was, laying on a bedroll beside a fire, dream-drunk and pulling air into his lungs. The cool clean air did nothing to quench the ache in his throat though.

"You won't catch me…" he croaked. The pain made him wince.

"Don't speak," Mercy said.

She sat beside him. Francis was there as well, his unfathomable dark eyes staring at Jim, as if in search of a sign. And someone else was there as well. As his vision cleared, Jim could make out the kindly eyes of old Charlie Snow Owl.

"Well, there you are now, Jim Hawkins," Charlie said. "Back among the living."

"…Am I?" Jim croaked.

"Don't talk," Francis said. "Your neck nearly broke from the hanging."

The hanging. Jim remembered now. Dangling like a fish on the

THE RIGHTEOUS AND THE REST

line while the breath slipped out of him completely, in a way he'd never known before. The memory of it made him gasp and choke.

He coughed and motioned for water. Mercy handed him a skin and he nearly drained the whole thing in a gulp. The cold water was a salve for his throat, though the comfort lasted but a moment; replaced by a tingle of pain prickling at the skin of his neck.

"Lizzy..." he croaked. "...Where..?"

"With Greer," said Francis.

"You remember what happened?" Mercy asked him. He realized it was a command, not a question.

Jim felt his neck. It was sore inside and out. When he took his fingers away, they were spotted with blood.

"You'll have a wound, that's for sure," Charlie said. "Should scar up nice and pretty. Mark you till the end of your days, I'm afraid. But the good news is, those days ain't numbered yet."

Charlie seemed more reassured by that statement than Jim ever would be.

"...Need to go," Jim's voice sounded like he'd been gargling with razor blades. "...Catch up... to Lizzy."

"Now hold up there son," Charlie pushed Jim back onto the bed roll. "You've been dead nearly a whole day. You need to rest."

Jim looked at Mercy and Francis.

Mercy seemed to read his mind. "Yes, it's been a day since you was hanged. Lucky for you that Finch feller ain't no knotsmith, else you'd be in that grave for sure. I rushed to get Charlie here, who worked a wonder on you. Francis stayed and watched over your body, so as not to let the animals of the Switch get to it."

They could tell by the look on his face that Jim was incredulous, perplexed, slightly afraid, but mostly uncertain.

"...You... guarded...me..?" he looked at Francis.

He nodded.

"I'm sure you have questions," Charlie said. "And we'll answer them, best we can."

"Where... where are we?" Jim sipped some more water.

"Nowhere-In-Particular," said Mercy. "Which is a shame, as we really should be headin' on to Anywhere-But-Here."

Jim looked up and saw the hanging tree over his head. The graves they'd dug had been put to use, as Francis returned to shoveling the remains of the revenants who hadn't gotten up and lumbered after their captain into them.

"What... danger?" Jim asked.

"Swann is still out there." Francis deposited another load of bones into the grave. "He's regrouping."

"I think we'll be safe here for a spell," the look on Charlie's face said otherwise.

"I don't know of a place we can be safe, so long as Johnny Rev is out and about," Mercy said.

"There is no safe place to hide from Talbot Swann. He has sawdust where his heart should be. We need to be gone from this place," Francis added. "We need to find Lizzy."

"I understand your desire to be all heroic and such but we haven't a clue where Greer has taken her," Mercy said. "And even if we did, we ain't got enough provisions for more'n two days, best guess. And should we find them by chance, then what? We got nothin' but our own wits as a plan, and seeing as how they got us into this mess, I'm not sure trusting them to get us out is such a fine idea."

"So... what now?" Jim croaked.

His throat was feeling slightly less like he'd swallowed a cup full of broken glass but that wasn't quite enough to carry on a decent conversation, let alone plan the revenge that was smoldering in his heart.

"Did you not hear what I said?" Mercy looked at him hard. "We need a lot of questions answered before we settle on a plan, whether it's a foolhardy stand against unbeatable odds or a sensible and hasty retreat."

"But... Lizzy!" Jim croaked once more.

"Mercy is right," Charlie stood and moseyed over to the pile of revenants laying motionless beneath the tree. "We need answers first."

"And where do we get those?" Francis asked.

Charlie examined the corpse Francis was burying in the grave Jim had dug.

"This poor feller," Charlie knelt down and looked at the sack of bones wrapped in a Confederate uniform.

This soldier was already pretty far gone, with a thin bit of dried skin stretched across a mostly empty skull. Francis slid the shovel under him and heaved him into the grave. He toppled in piece-by-piece, though his skull rolled away under a mesquite bush beside the hanging tree.

Charlie retrieved the skull and looked at it thoughtfully for a moment. "You've been dead for a while, that's for sure. Wonder what you seen, huh?"

"He don't seem to be in a speaking mood," Mercy said.

"Shame," Francis hefted his shovel. "If he were, maybe he could tell us what Greer is up to."

"I'm mighty curious about that myself." Charlie returned to the campfire and set the skull on one of the rocks that ringed their fire.

"Francis, what can you tell us about Greer's army?" Charlie asked.

"Not much. I was a hired scout, three years back. The General was a petty criminal then, leading a gang of about two dozen raggedy-ass Rebs. All he talked about was setting up a new Confederacy down in the Caribbean where he could raise an army and then come back for round two of the War. Never more than talk though."

"Seems he's done talking and put words to action," said Mercy. "Where'd he learn this trick, raising revenants?"

"That's a fine question," Charlie stood and clapped his hands.

"Let's see if we can't get some answers straight from the skeleton's mouth, as it were."

Charlie picked up a smoldering stick from the fire. He wet his fingers and extinguished the bit of flame at the end. Using the charred bit of wood, he covered the skull with soot, humming and chanting as he drew symbols over the last thin bit of skin on the dead man's skull.

He placed it in the fire, and they watched as the skin burned away, leaving a gleaming white skull, with the eye sockets lit by coals.

Charlie reached into the fire and plucked the skull out. He set it on the rock before him and waved his hand to extinguish the bits of flame that clung to his sleeve, and sucked his singed fingers.

Charlie Snow Owl stomped and swayed, humming to himself. The humming turned to a low throaty keening, rising eventually to a shrill and blood chilling howl.

The hair on Jim's arm stood on end.

Charlie let out a whoop and shouted at the skull, "Wake up you!" And he hit it with a stick from the fire.

The skull rattled and sighed and then its jaw opened, coughing up a lungful of dust.

"Ay!" the skull coughed. "I'm awake?"

"That you are, son," Charlie said. He threw the smoldering twig back into the flames and sat. "You know where you are, soldier?"

"No sé," said the skull. "And what ya mean, soldier?"

"Hmm," Charlie stroked his chin. "That's an interesting twist. I don't suppose you know who raised you up from the grave and for what purpose?"

"No sé," said the skull. "This is all news to me."

"What do you remember?" Francis asked.

"I remember a woman. She liked to smile and I made her laugh. Think she was my wife. And there were two boys, ours as well. We worked a hacienda outside Juarez."

"Oh sure, fine country out that way," said Charlie, as if he'd done nothing more than strike up a conversation with a feller on the train.

"You know anything more?" Mercy asked.

"The boys, their names were Benito, and Estancio... My wife was Amelia..."

"Do you recall anything more about the General, the one who raised you out of the grave?" Francis asked.

"Oh, sí, sí let me think... I had a sickness in me. Grew weaker by the day until I could hardly move. Then they laid me down and I was comfortable for a long while, without a care in the world. By and by, some voice called out and bid me get up. Didn't seem to have much choice in the matter. They dressed me in some rags and handed me a rifle. Funny though, because I could never shoot worth a damn when I was alive..."

"Who is they?" Jim asked in a low whisper.

"Dios mío! You sound worse than me!" the skull let out a wheezing laugh. "Don't remember the man's name. We called him Generalissimo."

The four of them exchanged a look.

"I was dead, then became a soldier, you say? Ain't that just like me, get things mixed up like that."

"You sure you don't remember nothin' more 'bout this General who ordered you about?" Mercy asked. "How many other soldiers were there? And where they come from?"

"I'm not normally a withholding sort," said the skull.

"Go easy on him, Mercy," Charlie patted the skull gently. "He's had a time of it. What's your name, son?"

The skull hemmed a bit as if trying to recall. At last he said, "Juan Jesus Del Campo. Though everyone called me Gordo."

"Gordo it is," said Charlie. "You help us out, Gordo, and I'll see you get a proper burial back home in Juarez, if'n the Four Winds will have it."

"Ándale!" said Gordo.

"Now if we're all done, talkin' about the weather, I think we—"

Mercy was silenced by a gesture from Charlie.

He tilted his head, listening. "Someone's approaching fast. And they aren't as far off as I'd like."

"...'Towering genius disdains a beaten path. It seeks regions hitherto unexplored'," said Abraham Lincoln.

"Right, time to skedaddle," Mercy grabbed her gear and had it tied down to Abraham Lincoln's saddle in a moment.

Francis helped Jim up and onto the back of a yellow and white stallion that he recognized as Swann's own horse.

"This is Sebastian," Francis told him. "When Swann run off, he stayed behind. He's a good horse. He'll mind you."

Jim patted the horse's neck. He made a friendly, nickering sound.

Charlie doused the campfire with sand, then stuffed Gordo into a gunny sack.

"Ay! Who turned out the lights?"

"Shush now, Gordo." Charlie mounted Shadow behind Francis and they were off, running through the woods.

Scarcely had they left when a large crow swooped down through the trees, and came to a landing right beside where the campfire had been but a moment before. The enormous bird cocked his head to one side, listening cautiously. He scratched at the remnants of the campfire with one talon.

Captain Swann emerged from the trees on horseback, having acquired a new steed. He dismounted and watched the enormous crow shuffle and scoot about the camp.

"What see you, Lieutenant Daw?" Swann said. "Were they here?"

"Here and gone again, Captain Swann, sir," said the Crow.

The revenant contingent arrived with Finch and Hoots in the lead.

"We find 'em, Cap'n Swann, sir?" asked Finch.

"We have found nothing, as usual," said the Captain. "And were

I to find anything, you would know or not know at my choosing."

"Just askin'..."

The crow pecked at the ashes in the campfire with his beak and tasted them. He hopped a few paces in the direction Jim and the rest had gone mere moments before.

"They go this way."

"Are you certain?" asked Swann.

"Jack Daw knows. Jack Daw smells. Jack Daw sees."

"Jack Daw takes his Got-Danged time doing all three!"

Hoots groaned to Finch. Swann marched up to the recalcitrant duo. Finch flinched. Hoots stood still.

"You got something to add, soldier?"

Hoots groaned again.

"Hoots here says you should take it easy on our friend the crow," said Finch. "Lt. Jack's done nothin' but lead us to the promise since he joined up, and he is a credit to his breed."

"I care not for his or your feelings on this or any other matter."

"Begging your pardon, Cap'n Swann, sir, but we'd all work a lot better with a word of encouragement, now and again."

"The General ordered them dead and yet, they still live! Long as the fugitives elude us still, you will work as hard as you can or I will return you both to the grave from whence the General fetched you. Do I make myself clear?"

Hoots grunted and nodded.

"Aye, sir," added Finch.

"They close!" Jack said and leaped into the sky.

Swann mounted his horse and drew his saber.

"We ride!"

Swann charged after the enormous bird, with Hoots and Finch straggling behind.

Jim and the others followed Mercy through the woods, heedless of where they might end up. Sebastian turned out to be a vast improvement over Jim's former steed, whose name he now could not recall. This was a fact Jim regretted as much as the fate of the poor animal.

He hadn't been a bad horse, and Jim wouldn't wish that end on any creature, except maybe his damned brothers. This in itself was a marked change in opinion, one he would spend much time mulling over the next few days.

Jim was not completely naive; he knew Travis had the habits of a scoundrel. Ma and Pa had commented on them for much of Jim's life, and in their own way, tried to correct them. Travis being fourteen years Jim's senior, he'd provided him with a bevy of examples of what not to do as a boy and later as a full-grown adult.

But Jim, like their mother, had a spark of hope that he would one day come around, find his purpose, or at least a facsimile of such, and settle down. Now, after the events of but a single night, Jim feared such a benign fate was beyond his oldest brother's reach.

Edmond was likewise a study in contradictions. He aspired to humility, as one would expect from a preacher, but always found himself in one vainglorious situation after another. Many of these, now that Jim came to think on it, were instigated by Travis. Despite his outward appearance as a community leader, Edmond was but a follower, always chasing after his older brother's coattails. Of the two of them, Edmond was the one Jim had the most hope for a turn back towards reason. Whether the preacher from Texarkana had the gumption to do what would be necessary was another matter entirely.

As for Francis, he had been eyeing Jim since they left the hanging tree. Jim couldn't say why, exactly but his look was unnerving.

"It's impolite to stare," Jim said. His voice would keep a touch of gravel for some days yet.

"Apologies, James."

Francis looked away, up at the sky, down at the road. After a while though, he returned to scrutinizing Jim with side eyes.

"I got some dirt in my hair?" Jim asked. He lifted his hat and shook it, smoothed over his hair.

"He thinks you're gonna turn into one of them revenants," Mercy called from the front of the line. She didn't even turn around.

"Why would I do that?" Jim asked.

"You were dead," said Francis. "It's rare for someone to come back and when they do, they are always... changed."

"Changed?" Jim thought for a moment. He supposed he was but was it really possible that he might turn into one of them slavering cadavers? He hadn't considered it. "Am I changed?"

"Of course you are," Charlie laughed. He turned to regard Jim, squinting as if looking through some invisible magnifying glass at him. "Anyone who goes through what you did is bound to notice a marked change in their ways. But as for you turning into one of them flesh eating revenants like the ones Greer commands, that is unlikely."

"Could happen though," said the skull sitting in Charlie's lap.

"Huh," Jim thought for a moment. "I hadn't really given the state of my eternal soul a second thought in all this. Never really thought much about my soul at all, if I'm being perfectly honest..."

"Most folks don't," Charlie said. "Though what you should be concerned about is the state of other people's souls. And by people, I mean all things. Everything's got a bit of soul, and how you treat 'em, well that determines the state of your own soul."

"Some theology," Mercy grinned. "That's the Golden Rule, you old fraud."

"That's all any religion is," said Charlie. "Everything else is commentary."

"You sure we're headed in the right direction?" Francis asked, changing the subject.

They had camped rough the night before, sleepless and alert for any sign of their pursuer, and now it was approaching midday.

They had diverted enough from the road that the hollowness of their bellies outweighed the general concern for their safety. They had salvaged what they could from the hanging tree but there was little more than Mercy's sidearm and rifle, Francis's hunting knife, and the sword that Jim had been gifted by the dead soldier.

This surprised Jim. Travis had been hell-bent to possess the sword when it was given to Jim, only to lose all interest when the opportunity to claim it outright presented itself. That Travis had abandoned it in the same grave he intended for his brother was another tally mark in the column of Jim's ire.

"Don't you worry none," said Mercy. "By tonight, you'll be swimming in beer and resting your head on a feather pillow."

"Shoot, I like the sound of that," said Gordo. The chatty thing had insisted on seeing where they were going, despite having neither eyes nor any more wherewithal than the rest of them.

"So we're headed somewhere safe, then?" Jim asked.

"Safe is relative, out here in the Switch." Mercy led Abraham Lincoln along a narrow trail at a leisurely gate. "But Ol' Davey's Freehold is a place known far and wide. Known the owner, Davey since I was a little boy. Heck, he was one of the first people to see me for me. Gave me my true name. 'Mercy!' he'd say upon seein' me approach, 'it's them Nightingales again!' That's what he said, and that's what I called myself when it come time to be my own true person."

"We're heading to Davey's?" Charlie perked up at this. "Well now, why didn't you say so? I haven't seen Ol' Davey in ages! Wonder if he'll have any of that peanut brittle he used to make..."

"Wouldn't be surprised in the slightest. After what we've been through, a night of rest at Davey's will be a genuine balm to the soul. You... wait and... see..?"

They exited the woods onto a narrow dirt lane, rutted by wagon wheels and beaten smooth by hoofprints. Ahead, there stood a holler, with a cabin at the center. It stuck out on a small knoll, overlooking a steep bluff. Beyond this, was stretched a vast expanse of desert.

As they neared, the visions of beer and featherbeds evaporated like heat ripples on the road.

The cabin, or what was left of it, lay in a heap of blackened timbers. The house was—or rather, had been—a wide log cabin standing on a platform. But this had collapsed under the weight of some unspeakable calamity. The walls were scorched and the roof was a pile of splintered shingles now laying in what had been the storeroom.

The goods were spilled, burned, spoiled, or scattered into tatters, picked over as much by wild animals as opportunistic folk.

They all dismounted. Mercy ran to the edge of the heap, standing as still as Jim had ever seen her. The rest approached with caution. But there was nothing for it—the place was a ruin.

Francis placed a hand on her shoulder. Mercy flinched but turned away. She looked neither at them nor the ruins of the camp.

"Ya'lla liked Davey. He'd run this trading post since... well, since forever. He and his kin were trappers and furriers, going back to the early days of settlers out in these parts. He befriended the natives and traded with them as well as anyone else. Always had a warm bed for a weary traveler. Didn't care where you'd come from or why you were heading away from there. He..."

Mercy grew quiet, choking back the tears.

"...When we escaped the plantation, his place was a stop on the underground railroad. Dozens of folk like us, fleeing for our lives found comfort here. It was the last homely house most of us knew. But when you reached Davey's freehold, and saw that big gap-tooth grin and bushy beard, you knew you were safe. He helped my family. Was my family."

"Perhaps he moved camp when this old shack burned down?" Jim said. But he knew it was a hollow hope.

Mercy shook her head. "I like your optimism, Young James

Hawkins," she wiped away her last tear.

Jim didn't know how much optimism he had left. There was a good chance, now that the words had left him, that it was exhausted.

Still, they searched around the ruins for a sign that might suggest survivors. Instead, they found the bodies of Mercy's friend and his family. There weren't much left, due to the fire, and animals having scavenged the remains, but Mercy was able to identify Davey by the red kerchief he used to wear. This she pocketed.

Then they fetched shovels and set about digging a couple of graves under an old oak tree.

Once their grim business was done, they set up camp beside the ruins of the freehold. There was a narrow creek that Davey had dammed up and built a small water wheel beside. It was still now, and quiet, like the trees and the woods surrounding them. Before long, Jim fell asleep beside the fire.

His sleep was fitful though; filled with dark dreams of slithering things in the night, and moonless paths through a landscape filled with bones and shadows.

Mercy remained awake though, taking the first watch, as she would be unable to rest most of the night anyhow. Francis was curled up asleep beside the fire, one hand on a knife. Charlie fell asleep sitting beside the fire. Even Gordo stopped his chattering after a while and grew quiet, if not restive.

Sometime after midnight, Jim startled awake. Sleep brought little relief to him, as sinking into the darkness reminded him of the vision he'd had of the black bog and the Black Rider. He sat up and surveyed the campfire. The only person unaccounted for was Mercy.

A quick glance over at the trees found all their horses tied up one to another, though Abraham Lincoln was the only one awake.

"Mr. President?" Jim whispered. "You see where Mercy went?"

"...'When I hear a man preach, I like to see him act as if he were fighting bees'..." said the horse. So maybe he wasn't awake after all.

Jim took his saber and scouted around the perimeter of their camp.

He found Mercy beside the graves of her friends. She sat on a barrel, cleaning her sidearm, mulling over something. Though mulling wasn't exactly the right word.

"You going hunting?" Jim sat beside her on the ground.

"Soon as I see that no-good-so-and-so, Talbot Swann, I intend to shove this barrel down his throat and pull the trigger 'til it goes click."

"Seems everybody I know is in a great hurry to shoot a feller," Jim sighed and shook his head.

"You think he ain't got it coming?"

"Didn't say that. But killing seems like one of them things you should be certain about before you go making an awful mistake." He rubbed the raw spot around his neck.

"Oh, I intend to remind him of his mistakes, forthwith." She slapped the chamber of her Navy Colt closed and holstered it.

"Now Mercy, we don't know it was Swann and them who burned down the freehold," Jim said.

"Don't we though?"

"Swann deserves much scorn, and little pity, but killing him will not bring back your friend."

"It'd make me feel better though."

There was but a half moon, and Mercy could still feel the weight of his stare, if not see it clearly.

"For a bit, at least," she said.

Jim leaned back, resting on his elbows.

"I know this ain't about exacting revenge," Jim said. "You're hurting for the loss of your friend. Want to talk about it?"

"No."

He nodded. "Good. I ain't got any sense about death or loss or grief. It's not something I'm familiar with at all."

Mercy squinted at him in the dark. He smiled.

"Don't be a fool, Young James Hawkins." She kicked him with the toe of her boot.

"Ouch!" Jim rubbed his knee where she'd nudged him. "Yes ma'am, Tracker Mercy, ma'am."

She shook her head. "That wound a'yours is gonna itch awful come morning."

Mercy fished the red kerchief from her pocket and tied it around his neck real gentle, taking care not to chafe his wound.

"There. Now you look dapper to boot. Like one of them singin' cowboys."

"Oh. Does that mean I gotta get me a guitar?"

"Know what they say, music can save your mortal soul," Mercy smiled, "Though don't tell Francis, or else he might begin to suspect somethin'."

They both had a gentle laugh. Then they sat in companionable silence for a while.

By and by there came a rustling sound and murmuration of low voices from the other side of the trees.

Jim and Mercy gathered their weapons and crept up to the tree line surrounding the ruined trading post.

They found Charlie and Francis already there, watchful. Charlie held Gordo in one hand, and with the other held the skull's jaw shut to prevent him from chattering. Francis raised a finger to his lips and they gathered around, quiet as could be.

Several figures were hunched over the remains of the burned out ruins, poking through the ashes. The squawk of a bird alerted them to the presence of onlookers.

One of the figures, the tallest, shifted his stance; in the light of the moon, Mercy could see the glint in his black glass eyes.

"There they are!" Swann called. And out of the trees emerged a dozen revents, rifles at the ready. Swann drew his pistol and fired but the shot flew wide; though not as wide as Jim would've liked, as it grazed his hat and hit the tree behind them.

"Talbot Swann!" Mercy drew her colt and took aim. "Stand and deliver, you coyote faced son of a bitch!"

She opened fire, landing a hit directly into Swann's shoulder. But instead of blood, out of the hole poured a trickle of red sawdust. He stuck a finger in the wound to staunch the flow.

"Open fire!" bellowed Swann.

Francis grabbed Charlie and Gordo and pulled them down to the ground as a volley ripped through the trees, splintering the bark.

Jim drew his saber, for all the good it would do against bullets and rushed out to Mercy's aid. But she stood, shouting curses as she fired at Swann.

It was dark and the firefight chaotic, but brief. It was also inconclusive, as neither side appeared to have taken much damage.

"We need to go!" Jim said.

Mercy turned to him, her eyes ablaze with malice.

"Mercy. Let's go!" Jim whispered. She snapped out of her bloody fugue as another volley of rifle fire spit at their feet.

Jim held up his sword and managed through preternatural luck, to deflect two, three, then four of the shots that might have otherwise taken his or Mercy's breath.

Neither had a moment to comment though as the Revenants were upon them, groaning as they charged with bayonets.

Mercy and Jim hightailed it back to their camp, which Francis and Charlie had already struck.

Jim hopped onto Sebastian's back, and Mercy onto Abraham Lincoln's. They reared about, looking for an exit.

Abraham Lincoln jumped the short hedge that marked the boundary of the oak grove, and the high plains that stretched out beyond. Jim and the rest were right on her heels. As were Swann and his men, who followed after into the desert.

8
Moonshine & Magnolias

That night, Lizzy crept from her bed and down the steps, slipping out the front door. The moon was full and lit the fields of Blanchefleur like day, but still, she did not know which way to go. Every attempt to tread into the woods led her by some circuitous path, back to the house. But then, she saw it: a firefly blinking in the dusky night. First one then another, until a swarm of fireflies lit a path true and clear through the woods, into the desert.

Lizzy wandered through a parched desert, under an angry red sun. She walked until she came to the edge of a cliff. There, she could see from a great distance that a group of riders on horseback tried to outrun some swirling dust devil. In the lead, Lizzy saw a familiar face.

"Jim!" she called out. But the wind and the scouring sand ate her words.

She could see that the dust devil was not one of wind and sand but of feathers and beaks; her brother and the others were being pursued by a swarm of birds—crows, and cranes, and small raggedy pigeons—all cawing and pecking at his neck. She knew that if Jim could reach the safety of that canyon up ahead, he would have a chance to reach her. She went to call out to him, but every time she did, the wind would blow and the rasp of sand swirling between them would stifle her calls. Still, she yelled and yelled, hoping against hope that he might hear her...

Lizzy awoke to find someone lurking at the foot of her bed. It took her half a second to recognize that it was Haney.

"Montezuma's Name, girl! You dang near startled me!" Lizzy sat up and rubbed her eyes.

"Sorry about that, Miss Lizzy," Haney smiled. She went to the window and threw open the drapes. The blaring sun wiped away all memory of her dream.

"The General insists on an early rise, to greet the morning."

"I'm sure he does," Lizzy sighed.

"And where is the General this morning?"

"Oh, General and his officers are tending to business," Haney said as if that explained anything at all.

"And what business would that be?" Lizzy offered her a perplexed expression.

"Oh I couldn't say."

"Can't you though?" Lizzy asked.

"I'm sorry Miss Lizzy but I don't know nothin' about the General's business!" She averted her gaze and Lizzy realized she'd been short with the girl.

"Of course, Haney, I apologize," Lizzy said. "Morning sickness makes me crabby."

She turned herself awkwardly until she reached the end of the bed. With Haney's help, she slid her feet to the floor.

"Woo wee!" Haney grinned. "You get bigger in the night, Miss?"

"I think I did?" Lizzy looked down at her belly, which by her own reckoning, was nearly twice the size it had been when she'd gone to sleep the night before.

"Happened to my Sister," Haney said. "Could hardly tell she was with chil', then boom! Big as a boat! Gave birth to twins."

Lizzy didn't want to think about that possibility. Instead she said, "So what's for breakfast 'round these parts?"

Haney helped her dress and soon, Lizzy set about her first day of captivity at Blanchefleur.

Despite her misgivings, it didn't take long for Lizzy to settle into her predicament. It wasn't resignation—she would be damned if she gave Greer that satisfaction. But weeping and gnashing her teeth and rending her dress wouldn't get her anything but puffy eyes, an aching jaw, and a mess of mending work to be done.

Instead, she set about sussing the boundaries of her situation. And that meant exploring the Manse, to see what the old house had to offer.

Now Lizzy, having been born and raised on a cattle ranch, knew a thing or two about the ways of a working farmhouse. The Hawkins farm employed a few servants, such as a cook and a maid, plus a dozen farm hands.

But Blanchefleur was another world entirely. By her estimate, there were some two dozen house slaves. These included the maids and kitchen staff, who answered to the housekeeper, Miss Rachel, and assorted footmen who answered to the butler, Robbe. He skittered from one room to another whispering orders from the General in a sure, even voice.

"Good morning, Miss Lizzy," Robbe greeted them with a wide grin as Haney led Lizzy into the dining room. "My, you look positively radiant this morning."

Haney had helped her to dress in a cotton day gown with layered sleeves and a high collar. There were ruffles and petticoats and a shawl and by the end of it all, Lizzy felt less like she'd been attired and more like she'd been wrapped up like a present under the Christmas Tree.

"Thank you, Robbe… was it?"

"Indeed it is, Miss. I trust you slept well, m'lady?"

"Uh, yes I think I did," Lizzy said. This answer gave Lizzy pause because it was the truth.

It had been a week to the day since she and Francis had run off from her home in Texarkana, and she had not known a moment's comfort. Upon reflection, Lizzy realized she had slept deeper, and more thoroughly then she had in some time, despite her growing belly.

"Excellent!" Robbe snapped his fingers.

This startled Lizzy for half a second, before one of the footmen in blue livery appeared at Robbe's elbow. He pulled out the chair for her.

"Miss Rachel takes pride in her housekeeping and she will be awfully happy to hear that you slept well. The General likewise, of course."

"Oh, the General takes an interest in how folks sleep around here, does he?" Lizzy asked.

She poked at the food on her plate. The eggs looked good and the bacon smelled heavenly. She took a tentative bite, following that up with a hearty forkful.

"Oh yes," said Robbe. "The General takes a profound interest in your well being. In fact, the General was telling me earlier this morning how he wanted regular updates on your condition." A proud smile rose to his eyes.

"My condition?" Lizzy said.

Robbe cleared his throat and motioned gracefully to her swelling belly.

Lizzy looked down at herself as if noticing it for the first time. "Oh my, when did that happen?" Lizzy chuckled.

Robbe waited a half second, to make sure it was a genuine chuckle before adding one of his own.

"Oh, I see we will have to keep a close eye on you, Miss Elizabeth!"

"Not too close, let's hope," Lizzy smiled. "A girl does like her privacy, after all." Lizzy tucked into her breakfast.

"Oh, yes of course! I didn't mean to... that is I... the General would never... Ha!" Robbe's smile melted away. "I... have chores to attend to. Should you need anything at all, do not hesitate to ask for me. Haney will know how to find me."

He offered Haney a wink and a nod.

"Now if you will excuse me, Miss," He bowed and held it for a moment too long before Lizzy realized she'd missed her cue.

"Oh! Yes. Sorry. Thank you Robbe, that's... all?"

He nodded once more then left by way of a servant's door.

The servant's door led down a set of stairs, into a long narrow passage that ran back to the kitchen. To either side were storerooms. Robbe's office was also located here, though it was more of a cramped cupboard with a narrow desk and stool, lit by an oil lamp that never seemed to throw enough light to fill the room. Robbe rarely worked there anyway, as he preferred to work on his feet.

As Robbe approached the kitchen, he was met by a trio of footmen in blue livery. They stood taller and straighter as he approached.

"Morning, gents, what's the news of the world?" Robbe said, not stopping. The trio of footmen fell in behind him like ducklings behind their mother.

"Finished polishing the silver, as requested." The first footman, Connor, held up a spoon.

Robbe plucked it from his hand like picking a daisy. He inspected it as he maneuvered around a scullery boy who was rolling a barrel into the kitchen. Robbe smiled and checked his teeth in the curved mirror of the spoon's bowl. "Excellent," he handed the spoon back to Connor. "What else?"

"Laid in an extra cask of wine, per the General's request." The second footman, Franklin, handed Robbe a tin cup.

Robbe sipped, and swished the contents around in his mouth, spit it back into the cup.

"That'll do for the officers in the evening, but for the General's big to-do, I want that last case of the '59 brought up. Yes, Franklin?"

"Yes, Mr. Robbe."

"Here's the Cook's list, Mr. Robbe." The third footman, Henry, offered a folded piece of paper. "I took the liberty of alphabetizing it for—"

"You did what now?" Robbe stopped short and looked hard at Henry. "And who asked you to read my list?"

"Oh no sir, I just rearranged them so the shapes were all the same-like."

"And you did this somehow without reading the list?"

Henry hadn't thought about that and bit his lip.

Robbe snatched the paper from the footman and scanned it. "You got your 'I's before your 'E's, Henry. Sloppy. If you're going to break ranks and show off in such a dangerous fashion, at least be thorough enough to be right. Yes, Henry?"

"Yes, Mr. Robbe, I just…" He let the words wander off.

"No you just didn't think, Henry, is what you just did not do. There'll be no more justin' 'round here, less we have an outbreak of notions. Do you understand?"

"Yes Mr. Robbe!" sang the chorus of footmen. Though Connor and Franklin jabbed Henry with their elbows.

They set off at double time now to make up the distance.

"What's the status of that leaky water pump?" Robbe asked.

They turned the corner and entered the parlor. The maids had been thorough and already cleaned up from last night's revelries with the return of the General and his men.

No answer.

Robbe stopped. The three footmen stopped a half second later, stumbling into the back of one another. Robbe looked around. "Where's Andre?"

The other three footmen looked at one another. They looked at Robbe. It fell to Henry to be the bearer of bad news.

"Uh, Andre, is… workin' on that pump now. I expect…"

"You expect?" Robbe turned to Henry, who averted his gaze. "Show me what you expect, Mr. Henry."

"Yes'r," Henry gulped and led Robbe and others back down a servant's passage.

The Cook, Miss Coffie, kept a small herb garden out back of the kitchen. There was a flagstone path that ran from it to the kitchen door, beside which stood, for as long as anyone could remember, a leaky old pump.

Samuel crouched in front of the pump, using a wrench to loosen a nut. At least, that was the plan.

"What's taking so long?" Andre asked. He leaned on the wall beside the kitchen door.

"You wanna do this?" Samuel said.

"And get my fine suit dirty?" he brushed a speck from his shoulder and adjusted his cuffs. "No thank you."

The back door opened and one of the maids, Sarah, came out with a pail full of dirty water.

"Well good day, Sarah," Andre smiled, all teeth. "What brings you out and about this fine morning?"

Sarah shook her head but smiled at Andre. "Work. Which is more than I can say about you."

She and Samuel both chuckled as she dumped the contents of her pail into the garden.

Sarah watched Andre carefully as she made her way back to the kitchen door and shut it behind her. Andre watched her go, and couldn't help but smile even after she was gone.

"You see that?" he asked.

Samuel strained to turn that blessed nut, rusted in place.

"I ain't see nothin' but a fool up to no good."

"Me?" Andre said, mock shocked. "Never! You done yet?"

"How did I let you talk me into doing your work for you?" Samuel grunted.

"I'm shocked—nay—offended! That you would accuse me of tomfoolery. Chicanery, even!"

"Didn't answer my question," Samuel said. He paused to wipe his brow.

"You know I ain't technical minded. I'm a people person."

Samuel gripped the wrench in both hands and gave a mighty push, loosening the nut.

"Finally!" said Andre.

"Yes, after all your hard work," Samuel sprawled out to catch his breath.

"So," Andre flopped onto the lawn beside his friend and whispered conspiratorially, "you of course will be throwin' into the weekly pot, yes?"

"Is that why you had me come up here?" Samuel said. "Shake me down for money for your irregular card game?"

"No!" Andre smiled. "Well, not the only reason, of course." Andre nodded to the water pump.

"Come on!" Andre said. "I got half the field hands in on this! It's gonna be grand! And Henry! Henry said he's throwing two whole dollars into the pot! You tellin' me you're gonna walk away from a chance at taking that turnip head's money?"

"As entertaining as it is watchin' you lose all your money at cards, think I'll pass." Samuel proceeded to unscrew the nut and replace the washer, which was, he suspected, the root cause of the leak.

"My own friend, shootin' down my dreams," Andre looked up at a single white cloud scudding across the blueness of sky. "You know this is no mere card game."

"Oh, this again," Samuel shook his head.

"Whatcha mean, 'this again'?"

"This whole notion that you're gonna win a card game against the entire House…" Samuel wrestled with the pump a bit, checking the gaskets before he began to assemble everything. "…and somehow buy your freedom. It's never gonna happen."

"Ye of little faith!" Andre scoffed. "You think I want to spend the rest of my days sayin, 'yes'r' and 'nos'r' to the likes of the General? Fixin' water pumps that I ain't even aloud to drink from? Polishing some other man's silver? That all there is? Don't know 'bout you, but as for me, I'm bound for glory!"

"The prospect of glory seems to have eluded you once again, Andre."

He and Samuel looked up to find Robbe standing over them. He was flanked by the three footmen, all scowls.

"Mr. Robbe!" Andre took his hands out of his pockets. "I was about to come find you! Me and Samuel here been workin' on this pump all morning and nearly got it fixed up."

"You have been working on it, have you?" Robbe asked.

"Of course! I needed Samuel's help though. You know how these things go."

"I do indeed, Andre." Robbe looked at the pump. Samuel had replaced the washer and was tightening the nut that held the pump handle in place.

"All sorted, Mr. Robbe," Samuel took a kerchief from his overalls and wiped his face with it.

"Not a squeak, yes?" Robbe said. He gave the pump a few tentative turns. There was indeed, not a squeak, and after three or four pumps, it began to pull clear water once more.

"See!" Andre said. "All fixed."

"Hmm," Robbe said. "Samuel. Don't you have work to attend to?"

"Of course, Mr. Robbe," Samuel patted Andre on the shoulder and headed down the hill, back towards the fields.

"I count on you, Samuel?" Andre called after him.

Samuel waved a dismissive hand over his shoulder.

"I'll count that as a yes!" Andre grinned.

"And what tomfoolery are you two miscreants planning?" Robbe looked at Andre.

"Oh. Bible study, for sure."

"Of course," Robbe said. "Now, what shall your punishment be for shirkin?"

"Wha..?" Andre's voice caught in his throat. "Naw sir, there's been a little mistake, you see—"

"Are you saying I am in error, Andre?" Robbe said.

Miss Rachel exited the kitchen door and they all turned as one to face her.

"And here I thought it was a gaggle of cats making such a fuss out here!" Miss Rachel looked at Robbe.

"I have this matter in hand, Rachel," Robbe said.

She placed her hands on her hips.

"Miss Rachel," he corrected himself, straightening his cravat. "Etiquette of course…"

"What I thought," she sighed dramatically. "Why you waste time with these triflin' fools? Get back to work, the lot of ya!"

The footmen nodded as one and shuffled back through the kitchen door in a train of elbows and knees and whispers.

Once they were alone, Robbe crossed his arms and stared at Rachel. "I dislike you undermining my authority in front of the help."

"The help!" she chuckled coldly. "Look at you, suddenly a member of the family, are we?"

Robbe cleared his throat. "The General relies on me… on my clear-eyed advice. I'm not merely some Butler, I'm—"

"Let me stop you right there," Miss Rachel said. She raised a finger, circling around his face to point at his nose. His eyes crossed, following her fingernail. "You ain't nothin' to that man but an extension of his tiny little finger."

"And you are something more?" Robbe smiled like a cat. "Oh, my apologies, Miss Rachel. Let me get back to my work, Miss Rachel. Thy will, Miss Rachel."

He bowed and headed for the kitchen door. He glanced back at her. Miss Rachel held up her pinky finger and pointed it at him.

Robbe returned to the foyer in time to find the General and Doc Hatchet. They were kitted out for riding.

"Ah, Robbe," the General called him over.

"Yes'r?"

"Robbe, the Doctor and I are heading out to survey the western field. We shall be about it for the rest of the morning, and return for luncheon, which I would like served promptly at noon." The

General turned, raised a finger as a thought occurred to him. He turned back to Robbe.

"I shall endeavor to inform Miss Lizzy that her presence will be required," Robbe bowed.

"Inform Miss Lizzy—ah, yes." The general smiled. "Very good. See to it."

"Thy Will, General," Robbe bowed and then went in search of Miss Lizzy.

He found her on the back porch, with Haney. They were heading out as well, though Haney was having considerable trouble tying the bonnet under Miss Lizzy's chin.

"...I don't need no hat," Lizzy said, keeping her voice even. "The parasol will do, Haney."

"Yes Miss," Haney curtsied and then helped her down the steps.

"Ah, Miss Lizzy I..." Robbe started to say something, but Lizzy pretended not to hear, and instead hurried down the lane.

"Oh. Yes, of course. Upon your return then!" he called after.

Haney had to run to keep up with Lizzy, who held a parasol over her shoulder like it was a rifle and she was marching off to join the company of St. George.

"I think Mr. Robbe was... tryin'a get... your attention, Miss Lizzy..." she huffed.

"That would appear... to be his problem... not mine," Lizzy puffed.

"Are we sure we should keep up... this pace, Miss?" Haney said, a bit out of breath.

"Nonsense... fresh air is... good for a body..." Lizzy huffed and puffed, yet strode on. "Especially a body... in my condition... Sides, I want to see this here... Blanchefleur... for myself..."

So they strode on into the morning.

In truth, Lizzy was impressed with the size of the place. There were assorted grooms, stable boys, sugar makers, coopers, washerwomen, and field hands. Every morning before dawn, the slaves were up and about, cooking, sewing, and working the fields, hoeing, weeding, tilling, and tending to the livestock.

It was, in short, a real life plantation. This fact startled Lizzy, as she was sure (or at least had been told by her father, which amounted to the same thing) that all the plantations had been sold off after the War and the slaves freed. And yet. Here sat Blanchefleur, like it was 1859 and not a day later.

More concerning to Lizzy was that every time she attempted to voice her concerns about the slaves, all that came out was a sneeze—and then the words would vanish from her mind.

Still, she was determined she would reach the edge of something; to know that this world had a boundary she could touch and see, if not cross. That thought at least clung to her like a burr to her dress hem. And she would keep it there to prick her motivation as needed.

Lizzy marched all the way to the woods on the East side of the plantation, and then decided to follow them around till she reached somewhere else.

By and by, they came to the blacksmith's shack. There, Lizzy's eye was caught by a decorative wrought iron arm.

This one had delicate curlicues at one end with a coil in the middle and a snake's head with bared fangs that served as a hook for a sign or what have you. It also had two curious horns atop it's head and a hole above the indentations that marked its eyes. It stuck out above the door to the shack, as if advertising the craft, or to scare away something else, Lizzy did not know. But it fascinated her in a way she could not readily put into words, like something from a dream (...*The moon illuminated a woman wearing a dress and veil, sitting at atable. A deck of playing cards sat before her. One after another, her thin hands turned the top card. Ace of Hearts. Nine of clubs. Ten of diamonds. And from her mouth, slithered a large and glistening snake with horns and a crystal set in its forehead…*).

"The horned Serpent…" she whispered to herself.

The Horned Serpent. Tezu had told her stories of the beast, but it was just a legend, some native tall tale, like the Thunderers, or Skinwalkers. But then, revenants had been just such a tall tale until a few days ago.

An older man with weathered skin looked up from the anvil.

"Sorry Miss, didn't see you there," he wiped his hands on his apron and ambled over, all smiles.

"Help you with anything, Miss?" asked the blacksmith.

Lizzy was brought up short, so lost in thought that it took a moment for her to find her tongue.

Haney arrived just then and made introductions. Ben was an older man with a bit of gray in his hair and the sort of twinkling eye that reminded Lizzy of her favorite uncle back home.

"I was admiring some of your work. That is quite a piece," Lizzy nodded to the snake-shaped arm over the door.

"Thank you, Miss," He grinned and wiped his brow. "Rather like that one myself. Made it for the General, though he had other ideas, so's I hung it up there. Keeps the crows away. Why don't you sit a spell, Miss," he offered Lizzy a stool.

It wasn't much but it was the only seat in the shack. Also, Lizzy was now feeling the folly of her plan to march about at such a pace, and so sat.

"…And this here's Samuel, who's been out loafin', as usual," Ben smiled as his apprentice arrived.

"I wasn't loafin'. Miss," Samuel nodded to Lizzy. "Been up at the Manse, fixin' the water pump for Miss Coffie. You must be Miss Lizzy."

"I am. And Ben here speaks highly of your skills. I've always been fascinated by smithing. Turning rocks into tools by the judicious application of fire strikes me as the closest thing to real alchemy humans have ever found. "

"Oh, that is a fine way of putin' it. Just don't go askin' me to spin you some gold!"

"You'll have to excuse the modesty from this one," said Ben. "Go on, show Miss your project."

"Nah, she don't want to see that," Samuel grew bashful, thrusting his hands into his apron pockets.

"Oh please share!" Lizzy smiled. "I'm so awfully tired of looking at needlepoint. I'd love to see whatever project you've got to hand, even if it's an outhouse doorknob."

"It's quite a bit more excitin' than that," Ben chuckled.

Samuel fetched something wrapped in oil cloth from a shelf behind him. He laid it on the table and unwrapped a small six sided box made of finely polished brass. There was a ring on the top and a pattern of holes on the sides.

Samuel lifted the ring, which raised the finely articulated shutters on all six sides of the box. He held it up for Lizzy to see.

"Oh my, is it a lantern?" she asked.

"Yes'm." Samuel gripped the base and twisted it. The lantern clicked and ignited, spilling a bright light around the dimly lit shop.

"Oh, it lights itself?" Lizzy said in astonishment.

"There's a flint set in the base. Give it a twist and it ignites the wick. The shutters can be adjusted to let in as much or as little light as you want."

Samuel demonstrated by turning the ring again, lowering the brass panels over the glass. There were a series of pinholes in each panel, and these cast tiny stars around the shop.

"This is amazing," Samuel," Lizzy said. "You have a genuine knack for invention."

"Oh t'ain't a thing ma'am, somethin' to pass the time is all."

After making their goodbyes, Haney led Lizzy down a narrow dirt path. The day was warm and bright, and Lizzy was growing tired, so let Haney lead her back to the manse.

To one side was a long field, in which two dozen field hands stopped picking cotton. Lizzy supposed this was how Greer funded much of his military operation. She wondered, did folks who purchased his cotton knew to what ends the General was putting their money? Did they care, even?

The sun shone down on their backs and the air buzzed with activity. As they passed by, Lizzy heard the field hands singing:

> As I went down in the river to pray
> Studying about that good old way
> And who shall wear the robe and crown
> Good Lord, show me the way!
>
> O brothers, let's go down
> Let's go down, come on down
> Come on, brothers, let's go down
> Down in the river to pray

The field hands were under the care of Tristan, the Overseer. He wore a straw hat and overalls and carried a whip wound about his ample waist. He was accompanied by the Commandeur, a stout, dark skinned man who cut a fatherly figure to one and all. He was called Little Tom and he stood beside the Overseer, who sat atop a pony that looked barely large enough to hold his girth.

"Ach! At this pace, you'll neveh see the end of the day!" Tristan bellowed in a Scottish brogue that frequently revealed its Southern origins, especially when he drank, which he did much of the time.

He hopped down from the pony and marched up to the nearest hand.

"Is the shovel na to yer likin', Alphonze?" Tristan grabbed the tool from the worker's hand.

"Nos'r," Alphonze avoided his gaze.

"Then why tis it that ya move so slow? Is you shirkin'?" Tristan narrowed his eyes.

"Nos'r, I'm not shirkin!" Alphonze said. He took the shovel and returned to work double-time.

"That's fine work you're doing then," said Tom. "Give it a little more shoulder!"

Alphonze leaned into the shovel and turned the thick soil over in a great clump.

"There now, You got it!" Tom grinned and slapped the man on the shoulder.

Lizzy had stopped to watch the exchange, more curious than anything else.

"Who is that rat-faced little blaggard?" She asked Haney.

"Oh that's Tristan, Miss. He's the Overseer and the General's cousin, twice removed? Though I never was so sure what removin' was, so maybe he's closer kin than that…"

"That man ain't kin to nothing but a snake," Lizzy said.

Tristan noticed her first and waded out of the muddy row to smile wide and tug on the brim of his straw hat.

"Ma'am," he said. "I'm Tristan. You must be the new lady, Miss Elizabeth."

"That is my name," she said. "Though I don't know anything about being any Lady."

Tristan took this as a self-deprecating bit of chit chat. Lizzy was serious though and fixed her jaw to show it.

She turned to regard the other man. "That would make you the Commandeur?" Lizzy asked.

"Little Tom, Ma'am," he touched the brim of his hat. "You know your way 'round a plantation."

"Grew up on a ranch. They're more alike than not. Nice to meet you. Lizzy Shonka," she offered him a hand. He looked at it for a moment.

"It don't bite," she smiled.

"Sorry Miss, I'm sure that I look afright," Little Tom wiped his hands on the leg of his trousers.

"Nonsense. A little dirt never hurt nobody. 'Sides, I learned to muck a stable before I could read or write."

She offered her hand again. Tom took it gently and shook.

"Haney showing you all the sights, I see," Tristan said. He offered Lizzy a hand. She looked at it pointedly but did not shake it.

"She is. And we must be getting on," Lizzy nodded and then opened her parasol once more. "Good day, Tom," she smiled.

"Tristan," she did not smile at him, nor ever would.

He turned on the field hands who had gathered to see the Miss. "Back to work, the lot a ya!"

"You heard 'em!" Tom smiled. "Let's get to it!"

Lizzy and Haney were half way up the lane heading back to the house when the little boy Lizzy had seen the first day ran up, breathless.

"Hi Miss Lizzybeth!" he said.

"Well hello there. And what's your name?" Lizzy smiled at him.

"It's Tandy, Miss and I picked these fer you!" He thrust a handful of wildflowers at her.

Lizzy chuckled and took them. "Oh how lovely! Haney, we must find a vase for these, don't you agree?"

"Yes Miss," Haney said. She nudged Tandy, "Now run along and be useful Tandy."

"Yes, Haney," Tandy rolled his eyes. Then a thought occurred to him and he grinned, "I'm gonna go catch frogs!"

And he ran off, heading back towards the pond.

Lizzy watched him go, thinking about what a great time he must be having. But her smile faltered when she remembered that he too, like Haney and all the children born here, were destined to grow up apparently unaware of their freedom.

They were to a one, kept in bondage by nothing but a quirk of fate, with no respite but that which picking flowers and hunting frogs could provide. Tandy, who was but a child of six if he was a day, already had his fate written for him; destined to a life of drudgery, to live forever in fear of one misstep, one bad day, either his or Greer's. And then what?

General Greer had created an impressive tableau here at Blanchefleur, to be sure, but it was still just a show. The other officers and especially her brother were taken in by it, because it showed them what they always had wanted but were never allowed to have, whether by custom, aptitude (or its lack), or fortune's disregard. But Lizzy saw Blanchefleur for the moonshine it was, because what it offered her was not something she wanted.

Lizzy had been expected to want it all—the Big House, the kindly and cheerful servants, the dresses, the drama—but in fact would have none of it. Truth be told, Ma and Pa Hawkins had been at their wits end with regard to Lizzy and her temperament. She was far too comfortable, donning trousers and a field hand's hat and chasing down stray calves, or pestering her father to show her how to run the family business (an argument he almost gave into, seeing as how Travis was disinterested).

Ma had tried to cultivate in her ladylike sensibilities, but they rarely took, and those that did, were seen by Lizzy as performance. The Elizabeth Hawkins Pageant of pretending to care about cross stitch and play the pianoforte and whatever else it was expected of her to do. It wasn't that she hated these things, or rejected them outright. She gave being dutiful a try. It simply wasn't for her. She could work the ranch as well as her brothers and being short of hand, her folks let her. And on those rare occasions when she was expected to perform, sans culottes and smelling like a bed of flowers, she put on the show. She did it for others, and it pained her to realize that so many folks who were deer to her, did not know her heart.

And then she met Francis. And all desire to continue the Elizabeth Hawkins Pageant of so-and-so, etc. blew away in a strong West Wind.

Even though Greer had concocted a scene to make it appear as if her presence here at Blanchfleur had been her choice, it was not. Lizzy knew when she was being led about and the General had done a thorough job of it; and not just her. Lizzy could see that Edmond and Travis were as likewise manipulated, though the enticements may have been different.

And she decided, somewhere between being shown the stable full of horses, and the slaves singing as they worked the fields, that she would have to find a way to show her brothers how they were being misled. Only then, could she rescue them, and herself from this hell of a moonshine and magnolia dream.

"Haney, are you and Tandy—" Lizzy was about to say something but suddenly sneezed.

"Bless you miss."

"Thanks," Lizzy sighed. "What was I sayin'?"

"I don't know, Miss. Was it important?"

"I suppose not, less I would remember it." Lizzy handed the flowers to Haney, and led her up the steps to the house.

They had barely set foot inside before they found Robbe, looking tense as usual.

"Ah, Miss Lizzy, there you are!" He called and waved from the top of the stairs. He tripped on the steps as he ran down to meet her.

"The General has requested your presence at luncheon, which will be served shortly."

"Lizzy sighed. "Inform the… General that I will not be attending. I have instead retired to my room to lie down for a spell."

"Oh yes of course Miss. However, I was informed by the General himself that… your attendance is required."

He smiled thinly, and Lizzy could see it pained him to the very soul to be put in this predicament; stuck between a demanding master and hard-headed mistress.

"Of course. Inform the General I shall be there, but late."

"They will, Miss Lizzy." Robbe bowed and then scuttled away.

"Let's get you dressed for luncheon then, miss," said Haney.

"Yes, let's," Lizzy sighed and headed for the stairs. "But not too quickly. I intend to be very late."

As they reached the landing, Lizzy's eye caught a shadow at the end of the hall.

"What's in that room?" Lizzy nodded to the room two doors down from hers. She had noticed it before but kept forgetting to ask about it. As if once it was out of sight, it was out of mind as well. Though the large windows at either end of the hall cast enough light to see, and there were gas lamps at regular intervals for the evenings, there was a pool of darkness in front of this particular door.

"Oh we're not permitted to go in there, Miss Lizzy," Haney said.

"But what is in there?" Lizzy asked.

"I'm sure I don't know," said Haney.

"But how is it there's an entire room you've never been in?" Lizzy asked.

Haney looked confused. "I'm not permitted in several rooms, Miss. Master's office, the billiard room, another gentleman's bedroom—why, it wouldn't be proper!"

"But that is no gentleman's room, is it?" Lizzy asked.

"No, miss."

"So whose room is it?"

Hany once more wrinkled her brow in confusion. "I'm sure I don't know."

"Of course," Lizzy sighed, exasperated. "It must have something to do with—" Lizzy sneezed.

"Bless you, Miss. Would you be needin' some tea? Sounds like you might be catchin' cold."

"I'm fine, Haney," Lizzy spoke the words, but they felt false. She was far from fine. She was frustrated by something she could not define, or even recall, and every attempt to do so caused the words to vanish like morning dew.

They had reached the end of the hall, outside the billiards room when the door opened. Into the hall stepped a string bean of a young man, his dark skin contrasting the light blue livery that identified him as a footman. He bore a silver tray on which was balanced three empty glasses. As the ladies approached he smiled and nodded and shut the door to the billiards room behind him.

"Haney, you keeping out of trouble?" he grinned.

"Of course," she said. "Miss Lizzy, this here is Andre."

"Miss Lizzy," Andre bowed. "Though I'm sure you don't recall, we was introduced last evening, upon your arrival."

"My apologies for not recognizing you. It's been a whirlwind of a time," Lizzy said. "I admit I haven't quite matched every face to a name yet."

"That's to be understood and most names won't be worth remembering nor faces. Especially hers." He nudged Haney with his elbow.

She scowled at him and nudged him back, nearly toppling the trio of glasses balanced on his tray.

Lizzy couldn't help but smile.

"Sorry Miss," Andre said, straightening up. "I forgot myself for a moment there."

Haney stifled a giggle behind her hand and straightened her skirt. "Won't happen again, Miss Lizzy."

"Nonsense," Lizzy said. "You two must be siblings, am I right?"

"How'd you guess?" Haney said, flabbergasted.

"It don't take a deck of cards to read that fortune," Lizzy said. "You remind me of my own self and my little brother, Jim. He and I…"

Lizzy grew quiet as a flood of memories washed over her, of mis-tied laces, arguments over a swing, and other such moments that were gone now, lost with her brother's life.

"...I'm sorry." Lizzy choked back a tear. "Ahem. My brother Jim, he and I… we was like the two'a you in continence."

Andre produced a handkerchief from his pocket and presented it to Lizzy. She blew into it and dabbed her eyes.

"My, you are quite prepared, Andre," Lizzy smiled.

"Of course, Miss. As a footman ought to be. Now if you need anything—anything at all—you let me or Haney know and I'll see to it."

Andre nodded farewell and set about his appointed tasks.

"Well come along then, Miss," Haney said.

They headed to Lizzy's room only to find Edmond and Travis to round a corner and begin making a thorough inspection of the mysterious door she had noted earlier.

Lizzy stalked up to them as Travis was bent over, looking at the lock on the door.

"They keep the silverware downstairs, ya ninny!"

"Lizzy!" Travis straightened up.

Edmond took off his hat and smiled. "I trust you are… uh settling in then?"

"I'd say I was making myself to home, but not nearly as much as the two of you."

"We were… inspecting the details is all. Fine bit of craftsmanship this," Travis ran a hand along the door handle. "Don't make 'em like this no more, do they, Edmond?"

"Uh, no. I suspect they do not."

"Uh huh," Lizzy scowled. "I know you're up to something."

Edmond looked aghast. "I? Never!"

Lizzy shook her head. She turned to leave.

"Go on then," Travis waved her away. "Why don't you go get changed or something? That's right, run along now!"

Lizzy stalked back to them, hand raised as if she was about to slap them both. Haney stepped between them, and smiled.

"Miss Lizzy, we have other duties to attend to, if you recall."

Lizzy exhaled a great breath and crossed her arms.

"Of course, Haney, you're right. Let's go."

She turned and left her brothers to their business.

Travis turned his attention back to the door. It was an imposing bit of construction, made of heavy wood, lacquered and stained a dark reddish brown, with brass fittings.

"I reckon it's gotta be in this here room," Travis knelt to examine the door frame and the lock. "Though Hannibal and all his elephants would have a time getting through this thing!"

"What is in this room that has fixed your attention?" Edmond asked.

"Why, gold, son!" Travis winked at his brother. "Or silver. One or the other, makes no difference which."

Edmond made a noise as if he had a fish bone stuck in his throat. "And what makes you think our threadbare General has a stash of gold hereabouts?"

"Why, how else does he pay for all this?" Travis gestured to the hall, the manse and environs.

"Of course. Your logic is sound, as always," Edmond sighed. "But perhaps stealing from our new lord and master is perhaps not in our best interests?"

"Are you saying there ain't gold in here?" Travis asked.

"This gold—hypothetical, as it is—is beside the point. What I am suggesting is that we face a genuine conundrum, one which would not be lessened by adding thievery to the mix."

"I've thought through all the angles, there Edmond old boy," Travis said. "Quit yer worrying!"

"So it has occurred to you then that there is but one man who stands between us and escape from this interminable situation with our dear sister?"

THE RIGHTEOUS AND THE REST 141

"You talkin' about Jesus?"

"General Greer, You ninny!" Edmond hissed.

From around the corner appeared Miss Rachel.

"Can I help you gentlemen? Perhaps you were looking for the Billiards Room? I believe some of the other officers are gathered there for a spirited game." She motioned down the hall.

"We were actually just—" Edmond waffled until Travis took his hat from him and handed it back to him.

"That's the billiards room? Over yonder? See Edmond, I told ya it was this aways!"

Travis stalked off. Edmond smiled and turned his hat around in his hand. "Thank you, Miss Rachel. Fine name. Biblical, even. But of course you knew that. One of my—if not even my most favorite name. From the uh—"

"Come on son, before you step in it some more." Travis took his brother by the sleeve and dragged him towards the billiards room.

Miss Rachel waited for them to leave before she drew a circle around the lock with her finger. The door shuddered of its own accord, and the lock mechanism clicked. Miss Rachel nodded in satisfaction, then returned to her chores.

9
The Bells Of San Catrina

Mercy and them rode single file, passing through scrub brush and mesquite, over rocky hills and down dusty gulches, brushing against cactus, wandering in and out of heat ripples under a sky so incandescently blue that it lit up the backs of their eyelids when they blinked. The cicadas clicked at the few clouds wandering overhead and the sun glared back.

By the afternoon of the fourth day, they all decided that they were in dire need of a place to rest. The horses were exhausted, and though they had evaded Swann and his men thus far, they knew that it was only a matter of time before the indistinct smudge of dust at their backs arrived full of spite and malice. Them being dead meant Swann and his brigade didn't stop for water or food or sleep. They would pursue them into the desert and would keep at it, till the ends of the Earth and beyond. And as Mercy had pointed out, there were other things that stalked by night, hungry and full of thirst.

It was getting on towards the evening, when the sun stooped low, about to kiss the mountains, that Jim spied the fireflies. At first they were nothing more than a few tiny pinpricks of light that blinked in the dusk.

But soon there were more, and then dozens, hundreds blinking out a path through the growing darkness.

"Do you see that?" he asked.

The rest of them could make little more than shadows and the settling dusk beyond.

"What are we supposed to be looking at?" Francis asked.

"Fireflies," Jim said. "Lightning bugs, if you like. I heard stories of fireflies leading folk to safety when lost in the woods."

"Let's follow and see where they're leading us," said Charlie.

With no other recourse, Mercy diverted them until the sun was behind the mountains. The blinking trail of fireflies lit a path through the twilight.

"There's a safe place to rest ahead!" Charlie said.

They rode on, cresting a hill. Jim's ears were greeted by the sound of church bells faintly ringing.

"Are those… bells?" Jim asked no one in particular.

Charlie called back. "There's a place up yonder!"

Below them, in the waxing dusk, stood the old stone walls of a mission. There was nothing else around for miles but scrub brush and sage, with the purple mountains behind them. The fireflies lit the way straight and true to the mission's front door.

That great black crow of Swann's flew out ahead of them, diving towards the desert floor, turning and swooping back into the sky, wheeling over their heads. A moment later came the sound of hoofbeats from behind.

Francis nudged Shadow on. "Almost there," he whispered.

They took off at a gallop with Swann and his men hooting and hollering. But sure enough, as Jim and the rest neared the shadow cast by the mission walls, the Bird Brigade doubled back at a sprint. Even the crow, Jack veered away before he passed over the Mission.

"Now where are they going?" Jim said. He called after them, "cowards!" and his words echoed across the way.

They found the old wooden doors of the mission standing open. By the look of things, they had been left this way for a long time. The roof of the parish hall had fallen in, and the living quarters were either empty, or had become warrens for desert animals. The roof of the stable was intact though, as was the church, which meant they and the horses would both have some cover for once.

"Curious sort of mission, out here in the middle of plum nowhere." Mercy dismounted first and walked the horses into the courtyard.

A large rose bush wrapped the base of the statue, which depicted a skeleton in an old dress of faded green taffeta with poofy sleeves and a broad-brimmed hat atop her skull.

"I am unfamiliar with this saint." Francis peered close at the statue, wrinkling his brow.

"That is Santa Catrina," Charlie explained. "Patron of them who were killed by violence. She won't hurt you, less you hurt others."

Francis made a face but said nothing more.

They set about securing the Mission. It wasn't a large place. Four rough stone walls with some cactus growing in the corners and a churchyard overgrown by the same rambling rose bushes.

"Odd that Swann and his men won't come close to these old walls," Mercy said. She and Francis were devising a way to close the gate and bar it, in case this circumstance changed.

"That is not the only thing odd about this place," Francis said. He heaved the left hand door out of the rut in which it had sat. Together, he and Mercy managed to lift and push the old door into place in the arch.

"You care to elaborate?" Mercy asked. They took a breather before wrestling with the right hand door.

"A feeling," he said. "As if we're being watched…"

Mercy squinted into the twilight but all she saw was a few yellow owls' eyes looking back at her from the rafter of the stable.

"I've been spied by worse," she said.

By the time Mercy and Francis had secured the gate, Charlie and Jim had set camp inside in front of the old wooden church door. Charlie was roasting some cactus palms, which he'd stripped of spines and skewered on a stick over the fire.

When the food, such as it was, was ready, Francis took his portion and grabbed his bedroll.

"I will stand watch."

"All on your own?" Jim asked.

Francis slung his bedroll over his shoulder, shifted the plate of food to his other hand and hefted Gordo.

"Gordo and I will manage," Francis said.

"Do I get a say in this, amigo?" the skull asked.

"No," Francis said.

With Gordo in hand, Francis set his bedroll under an old Mesquite tree near the gate. It wasn't long before they saw the shadows cast by his own fire.

"So, what's Francis's story?" Jim whispered.

"Francis is a complicated man," said Charlie.

Mercy laughed. "There ain't nothin' complicated 'bout Francis. He was driven to a life of desperation and strife, and is seeking a redemption of sorts, to earn the love of the woman who loves him. Simple."

"I don't think that's a simple matter," said Charlie.

Jim shook his head in agreement.

"I mean, devil's in the details, ain't he?" said Mercy. "Francis was one thing, and now is trying to become another, better thing. That ain't hard to understand."

"I defer to our local expert on becoming another thing," Charlie raised his nearly empty water skin in a toast.

Mercy rolled her eyes and laughed him off.

"What's he mean?" Jim asked. "About becoming another thing?"

Mercy looked at Jim across the fire.

"Some folk are born a bit crooked in their skin," she said. "If they're lucky, and brave, they figure out who they are and get their skin on straight. And if they're real lucky, they can make the rest of the world see them the way they see themselves. But that's a mountain that takes a long time to climb."

"Francis is unsettled by some of his past actions and our host," Charlie nodded to the statue beside the gate. "Is a reminder of those things."

"Yeah but it's just a statue, ain't it?" Jim asked.

Mercy shrugged.

"Some things are more than what they seem," Charlie said. "Other things are exactly as they appear."

"Well if you two ain't cryptic as the day is long," Jim sighed.

After their meager dinner, they doused the cook fire and retired inside the church. There, they moved some of the old rotten pews and swept the stone floor enough to roll out their beds.

Jim lay there a while, looking up through a small hole in the church roof. The tower was above, but it had long since crumbled to a finger of stone pointing at the moon, the bell lost to bandits, or time. It took him a good long while to discern why this bell tower had grabbed his attention. It wasn't until he was about to drift off to sleep that he recalled hearing the sound of bells as they had approached.

"...where's the bell then...?" he muttered and fell asleep.

Francis and Gordo had been sitting watch for a short while before Gordo said, "So, do you want to talk about it, amigo?"

"No," Francis said.

He continued to stare into the flames of the small fire he'd built under the mesquite tree. The flame danced in the breeze.

"I'm remembering things now," Gordo said after a while. "From when I was reclutado."

"You want to talk about it?" Francis asked.

"Si."

"Mercy and Charlie and Jim are right inside."

"That some sort of joke?"

Francis shook his head.

"I remember having the Generalissimo's voice in my head,"

Gordo said. "How it was always there, interrupting any other thought that might occur. After a while, you stop fighting it, and let that puto have his way."

"It is not Greer's voice that haunts me, Gordo."

Francis glanced back through the open door. The statue of the saint stood in a pool of darkest shadow, but the stone skull, polished from years of wind and rain, shone brightly in the moonlight.

"Ain't it though?"

"Greer's is but one of the voices I hear," Francis turned back to look into the fire.

"You gonna make me guess the others? Cus you and me, hombre, we got all night."

Francis was quiet for a moment.

"I hear Lizzy calling out for me, in my sleep. I hear my father's voice from a long time ago. And I hear the voices of all the people I… They whisper their last words in the wind. It doesn't matter how far I ride or what I try to do, I can't undo the things I've done."

"None of us can, Jefe," said Gordo. "We try to do better, estoy cierto?"

"Perhaps. But I've done some things that shouldn't be forgiven."

"Forgiveness? That ain't for you to decide," Gordo laughed dryly.

"I know. That's what I'm… Never mind."

A westerly breeze rustled the dry grass.

"But you found a reason to try though," Gordo said, "and that's gotta count for somethin', right?"

Francis did not answer.

At that same moment, Talbot Swann was waiting for an answer to a question of his own. He sat on an old Mesquite log at the bottom of a dry creek bed that ran through the desert like the shadow of some giant snake. He and his brigade of revenants had regrouped there to devise a strategy for smoking them out of that Mission.

"...They ain't got no more than a few bullets between them," said Swann. "So tell me again, Mr. Finch, why should we not simply attack?"

"Well sir, it's like this..." Finch started to say, but the words fumbled in his brain.

Hoots made a few short declarative sounds and hand gestures, the overall impression of which gave him the appearance that he was having trouble churning butter.

"...Right, I was just about to mention that part," Finch said after pausing to let his companion finish. "Hoots and I are concerned about the mission and it's, er, Mission, as it were, sir."

"I don't follow," said Swann.

"No sir, I doubt you would," Finch said.

"And what pray tell, does that mean?" Swann's black glass eyes twinkled in the moonlight.

"Nothing sir. Just that place, it's got an awful pall about it. Real wholesome and spiritual like, I guess is how you'd put it?"

Hoots shrugged.

Jack squawked. "The Saint of bullets and bayonets watches over those walls," said the crow. "And She does not take kindly to trespassers."

Finch nodded. "What he said."

"You mean to tell me that this place, because it has a holy name to it, has rattled your innards to jelly?" Swann twisted his face into his usual sneer.

"Well, when you put it that way..." Finch said.

Swann took off his hat. He smoothed his greasy hair down and took a deep breath before he proceeded to thrash Finch about the head and shoulders.

Swann paced three steps, turned and paced back.

"What we need is a way to make it a surgical strike," he said. "Get in and out before the saint knows we're there."

Hoots mumbled something.

"Yes, good point, Hoots here says it might work if we had someone on the inside to open the gates and invite us in."

"Hmm, I see," Swann said mulling over the idea. "What we need is someone persuasive…"

Finch nodded in Lt. Jack Daw's direction. Then he stuck his thumb at him and nodded some more.

"Someone with the whits to carry out such an intricate plot."

Swann wheeled around and aimed a finger at the crow. "A volunteer presents himself!"

"Me sir?" The crow shook himself.

"The very same, Mr. Daw."

"Well I don't know…" said Jack.

Swann drew his pistol and cocked it. He held it for a moment pointed at the moon before slowly aiming it at the bird.

"When you put it that way…" Jack sighed.

He flew out of the dry creek bed and into the night, soaring across the wall of the Mission and into the ruined church.

There, the crow alighted on the back of a pew.

"Pss! Hey," Jack Daw hissed.

Jim pushed himself up on his elbows and looked at the crow.

"What is it, bird?" Jim yawned.

"I got a proposition for you," squawked the crow.

Never one to look a gift horse—or crow—in the mouth, Jim decided to at least hear him out. "Shoot."

"What's say you open that gate for me, huh?"

"The front gate?" Jim sat up. He looked back at the crow and noticed it had a white streak down its left wing. "You're that crow what works for Swann."

"Lt. Jack Daw, at your service," the crow bowed.

"Right, Lieutenant. So why would I do that? Help you, I mean? Ain't your commanding officer and his brigade of revenants out there waiting to slaughter us?"

"Slaughter is a harsh word," said the crow.

"So You ain't just waiting to kill us?" Jim asked.

"Well. Didn't say that…"

Charlie sat up and squinted at Jack Daw. "Oh, it's you," He groaned and shook his head. "James, why are you listening to this wretched creature?"

"Wretched?" If a bird can be said to frown, Jack did it just then. "Who's wretched?"

"You are in league with that sorcerer, Greer!" said Charlie. "And against not just your own kind, but all life. I call that a wretched thing to do."

"Oh well, when you put it that way, sure those aren't whatcha call, savory activities, I admit. But it don't mean I am myself, a wretch."

"You're saying your actions don't speak to the condition of your soul?" Jim shook his head. "I find that argument faulty in a number of ways."

"A body has to eat, don't they?" said Jack. "Same with crows as it is for humans. We're people too, ya know."

"But crows is crows," said Jim. "Being a crow, that's your job. And as I understand it, you're an important part of the food chain."

"Well I don't mean to brag," Jack stretched his wings and preened.

"What do you get working with Swann and Greer and them? Can't imagine they treat you all that well."

"I do all right," sniffed Jack. "Revenants attract all sortsa carrion, so it's like having a traveling buffet."

"Three squares on the regular is nice," said Jim, thinking about the last time he enjoyed such an arrangement. "But there's more to life than that, ain't there?"

Jack said nothing for a long moment, just scratched at the church pew for a moment in thought.

"So that's a no on opening the gate then?" Jack said at last.

"That is a no," said Jim.

"Thought so." Jack stretched his wings. "Oh and The General ain't no sorcerer," said the bird. They could almost see the sneer on his beak.

Then he flew into the night.

"If Greer ain't waking those revenants, then who is?" Charlie asked.

Jim would lie awake for some time, pondering, listening to the sound of bird's wings fluttering through the night.

Lt. Jack Daw flew over the Mission Wall, letting the cool desert night air wash through his feathers. The long black snake of the dry creek bed lay below him.

"What else is there?" he said to no one.

Jack fluttered to rest on a log beside Swann.

"Report," he said. "Tell me you convinced them to open the gates, so that I may spare your wretched life."

"...Whose wretched then?" squawked the crow.

"Enough prattling," growled Swann. "Report. Will they open the gate or not?"

"Yeah, about that..."

Just then a sound reached them. It was the ringing of the church bell. Faint at first, it grew louder, drawing their attention to the side of the dry creek bed. Peering over, Finch and Hoots and Swann watched as a long line of fireflies approached the Mission. Jack fluttered over to land on Swann's shoulder and watch along. As the lights reached the gate, it slowly opened, whining on rusted hinges.

"The gate!" Jack cawed.

"At least one of you isn't completely useless," said Swann. He turned to Finch and Hoots. "Ready the men!"

Jim had no idea what time it was when the sound of a bell tolling woke him once more.

"I'm up!" Jim bolted upright. "Stop with the bells already, I said,

I'm awake. What is it this... time...?"

Through the open church door streamed a beam of silver light, too bright for Jim's sleep shrouded eyes. He had to blink several times to focus but when he finally could see again, there before him danced a flickering twinkle of light. At first, it looked as if the fireflies had come to call again. But the twinkling lights expanded, taking on the shapes of people. One in particular became an old woman. Jim watched, more curious than afraid.

At least two dozen such apparitions appeared all around them in the church. They looked as they had in life, wearing the clothes they were buried in. Or, Jim supposed, the memory of clothes.

"Mercy!" Jim hissed. He kicked the pew she was sprawled out on. She startled awake, coming up with her pistol cocked.

"Don't think that'll do any good," Jim whispered.

Mercy took one look at the glowing translucent faces gathered around them.

"Suppose not..." she lowered her pistol.

"Charlie?" Jim looked over to find him wide awake but laying on his bedroll beneath an iron candelabra. Three children were gathered around him, poking him and tugging on his hair.

"Yes, Jim. I see them."

Up at the altar, there appeared a monk. He had been a kindly old feller in life, with a white beard and close cropped white hair and a wide smile.

The ghostly old woman who had been looking at Jim drifted over to the monk, chattering away in Spanish.

Several of the other ghosts added to her speech, until the church was filled with the echoes of voices.

"Any idea what they're on about?" Jim asked.

Mercy shook her head. "Alls I know how to do is cuss in Spanish."

A skull floated through the church door. As it entered, a body materialized, faintly at first as if gathering itself out of starlight and shadows, until he looked as he had in life, a portly feller in a poncho with a great bushy mustache.

"¡Hola, muchachos!" he said.

"Gordo? Is that you?" Jim asked.

"Si!"

The monk turned to Gordo and made some sort of prepared speech. They had a brief chat and then the monk turned and said, "Bienvenido el forastero! Como estas?"

"Gordo?" Charlie said. He sat up and shewed away the trio of little girl ghosts who were playing with his braided hair. "Any idea?"

Gordo turned, his eyes glowing softly. "Si. They say they have been waiting here for someone to come."

The Monk spoke excitedly in a long stream of words.

"Slow down, Brother, I'll tell them," Gordo said.

"Tell us what?" Charlie asked.

"Well, from what I've gathered, they were a simple farming community. Brother Jerome here—he's the monk—he was the sort of leader here, helping the locals with both their spiritual life and other more practical needs."

"What happened to them?" Jim asked.

"Same thing that happens to us all, eventually," Gordo said.

And then what happened?" Charlie asked.

Gordo and Brother Jerome had a long conversation in Spanish. Eventually, Gordo looked at his friends. "They had el objeto and well, most of them decided to keep on with the work. Gives them something to do, I suppose."

"And what is it they do?" Mercy asked.

"They care for weary travelers who happen by the mission.," Gordo said. "And we're welcome to stay as long as we like."

"Tell them we appreciate that," said Jim. "Only, do they have food and water?"

Gordo translated the question. They all replyed with smiles, especially Brother Jerome.

"He says they have all we can eat and then some!"

"Well that's a mighty fine turn for once," Jim said.

Gordo relayed the message.

The monk drifted to the church door and disappeared through it. He was followed by the others.

"He says to follow him."

Jim found his boots, and they all headed for the courtyard. Mercy and Charlie ran after.

Brother Jerome led them into the courtyard. The mission doors creaked open of their own accord and through the great stone archway came a procession of fireflies, each one growing a body and turning into a ghost. The nearly full moon cast its silver light, strengthening them, giving them weight and solidity, so that they were more than mere wisps of smoke, but people.

Under the watchful eye of Santa Catrina flowed a procession of lost souls: men and women and children form across the land, settler and native alike; banditos dripping blood from their mustaches and hunted soldiers; coyotes and bears and older creatures, the likes of which had not been seen in eons. They strode through the gates in groups and by themselves, called by the bell tolling across the desert.

Jim and Mercy and Charlie stood in the courtyard as the spirits surrounded them, drifting towards a covered walkway that ran beside the overgrown garden. Several of the Mission's residents were there, setting dishes on a long wooden table.

There were plates of tamales and roasted beef, potatoes mashed with butter melting in a pool on top, steaming bowls of corn chowder, menudo, and beans. A platter of freshly grilled tortillas floated by, practically lifting Jim off the ground with the warm corn meal smell of it.

Jim and Mercy ran to the table, grabbed plates and began piling them high.

THE RIGHTEOUS AND THE REST

"Now hold on a minute," Charlie said. "You can't go and accept food from the dead."

"I fail to see why not?" Jim mumbled around a mouthful of bread. "They ain't using it! Tell 'em Gordo. Tell them we're happy for the hospitality."

Gordo translated Jim's Thanks to the monk and the gathering ghosts.

Mercy caught herself about to take a bite of food and shook her head. She set the plate down. "While it would be polite under the usual circumstances, I think we should follow Charlie's lead on this, Jim."

"Now I may not know all the ways of the Switch," Jim grabbed another tortilla and rolled it up, "but I know it's inhospitable to turn away help when it's offered."

"Gifts from the dead come with strings attached," added Charlie.

Jim offered a quizzical look to the old Medicine Man. He nodded in the direction of the garden.

A tangle of rose bushes stretched around the wall and ended at the foot of the saint. Spaced out around the bushes were small plots.

From the shadows emerged several large owls. They were bigger than the usual sort of barn owls Jim was used to spying back home. The tallest among them stood almost up to the brim of Jim's hat, while the smallest was only about waist high. Still, they wore long brown robes and fell into a semicircle behind Brother Jerome, moving ominously towards them, wings outstretched, beating the air.

"Oh, hullo there fellers," Jim set the food down and touched the brim of his hat. "You sure are big owls, ain't ya?"

The owl monks gathered around Jim and the rest staring through them with large yellow eyes. It took Jim a moment to realize they were pushing them, albeit gently, towards the open graves beneath the rose bushes.

"Now wait just a ding dang minute!" Mercy said.

"Gordo, what did you tell them?" Charlie asked.

Gordo said something in Spanish to Brother Jerome. He replied and Gordo translated.

"Brother Jerome says some folk wonder till they get good and lost. Then they come here. They help them find a new purpose, in service to the Saint. All who perform a night's work, are granted bread and blood."

"Bread and... blood?" Jim and Mercy exchanged looks.

"Still think all hospitality is good hospitality?" she asked.

"What do they mean by a night's work?" Jim asked Gordo.

Brother Jerome pointed to the half dug graves under the rose bushes and clasped his hands, bowling his head.

"You dig a grave, you then are offered the peace of it. Oh, the piece of the grave!" Gordo chuckled. "That makes sense now."

"Oh, that seems... kinda peaceful..." The food Jim gobbled down was making him sleepy. His bones felt heavy, like they were made of lead. The idea of lying down everything and falling into deep sleep there under the rose bushes suddenly seemed like a fine idea to Jim. He didn't know why he hadn't thought of it sooner.

"But we've got places to be. Ain't we, Jim?" Mercy tried to shake him out of his stupor.

"Nah, it's still dark out," Jim said dreamily.

"Not as dark as all that," Charlie said. He pointed at the lightening sky over the Mission wall. "By my reckoning, we got ourselves but a short while before dawn breaks."

"I think we got ourselves another little problem," Mercy said.

They all turned to the Mission gates. No one had bothered to close them on account of the spirit parade. But now through that stone arch trotted a familiar figure on horseback. Captain Swann looked around at the assembled faces. Lt. Jack Daw sat on his shoulder.

"What a festive atmosphere!" Swann slid from his saddle and stalked up to Jim and the others. "Hope I'm not intruding any."

Brother Jerome floated over to Captain Swann, shouting something in Spanish.

Gordo translated for him, "This place is not for you!"

"But I do not care a lick for you or your Mission," Swann spat. "I go where I please, and do as I please!"

Swann drew his pistol and pointed it at Jim. He cocked it.

"Anybody got anything else to add?"

A shadow crept in swiftly through the door and grabbed Swann from behind. Francis rolled him into the dirt, with his knife to Swann's throat.

"I got one last word for you, Swann!" He hissed. A trickle of red sawdust drifted from a thin slit in Swann's neck.

"Tezu, my old friend!" he laughed. "Will tonight see your revenge upon me at last?"

Francis adjusted his grip on the knife handle. "Let us find out."

A sudden breeze rustled the rose bushes and brought with it the sweet breath of the roses that grew at the foot of the Saint's statue. A hollow sound, like a voice whispering from the gloom of the courtyard's four corners followed, echoing off the stone walls.

It was Santa Catrina who whispered. The statue hitched up the hem of her ragged skirt and climbed down from her pedestal.

The horses Swann had cajoled into service all balked and ran out into the desert.

"What sorcery is this?" Swann looked at Charlie.

"You are in Her mission, Talbot Swann. And you've been disrespectful of those she calls her own."

"Brigade!" Swan called. "Do what you do!"

The revenants turned and advanced on the Saint but she glared at them with empty sockets and clicked her stone teeth. The Revenants froze.

"I said attack!" Swann shouted.

"Well Sir, I'd rather not," Finch muttered.

Hoots groaned in agreement.

"I said attack, hang it all!" Swann ordered.

"Cowards," Squawked Jack from his shoulder.

The revenants inched forward, leveling their rifles.

The Saint of bullets and bayonets grabbed one revenant by the neck and dragged him, kicking and struggling to the well. There she threw him in. A flash of light and burst of smoke that smelled of sulfur and fire belched from the well's mouth.

The host of owl monks ran after the remaining revenants, flapping their great wings and nipping at them with their razor sharp beaks. They chased them through the gate, making a horrible ruckus, all hissing and spitting as they went.

Swann scrambled out from under Francis's blade and ran after them, cursing and swatting at their heals with his hat. Their hollering echoed for miles.

The Saint turned and glowered at Francis, who stood in the Mission's doorway.

Francis dropped his knife. He fell to his knees and sighed as a single tear rolled down his cheek.

"I submit myself to you, Santa Catrina," Francis whispered. "Be merciful. Be quick."

Jim ran to stand before Francis and the Saint.

"Now Ma'am, I don't want to intrude but Francis here is my… Well, he's my brother. And I know he ain't led what you'd call a life of the straight and narrow path, but who among us has?"

The saint loomed over them. Jim could feel her gaze fall upon him. He felt naked, and ashamed in the predawn light. After the longest moment of their lives, the Saint strode back to her pedestal and climbed up to stand watch. And she moved no more.

It was about then that Charlie pointed East where they all saw a creeping light, faint at first, rising over the old stone walls.

"Hate to change the subject, but we need to skedaddle!" Charlie said. He ran for the stables.

Brother Jerome gave an earnest and short soliloquy.

"You have many burdens, James Hawkins," Gordo translated for him. "But not all of them are yours. You can lay them to rest here, if you wish."

The thought of rest appealed to Jim, but he knew that if he abandoned Lizzy to her fate now, the thought of it would eat at him for all his days, and then some.

Charlie returned from the stable leading the horses.

Mercy mounted Abraham Lincoln.

"Jim, you ready? Jim…?"

"One moment, Mercy," Jim said. He turned to Brother Jerome. "I wanted to say…"

Brother Jerome smiled and said something in Spanish. Jim didn't catch the words, but he understood the meaning that passed between them as he faded into the morning light.

"Come on, Jim," Mercy said. "I still got some living to do. As do you."

Jim, still a bit groggy but feeling more like himself than he had in days, found the saddle on Sebastian's back a wake up call. Charlie, who sat behind Francis on Shadow's back, reached out and grabbed Gordo's skull as his body vanished.

"Come on Gordo. Don't want to lose you," Charlie patted the skull.

They set out as the sun rose, the bells of the Mission ringing out their departure. It wasn't until they were a good mile away, cresting a hill that they stopped and turned back to have one last look.

But where the mission had stood the night before, there was nothing. The sun rose over the mountains, the empty desert stretching forever, and the sound of the bells of San Catrina echoing on the breeze.

10
Southern Volunteers

Lizzy waited until midnight. By then, everyone upstairs had retired, and she had dismissed Haney for the night, which meant there would be no one to see her snooping about. At least, that had been the plan. But soon as she stuck her head out of her bedroom door, she heard footsteps and muffled whispers approaching down the hall. She ducked back inside, but left the door open wide enough for her to observe who was making the rounds. By the light of the gas lamp beside her door, she could make out the familiar profiles of Travis and Edmond.

They passed her by and headed straight for the mysterious door at the end of the hall. There, Travis knelt and appeared to kiss the doorknob. Though from Edmond's admonishments, Lizzy got the idea he was attempting to pick the lock.

"That is not the way it is done!" Edmond hissed.

"Oh quit yer yappin'!" Travis retorted.

They lingered another moment to engage in fruitless handle jiggling, before giving up for the night. They headed back down the hall to the billiards room, where the rest of the officers were carousing.

Whatever lay in this room must be of some particular interest, to arouse the curiosity of her older brothers. Lizzy loved them in a way, though had never been bamboozled by their lack of wit.

Once they were gone, Lizzy crept down the hall to the mystery door. It was locked. She recalled seeing Miss Rachel walk about with an iron ring full of keys, one of which no doubt, opened this door.

THE RIGHTEOUS AND THE REST

Lizzy stood there in the dark, pondering her next move, when the sound of footsteps approaching brought her out of it. She lay as flat as her belly would allow against the shadow-draped wall and watched as a round little shadow paused on the landing. By the sound of his wheezing, Lizzy identified him as Quartermaster Gates. He paused a moment before making his way down the creaking stairs. Lizzy peered over the banister into the foyer in time to see Gates meet General Greer. They left by the front door.

Lizzy crept down the stairs. The fourth step from the top creaked loudly as she stepped on it. She froze, fearing the worst. But the men in the billiards room were laughing heartily at some off-color remark Travis had made. Lizzy exhaled, and rushed down the stairs and out the front door.

Lizzy caught up to Gates and the General at the edge of the woods on the eastern side of the plantation. It was dark and there was but a sliver of moon. Luckily, there were a few fireflies about, lighting up the trees as they flitted hither and yon. From the glow of the fireflies, Lizzy saw them meet first a tall lean figure she identified as Doc Hatchet, and then a mystery figure in a dress and veil. Lizzy could not make out the particulars of their conversation as it was brief and she was upwind. But clearly something had been decided, and after a moment this curious group set off along a narrow tree lined path leading through the woods.

Lizzy followed after them until the woods ended abruptly, at the edge of a wide swath of sandy desert scrub. She waited for them to move on before easing herself down the steep slope. They were now some ways ahead of her, but illuminated by the crescent moon, they were easy to locate, as was the village they approached.

Eventually, they came to a small graveyard surrounded by a short iron rail fence. A cloud of smoke from a nearby chimney smudged the night sky. Greer showed no regard for the fence and simply stepped over it, as it was low and more decorative than practical. Gates opened the little gate for Doc Hatchet and the veiled woman, and once they had entered, shut it behind him. Gates remained outside, whether to observe or keep watch, Lizzy could not tell.

She watched from behind a gnarled old mesquite tree as Greer navigated the graveyard with a bucket, scooping out handfuls of the night soil and sprinkling it over the graves. But, not all the graves. The veiled woman would raise a lantern she carried and read the meager headstones, shake her head at this one, and nod in favor, pointing at another, which Greer would deconsecrate, as it were.

When he was through, Greer took a knife from his belt and slit a fresh wound into the heel of his left hand. Aided by the doctor, he made sure each headstone they'd marked received a few drops of his blood. Once this was accomplished, Greer and Doc Hatchet retreated to the other side of the small fence with Gates.

The three men proceeded to stomp their feet and chant in some language Lizzy could not recognize. Whatever the case, it rose in crescendo to the beat of Quartermaster Gates, who kept time on the empty pale.

The din was so loud that a few lights came on across the way, in the village. They paid them no mind and continued to chant until a wind blew in from the East. It smelled of dry leaves and dead things.

The veiled woman set her lantern on the ground at her feet. She stood to her full height and chanted as well. She reached out as if to snatch the wind from the sky. The wind reached a climax and she shouted,

"get thee up, you lazy bones!"

The wind stopped.

Gates stopped drumming on the bucket.

The whole wide world stood silent and still.

Lizzy peered as close as she dared.

Greer stepped into the graveyard. The woman lifted her veil and Lizzy saw that it was Miss Rachel the housekeeper. She and Greer peered at the marked graves, waiting.

And then: the ground rumbled and from first one grave, then another rose a pale hand, pushing through the soil. It took several minutes for the deceased men to scrabble out of their graves.

As each emerged, Miss Rachel approached and stuffed a portion of the contents of a pouch she wore on her belt into each of the hungry corpse's mouths. In turn, a single firefly crawled out of each mouth, blinked and fitted away in a lazy circle. Miss Rachel took a glass jar from her robe and caught each of the fireflies in turn. As she did, the corpses took up a regimented posture, lining up along the tiny fence, which barely came up to their thighs, awaiting orders.

Once the lot of them were up and out of their graves, Doc Hatchet reviewed the recruits, checking their teeth to make sure they were not given over to rot and ruin. Gates turned the bucket over and used it as a stool. As the Doctor found each new recruit to his liking, he'd say something to Gates who would scribble a note in a small notebook balanced on his knee. Once Doc Hatchet was satisfied the revenants were up to snuff, he nodded to the General.

He in turn ordered the new recruits to Forward March. Gates opened the gate and beckoned the new soldiers out of the yard. They fell in behind Greer who marched into the village. Miss Rachel, Doc Hatchet, and Quartermaster Gates took up the rear.

Lizzy waited for three beats, trying to decide if she should follow or not. Curiosity getting the better of her, she crept after them, sticking to the shadows as best she could.

As they neared the village, General Greer called out in a military cadence, "Hup, two three, four! Come and see the soldiers march!"

Doors opened and startled, half-asleep folk peered out. Lizzy crept around the side of a blacksmith's shop, the hearth now cold, and watched from the shadows.

The newly resurrected soldiers entered the single lane that

served as the village's thoroughfare and were greeted with shrieks and wails from the mouths of their former families.

"Company... halt!" barked the General.

The revenants staggered to a lazy stop in the middle of the road, right in front of the adobe walled church. The priest, his face as stark white as those of the dead men before him, took a tentative step forward.

He looked over the familiar faces of the dead, his eyes streaming and lip quivering. Greer sauntered up to him, tying a soiled length of cloth about his cut hand.

The preacher turned to him and said in a thick, Spanish accent, "Jesu Christo, what have you done, señor!?"

"What needs doing, Father," Greer smiled. "And nothin' more than our Lord and Savior might've done himself. For you see, I am on a mission, as it were. Now, it might be a bit more profane than the one Christ set about, but I see it as my God-given duty and I am bound for glory."

Greer stepped back into the street and addressed the growing crowd, who were aghast at the blank stares on their dead men's faces.

"To that end, I need your padres e hijos here," Greer announced. "They have been volunteered into the service of a noble cause. But fear not. When I succeed in my endeavor, your menfolk will be returned to you, little worse for the ware, but to sleep forevermore, consecrated in the ground of a Nation made whole and great once more!"

Someone's abuela, her hands clenched in fists of rage, stepped toward Greer and spat on his boot. She proceeded to curse him out in Spanish, until she reached the last bit,

"...You monster! Put our boys back in the Earth and leave us alone!"

"Wish that I could Granny, wish that I could," Greer said. "But your boys have been called to a higher purpose. Now."

He turned back to the crowd.

"I will give you a moment to say goodbye to your sons, husbands, and fathers, and then we need to get back and make preparations." Greer cast a steely eye over the gathered families.

There was maybe four dozen folk present. And out of them, most of the menfolk were but children, and some older men, stooped from years of labor. A woman and her two children rushed forward, crying and made to hug one of the Revenants. He was recently buried, judging by the lack of decay in his features. But he did not recognize his wife and boys, or if he did, had no leave to show them a sign. Still, his children cried and his wife raged, threw spanish curses and clumps of dirt at Greer.

He merely wiped the dirt from his uniform and approached the family. He knelt and addressed the two young boys, their faces stained with tears.

"Fear not, young'ens. For your father has joined a righteous cause. Know that he goes to free a dark and benighted land from tyranny!"

Greer stood and motioned to Gates. He gave an order and the revenant conscripts turned as one and marched down the lane, towards the woods and the camp, the General leading them. Doc Hatchet doffed his hat and then followed them down the lane.

Miss Rachel lingered and raised a slender finger to her lips as if shushing a child. The families all grew quiet, their sobs choked in their throats.

Lizzy waited as long as she could, till her hands stopped trembling, and then she wiped the tears from her face and headed back through the night after them.

Waking up the following morning was more of a chore than Lizzy was prepared to perform. Somehow she managed to rouse herself and with Haney's help, set about her day.

The details of what she had seen in the woods faded, as if it had all been a dream. She was certain she had seen what she had seen, and the proof was in her shoes, caked with mud and grave dirt. She'd had to carry them inside when she returned to the manse last night. Lizzy had prepared an elaborate excuse, about visiting the horse corral after dusk with her brothers but found the story was unnecessary. Haney simply took the shoes away to be cleaned. Lizzy found them, like new, waiting for her that afternoon when she returned to dress for luncheon.

But it did confirm her suspicion that Greer was planning a large military offensive. He had the plan—being a Confederate revanchist made his target obvious. And now he had the army, one that wouldn't blanche at the horror of war, or question orders. Soldiers who wouldn't stop executing those orders, ever. Still, the question remained, what could Lizzy do about it?

By that afternoon, Lizzy found herself loitering on the front porch, attempting to evade small talk from the officers, who circled lazily like flies.

Travis was there of course. He comported himself like a seasoned vet in his borrowed uniform, puffing his chest up while discussing military tactics with a dough-faced gentleman in his sixties whom everyone called Dillford. He then switched to flirting with the maid, Sarah, when she arrived to refresh everyone's drinks. She refilled Travis's glass. He took a sip and held it up to the light, smacking his lips.

"My, that is a refreshing beverage! Did you make this lemonade yourself?" Travis asked.

"Nos'r," Sarah smiled and looked away. "I carry the pitcher is all."

"And you do a lovely job of it," Travis said.

Lizzy could not help but notice the look of terror behind her eyes. Travis did not see it of course. No man there did. But Lizzy had seen it before—felt it herself whenever pa's old friends came by the ranch and she would have to smile at their wolfish intentions hiding beneath sheep's compliments.

Sarah laughed behind her hand, and then looked around, for other glasses to fill, and any avenues of escape that they might afford her.

The General arrived with the rest of the officers in tow. He stomped up the steps and took a glass offered by Sarah, who bowed her head, looking away.

Greer did not notice.

But what Lizzy noticed was the bandage on his left hand.

"Evening Miss Lizzy," the General took off his hat and nodded. "I trust you have had a pleasant day thus far?"

"Of course, General," she said. "Though it would appear your day has been more eventful. What did you do to your hand?"

"Oh, this?" Greer held up his bandaged mitt as if noticing it for the first time. "A scratch only. One of the occupational hazards of the professional soldier, I'm afraid. We're always managing to draw blood one way or another."

He chuckled. Lizzy did not.

"I suppose you will have to get used to such sights as minor wounds. The sight of blood can be overwhelming to some, but to the true patriot, it is invigoratin'!"

"Yes, well I wouldn't know of such things," Lizzy turned abruptly away and returned to her seat on the porch.

"Hmm. Yes, well, I understand Miss Coffie has prepared us a special meal this eve. Let us away to enjoy ourselves." Greer looked around the porch. "Are we not all accounted for? Who is amiss?"

"Edmond," Travis looked at his empty glass, around the porch for Sarah. Alas, she had gone. Disappointed, he turned back to Greer. "He hasn't returned yet."

Greer sighed. "And where is the Reverend?"

"Last I saw, he was headin' down to Camp Able. Still preachin', I expect."

"That's what you expect, is it? Perhaps someone should go fetch him then, shouldn't they?" suggested the General. He looked pointedly at Travis who ignored his look.

"I'll go get him," Lizzy hustled down the steps and around the side of the house before Haney could stop her.

"Where are you going Miss Lizzy?" Haney huffed and puffed as she caught up to Lizzy. She was heading across the southern pasture and due to her immense dress, she was making slow work of it.

"If I know my brother," Lizzy stepped around a cow patty not quite as gracefully as she intended, "He's lost all track of time administering to his flock."

Haney nodded and led the way.

Sure enough, Lizzy found Edmond around back, past the slave quarters. He was standing inside the ring of trees that served as the demarcation line between Blanchefleur propper and what the soldiers called Camp Able.

That is how Greer and the rest of the officers referred to the field southeast of the manse, where they corralled the revenants. Though it wasn't a camp of any sort, but an empty field, churned to mud and dust by the wandering footsteps of the unsleeping soldiers. They had broken ranks and were mulling about in small herds that sort of resembled platoons, though there was no leader per se.

Edmond stood beneath an oak tree, Bible in hand, attempting to get to the end of a sermon. This one was on the Widow's Mite, which Lizzy had always found dreary and moralizing, even for a sermon. Judging by the reception given by the Revenants, they were as interested as Lizzy had been in her Sunday School lessons.

"...And this is why you should endeavor... endeavor always to be cheerful of heart and to care for those less fortunate than yourselves," Edmond offered a thin smile and slapped the book shut. He turned to find Lizzy and nearly burst into tears.

"Oh thank heavens, sister!"

"I come to fetch you for supper," Lizzy said. "This your new flock?"

"Indeed," Edmond mopped his brow with a hanky. "The General has tasked me with ensuring that their souls are well cared for but I..." Edmond looked around as if there was anyone within a hundred yards of the scene but the three of them.

Haney loitered several feet back, as she was uncomfortable around the Revenants.

"What's the problem Rev, your new flock not up to snuff?"

Edmond hemmed and hawed a bit but eventually, he said, "...I am not sure the Revenants have souls." He looked as startled by the admission as if he'd informed Lizzy that the General's pigs all had wings and were currently flying South for the winter.

"Whatever spark of divine grace that enlivened their bodies in life has long since departed, leaving behind naught but a sort of... animal drive. I must admit I am not versed in the theology of the Switch enough to know how to put it. They go through the motions of one who lives but lack any sort of driving force. They are but bodies in motion, without internal... spark. I do not know how else to describe it."

"They're dead, Rev. Ain't got any aspirations, now do they?"

"That is it!" A faint smile appeared on Edmond's lips. "They lack aspirations. But how does one go about sparking aspirations in the uh deceased?"

"I don't know, sounds to me like you found the perfect parishioner." In his face, Lizzy saw a real sense of struggle, and the bags under his eyes were dark and denoted his soul's own restlessness. For a moment, she felt bad for her brother. But only for a moment.

"That is unkind, Lizzy. You have become quite the curmudgeon of late, I must say."

"Can't imagine what might've driven me to it."

"It is not helpful, is all I am saying."

"Yeah well, ain't my job to help, is it? You made your bed, theologically speakin', so you can lie in it. Come on Haney. Supper is waitin'."

Haney was pleased to lead them out of the field back towards the Big House. She skipped ahead of them, which let Lizzy and Edmond have a moment alone.

This was the first such moment they'd had since Lizzy's capture and his indenturement.

"I apologize for worrying you so," Edmond whispered.

"You betrayed me and my husband."

"Husband? You two were married by a preacher, were you?"

"Our vows were consecrated under the full Moon and witnessed by fireflies," Lizzy held her chin high. "May not hold up at the county courthouse, but it was true enough for us. If'n you or even God Almighty got a problem with that, you both can keep it to yourselves. And now I got no more on the matter to say to you, Edmond Ezekiel Hawkins."

They walked in silence a while before Edmond tried a different subject.

"I do hope the General has laid out a spread, as the morning's work has famished me. And I must say, you do look lovely. I see that you have dressed for the occasion."

"Haney put this old frock on me. Is this not how a Lady dresses for luncheon in the antebellum?" Lizzy stopped. A lone cloud wandered overhead, casting shadows as it passed between them and the sun. "Wait. What occasion?"

"Oh," Edmond wilted. "I should not have said anything..."

"Haney!"

Haney stopped in her tracks and turned on her heel.

"Yes'm?"

"What occasion is my Got-Danged brother here not informing me about?" Lizzy stared at the poor girl hard, hands on her hips. Lizzy didn't like to deploy the full power of the Hawkins stare but like their mother, she realized long ago there were times when it was called for.

"Well, Miss Lizzy it… it ain't really my place to say."

Haney looked at Edmond, who shook his head in agreement.

They returned to the Manse in silence, making their way up the front steps to find that the dinner bell had already been rung.

In the dining room, Lizzy found a seat for her waiting at Greer's left hand. Andre the footman pulled the chair out for her.

Edmond took his seat down the table half a ways, beside Doc Hatchet. The two had become fast friends since their arrival at Blanchefleur and they fell into easy chitchat.

Travis sat at Greer's right hand and avoided making eye contact with Lizzy as she took her seat.

After a brief prayer muttered by Edmond, dinner was served.

Dinner conversation was the smallest of talk, mostly concerning a coon hunt the officers were planning for that evening. After a while, the General returned once more to his most warmed-over topic, that of the War and what would come after. This reminded Lizzy of something she had intended to ask before. She decided now was as good a time as any.

"…You've mentioned these Powers that guide you," she paused to dab her lip with a napkin. "What are they, exactly? And do they have anything to do with wherever it is you and your officers disappear to every morning?"

Travis and the other officers shared an uneasy glance around the table. It was pointedly not remarked upon by anyone there present.

After a moment's silent contemplation, Greer nodded. "My, you do have an astute eye."

"Well if you don't want to tell me, that's fine."

"Forgive me, Mrs. Lizzy. I find your gradual warming of mood over these last few days as refreshing an occurrence as a summer breeze."

"You could just say I don't know," Lizzy smiled thinly and took a bite of her dinner. Tonight's meal was a succulent roast bird of some sort.

"It's merely been a spell since I had anyone ask about such matters," said The General. "The theology of it escapes me, to be plain. However, as I understand it, the heathen Powers who call these wild places home are willing to offer their influence, should a soul be amiable and ask sweetly."

Greer paused to sip his wine.

"It's much like courting a prospective mate. The Powers like to be wooed. And if you leave them for too long they may grow jealous and wrathful. Best to go and call on them, one neighbor to another."

"And that's how you do it then?"

"Do what, ma I ask?" Greer's jovial smile faltered a bit.

"Engender such devotion in the men under your charge, of course."

Greer chuckled. "You are a sharp one, Mrs. Lizzy. I'll admit, the particular Power to whom I must pray grants me charge over certain, shall we say, tight-lipped men. But the rest are devoted to me as much as to our singular cause."

"It all comes back to that mission of yours, doesn't it?" Lizzy set her fork down.

"Indeed it does. It is the fire that stokes the boilers of my fervor. I know you do not share that fervor and it may surprise you to know that I shall never require your devotion to the cause."

"Really? You don't want true believers in your choir?"

"In the choir, yes. In the pews? It is neither a requirement nor a hurdle. Everyone shall know peace when I am through. They shall all have a place in the proper order of the world. Faith is not a requirement, only obedience."

"Oh, is that all?" Lizzy picked up her fork.

"Come now, you are a smart woman. Smart as they come, I

reckon. Do you not already benefit from the many contributions me and mine have brought into this world?"

"I do no such thing!"

"I disagree." Greer smiled ruefully. "You come from a farm, do you not? And while I'm sure you and your brothers do your fair share of work, it is not your lot to weed the garden or cook the food, but those whom we rightly put in their place to do so for us."

There was a kernel of truth to his words. As a woman, she was not expected to work the fields or mend the fences or perform much of the physical labor about the family homestead. And while she had her tasks and roles to play, they were more manageable than say, Natty Meg, their cook, or even Bethany, the maid.

"A farm is one thing," Lizzy said. "And Pa does not engage in chattel work or bondage. Our workers are free folk, to a one, and well compensated for their labor."

"Are they now? Truly?" Greer took a bite of his meal.

She looked at Travis and then at Edmond. Both avoided eye contact.

"They are," Lizzy picked up her fork. She set it down again. "Besides, you're talking about ordering a whole society! Yoking free souls and grinding out their lives in ruin and work!"

"Empires are built on the backs of the poor and wretched, it is true." Greer set to cutting his meat from the bone. "But is that not the God-approved order of the world? That the wretched and the elite shall both serve their appointed task, to elevate one another with glorious purpose?"

"And you think you'll simply return home after the long years in the wilderness and what? Ascend some seat of power?"

"I myself will not live to see that glory, alas. That is not my fate. I do what I do for the future generations," he nodded at Lizzy's swelling belly. "Eat up, Mrs. Lizzy. For you will be a mother to not just a babe, but to a new world!"

"It is an exceptional burden you place on others," Lizzy whispered.

"We all have our burdens to bear," Greer wiped his mouth on his napkin. "Though is it not also the way that we should share them with a partner?"

"I suppose it is." Lizzy did not like the way the General smiled at her. "What are you getting at, General?"

"I have given the matter much thought," Greer gestured.

Andre took the carafe of wine that had sat in the center of the table and poured out two glasses. He handed one to Lizzy and the other to Greer. The other servants likewise delivered wine glasses to the officers.

"As unconventional as it may seem, given the circumstances, I think you could have a greater share in the glory and purpose of the world in which I aim to make," Greer stood and raised his glass. "To this end, I wish to formalize our arrangement."

"What arrangement would that be?" A cold fear gripped Lizzy by the stomach. "I am your prisoner, sir."

"Prisoner?" Greer looked genuinely shocked. "No! A captive only, in the traditional sense. The necessities of politics makes our meeting a fraught one, but that does not mean we must remain in such a stifling arrangement."

Greer shifted in his seat so that he could look at Lizzy in full. He wore the most curious expression, one Lizzy would later identify as admiration.

"I have granted you a modicum of freedom and you have been kind enough not to abuse it. Furthermore, I have broached the matter with your brothers and they have granted their permission and blessing."

"They have done what now?" Lizzy shot a look at Edmond and at Travis. Edmond looked away. Travis stared at her wearing the sort of smile one would find on the face of a wolf.

"I intend to bestow upon you every measure of power that a lady of the South could want," Greer stood and picked up his glass of wine.

"Miss Lizzy, I intend to make you my wife. You may celebrate now." Greer took a gulp of wine.

The gathered officers cheered. As did the servants.

Lizzy didn't know what to say—could say nothing.

"Given your delicate condition, I will of course make every accommodation I can, within reason. You will have no cause to alarm, I will not press my advantage or make any liberties while you remain with child. As to the details of our wedding, I will leave those to you. Now if you will excuse me, I have matters to attend to. Evening, Miss Lizzy."

Greer took her hand in a gallant gesture and kissed it. He then left the dining room.

Lizzy sat there a while longer as the officers in turn offered their well wishes. Edmond offered her a weak smile and mumbled some bit of scripture before he slipped away. Travis left shortly thereafter, offering neither his blessing, nor even a word at all.

After thanking all her well-wishers, Lizzy retired to her room. Haney saw her up the stairs.

"Thank you, Haney, but I think tonight I'd like to be alone. I have much to ponder."

"Yes, Miss," Haney curtsied and lingered a moment. Lizzy could tell she wanted to say something but couldn't form the words.

Lizzy made to go in but turned back. "Haney…"

"Yes, Miss?"

"I would like to write a letter. To my parents, updating them on our situation. Could you find me some stationary and an ink pen?"

"Of course, Miss," Haney beamed. She rushed over to the desk and began to rummage the drawers.

"The General says letter writing is a dying art form. I myself have never learnt it but I find it frightfully interesting, how folks go about making those letters with the curlicues and such. Here we are, Miss."

Haney had set out several sheafs of paper, a pen, and an ink well.

"Thank you, Haney, that will be all."

"Goodnight then, Miss Lizzy," Honey said. She lingered a moment more, in case Lizzy needed something. Once it was apparent she did not, Haney shut the bedroom door behind her.

Lizzy did not like using Haney as a tool for her subterfuge, but she had been mulling a thought all through dinner: if she could not speak her thoughts on the house and its peculiar ways aloud, then perhaps she could write them out?

Lizzy wasn't much of a wordsmith but after a moment or two she recalled how to fill the ink pen and then spent another minute making little splashes and drops all over the first page. But she managed to write the word SLAVE in big capital letters, which proved to her she could write what could not be said.

Whether anyone would ever read it was another matter but one that was not for her consideration at present. She had something to say and if only the paper would read it, then that was how it would be. For the sake of her own sanity, Lizzy decided to make her statement in the form of a letter.

"It was good enough for the Apostles, it oughta be good enough for me," she surmised to no one.

She decided right away to whom she should address her most desperate epistle:

Dear Jim,
I know you will never read these words on account of you being dead most likely. I find myself in a strange ~~circams~~ circumstance and must tell someone and you was always the one who would listen out of all my brothers so its on your dead ears I lay this message. General Greer has a plantation house he calls Blankenflower (I don't know the right spelling but it means 'white flower' in french) and it is full of slaves.

I know that doesn't sound right on account that the slaves were all freed fifteen years ago but it is the truth. There are some sixty or more souls kept as slaves here against the will of God and the laws of the land.

Lizzy filled four more pages of chicken scratch as she poured her heart out onto the cream-colored paper. She wrote about the slaves, and about how they should be freed by someone, and what she knew of Blanchefleur and its ways and layout, even drawing a little map on the third page. After a while she grew tired and the energy of putting all those words onto the paper drained her. She closed the letter by saying,

If your spirit somehow reads these words I want you to know that I always loved you best. And if the shade of my love is beside you as I hope he is, tell Francis that I love him too and will until my dying breath.
Yours,
Liz. Shonka

Then she folded the letter up neatly, placed it in the drawer of the desk and stood before the window. She found the evening star, Hesperus, riding low in the night and offered a prayer to it that someone, somewhere would know her plight and bring aid, for herself and the slaves of Blanchefleur, and to her dead brother and husband. After that, Lizzy lay on the bed and cried herself to sleep.

11
A Dollop Of Thunder

Jim and the rest rode on. Under the blaring eye of the sun. Across scorched desert. Through the night and into the next day. It had been three days since they left the Mission, near as Jim could figure. Though there was some disagreement on the matter—Mercy and Francis were certain that only two nights had passed and this was the third day. But Jim and Charlie were of the opinion that they had been on the spur for three days already.

"I distinctly remember three sunrises since we left," Jim said, scratching at his neck.

"Now that's just bad time keeping, that is," said Mercy. "What say you Gordo? You're the tiebreaker."

"Time is el espejismo," said the skull. "I never rely on it for telling me anything."

"There you go!" Charlie grinned

"Ah, what do you know," Mercy huffed. "That's what I get, asking a dang skull what time it is..."

However many days it had been exactly, only the Four Winds knew. But it was on an afternoon (they all agreed on that) when they found themselves at a crossroads, beside a small grove of sycamore trees. Here they made camp. They were now completely out of food and had but one skin of water between them.

"We can't go on like this," Francis scanned the horizon in search of something, anything. "Not without water."

"But taking a night off the road to go in search of some will only slow us down," said Mercy.

Charlie nodded. "I don't like it either, but I don't see what other choice we have."

Abraham Lincoln whinnied to get their attention and they heard the horse grumble under his breath, "'It is not best to swap horses while crossing the river'."

"En serio?" said Gordo.

Charlie had set him upon a rock under the tree beside their campfire.

"If we stay too long, we may never find the road out again." Jim swayed a little on his feet. "...And I for one have an appointment to keep."

Jim's insistence that they continue on to wherever this road ended had become his sole motive. The others had each in turn taken note of his newfound zeal and it was beginning to worry them. That and the fact his eyes remained closed longer and longer each time he blinked.

Jim sat in the shade of a sycamore tree, his head nodding. He caught himself, and bolted upright once more.

"You feeling alright James?" Charlie looked in his fluttering eyes and found his pupils wide and eyes glassy.

Jim, your neck," Mercy pushed the bandana she'd given him aside. They found the wound from his hanging had turned angry and red.

"I'm fine," Jim pulled the bandana back into place.

Mercy and Francis exchanged looks.

"Said I'm fine! Now let's mount up," Jim swayed a moment. Shook himself awake.

"Jim," Mercy placed a kind hand on his shoulder and looked him in the eye. "You need rest. You can't go on like this, letting the circumstances gnaw at you so. Truth is, we don't know where Geer has gone with Lizzy. And fretting over it ain't helpful to anyone's sanity."

"So what are you sayin'? You want to turn tail and run off somewheres? Where can we go that they will not follow? And where, Mercy, would you have me go to forget my sister's fate?"

"Now hold on there, Young James Hawkins," Mercy's stare turned hard. "No one said anything 'bout given' up."

"Maybe not in so many words, but would you give up if you could? After all, this is but custom to you. I paid you for your services. If'n you want to leave, by all means!"

"First off, Mercy Nightingale don't run out on a job," she said. "And second, if you think you are but custom to me now, after what we been through, then you can go back and crawl into that grave we fetched you from!"

"No Power will put me in the ground!" shouted Jim. "I will chase that bastard 'round the world and back again, if it means finding my sister! And if none of you will help me, I'll do it alone."

"You forget yourself, Jim," Francis said. "There are others whose fates are tied to Lizzy's. But until we escape from Swann and find some clue as to where Greer has taken her, we are lost."

"And if you're dead of thirst or infection, you can't fight the good fight," Charlie added.

"I know," Jim sighed. The fire left his blood. "And I didn't mean… I'm sorry, Mercy. And everyone."

"You are a maddening feller, Young James Hawkins," Mercy shook her head and smiled. "But you mean well, that we all know. And it's high time you knew what we stand for."

"I do know, and thank you for standing with me. I have become less… circumspect since we set out on this quest."

"You have not become less of anything, James," Charlie smiled. "You are more yourself now than you have ever been."

"Y ahora qué?" Gordo said. "Now about those supplies…"

They were deep into weighing the pros and cons of the situation when they were distracted by a tuneless humming, like some great swarm of bees approaching. They turned as one to find a traveler

THE RIGHTEOUS AND THE REST

coming along the East-bound road.

A spindle of a man with a gravelly voice and a stovepipe hat sat in the front of a wagon led by a team of mules. By and by, he drove close enough for them to make out the advertisement painted on the side of his wagon in large careful letters:

> *Dr. John Picadura, Esq.*
> *Purveyor of Fine Elixirs & Tonics*
> *All Manner of Ailments Treated*
> *5¢ a Scription*

He pulled his mule team to a stop in front of Jim and the rest and ceased singing. He offered them a wide grin.

"Any of you, by chance, lawyers?" he croaked. "Or in some fashion familiar with the legal arts?"

They all shook their heads.

"Excellent!" The man hopped down and doffed his hat. "Dr. John Picadura, as the signs and portents have spoken about." He knocked on the side of his wagon. "Don't suppose any of you would be in need of my services this fine day?"

"As a matter of fact…" Mercy said.

Jim scowled.

"What? He's a medical doctor," Mercy said. "Can't you read?"

"I am indeed." Dr. John looked Jim up and down. "And by the looks of things, you all are in dire need of my expertise."

"No sir," Jim clenched his jaw. "I think we'll manage."

"Have no fear, young sir, I understand your skepticism completely. 'Tis a wide and unruly world out there and you never know who is around the bend. But let me put your mind at ease by waving my customary examination fee."

"See? A real whatchamacallit, Heracles," said Mercy.

"I think you mean Hippocrates," corrected Jim.

"Oh, my apologies, college boy," Mercy rolled her eyes.

"Ah, a learned man!" Dr. John smiled. "And what area of knowledge are you engaged in, my young friend, eh?"

"I was studying medicine, least until circumstances got in the way…"

"And a fellow practitioner of the surgical arts, no less! Well then, as our mutual master Hippocrates would agree, you'll understand the need for proper medical attention when it is called for. So what seems to be ailing thee?"

Charlie exchanged looks with Francis and Mercy. They both shrugged. Charlie waved the Doctor over to the sycamore tree. Jim sat there holding Gordo in his lap, stroking the skull like it was a puppy.

Dr. John made a brief examination of the skull. "My, oh, my. I'd say we have ourselves a bad case of being stone dead."

"Will… will I make it, Doc?" Gordo moaned dramatically, but then caught himself in a cackle that rattled his mandible.

"I'm afraid there's not much I can do for your talkative friend here. However, I notice you, my young friend, have a bit of a problem with your neck."

"Yeah, I was hanged," Jim coughed. "Got better through."

"Ah that explains the redness and swelling," Doctor John offered a smile. "Believe I have a poultice that will clear that right up. But as to the other matter, well…"

"What other matter is that, Doc?" Charlie asked.

"Well, I don't intend to pry. Folks got their own burdens, of course, but I will say this: no man may unstoop his own shoulders."

"The hell does that mean?" Mercy asked in a low whisper.

"It means, my dear, that I can fix whatever else it is that ails the rest of you. A little bit of the ol' Kickapoo Joy Juice, perhaps? One snort, and you'll be right as rain!"

They handed a silent look around the circle, which served as discussion on the matter; Dr. John, well versed in most forms of nonverbal communication, clapped his hands and smiled. "Well then, say no more!"

The doctor headed for his wagon. Stopped, turned.

"There is however the matter of my 'scription fee."

"Thought you was gonna wave that?" asked Mercy.

"The examination fee is gratis, My dear. However the 'scription fee is another matter entirely. A man must eat, after all."

Jim, Charlie, and Francis looked at one another.

"I'm tapped," Francis whispered. "Jim, what you got?"

"I spent my last silver dollar securing the services of Mercy," Jim said. "Surely, one of us's been holding onto some last penny, tucked away somewhere?"

"I don't have much use for money," Charlie scratched his chin.

"If'n you boys haven't got the currency, I will accept barter in lieu of payment."

"Yeah, we ain't got any of that neither," Jim said.

Mercy rolled her eyes. "Doc, how about some Grade A Spirits?" From her saddle she took the jug of liquor she'd been hauling since Pawhuska, the contents of which had quelled that dead soldier they'd found, and whose sword Jim still wore on his saddle.

"My dear you are an angel!"

Dr. John fetched an old jam jar from his wagon. Mercy poured a nickel's worth of her spirits into it. The Doctor held it up, swirling it around, studying how the light bent inside of the jar.

"Marvelous!"

Francis, out of curiosity, had gone around to have a look through the canvas flap that covered the back of the Doctor's wagon. True to his advertisement, the inside was full of bottles, jars and all manner of vessels, each containing powders, unguents, ointments, and elixirs. There was even a large brass sphere connected by a coil of wire to a complicated-looking machine.

"Ah, I see you've noticed my electrochemical device!" Dr. John winked. "It's a wonder of the modern age, sure to revolutionize medicine. As soon as I figure out how the dang thing works. Say," he turned to Francis, an earnest curl to his mustache, "You wouldn't want to help further the boundaries of medical science, would ya?"

"No thank you, Doc," Francis said. "While I am curious about the workings of that contraption, the thing I was noticing was that hunting bow on the back wall."

"Astute eye my friend!" Dr. John climbed into his wagon, headless of the shelves full of glass and ceramic jars, returning a moment later with the bow in hand.

"This particular item was given to me in trade for performing a rather tricky appendectomy on a Chocktaw feller. Said it was a genuine Spirit Bow, like his granddad used to war with. Now, being a peaceful soul and a law-abiding man with no quarrel against anyone, save perhaps a certain squire who has ascribed a wayward writ against me, I have little need for weaponry of this nature."

With a flourish, Dr. John handed the bow to Francis.

"I couldn't accept such a gift," said Francis.

"Nonsense! To tell the truth, this here bow has been haunting me. It appears in my dreams, telling me to find the one to whom it belongs. You, sir, look like the sort of fellow who might appreciate a fine, handcrafted weapon, and one that comes with a commandment from the Spirit World. Now, I'm not saying it was fate that we found one another, but being a man of some knack, I know not to question the way the Four Winds blow."

Francis nodded. He rummaged in his saddlebag and rummaged around until he found a small cowrie shell. He returned and placed this in the Doctor's hand.

"It's tradition that a weapon be not given, but exchanged."

"I appreciate and accept your exchange, feller." Dr. John placed the cowrie shell on the nearest shelf in his wagon, beside a bottle of Swamp Root.

"Is that really advised?" Jim asked. "Buying a bow with no arrows to shoot."

"It has arrows," said Charlie. "You just have to find them."

"Sooth!" Dr. John emerged from the back of his wagon with a mason jar of cloudy liquid. "I knew I had retained a quart or two of the good stuff!"

Mercy shrugged. "Well, not like we were going anywhere today."

"Oh, you'll certainly travel a bit, I assure you!" he poured spoonfuls all around. He then wiped the spoon on his trouser leg and measured out another, which he then gulped down.

"Sampling the wares, doc?" said Gordo.

"A good doctor always makes sure the stock is up to snuff. Also, who among us doesn't need a bit of medicine from time to time?"

"What exactly is this?" Jim asked. He looked at the mason jar but as far as he could tell there was nothing inside but a bit of moonshine.

"This here is an elixir of profound curative power. It's a distillation of a particular variety of mushrooms commonly found growing in cow patties, cleaned and distilled in grain alcohol."

"Ah, Vision Juice," Charlie nodded. "I've been known to brew a pot or two of the stuff myself."

"You sir, are a kindred spirit and I like you. You will of course attest to our more skeptical friends here that this is the perfect medicine for treating all manner of problems, be they gastrointestinal or psychoanalytical. I myself take a dose now and again, to keep my vision clear. In fact..." The Doctor looked off in the distance for a long moment, scrutinizing some clouds that were scudding along in a westerly fashion, right where the sky grows brightest before it meets the horizon. "...In fact, I'd recommend a gulp for each of us. Looks like it's going to be a stormy night."

"I see no storms," Jim said, shielding his eyes with his hands and following the Doctor's gaze.

"All manner of storms come and go this time of year. Some seen and others un. Best to gird oneself for all possibilities."

"Possibility of what?" Jim asked.

Doctor John waggled an eyebrow. "That is the question, ain't it?"

He poured out a measure in mismatched teacups, one for each of them.

"Slanche!"

And they all knocked it back.

Doctor John made a poultice of sunflower heads, tobacco, and a few other ingredients whose origins he was reluctant to divulge, but, he assured them, would do the trick. This he affixed with a plaster to Jim's neck. Soon, the fever had left his blood and he felt cooler to the touch.

Charlie found an old drum in the Doctor's wagon and set to pounding out a rhythm that sounded to all like the heartbeat of the world. The Doctor took off his shirt, found some bells, and together with Francis, Mercy, and Jim they all danced to that eternal rhythm echoing through their veins.

Sure enough, as Dr. John predicted, a storm blew in some time after sunset. Great gusts of wind swept across the plains and a wall of clouds belching bolts of lightning moved towards them. Jim, Francis, and Mercy felt the exhilaration of the evening and they stripped down to nothing but their boots and ran out into the desert to meet the storm. Jim felt compelled to bring his sword along and brandished it at the clouds as they ran.

Overhead, giant purple and black clouds swirled, forming into shapes of enormous birds, their swooping, gliding, and diving illuminated by the lightning that licked the distant ground.

"Thunderbirds!" Mercy whispered reverently. Though she may have shouted the word as far as Jim could tell with the wind in his ears.

For surely, that is what they were, plain to see for all: great birds made of clouds shrieking lightning and cracking thunder with the beat of their wings.

Francis ran out into the desert, chasing the flashes of lightning and before they knew what they were doing, Jim and Mercy ran after.

Out on the plain, they saw the clouds galavanting above the silhouette of a mountain in the distance. Before them, on the desert plain stood a woman. She wore a dress of black feathers that glistened in the light cast by the storm. Her face was dark but her eyes were electric blue and her headdress was a bird's skull wreathed in flame-colored feathers.

The woman moved in between the flashes of lightning, appearing here and there, far away and then up close. She appeared in the distance, at the foot of the mountain and Jim brandishing his sword at the clouds gave chase.

He ran for what felt like hours, until he reached the woman at the base of the mountain.

There, she pointed towards the mouth of a cave. It was little more than a crack in the great wall of stone, and Jim had to stoop to get inside but once he did, he found the passage was tall enough for him to stand.

Jim wandered deeper into the cave. It was dark, but there came a faint glow from his saber. He held this out in front of him like a torch and with his other hand, guided his path along the stone walls. The passage wound around and down until he was certain he had traveled into the center of the very earth. Eventually, he came to the end of the tunnel. Instead of a hard stone wall, however, there was a wooden door, set in its frame as if that was the perfectly natural thing to find below the pillars of the Earth.

Jim turned the handle, pushed it open, and stepped through into a large and well-lit hallway. The hall was that of some well to-do house, lined with pictures, though he recognized none of the faces. Under his feet, instead of damp stone rock, was a carpet over a wooden floor, polished and smelling of wood oil and varnish.

Jim wandered along this hall, until he came to a room.

The door was open and inside there was a faint light cast by the moon through an open window. The moon illuminated a woman wearing a dress and veil, sitting at atable. A deck of playing cards sat before her. One after another, her thin hands turned the top card. Ace of Hearts. Nine of clubs. Ten of diamonds.

Jim peered at the woman, trying to make out her features beneath the veil.

"Lizzy? Is that you…" He lifted the edge of the veil to find a skull with pitiless empty sockets. The skull swiveled up as if to look at him and from her mouth, slithered a large and glistening snake with horns and a crystal set in its forehead.

Jim gripped his saber tight and took a step back.

The horned serpent fell from the skeleton's mouth, coiling into the shadows.

"You, serpent!" Jim yelled in a quavering voice. "I am not afraid of you!"

"You lie!" hisseed the serpent. "I can smell your fear!"

The creature's long tongue darted out. Jim swatted it away with his sword. The serpent hissed and reared back. But Jim was faster and he struck first.

Jim felt a sharp pain and looked down to see the blade of the sword protruding from his own chest.

The Horned Serpent was gone, if he had ever been there at all. Jim pulled the sword from his chest and laughed. He laughed and laughed, and cried…

Francis and Mercy found Jim kneeling on the dry cracked earth, weeping. They picked him up off the ground and held him up as the rain came to greet them. The rain cleaned away Jim's tears until he felt empty. He was no longer angry, or afraid, a fact he had refused to admit even to himself. He was simply alive.

Jim reached out a hand and Mercy took it and they held onto one another as the wind and rain and shrieks of thunder washed them clean. Soaked to the bone and in awe of every breath, the three of them ran through the rain, slipped in the mud, and whooped back to the shrieks of the Thunderbirds swooping overhead.

Jim would recall this moment until the end of his days, the night he first saw the majesty of those great Powers of the sky move with ferocity and grace.

In the morning, Jim and the rest woke a little worse for wear. Jim complained of a headache, for which Dr. John prescribed a spoonful of his patented cure-all, which he doled out to each of them, and which tasted to Jim suspiciously like moonshine. He said as much to Dr. John.

"Taste of the poison is sometimes the cure," replied the physician.

Dr. John checked Jim's wound and found it satisfactory. "You're on the mend my boy, though I'd avoid getting tangled in any more nooses if I were you."

They then tucked into a meager breakfast. This consisted of beans, hard biscuits, and coffee, with some nopalitos provided by Charlie. Jim was skeptical at first about eating cactus, but with the spines removed and fried up in the doctor's cast iron pan, they were quite tasty; Jim suspected they would go well with scrambled eggs and coffee.

After breakfast, they packed up their camp and made ready to leave. The Doctor made them a generous gift of one skin of water and some venison jerky.

"It ain't much, but it'll see you to the nearest settlement, about 40 miles due West, as the crow fly." Dr. John climbed up behind his mules and waved to them as they headed out on the Eastward road. "Fare thee well, friends, and be safe, as you are venturing into dangerous territory. Francis, keep that bow close. I hope you can find your arrows!"

And with that, he prodded his mules onto the North road, humming a jaunty tune.

Mercy led Jim and the rest due West, towards a settlement she knew of where they might find some water and rest, maybe sort out their next move. They weren't any closer to learning the location of Greer or Lizzy and the situation was growing dire. Even though they'd decided unanimously to not discuss it, it was plain to see that they needed a sign or new information soon, lest they become permanent fixtures out here in the switch.

They passed through scrub brush and mesquite, over rocky hills and down dusty gulches, brushing against cactus, heat ripples, and a sky so incandescently blue that it lit up the backs of their eyelids when they blinked.

All the while, Mercy was plagued by an unrelenting tingle at the nape of her neck. She spent most of the day looking over one shoulder or the other, but all she could discern was a smudge of dust on the horizon.

When they stopped to water the horses around noon, Jim noticed her looking over her shoulder. "What is it?" he asked, quietly.

"Someone's trailing us," she nodded to the smudge on the horizon.

Jim squinted, looking real hard for a sign or detail as to what it could be. "Perhaps it's merely a dust devil?"

"If I can't tell a dust devil from a tail, I'd best hang up my tracking boots."

"What should we do?" asked Jim.

"Nothing to do but ride hard and hope to outrun them."

"Them?" Jim asked.

"Swann and what's left of his revenant troop," Francis said.

"Shoot, they don't give up, do they?" Jim scratched his neck. It was at that stage of healing where the scabs itched something fierce.

"They will never give up," Charlie said. "The dead are often tormented by the living. They know what awaits them on the other side, and that knowledge can drive the dead mad. That is their curse."

"Yeah well, it seems to work both ways, don't it?" said Jim.

They mounted up once more and headed for a canyon pass that lay to the southwest. The walls were steep, which turned the bottom of the pass into a world of perpetual twilight. Down here, owls hooted at noon, and the cactus grew tall, as if reaching for the sun that lay beyond the lip of the canyon wall.

for a canyon pass that lay to the southwest. The walls were steep, which turned the bottom of the pass into a world of perpetual twilight. Down here, owls hooted at noon, and the cactus grew tall, as if reaching for the sun that lay beyond the lip of the canyon wall.

From what Jim could tell, they were alone. but a holler and a cackle echoed down the canyon, tinged with a cold glee.

"Tell me that was an owl," said Jim.

Francis shook his head. "Swann and his Brigade appear to have spotted us."

"Good," Mercy nudged Abraham Lincoln into a trot.

"Good?" Gordo said. "¡Vaya! What does she mean by 'good'?"

"Don't worry none," Charlie whispered to the skull. "Best if you go to sleep for a while." Charlie hung onto Francis. He whispered to Shadow, urging the horse on.

Jim saw shadows of men on horses on the canyon walls. They'd evidently lit torches and the flames were casting gaunt warnings ahead of them.

"Oh, that's more ominous than I thought it'd be!" Jim said. He spurred Sebastian into a gallop.

They raced down the narrow canyon. Soon, the sandstone walls were so close, Jim could almost reach out and touch both at the same time.

They came to a large boulder that created a fork, with two narrow passages to either side.

"We need to split up," Mercy said. "Charlie and Francis, head right. Jim, you're to follow me left. Comprende?"

Jim and Mercy took the left-hand path, winding through a bramble patch and emerging around the end of the path at a small spring. They waited for the others. But they did not emerge from the narrow crevice that, presumably, led back along their path.

"You think they got lost?" Jim asked.

Over the canyon wall swooped a now-familiar shape of a crow in flight. Jack alighted on Mercy's saddle horn and ruffled his feathers. Mercy drew her Navy Colt and aimed it at the bird.

"I'm in no mood to be trifled with, crow. So I'ma count to three. One."

"I come with a message," Jack said.

Mercy cocked her pistol. "Two."

"Wait!" Jim held up a hand. "Let him speak."

"The Captain, he treats me something awful. It's beneath my noble bearing as a crow and so I aim to find a new line of employment."

"We're all real proud of your turn of heart and all," Mercy holstered her gun. "But less'n you got an idea on how to help us, I'm not seeing any real advantage here."

"Your friends are in danger," said Jack. "Swann has set a trap for them. And for you." And with that, Jack flew off, circling into the sky once more.

"Helpful," Mercy frowned.

"Well, at least we know, right?" Jim said.

Mercy shot him a look. They headed into the crevice at a trot.

The path was narrow but clear, and there weren't any side paths for them to get lost on, which made it doubly vexing that they had not yet caught up to Francis and Charlie. When they did locate their wayward companions, the source of their hindrance was all too clear.

THE RIGHTEOUS AND THE REST 193

Francis and Shadow were mired up to the horse's flanks in quicksand. Charlie, in an attempt to rescue them, had waded in, only to get snared by the trap himself. Before long, they were neck-deep in the quicksand and sinking fast.

"What in tarnation are you two doing in there?" Jim huffed.

"Going for a swim, what's it look like?" Charlie said. "Don't stand there, gawkin', give us a hand up!"

Jim dismounted and scrambled up a boulder, while Mercy threw him a rope. Mercy managed to grab hold of Shadow's bridal, by looping the loose rein around the butt of her rifle. She tugged on the leather strap with all her might, until the horse budged ever so slightly.

A shrill laugh blew on the wind. They all froze and searched the canyon walls for some sign. This had the positive benefit of slowing their descent into the quagmire. But only for a moment.

A figure appeared on the lip of the canyon wall. He was a shadow with a large bird on his shoulder and a wide-brimmed army hat on horseback. But Francis knew that silhouette well. The shadow was accompanied by several more men loping at his back. The wind changed direction, dipping into the canyon, and they all smelled the tangy scent of corpse breath upon them.

Jim pulled and Francis came free of the quicksand. He scrambled up the boulder, and took the bow from off his back, where he had been carrying it.

Jim watched as he shut his eyes and slowed his breathing.

"Seems your journey's at an end, Tezu!" Swann's voice echoed down into the canyon like some malevolent specter haunting their every step.

Francis drew the string of the bow tight and aimed for the shadowy figure looking down at them from the canyon wall. Swann drew a pistol and they all could hear clearly the sound of the hammer drawing back.

Now!" Cawed Jack.

They pulled: Jim on the rope, Mercy on the reins, Francis on the bow of his string.

"Why, you traitorous so-and-so!" Swann shouted.

A shot rang out but in the ensuing confusion, Jim had no idea at first where the bullet landed. But he would later swear he saw an arrow fly straight and true towards Talbot Swann.

The Captain reared back, clutching at his face and screaming. There was confusion among the revenants now. They panicked, spooking Swan's horse, setting him to cantering on the lip of the canyon wall. The gravel under the horse's hoof gave way and the ensuing avalanche of loose rock and dirt startled the mired horses.

Together with their new burst of fear and Jim, and Mercy's pulling, Shadow and Charlie lurched free of the quicksand. The rocks slid. Dust and debris flew and everyone ran for the mouth of the canyon.

Looking back, they saw that their places in the quicksand had been taken by Swann and his men. They were already up to their chests, Swann's horse barely visible.

Swann was in bad shape. His left eye had been taken out, leaving a crater of red sawdust and mangled flesh. He screamed and thrashed about, which only made them sink faster.

"I do not like the looks of this!" shouted Finch. Hoots grumbled something but no one could understand what he had said.

That was when Jim found where Swann's bullet had ended up. Jack Daw lay in a shadow of the canyon wall, wings splayed, silent.

Another crow swooped down into the canyon, followed by a second and third, then more. In a moment, there were dozens of crows circling overhead. The ones who had landed formed a circle around Jack's fallen body. They spread their wings and howled a long and piercing shriek into the sky. The caw was picked up by the other crows swooping and circling above.

Charlie and Mercy and Jim and Francis gathered at the edge of the quicksand.

"That there is a crow funeral. I've attended a few in my time and when they sound like that?" Charlie shuddered.

"You are in a state," Mercy said, leaning over to gloat in Swann's face. "I'd offer you a hand out, but my mamma didn't raise no fool."

By then, Swann was up to his chin, with but one arm free. He grasped at the air feebly. "I can make it worth yer while!"

"Nothing you can say now will save you," Francis glowered at Swann.

"Now hold on a minute there," Charlie said. "The Captain here might know the road to Greer's location. That information might be worth a trade."

"Yes!" Swann shouted. "I know where the General is! Free me and I'll tell you!"

"Well see now that's not good enough," said Jim. "How about you tell us, then we'll free you?"

"What?! That is an absurd proposition!" Swann's voice rose into the octave of panic.

"Suite yerself," Jim ran a finger along the brim of his hat and turned to leave.

One, two, then three crows alighted on the boulder looking over Swann. Their dark eyes gleamed with a cold fire.

"Blanchefleur!" Swann shouted. "The General is at his family manse, at Blanchefleur! Now, get me out!"

"Blanchefleur?" Jim raised a skeptical eyebrow. "You're spoutin' gibberish."

"It's not gibberish," Charlie said. "It's French."

"It is the General's estate, or so I have been told," Francis said.

"You know where to find this place?" Mercy asked. "'cuz I ain't never heard its name before."

"It is difficult to find," said Francis. "But I believe I know the way."

"Right, well then," Jim mounted Sebastian. The rest took to their own horses and they headed out of the canyon at a slow walk.

"Wait!" Swann screamed. "What about me?"

"What about you?" Jim said. "You take us for fools, making deals with devils. Shoot."

Jim reached into his saddle bag and took out a coiled length of rope that he'd carried with him from the hanging tree. He tossed the rope to Swann, who caught it in his free hand. One end was tied in a noose. The other end dangled into the quicksand.

"I give you the same kindness you showed me," he said.

As they left the canyon behind them, they could hear the shrieks of birds and feel the whispered flight of a hundred wings diving out of the sky.

By the time Jim and the rest exited the canyon, and found their way back to the road, Swann's yelling and shrieking had stopped.

They headed west into the afternoon light. A little worse for it, but they were every one of them intact, if a bit soiled by the quicksand and frazzled from the encounter.

Roused as if from a nap in the crook of Charlie's arm, Gordo the skull snorted and said, "¡menos mal! What did I miss?"

"Back to sleep, you," Charlie said as they headed out of the canyon.

12
Down To The River

The next morning, Haney couldn't find the blue ribbon. That is how she would remember it later, and how everything that came after was the result of misplacing that blessed piece of silk.

All she knew was that the General wanted Lizzy to look her finest, and that meant dressing her in the blue and white gingham dress with the pretty frills around the sleeves, and that meant the blue ribbon to match, tied in her hair. But where had the ribbon got to? Haney turned the room upside down in search of it.

Lizzy knew nothing of this. She simply sat at the dressing table, looking at her puffy eyes and wondering how she had gotten herself to this point.

Every decision at the start had seemed right—running away with Tezu had been the single most right-feeling turn in her entire life. And yet. Here she was, prisoner in a got dang plantation house, her husband and youngest brother dead, and the other two up to their ears in cahoots with her captor. It all made her want to scream and break things, starting with the silvered glass mirror in front of her and ending with the manse in flames.

Thus preoccupied, she didn't notice Haney's distress until the girl hissed, "...Bother and fuss, where did it get to!?"

"What's the matter?" Lizzy asked. Judging by the young girl's scared eyes, she was momentarily concerned that something untoward had occurred. "Has the General declared himself emperor of the sky now?"

"No, Miss Lizzy," Haney huffed. "It's just I can't find the blue ribbon."

"Is that all? Great Montezuma's Ghost, you have a way of spookin' a soul! Look in the desk, left hand drawer."

Haney went to the small writing desk by the window and opened the right hand drawer by mistake. She was about to shut it when she saw the folded sheaves of paper laying there. She took these out and unfolded them, examining the shaky hand like she could make sense of the words they had written.

Though this epistle's true contents escaped her, the shape of the letters spelled out a sadness and a longing that Haney could not put into words. And for the first time ever, she wanted to know what those written words said. Needed to know. Something about it ached in her soul and she knew Miss Lizzy shared that ache too.

"Find it?" Lizzy asked.

Haney folded the letter and tucked it into her skirt. "Uh…" she opened the left hand drawer. "Yes'm. Right here."

Haney was distracted the rest of the day. She nearly spilled the chamber pot on her shoes and barely heard a word Miss Coffie said to her as she prepared Miss Lizzy's plate for luncheon. Every spare moment was spent looking at the letter, trying to decipher the letters and connect them to sounds. She knew full well that if she was caught with the letter that she'd get a whipping, but still, she felt like it was worth the risk, if only she could learn what the letter said. With this in mind, Haney decided to ask for help from the only person she knew who would neither rat on her to Miss Rachel, nor turn his nose up at the prospect of bending the rules.

It wasn't until after supper that Haney found Andre. He and some of the other footmen and field hands were round back of the kitchen, where he'd set up an improvised card table, which consisted of an old plank balanced on a barrel. He was mid game with the other footmen, Harry, Steven, and Franklin, plus Samuel, of course. For if Andre was up to something, it was sure to involve Samuel as well.

"...bet's to you, Hen ol' son," Andre grinned wide. "Though might as well fold now."

"Some poker face ya got there, 'Dre," William shook his head and threw in his hand.

"Why you do this to yourself, Andre? It's unseemly?" Samuel tossed three coins into the pot. There wasn't much in the middle of the table, but for them it was everything they had.

"I got aspirations," Andre said. "Ain't a man allowed to dream a little?"

"Sure. But there's dreamin' then there's whatever delusional fancy this is."

"Says you," Andre threw down four Queens. "Bachelor's Dream, boys!"

A chorus of groans as Andre raked in the pot.

"One of these days I'm gonna figure out how you do it," Samuel shook his head.

"Do what?" Andre smiled. "Beat you at every hand?"

Haney arrived to find them falling about the place.

"Andre, I need to talk to you," Haney said.

"Go on, Andre," Franklin said, catching his breath. "Sit this one out, give the rest of us a chance to win for once."

Andre waved a dismissive hand. "Nah. Haney can wait a spell."

"I cannot!" she yelled.

Andre waved her quiet. "All right, no need to panic."

Andre handed the deck to Samuel. He expertly shuffled the cards.

"Finally, someone who knows what they're doin'!" laughed William.

Andre followed Haney around the corner, to where the old water pump sat beside the back door to the kitchen.

"What's it all about?" Andre whispered. "You look upset."

Haney wrung her hands and tried to find the right words. "I… I found something and I need you to tell me what it is. Or what it means. I don't know!"

"Alright. Tell me. I'll see what I can do."

"Okay…" Haney took a deep breath. "But you have to promise me—really promise—you won't tell nobody! Not even Samuel."

"Now what could be as bad as all this?" Andre tried a brotherly smile, only for it to fall flat.

"Promise!" Haney said.

"I promise," Andre said. "Now what is it?"

So Haney showed him the letter. The thing was, Andre couldn't read neither.

Andre looked over the pages. "It's a letter."

"I know that! What I want to know is, what's it say? And to who?"

Andre shrugged and handed the letter back to her. "How should I know?"

"Well, ain't you as useful as wings on a pig!" She snatched the letter back.

"I don't know what to tell you, Haney. I can see it means alot to you but… did Miss Lizzy write this?"

"I reckon she did, yes," Haney said.

"And you think it's important to her?"

"I don't know much," Haney said, "but it seems to me folks tend to write their most important stuff down."

"Can't argue with that…" Andre sighed. "Look, maybe it's nothin'. Maybe she's homesick and wrote herself a letter. In which case, you'd best put it back where you found it, in case she goes lookin' for it."

"Yeah, I guess you're right…" Haney said.

"Oh na what's all this?"

They both peered around to find Tristan the Overseer had stumbled upon the card game. He arrived in a cloud of cigar smoke from one of Greer's cigars, which they all knew he liked to pilfer.

"Ach," he exhaled a cloud of cigar smoke. "You lot're throwin' cards and didn'a think ta invite me? That's bad manners, that is."

Andre sighed and took Haney by the shoulders.

"Look I gotta sort this out before Tristan demands all our money. I'm sorry, Haney, maybe it's for the best you don't know, eh?"

Andre gave her a hug and then ran in to try and salvage the game.

"Well now Mr. Tristan, we was just warming up, till you arrived," Andre said as he arrived back at the table. "How's about you deal him in, Samuel?" Andre winked at his co-conspirator.

"Now here's tha one with brains," Tristan grinned. Though the grin didn't quite reach his eyes, which remained cold and heavy, like lead.

Andre took a seat, and so did the overseer.

"Well now, where's the hospitality then?" Tristan took a long drag on his cigar. He looked around, until one of the footmen took his meaning.

William pulled a bottle of moonshine from beneath his stool. "Saved some for you, of course."

"Now that's more like it," Tristan snatched the bottle and took a gulp. He kept it balanced on one knee the rest of the game.

"Right, my deal, is it?" Samuel took the cards from Franklin, who was about to start dealing and took matters into hand.

Tristan looked over to find Haney peering at them from around the corner.

"You like watcha see, girl?" He winked at her.

Haney made a face.

So did Andre, though his veered more towards anger than disgust. He forced himself to smile when Tristan turned back.

"She's turned bonny, ain't she?" He took a swig of moonshine. Then he glared back at Haney. "Go on girl, 'lest I get some notions of me own!"

Andre looked at Samuel and winked, which was code for, *fleece this fool?*

Samuel scratched his ear. This meant, *already on it*.

None of the other footmen knew their codes, which they'd devised when they were children, as a way to pass secret messages. When you knew someone as well as Andre and Samuel know one another, even the gestures themselves were unnecessary. They would have gotten the gist of it from the way Samuel turned the cards. He had a knack for it, which was why Andre had wanted him in the game in the first place.

"We playin' then?" Tristan drawled sloppily, a bit of southern twang creeping out from under his Scottish brogue.

This will be a cinch, Samuel told Andre by rubbing chin.

They managed the next few hands, slipping each other signals when to stay, when to call, when to raise and fold, until they'd relieved Tristan of most of his money.

"I didn't know better, I'd say ya'll were swindlin' me," Tristan chuckled and drained the last of the hootch. "But that would be an excershize, an excursion, um, an excorcise in futiliteh, na wouldn'a it?"

He laid his cards out in front of him. He had a pair of Jacks.

"Now how can you say that, Mr. Tristan?" Samuel grinned and threw down two pairs, aces and eights.

Tristan grumbled something—whether gibberish or Scottish, none could tell—and stalked away from the table in a wobbly line. He wandered off into the treeline and fell into a patch of clover, cussing as the cherry end of his cigar scorched his pant leg. He swatted at it a moment, then lay still.

Curious, Andre and the others crept over to find him snoring in a patch of poison ivy. They fell over one another laughing. Samuel smiled, but couldn't help but feel a little hollow inside for it.

"You two must be the bravest coupla sons of so-and-so's I ever did meet!" William shook his head and grinned.

Andre turned to Samuel. "What's he mean by that?"

"He means Tristan is gonna find some way to retaliate, on account of us cleanin' him out," Samuel sighed. "And an awful petty revenge it will be."

Andre made a dismissive gesture. "That's tomorrow's problem. Now pass me the hooch!"

The next afternoon, Lizzy and Haney were on the back porch, attempting to find some semblance of shade. The day had grown hot and the font of the house was bathed in sunlight, making the font parlor stuffy.

Lizzy had decided to try and take her mind off things with a bit of piecework. To that end, Haney had found some needlepoint that had been left unfinished by some ancient visitor to Blanchefleur. Lizzy retired to the back porch where she set about losing herself in the fiddly work of sorting it out, but it wasn't doing the trick.

No matter how hard she tried, Lizzy couldn't forget what she had seen and what she knew and how it all contradict one another, which made her want to tell someone, though every time she tried, she would sneeze and forget what she was upset about, only to pick up the needlepoint once more and immediately become frustrated again, as the loops of thread reminded her of so many loose ends. And then the whole cycle would start again.

Haney was, alas, no help. She had lay awake half the night in her cot, trying to make sense of the tangled loops and lines of the words on the pages. In her dreams, she could see their shape unravel; sometime before dawn, she woke, convinced she'd deciphered the letter's meaning, only to look over it once more in the light of dawn and find the same inscrutable letters she could not name.

Haney had decided that she would slip the letter back in the drawer when she dressed Miss Lizzy. However, when the time came, she had been so busy that she had forgotten. At least that's what she told herself.

She held the letter, folded tight into a small packet in her apron. Even now, she could simply make an excuse, say that she had forgotten the scissors or some such, and return to the room and place the letter in the drawer and forget about it. But she didn't do that either. Instead she stood there beside Lizzy, thinking about it until the sound of muffled ruckus from the yard reached them.

They ran to the edge of the porch and found two of the field hands shouting to the footmen and maids, who had come out on the second story balcony to see what the hubbub was all about.

"What is happening?" Lizzy asked.

"Don't rightly know, Miss," said Sarah.

She'd run downstairs and was a bit breathless, though that may have been more Andre's doing, as he appeared beside her a moment later, equally out of breath.

Andre said. "Something's afoot on the lawn."

Lizzy and the servants made their way down the back steps and around the side of the house. There they found quite the scene:

Tristan dragged Samuel, hands bound behind him, onto the lawn. The Overseer dropped a satchel at the foot of the steps. The General, Miss Rachel, and Mr. Robbe were already there. Little Tom struggled to catch up, as he'd gone to fetch Ben, and thus brought along the entire complement of field hands with them.

"What is the meaning of this?" The General asked.

"It is me sad duty to report that I caught this here miscreant attemptin' to flee into the woods." Tristan kicked the satchel forward, spilling its contents on the step. There were a handful of tools and a moldy crust of bread.

"It's untrue, General," Samuel said.

Tristan kicked him in the head and he tumbled into the dirt, hands tied behind his back.

"Is this true, Little Tom?" The General looked at Tom, who was out of breath.

"Na'sir," he said. "I didn't see it but I know Samuel, and he—"

Tristan cut him off with a look of disdain.

"These are serious accusations, Tristan. You have proof, I assume?"

"See fer yourself, General," he nodded to the pile of tools and the satchel. "I found 'em with these on his person. He clearly meant to make a run fer it, an' there's na doubt about it."

"It's not true!" Ben yelled and made to jump between Tristan and Samuel. But Tom and one of the bigger field hands held him back.

The General stomped slowly down the steps and knelt in the dirt beside Samuel.

"What do you have to say in your defense, Samuel?"

"I… I didn't run," he spat blood onto the grass. "I swear, General. Tristan give me them tools… so's I could fix 'em."

"Do you accuse Tristan of deceiving me then?" asked Greer.

"Nos'r, it ain't like that," Samuel said. "It were a mistake is all… a misunderstanding."

"You see the problem, don't you? It's your word against his."

"I… I am sorry as can be, General, Sir."

Greer stood. He ran a finger along the ring he wore on his pinky, making a show of being in deep contemplation.

"Sorry that you were caught? Or sorry that you attempted to run?"

"I…" Samuel realized a moment too late that there was no answer to this question that did not implicate him in some wrongdoing. He tried anyway.

"I am contrite, sir."

Greer shook his head.

"It's a sad day," the General said, addressing the crowd in a deep and fatherly baritone. "One of your own seems to have gotten a hold of some notion that there is another place in this world where he can run to, and escape the ever-knowing eye of the Lord and his judgment!"

The slaves, led by Robbe, shouted, "No! No one runs!"

Samuel's belly turned cold.

Andre and Ben both stood in the crowd, shaking as they tried to plead with their eyes. But there was no use. No one was looking at them.

"I cannot abide this sort of notional rebellion among my ranks. What would we become, were every frightful idea voiced out of hand? We would become like them bluebellies and their precious democracy, where every member of the rabble decries that his voice is worth a damn. And take my meaning thusly: your voice is nothing without mine. Do I not speak for the whole? Am I not your Master? And I am a noble one, I like to think. Fair and just."

Elkanah Greer paused here to chew on the tension a moment, as he deliberated.

"We must therefore, make an example of our Samuel," Greer nodded to Tristan.

He grabbed Samuel roughly and stood him up.

"My judgment therefore, is this: twenty lashes, live or die."

"No sir!" Ben jumped forward, trying to get to Samuel.

"It weren't his tools, but mine! I done it, take me!"

Tristan raised his whip hand to strike. Greer motioned and Tristan held his hand.

"This is a noble gesture, to be sure, Benjamin, but wholly inappropriate, don't you think?"

"No sir, I do not think it inappropriate!" Ben stood tall.

"Your loyalty is misplaced," Greer's eyes flashed. "You owe it to me! Not this scrap of a boy!"

General Greer made a dismissive gesture. Tristan smiled and dragged Samuel away from the house.

"Where are you taking him?" Lizzy demanded.

"Miss Lizzy," Greer clucked his tongue. "I am sorry that you had to witness such an event. However this is all part of the work of the land. And therefore, the domain of men. Let us away inside. We shall talk no more of this."

Greer motioned for Lizzy to lead the way inside. She did, reluctantly, though Haney whispered, "Miss Lizzy, I need to see to Andre!"

Lizzy nodded. Haney curtsied and ran to catch up to the procession.

"I see you have taken a shine to our Haney," Greer said. "I would caution you not to grow too attached, lest you become like our Ben there, too emotional to see the clear light of what needs doin'."

Lizzy said nothing. She headed inside.

Miss Rachel had stood as still as if she was carved from wood and watched the sentencing. But a voice in her ear whispered and she knew what needed doing.

"Sarah, keep everyone in the house," she said. Then she ran down the steps and sprinted as fast as her feet would carry her to the longhouse out back.

Every Conjure worth their salt keeps a root cellar. Never know when you're going to need a dose of Sweetening Potion, Hide-a-Jar, or mix up some gris gris for a bad case of What-Have-You. This is where much of the work of housebound hoodoo is accomplished, in roots and herbs and their power to ease and inflame. Miss Rachel's root cellar was under the boards of the second longhouse. There was a loose board in the back, through which she could quickly access a store of tinctures and sachets she had made for all occasions. No one knew they were there, but her.

And yet, as she reached the longhouse, there she found Travis and Edmond kneeling beside the fifth board from the left, the loose one that offered access to her store.

She ducked behind the side of the pit house. From there she could peer around the corner at them. Edmond stood, huffing and puffing and wiped his brow.

"There is naught here, brother. What could they have that you would want anyway?"

"Yeah, probably right," Travis stood.

The commotion caused by Tristan's arrival with Samuel grabbed their attention. They ran around the longhouse to see what was happening out front.

Miss Rachel was about to run for her cellar, to see if she had the sleeping drops she was sure were there. Perhaps they would be enough to drop Samuel to sleep as he stood at the post, and spare him the worst of it. She refused to think what might happen if she couldn't find the sleep drops or failed to deliver them in time.

She pushed the board aside and reached into her store. There sat several glass bottles and bundles of flowers and roots hanging to dry, and a small wooden owl that often spoke to her in dreams. But no bottle of sleep drops. Rachel remembered now that she had used the last on the night the General had returned, to soothe his road-weary mind and spare the household the torments of his night terrors.

Rachel began to cry then and smashed the bottles and ripped the dried roots down. A hand came to rest on her shoulder.

She turned to find Robbe kneeling beside her.

"There is precious little time, Miss Rachel," he whispered.

There were tears in his eyes. Robbe wiped them away and placed the board back over her root cellar.

"Come now," he offered her a hand. "They need us. They need you."

She stood and smoothed over her skirts, took a deep breath and bit her lip till it bled. The tears stopped and she turned to Robbe, jaw clenched tight.

"Well, ain't you just the most stopped clock ever."

They joined the rest in front of the longhouse. Haney caught up with them just as crowd as they reached the yard. These were three longhouses made of clapboard, and whitewashed clean, which surrounded on three sides a yard made of packed earth. On the fourth side sat a stone hearth, which they used for baking their bread. In the middle of the yard was an old wooden post.

The post had an iron ring set on the top. It was through this that Tristan had Ben pass the manacles. He did so, then stepped back three paces.

"Now now," Tristan said. "Lock him in good and tight."

Ben paused for a moment, then stepped forward. He fitted Samuel's wrists, each on one side of the manacle.

"I'm sorry," he whispered low.

Then he stepped back with the others. Haney and Andre stood beside him and the three of them held hands tight and watched. They were joined a moment later by Miss Rachel and Robbe. The latter stood a pace or two away but he lingered to witness.

Tristan ripped Samuel's shirt, exposing him to the waist. He leaned in and whispered, "This is for fleecin' me."

Then he drew his whip, which he coiled around one arm and raised to the heavens.

"Dear lord, 'tis yer hand that moves me!" he bellowed.

Then he proceeded to lay the lash on Samuel's back.

Tristan, who was well acquainted with the Torquemadan arts, paused for a three count between each strike, to ensure that Samuel would feel the bite of every hit and not become numb to the pain halfway through.

By the tenth lash, Samuel's back was already a mess of bloody stripes, some deep enough to expose muscle and bone.

After the twelfth lash, Samuel's feet gave way. Andre lurched towards him, only for Ben to grab him and hold him tight.

Tristan turned and waggled the whip in his face, close enough for Andre to smell the blood.

"Don't ya worry none, Andre, you'll get yours one day!"

Then he turned back and finished laying into Samuel.

When he was through, Tristan threw the whip to Tandy, who had stood in rapt fascination.

"Clean that," Tristan ordered.

Tandy looked around, unsure of what to do until Haney took him by the hand and led him away to the water pump.

"Best bring that back when ya through!" Tristan called after them. "S'my best whip and I won't have it gone missin'!"

Andre and Ben took Samuel down from the post. His back was

a bloody mess and his wrists cut and bleeding as well. But before they could wrap him up and carry him to the longhouse, where they laid out their dead, a pair of revenants loped out of the woods.

"Back now," Tristan ordered.

They all took a few steps back as the two reeking soldiers, held together by little more than their uniforms and some loose tendons, lumbered over. They wrapped Samuel's body in a tarp. Then the revenants carried him back the way they'd come, into the woods.

"Wait!" yelled Andre.

Tristan turned on him, hand raised.

"You got sometin' to add, do ya?"

"Nos'r, it's just… we want to bury him good and proper," Andre had to choke back the emotion in his voice.

"You'll do no such thing," Tristan said. "General's orders. Samuel's been conscripted. Lest you want to meet tha same fate, ya'll return to yer assigned work, all of ya!"

They stood there for a moment, the shock of it all washing over them.

"Am I gonna need to make another demonstration?" Tristan said.

"Come on now," Little Tom said in a low, calm voice. "Let's go back to work. Do a soul good. Come on…"

He ushered them back to their tasks in silence.

The rest of the day passed in a blur of busywork and half-hearted efforts. Haney wanted to scream and cry but she kept her head about her and finished her work.

After Lizzy had arrived at supper, Haney headed into the kitchen in search of her own. She had decided that Andre was probably right, and Miss Lizzy's letter was for her eyes alone and she'd best return it. Right after she ate, she would run it up to the room and stow it back in the desk drawer, where she'd found it.

Least, that had been the plan. But then she nearly ran into Little Tom, who was about to sit down with a bowl of cornmeal and some salted pork for his supper.

"Haney, love, where you headed under full steam?"

"Sorry, Tom, sir, a bit busy."

Well, ain't we all!" he sighed. "What you got there?" He plucked the letter from Haney's hand. She didn't even think to try and stop him.

Little Tom wandered over to the servant's table with his food and sat, perusing the letter while he spooned cornmeal into his mouth. Least, that was the intended destination. But the spoon never quite arrived.

He set his spoon down and looked at Haney.

"Where'd you come by this?"

"Found it," she said.

"Mmhm," Little Tom didn't take his eyes off her. "You know what this is, yes?"

"No, I don't." And that was the honest truth, for once.

Miss Rachel came in and surveyed the kitchen. "I see everyone is resting on their laurels."

"Having a bite of supper," said Tom.

"I'm just returning to work, ma'am," Haney curtsied, and made to leave.

"What's this?" Miss Rachel picked the letter up from the table. She glanced at it. "hold there a moment, Haney."

Haney found she could not move her feet, like they were stuck in ankle deep mud. She turned back to Miss Rachel.

"Ma'am?"

"We'll have none of this now, you understand?" Miss Rachel folded the letter and tucked it into her skirts. "Haney, run along to your chores now."

"Yes Ma'am," she curtsied quickly, then sprinted for the door.

"You gettin' a notion, Tom?" Rachel asked.

"Me? No ma'am," he said.

"You know what the General has to say on the matter of letters and the like."

"I do."

"Do you? None of you understand what the General has demanded of me. I want no more of this," Miss Rachel leveled a heavy gaze upon him. "Especially after today's… unpleasantness?"

"That what you call what happened today?" Tom looked at her hard.

She returned his hard stare, and said no more on the matter.

"Thy will, Miss Rachel," Tom returned to eating his supper and looking at nothing in particular.

Rachel deliberately put the letter's existence out of her mind until later that evening, when she was alone.

As Housekeeper, she was afforded the luxury of a private room. And through it was barely bigger than a cupboard and the bed squeaked, it was hers and hers alone. After the day's chores were complete she retired there before dinner preparations to have a quiet moment's contemplation. Most days, she would simply lie down and close her eyes and try not to think of any of the hundred little things that demanded her attention. But that day, there was but one thing demanding her attention in that quiet moment. Its existence suddenly became a thorn in her shoe.

Miss Rachel sat on the end of her bed. She lit the oil lamp and turned it up, casting as much light as possible, which was not quite enough to fill the room.

She read the letter twice, to make sure she hadn't misconstrued anything. The first time left her dizzy. But the second time, the words Lizzy had written only made her sad, then angry.

For a moment she was overcome by a whirlwind of feelings. Rage and despair and a sense of dread that made her a bit queasy.

She wiped a stray tear away with her palm and then smoothed over her skirts. She tucked the letter in her skirt once more, then blew out the oil lamp before leaving her room.

Rachel walked down a well trod path to the slave quarters. The long house was empty, but there wass a oil lamp casting shadows in the window of the small chapel that stood adjacent. There, Rachel found Reverend Hawkins leading a half-hearted memorial fro Samuel.

"...And that is why the Lord in his wisdom, tests our faith and resolve. But fear, uh, fear not! The love and the word of our lord is clear. We shall all meet again, in the next world, where our loved ones even now wait for us to, to join them. Ahem. Let us pray."

The servants were all gathered there bowed their head.

Tom stood in the back of the small church by the door. He didn't see Rachel come in until she stood beside him. Then he felt her tension, like a shadow had wandered in out of the rain.

"Rachel," he said in a whisper.

"Tom," she whispered back. "I would speak with you."

Tom glanced over her left shoulder. Rachel turned to find the General just then entering the chapel.

He stood in the back beside Tom and Rachel, until the slaves had finished singing their hymn. They then turned to file out, nodding to the General as they left.

"That was a mighty fine service, Reverend," said Greer as Edmond reached him.

"You think so?" He smiled thinly. "I... I wanted to let them know that despite the day's... events, that all was still right by God's ways."

"Your words, and the Lords, were a balm to their souls, Reverend, I'm sure."

Edmond stood there a moment too long, until an awkward tension was raised like the Holy Ghost between them.

"I have business to discuss with Miss Rachel," said the General. "If you'll excuse us."

Edmond nodded. Then he and Tom both left the chapel.

"This way, Rachel," Greer motioned to the door. "I have need of my conjure."

She walked beside the general but found that instead of the house, they headed around the back to the old potting shed. The general took a key from his waistcoat and unlocked the padlock.

He stepped inside and turned up an oil lamp that was there, casting stark shadows on his face. Rachel saw that a revenat guards stood at attention beside the door. He was stiff as a statue and reeked of peat and soil. Though that may just have been the shed itself.

"I have need of your skills once more, Miss Rachel." The General nodded to the table in the middle of the narrow room.

Rachel pulled back the tattered tarp to find Samuel's body laid out there.

The revenant guard shut the door to the potting shed.

Afterwards, Miss Rachel dedicated to take a walk. She had work at the house to finish but needed to clear her head. Root Work always made her a bit dizzy and out of sorts, but some time on the edge of the woods usually refreshed her, as if th eold trees breathed a little more of the life she had borrowed from her self back into her.

Thus refreshed, Rachel walked with purpose but did not at first know her destination. All she knew was she needed to move her feet.

Thoughts came and went, spun in circles but nothing could she snatch out of the air, certainly nothing that might make sense of her feelings. It was the light and the shadows of the trees marking the path to the blacksmith's shop. It made sense now that this was her destination, though she could not recall having set it as such. There she found Little Tom talking in whispers with Ben. They grew quiet as she entered the shack.

"How are you, Ben?" she asked.

"I'll be fine, Miss Rachel," he said stiffly.

"Did you read this letter?" She held it up for Tom to see.

He scratched his chin. "What if I did?"

"What letter?" asked Ben.

"Haney found a letter," Tom said. "Or so Andre told me..."

"Of course he did," Miss Rachel sighed. "Did he mention what the letter said, by chance?"

"No Ma'am," Tom shook his head. "Andre didn't seem to know. Neither did Haney."

"And I will ask you once more, Tom," Miss Rachel looked at him hard. "Did you read this letter?"

"Yes'm, I did."

"And do you take its meaning?"

"Yes'm, I surely do."

"And did you tell Ben what it said?" She looked at Ben for an answer.

"He was about to." Ben stoked the fire with a pair of tongs and starred hard at his old friend.

"Let him be, Rachel," said Tom, a croak of desperation in his voice. "He don't know nothin! None of them do. Not even Robbe. It's just us who knows."

"And is that something you want to change?" Rachel asked.

13
A Refuge For Scoundrels

The town of St. Simeon's Gulch didn't exist five years ago, but already it had three saloons, four taverns, two newspapers, a train station, and would soon boast the third-largest clock West of the Mississippi. This gigantic timepiece hung over the half-constructed town hall, still braced in its wooden frame, and hoisted over the heads of its citizens and visitors alike by a series of ropes and pulleys. It was a marvel of the modern world and Elkanah Greer hated it. He hated it almost as much as he hated the US Government and the taste of mustard.

Quartermaster Gates drove a mule team down the main street. Greer sat beside him, scowling at the city folk walking hither and yon, oblivious to him and his cause. In the back, Travis sprawled on a stack of empty flour sacks, his hat over his face, snoozing away. From her vantage point balancing on a barrel in the back of the wagon, Lizzy had a clear view of the whole place, from the barbershop to the train station, and all the people going about their lives on this clear summer day.

"So this here is St. Simeon's Gulch, huh?" Lizzy said, charmed by the vibrancy of the street scene.

"Yes ma'am," Gates glanced back at her over his shoulder. "It's gonna be a right fine town, once they finish making it."

On their way from the camp, Gates had regaled Lizzy with the finer points of the town's short but colorful history: St. Simeon's was founded by the Atchison Topeka Railway Company. They were in want of a place to build a station that could serve as a spur between their train line that ran West to Tucson and connected to their line that ran to Lubbock and points East. They found a relatively level spit of ground roughly halfway between the two in the recently established New Mexico territory and set about building.

The gulch that shared its name with the Saint of Orthodoxy was little more than a trickle of sweet water to the West of the city. It had served briefly as the seat of a Spanish mission, though that had been abandoned not long after it was built. Before that, it was rumored (but never proven) that Coronado himself camped by the gulch and named it after the curious saint who was famous for sitting atop a pillar in the desert for 37 years.

The town of St. Simeon's was a bustling little burg. Being there after weeks on the plantation made it a balm to Lizzy's senses. She had finagled herself a seat in the mule cart easy enough, claiming she needed, "things of a womanly nature," and since Greer was of no particular mind one way or the other on the subject, he approved her pass for the day. He was sending Travis and Quartermaster Gates on a shopping spree anyway, and decided she could accompany them.

"Do you not find this town positively charming, General?" Lizzy asked. She had decided that if she was to be his bride, she would make herself a shrew and burrow into his heart.

"Tis nothing but a phantasmagoria," Greer grumbled, "Constructed of strings and sealing wax and other fancy stuff."

Since setting out that morning, The General had been in a more prickly mood than usual. Gates had tried to ward Lizzy off small talk with hand gestures and pointed looks. But she was of a mind to pry.

"Now, Elkanah, that's no way to talk!" Lizzy said. "Is this not the epi-tome of the civilization you wish to save?"

"It is pronounced epito-me, my dear," Greer grumbled. "And all that is civilized to me is nothing but wisps of smoke."

After tying off the mules outside the dry goods store, Travis was roused and set to his watch. He helped Lizzy down from the cart while Gates made room for the sundries they would acquire.

"Now don't go wandering off, Lizzy," Travis said. He offered her a sneer the likes of which she had always found infuriating, ever since he perfected it when he was thirteen.

"Wouldn't dream of it, dear brother," she said curtly. "Merely intrigued by the to-do over yonder." She nodded in the direction of the town square. There was indeed a crush of people, all standing around watching something.

Lizzy, shadowed by Travis and Gates, whose curiosity had likewise been piqued, crept up to the edge of the road. There they had a good view of the parade as it passed.

There was a brass band sawing away at a loud march, a school house full of children let loose to run rampant with streamers and garland, the local fire brigade leading the fire wagon pulled by a brace of plow horses, carts loaded with hay bales that served as benches for the local farmer's association to sit on as they waved to the crowd, carriages and barring the flags of a dozen civic organizations, and a hundred local personages of note dressed in their Sunday finest waving to the crowds.

Travis tugged on the sleeve of the locals. "What's the hubbub?"

"Why, don't you know? The big cheese has returned!"

The feller went on to explain that Jebidiah Sanchez, the Cheese King of New Mexico Territory, had returned from Europe after a whirlwind tour with his award winning cheese wheel. This was no ordinary cheese of course; big as an ox and wider than a barn door, it had its own wagon.

Lizzy and Travis saw that the feller's description was no exaggeration. This wheel of cheese was easily as tall as a man standing on an applebox, with a rind thick as a fist. Though great wedges had been cut from it, no doubt by the sharpest cheese knives in Europe, and served up for the appreciation and appraisal of many a royal (including none other than the Queen of England herownself, who found the cheese delightfully sharp with a hint of walnut) it was still massive enough to require a team of six field horses. And they weren't small specimens neither.

Presumably, the dapper fellow with the waxed mustache who stood in the cart and waved to the onlookers was Cheese King Jebediah. He looked the part in his smart bowtie and felt hat.

"Oh, to be in Jebediah's shoes today!" The feller who had narrated all this to Lizzy and Travis bore an exalted face that was in stark contrast to the one worn by the Presumed Jebidiah.

For while he smiled, Lizzy could detect a particular sadness in his eyes. Perhaps he had realized that this was the pinnacle of his days here on Earth. Everything from this point on would be a slow, inescapable march towards ignominy, disregard, and eventually the grave.

"I feel for you, Jeb ol' friend," Lizzy said to herself.

General Greer straightened his coat, brushed his epaulets, and tucked his hat on tight.

"I have business to attend to," he said. Then he marched off towards the half-constructed hubbub of city hall.

"What's eating him?" Lizzy asked after the General was out of earshot.

Travis shrugged and said, "Business."

This was unhelpful. Lizzy looked to Gates for clarification.

"The General don't like going hat in hand, as it were," Gates explained. "Tends to spoil his pudding."

"I bet," Lizzy nodded. "If I were a man like that, proud of my pride, I wouldn't like to go begging neither."

Lizzy turned and headed for the dry goods store. Travis and Gates ran to keep up.

Had they'd lingered but a moment more, they might have recognized the group of stragglers who wandered into town on the parade's heels, right behind the little man with the bushy mustache and matching broom who was sweeping up after the horses.

"I know this town," Francis said. "It's run by a former Confederate. An acquaintance of General Greer's, as I recall. If we can find him, we may be able to find our way to Greer's house."

"Them's a lot of ifs," Mercy said.

"You said you knew how to get there already," Jim said.

"I said that I knew the way. The way involves finding someone who has already been there."

"Might have shared that information a bit sooner, don'tcha think?" Mercy asked.

"Makes no nevermind," Charlie added. "We're here, now. And here and now is where we need to be."

Jim took a deep breath. "So where do you reckon we could find this acquaintance of the General's that knows the way?"

"Suspect he's in City Hall, somewhere," Charlie said.

Mercy swatted him with her hat. "Why you encouragin' them in this fool endeavor?"

"Life is one big foolish endeavor," Charlie said. "Take the foolishness away and we got nothin' to hang our hats on."

By then, they'd found a general store and led the horses to hitching posts out front. Francis tied Shadow up beneath a juniper tree where there was some shade.

"Jim, let's not get our hopes up here," Mercy said. She hitched Abraham Lincoln to a post. "I know you and Francis want to get Lizzy back, but following every shootin' star ain't gonna accomplish nothin' but the production of a lotta tears."

"I for one think it's a great idea," Charlie was enthusiastic.

"Also, we don't have any other options," added Francis.

"Which means there's little chance it can go wrong," Charlie grinned. "So it's doubly lucky!"

"That is one way of looking at it, I suppose." Mercy sighed. "Fine. You two see if you can locate this Confederate feller. Charlie and me'll see the supplies. Then we'll all go get ourselves a pony! Meet back here in an hour?"

THE RIGHTEOUS AND THE REST

Francis nodded and he and Jim set off.

"What about me?" Gordo asked.

"You mind the horses," Mercy plucked him from Charlie's arms and set the skull on Abraham Lincoln's saddle. Then she followed Charlie up the steps and into the store.

"Well, how you like that, Señor Presidente," said Gordo. "I got a lot to contribute!"

"…'While man exists, it is his duty to improve not only his own condition, but to assist in ameliorating mankind…'" said Abraham Lincoln.

"See! Even the pinche horse gets it!"

Jim and Francis soon found themselves walking through a placid market, beneath the shade of a colonnade formed from elm trees, on the edge of the town square.

Everyone who couldn't find a place to stand and watch the parade was here picnicking on the lawn in front of City Hall, sipping lemonade under the summer sky, like they had no cares but when the fireworks would start.

"When I woke up this morning, I had no idea this is where the day would bring me," Jim said. He paused to look over a crate full of apples that an old woman was selling in the shade of a tree. She cast a withering glare, though not at Jim, he realized, but at Francis.

"You got something to say?" Jim starred the old woman down. She averted her eyes, but turned back to make sure neither of them ran off with her fruit.

"Mealy lookin' tubers anyhow," Jim dropped the apple back into the crate.

They moved on, ambling towards City Hall.

"I've noted a change in your demeanor, James, ever since we fished you out of that grave," Francis said. "You've become more… direct."

"Yeah, getting killed by your own brothers will change a man."

"Holding onto that grudge will only do you all in, eventually. Besides, not all your brothers would see harm come to you." Francis offered him a thin smile. For Francis, this was a florid display of affection, and Jim was appreciative of it.

"Says the man hunting down his wife's abductor," Jim turned to him and smiled.

"Good point. Maybe we both need to take a step back, for clarity's sake."

"I suspect that once everything is all said and done, clarity will come of its own accord."

They paused beside a tinker's cart.

"Wonder how much it'd cost to sharpen my blade?" JIm looked at the saber he'd been carrying.

A familiar voice called out from afar, "James Hawkins!"

Jim followed the sound of the voice across the green, to the other side of the town square. Something about their oafish demeanor was familiar but it wasn't until the lead feller turned towards them that Jim recognized the grizzled mug of their pursuer.

"Oh, Tezu!" called out Talbot Swann across the lawn. "I been lookin' fer you!"

Swann had seen better days. His skin was burned from days without shade or water in the desert, and his uniform, faded and frayed at the cuffs before, was now a grimey shade of ochre, baring the stains of the quicksand from which he'd slithered. While his right eye was still a gleaming black marble, his left eye had been put out and was covered by an improvised eye patch made from a ripped shirt sleeve. A smear of red sawdust speckled his cheek.

He drew his sidearm and fired a wild shot.

People screamed and ran in all directions. Jim and Francis, never ones to buck a trend, did likewise.

Finch and Hoots, looking no better than their Captain, opened fire with their own rifles, sending folks to duck and scurry as bullets obliterated produce and turned tables and chairs to splinters.

A cart of greens was overturned in the frenzy, and the owner could do nothing but cry for his lost cabbages.

Jim dragged the owner to the relative safety behind his overturned cart. There they hid briefly before Jim ran to catch up with Francis, who had sprinted across the road and was running along the shops, bullets chasing him.

Swann emptied his revolver into a wooden Indian in front of the tobacco shop, reducing it to matchsticks.

Francis and Jim met up in front of City Hall. The scaffolding and piles of lumber afforded them cover, though the clatter from the workers had ceased as the foreman tried to locate the source of the gun fire.

That source, in the form of Talbot Swann and his brigade of revenant outriders, came whooping and hollering across the lawn.

The workers dropped their tools and tackle, sending a pile of lumber clattering like a waterfall in front of the steps. Jim and Francis took the opportunity to high tail it in-doors ahead of Swann and his men.

Jim and Francis ran through the labyrinth of hallways of City Hall, Swann on their heels. Jim flung a door wide and they dove inside, only to find themselves in the stayed and stuffy courtroom of one Judge Parker.

A gruff voiced ranger with one eye sat in a chair beside the Judge's bench, recounting the details of how he'd tracked a wanted feller all the way to the Nevada Territory and brought him back.

"...there's where I caught up with ol' Johnny. Saw him shoot a man in Reno, just to watch him die."

Francis and Jim's sudden appearance turned the court to bedlam. Judge Parker banged his gavel till it broke and the lawyers both shouted, "Objection!" while folks in the audience hollered like they'd witnessed the murder, instead of the dry proceedings of its trial.

"Don't mind us, Your Honor," Jim said.

"This man's innocent!" Francis added. He nodded to the defendant, who was dressed all in black and sat at the table strumming a guitar.

They ran through the gallery and out the main door, back into a hall as Swann and his revenants thundered into the room.

The bailiff proved a formidable roadblock to Swann, at least till the former whipped the latter upside the head with his pistol.

Jim and Francis doubled back down the corridor, where Francis found an unlocked door. They ducked inside to discover they were in a cloak room.

Coats of all sizes and weights hung on either side but there was a second door at the far end. Jim and Francis crept towards it quiet as a pair of spiders.

From what they could make out through the sliver of the open door, they were adjacent to a corner office. High windows looked across the square, and an imposing figure stood behind a desk as wide as a steam engine.

"Who's that?" Jim whispered.

"Archibald McGill Fontleroy," Francis whispered back. "He's the mayor, and the man we come to find."

Mayor Fontleroy cut a striking figure. Rail thin, with a tidy silver-white mane of hair and mutton chops, he looked practically respectable in his deep blue coat and tidy cravat. He wore a small golden circle pinned to his lapel. Jim couldn't recall where, but the golden circle rang a bell.

Fontleroy stood behind his desk, looking at a folder full of papers spread open before him when there came a knock at the door. From their vantage point in the cloak room, neither Jim nor Francis could see the visitor, only hear his voice. But it struck them as a familiar one.

"Mayor Fontleroy, I'd like to have a moment of your time, sir?" the man said in his most obsequious purr.

"Anything for a constituent," The Mayor looked up from his paperwork with a smile. But his demeanor crumbled. "Oh shit. It's you."

"Now, now, your honor, is that any way to speak to an old friend?" The man approached the desk and they could see him clearly now. It was Elkanah Greer.

Jim went to draw his saber. Francis, more prudent, raised a finger to his lips and silenced Jim's hotheadedness. They continued to listen to the details of their conversation, safe, for the moment in their hiding place.

Fontleroy flopped into the high-backed leather chair.

"We are not now, nor have we ever been friends, Elkanah Greer," he sighed. "But I suppose you won't leave me in peace until I hear you out. So take a seat. And try not to besmirch the upholstery."

Greer flipped the tails of his careworn coat and sat in as dainty a manner as he could. His saber rattled in its scabbard against the fine mahogany of the chair.

"To what do I owe this... visit?" asked the Mayor.

"I come to you as one fellow Knight, seeking aid in this, our darkest hour."

"Cut the horseshit, Elkanah. Speak plain."

"As you know I am engaged in the long fight for our nation's honor. To that end, I require assistance."

"And I suppose by assistance, you mean money?" Fontleroy shook his head. "You old son of a bitch."

"Once you believed as I did," Greer said.

He stood and made a show of looking around the room and admiring the appointments. Brocade curtains, busts of men famous and infamous, and a few oil paintings on the walls. A particular piece caught his eye. It was an old and rather worn map.

"I look around and see a man of high position in the old enemy's stronghold. And I wonder how such a thing could be possible?"

Fontleroy chuckled ruefully. "I don't know if anyone told you yet, but we lost the war, Greer."

"The war? No. A skirmish only."

Greer stood and inspected a framed map on the wall. It hung beside the door to the cloak room, and showed the Southern United States and Mexico, along with the Caribbean. It was creased with age and there were several small pinholes marking various places that at one time had been of mutual interest to both men. Greer fingered the hole that had once upon a time marked Havana, Cuba.

"The fight continues. And with your support, I can return this country to glory!"

Fontleroy stood and paced over to the large bay window that looked out on the town of St. Simeon's.

"Out there are two thousand souls who respect me," he pointed out the window. "They follow the laws I help write. As a soldier in that godforsaken war, we accomplished nothing, Greer. We squandered blood and treasure on some foolish errand of pride! If we'd only kept quiet and put our people into positions of power, we could have subverted those snot-nosed... Yankees!"

"My, old age has turned your liver a darling shade of lily!" Greer spat. "You squat atop some bug hill and think yourself taller for it! But mark my words, the South shall rise again! That was the cause we Knights of the Golden Circle knew to be true!"

"You sorry son of a jackanape," Fontleroy marched over to the desk. He stared across the space between them. It might as well have been as vast as the Grand Canyon.

"You misunderstand me," Greer said, forcing a measure of calm into his voice. "I am not simply begging for alms, I also bring an invitation."

He produced an envelope from inside his jacket. This he handed across the desk to Fontleroy.

"I have at my command over one thousand soldiers, of a strength and determination that cannot be swayed. Not by propaganda, not by the heat of battle—not even by death itself. This is an invitation to a little soiree at my ancestral manse. There, I will make a show of my new army's prowess. I will also be wed to my new bride, who will preside with me over an empire the likes of which have not been seen since the fall of Rome! Light refreshment to follow, of course."

Fontleroy read the invitation.

"You're a damned fool, Greer! And worse, you don't even know it."

He sneered and threw it on the desk between them.

"The Knights of the Golden Circle expelled you years ago. If you hadn't been out galavanting in the wilderness like some savage, you might have seen how the world is turning in our favor. You sit in your own filth, dreaming of an empire like some old-world sultan. Hogwash! Meanwhile, we in the Golden Circle are building one from the inside out. In a few generations, we'll have subverted all the blessed institutions that those blue bellies have established. And we'll do it quietly. Without blood and thunder."

"You've become worse than a collaborator," Greer said. "You're a got-danged coward! I promise you glory and position of power in a new era and all you can do is whine and howl like a hit dog."

Fontleroy opened a drawer in his desk and removed a billfold. He counted out a dozen bills and slid them across the table.

"Here's your tithe, Greer," he said. "Take it and consider it a severance."

Greer smiled, folded the bills, and tucked them into his coat. He tipped his hat to his former friend.

"Tell all the boys back at Fort Sumter that their money will be put to the Cause."

"Rot in hell, you old fool!" Fontleroy said.

About then was when the door to the cloakroom flew open and

out tumbled Jim and Francis. They jumped to their feet and Jim drew his saber and brandished it at them both.

"Stand and deliver, you rascals!" shouted Jim.

Francis drew his hunting knife and held it to Greer's throat.

"Tezu, James. My, you two are a pair of bad pennies, ain't ya?"

"Greer, you know these two brigands?" Fontleroy said.

Jim turned his saber on him.

Fontleroy raised his hands.

"We are acquainted," Greer said. "Though I am at a loss as to how they came to be in your cloakroom."

"We have traveled far," said Jim, "through Hell and back, to find you, Greer!"

"You! You brought them here, Elkanah!" Fontleroy spat.

"I did no such thing! Last I saw of them, they were about to be hanged. Though it seems not to have taken."

"Tell us where Lizzy is or I'll slit your throat," Francis held his knife against Greer's neck.

Jim turned his saber on Fontleroy, who held his hands up, but inched towards the corner of the desk, where a particular drawer was within reach.

"Where is Lizzy?" demanded Jim.

"I don't know this Lizzy…" protested Fontleroy.

"I will tell you nothing," Greer spat.

Jim turned his attention briefly on Greer, which gave Fontleroy the opening he needed. He lunged for the desk drawer and came up with a revolver cocked and loaded. This distracted Jim and Francis enough for Greer to make a run for the door, which he slammed behind him.

"Great," Jim spat. "You let Greer escape!"

He turned back to Fontleroy, who had stuck his gun hand out a bit too far. Jim's saber slid against his hand, slicing off the tip of his finger.

This sent the pistol clattering to the corner of the room.

"Got dang it all!" Fontleroy howled as he clutched the gushing stump of his finger.

"Seems your blade is sharp enough," Francis said.

"Right, Fontleroy, let's have it. Where's Greer got my sister?"

"I don't know any sister of yours, or anyone named Lizzy!" Fontleroy slumped into his chair. His face was turning white.

Francis found a scarf in the cloak room and threw it to him to staunch the bleeding.

"Greer told you his plan," Francis said. "Now, where is he holding this party of his? My wife will be there!"

"He's got your wife, too? The blaggard!" Fontleroy sighed.

"They're one and the same!" Jim and Francis yelled together.

Fontleroy was turning a ghastly shade of pale.

"Lift that hand over your heart," Jim said.

"Who are you, some sort of doctor?" Fontleroy laughed but did as he said.

"I was gonna be, once upon a time…" Jim said. "But answer the question! Where is this shindig?"

"Why should I tell you anything?" Fontleroy had grown a bit more bold, now that the bleeding had stopped and the color was returning to his face.

"There are a lot of ways to make a feller talk. Not all of them involve bloodshed," Francis raised his knife. "But I don't know those ways."

"You're bluffing!" Fontleory huffed.

Jim raised his saber. A drop of blood slid down the blade. "We got but one question and you have nine more chances to answer."

"Greer's manse! There's a party, he's hosting it to show off some new army of his! But you can't get there without the invite, or having been there before," Fontleroy nodded to the envelope on the desk.

Jim picked up the envelope. Inside was an engraved invitation card:

Attend, Ye Knights Of The Golden Circle!
You Are Hereby Summoned To A Conclave Wherein Plans
Of A Mutually Beneficial Nature Will Be Put To Discussion
And The Marriage Of
Elkanah Greer & Elizabeth Anne Hawkins
Will Be Witnessed.
Refreshments To Be Served.

☞

Though the road be long and our trip a weary one,
the avenues of fortune will open to those
who dare to know, and to see, and to keep quiet.

"The hell does that mean?" Jim asked.

"You stupid ingrates!" Fontleroy laughed. "You Dolts! Greer is three steps ahead of you and you don't even know it!" His laughter grew shrill. "The Knights will have our day again, and there's nothing you or anyone else can do about it! And Greer will have your sister, or wife… or whoever. All because you have no idea how to point the way!"

Fontleroy pointed at them with his raggedy finger, wrapped in bloody silk and laughed.

Jim and Francis shared a look. Then Francis grabbed Fontleroy's hand and slammed it on the desk. Jim raised his sword.

Everyone could hear the mayor's screams out on the lawn.

14
The Blue Ribbon

Lizzy, meanwhile, was in the dry goods store, running Travis and Quartermaster Gates in circles. She had it in mind to make a break for it, jump in the wagon, and whip those mules till she reached Texarkana. But the reality of it was that she was trapped. Every time she found herself close to the door, Travis would appear beside her and ask some inane questions about pepper. If she even glanced at the door, Gates would wander past with a sack of flour and drop it at her feet, ask if that was enough, or should he get another.

But when the Marshall came in, Lizzy saw her fortune change.

He was an older feller with a white handlebar mustache and tin star pinned to the lapel of his tweed jacket. He smiled and made small talk with one of the clerks for a spell, which gave Lizzy a moment to steel her resolve.

She could—would—march up to him and demand his aid. Before she realized what was happening, she was walking towards him, a question forming on her lips.

The Marshall turned as she approached and tipped his hat. "Ma'am. Lovely day ain't it?"

"That it is, Marshall, sir. I'm in need of your assistance."

"Well I'm always happy to oblige a young mother," he said. "When're you due, by the by?"

"Hmm? Oh, few weeks or so, but I—"

Suddenly Travis was there beside her. She turned to see him smiling big and dumb.

"I help you, sir?" The Marshall asked, standing taller and looking him up and down.

"Nah sir. My sister here wandered off. Thank you, Marshall, for entertaining her while we wrapped up the provisions."

The Marshall looked at Travis in his confederate uniform. He looked at Lizzy and her pleading eyes. And nodded.

"Ah. Well, it won't do to wander off from your brother here, Miss. Not in your state."

Lizzy stammered, trying to say something. Anything.

"There a problem here?"

All eyes turned to find General Greer standing in the doorway. He was backlit by the afternoon sun, casting his shadow across the floor.

"This your wife, sir?" the Marshall asked.

"That she is, thank you," said Greer. "Hawkins, take her out to the wagon."

Travis nodded and escorted Lizzy towards the door.

Mercy and Charlie watched the proceedings from behind a couple barrels of molasses.

"...And that there is Lizzy," Mercy whispered as she caught Charlie up on the who's-who of it all. "Francis's wayward spouse and Jim's sister."

"Now Travis I know," whispered Charlie, "but who's that other feller, the one who looks like a badger dressed up in a suit?"

"That's General Greer!" Mercy said. Then they ducked behind the barrel as Greer's badgery eye scanned the room.

Jim and Francis rushed in, out of breath, hands covered in blood. They stopped dead in their tracks and stared down General Greer, Travis. And Lizzy.

She gasped, "Jim! You're alive!"

"Jimmy boy," Travis said. "Well, ain't you a surprise."

Francis dropped the bloody sack he was carrying. "Lizzy?"

"Francis!"

She wanted to run to him, to hold him.

"You're hair, you're wearing it tied up in a ribbon…" Francis smiled.

"I hate it so," Lizzy smiled.

"Well now, ain't this a fine reunion!" Greer smiled. "I wish it were under happier circumstances."

There came a thunder of boots up the steps as Swann and his men crowded into the drygoods store.

"Now I don't know what the problem is here!" said the Marshall, "but I want ya'll to git out!"

"Of course, sir," Greer touched the brim of his hat. "We was just leaving."

Swann and his men parted, allowing Greer to exit. He was followed by Travis, who wrapped his hand around Lizzy's arm like a vice and just about dragged her the whole way to the door. Once they were out of the store, Swann stepped back into the doorway, his whole body taking up the frame.

"Tezu, old friend. We keep meetin' like this."

"Right, you!" yelled the Marshall, "Get on now!"

He waved to the little girl who was minding the till.

She took a shotgun from beneath the counter, cocked the lever and aimed the gun at Swann. "You heard him. Git!"

Francis threw the bloody sack at Swann, who tumbled backwards as he caught it. This gave Jim and Francis enough room to escape.

Mercy and Charlie decided it was their cue to leave as well and so scrambled from behind the molasses barrels where they'd been hiding. Mercy made sure to push Swann back to the floor as she trampled over him.

"How do, Marshal," Charlie took the law man's feet out from under him. He'd drawn his pistol and the fall caused him to squeeze the trigger, firing a shot into the ceiling.

Jim and the rest caught up with one another on the general store's front porch.

"I see you got supplies!" said Jim.

"I see you made a right fine mess!" Mercy replied.

Francis grabbed the bloody sack from Swann and lept onto Shadow's back. He helped Charlie up and they made for the main road with Mercy on Abraham Lincoln and Jim on Sebastian right behind.

Having misplaced their horses in the quicksand, Swann and his men chased after on foot.

"Me cago en todo lo que se menea!" said Gordo, tucked in the crook of Charlie's arm, "Them again?!"

The crowd from the parade earlier had not yet thinned enough to allow an unfettered escape. In fact, Jim and the rest found themselves backed up behind the grand float, where Mr. Fromager and his gigantic wheel of cheese were coming in for a landing across from the General Store.

Francis managed to maneuver Shadow around the side of the great cheese wagon and scoot up beside the team of horses. He leaned over and whispered something in the ear of the lead horse. The horses bucked and tried to run in four different directions, which is no easy feat when one is tethered to three others and all attached by leads to a wagon.

The wagon's braces splintered, then broke and the horses wrenched themselves free. The wagon turned over sideways, spilling Mr. Fromager face-first into the dirt and sending his great wheel of cheese rolling down the street.

Abraham Lincoln and Sebastian managed a quick side step, and delivered Mercy and Jim safely around the cheese. Swann and his men weren't so lucky. The great wheel of cheese pinned them to the wall of the stables, where they wriggled breathless, like squashed bugs. Swann's black glass bead eye—the left one—popped out and rolled away into the dust.

Francis gave a loud whoop and a holler for joy as they rode off.

About a mile out of town, they regrouped behind a large boul-

THE RIGHTEOUS AND THE REST

der. From here, they spy the road while they made plans for their next move.

"We need ourselves a plan of attack," said Mercy. "No more damn fool iprovisin', ya hear?"

They all nodded, and agreed. But then Jim caught sight of Greer's cart picking up speed as it trundled down the road past their position.

"There they are!" he kicked Sebastian into a run.

"Now wait one dang moment!" Mercy called after. She sighed then nudged Abraham Lincoln on after him. "Montazuma, protect this dang fool before he gets us all killed…"

But despite the manginess of the mules, their speed was nearly preternatural. Gates managed to parley with the whip and forced them on at a rate heretofore unknown among pack animals. This forced Jim and the rest into a chase. After a mile or so, the cart careened around a bend, heading for a patch of gnarled old Mesquite trees.

Gates let out a great "Hiyah! Gi'yup!" and cracked the whip. The mules plodded on, diving into the mesquite thicket. In the back of the cart, Francis held tight to Lizzy's arm, lest she try and do anything ill-advised.

"Got 'em now!" Jim yelled and raced to catch up.

Only, the Mules didn't slow, or balk, but kept running at pace along a narrow game trail that weaved deeper into the thicket of trees. The trees parted; the thicket deepened.

Before anyone knew what was what, there went Gates, leading the mule cart at a breakneck speed into a vast and tangled forest. From the back of the wagon, Greer grinned and laughed.

The trees slid closed like some thorn shrouded door behind him.

"What the..?" Jim huffed.

Sebastian came to a short stop at the forest edge. Shadow and Abraham Lincoln did likewise, instinctively halting before they tumbled into the wall of thorns and stickers that now lay before them.

They watched as the sun set, and the cart bearing Lizzy and Travis and Greer disappeared into the improbable distance.

Jim kicked Sebastian into a trot and dove into that wild wood. Soon he was following a narrow game trail that split and doubled back, wound in improbable turns, ran down a hill and up the bank of a creek, and turned, and turned, and turned once more, until Jim found himself in a small clearing. Not a moment later, the rest caught up to him.

Jim got down from Sebastian and threw his hat in the dirt. "Got damn it! We had 'em!"

The mules couldn't keep up the pace for long and soon, the cart bearing General Greer and his company back to Blanchefleur slowed to the usual pace of a lazy donkey at the end of a day.

"That was a lucky break, no two ways about it!" Quartermaster Gates mopped his brow as if he'd done all the work.

Greer handed the reins to Gates.

"Hold them steady, Mr Gates. These lanes can be a might tricksy for those unaccustomed to their turns."

The General clambered over the boards, into the back of the wagon and knelt beside Travis and Lizzy.

"I can see you will pose a challenge to me and my ways, Miss Lizzy."

"Oh she excels at that, to be sure!" Travis chuckled.

Greer turned the full brunt of his ire on Travis.

"And you Hawkins! What sort of irresponsible tomfoolery were you up to?"

"Sir?" Travis feigned ignorance.

This gave Lizzy a momentary respite from the glare of Greer's attention. She scooted to the back of the wagon and made as if she were going to be sick.

As she expected, the two men ignored her.

"You had but one charge, did you not?" Greer bellowed.

"I did sir, but—"

Travis was cut off by a look from the General. "No excuses, Captain! You want to wear that rank, you'll act the part of a fightin' man! Do I make myself clear?"

"Yes sir, but—"

Greer raised a hand as if to strike him. Travis held from but raised his own hands in supplication.

"Sir! But if'n you would listen for one second—"

"What was that, Hawkins?" Greer's voice grew low like a rumble of thunder approaching over a mountain range.

The General harangued Travis and the others for another while, which gave Lizzy time to think.

The wall of mesquite brambles rising up on all sides had sparked a memory of long summer evenings spent at the carnival grounds in Texarkana. She had become quite adept at the ring toss. Even won the little carved wooden horse she'd been eyeing.

Lizzy loosened one of her ribbons. She slid it from her hair, tied a quick loop, and counted to three.

This allowed her nerves to calm a bit as she scanned the darkening trail behind them for a suitable target. Having spied one, she flicked her wrist, sending her loop of ribbon spinning into the darkness where it snagged on the thorn of a mesquite tree. She offered a silent prayer to the Four Winds that Francis and Jim might find it.

As the sun set, the thicket of trees seemed to grow around them, until the tall trees raked the dimming sky with their thorny limbs.

"That game trail was right here a second ago! Where'd they get to?" Jim looked at Francis.

"It's what Greer called a geas," he said. "No one can get to Blanchefleur who hasn't been there or hasn't been invited."

"Yeah but you said you knew the way!" Jim yelled. His anger

was palpable. His frustration only made him madder. "You said that feller, Fontleroy, he knew the way!"

"And he does," Francis said. "For he has been there before."

"Well then why didn't we bring him along?" Jim asked.

"We did." Francis held up the bloody sack. "Part of him, anyway."

Charlie peered around Francis from behind him, "What's in the sack there, Francis?"

In answer, Francis reached into the sack and pulled out Fontleroy's bloody stump of a hand. It was missing part of a finger but was otherwise intact. The invitation was in there as well, crumpled and smeared with blood, but still legible. Charlie gave this a once over, then read it a second time.

"...the avenues of fortune will open to those who know, and see, and keep quiet…" he scratched his chin in thought.

"What good is a hand going to do us?" Jim asked. He had calmed slightly, though his breath was still ragged in his chest.

"Now Jim, we steered you wrong yet?" Mercy asked.

"No!" he shouted, still angry, mostly at himself. "You have not!"

"'And having thus chosen our course, without guile, and with pure purpose, let us renew our trust in God, and go forward without fear, and with manly hearts,'" said Abraham Lincoln.

"Very encouraging, thank you Mr. President," Francis nodded.

Jim took a breath and exhaled slowly.

"Right, then. What's the plan?"

"Well, it's like Mercy said: we need steerin'!" Charlie said. "Let's see if I can get this to work…"

He hopped down from Shadow's back and walked the perimeter of the clearing, holding Fontleroy's hand in front of him. He slowly moved it about.

"Point the way now, Fontleroy," Charlie whispered to the hand. "Show us the avenue of fortune…"

After a few passes, the hand's index finger uncurled, pointing towards a game trail to the southwest. It was narrow and overgrown, barely big enough for ants to march single file down it without getting lost.

"See, Jim," said Charlie. "Not all hope is lost."

"If you say so," Jim mounted Sebastian and they formed a line, Shadow in the lead.

"Mercy, do you mind?" Francis asked.

"Not all," she said.

Francis nudged Shadow, who hesitated a moment, until Francis whispered to him, "I know friend, it looks daunting. But Lizzy awaits us on the other side."

Shadow snorted and cantered in a circle, building up speed and then took off down that trail. With each step the horse took, the way opened wider, trees swaying and the trail becoming wider, clearer, until they were racing down a road much traveled.

"It occurs to me that we don't really have much in the way of confirmation that this here... uh hand is pointing the right direction," Jim yelled over the thunder of the horses hooves. He was ostensibly speaking to Francis, though loud enough for them all to hear.

Shadow slowed to a walk and then stopped. Francis slid off his back and approached the tree nearest to their left. There, clinging to a mesquite thorn, was a thin blue ribbon. It was barely visible in the twilight forest, but it was real enough.

"This is Lizzy's," Francis said. He hopped onto Shadow's back. "They went this way!"

"See Jim, trust in the wind, and it'll always steer you true!"

"If you say so," he sighed.

Then they were off once more, racing down the path, into the setting sun.

It was in that deep twilight, after the sun had set but before complete darkness overtook the sky when General Greer and the rest returned to Blanchefleur. They were greeted by a ring of torches in the front yard.

The slaves had gathered on the lawn in front of the manse, in the same spot where, every midsummer's eve, Greer and his men would play bowls. The officers were there as well, along with Tristan, trying to hold the slaves back from the front porch. Edmond stood on the porch, attempting to deliver a sermon. Miss Rachel and Robbe stood beside him, stone faced and silent.

"...Now the Lord says... he says that the faithful servant, he uh, he—or she—does not ask for, for... Ah! General Greer, sir. Perhaps You could..."

Greer stomped up the steps, onto the porch, and looked over the angry faces of the slaves, both house and field, gathered before him. There was a wave of murmurs and shouts as he appeared in the torchlight.

But instead of saying anything, Greer merely stood there, on the porch, still as if he had been turned to stone, saying nothing.

Lizzy and Travis joined the General and the rest on the porch while Gates ran to help the officers. They were holding the line just in front of the house with improvised clubs and pistols, but only just.

The crowd quieted down as they waited for the General to say something. Eventually, and with much deliberation and perfunctory throat clearing, Greer stepped forward.

"What is the meaning of this?" He did not appear agitated, or concerned at all, but asked it as a simple question, as one would if they had been handed a menu in a foreign language.

It fell to Little Tom to step forward and speak for the slaves.

"We heard tell that all those... those like us'd been set free. This true, sir?"

"I see," Greer's smile faltered. "I had feared the day this pernicious rumor reached our ears. For that is all that it is. A rumor. And a got-danged vile one, at that. Some years ago, some Yankee scalliwag whispered into the ear of a more gullible folk then assembled here, telling them that the order of the world had been upended." Greer shook his head. "I had hoped to spare ya'll the frustrations and fears that come with this dangerous notion."

"But is it true?" Ben yelled from the crowd. Haney and Andre stood with him.

"It is nothing more than a campfire tale, the tallest I ever did hear," Greer chuckled, playing it off.

A wave of murmurs and disgruntled shouting washed over the slaves.

A voice rose up and said, "But we was told—"

Robbe stepped forward, tugging on his waistcoat and setting his jaw firmly.

"Told what now? A tall tale? For that's all this is! And for what purpose would such a story serve, if not to anger and inflame in you a hatred for those ardent masters of yours, the ones who set you free from barbarity in those distant Afrik lands? Why, it boggles description, what damage would be wrought to all of society, were someone foolish enough to entertain it longer than a moment!"

The murmuring subsided for a moment.

Greer waved a hand to shush them all.

The murmuring quieted down, but did not entirely stop.

"Your Robbe speaks the truth. And you should all listen well to him, for we enter grave territory indeed!"

"Is it the truth?" Tom leveled his gaze at Greer. "Tell us!"

Greer sighed. "I see I have been a bit too lenient of late. Perhaps we are all in need of a reminder of the proper order of things?"

Greer nodded to Travis. He stomped down the steps, drew his pistol, cocked the gun, and leveled it at Ben's face.

Everyone stood still, and quiet. Waiting.

Greer cleared his throat. Travis glanced his way and saw him bob his head to the left. Travis moved the pistol, pointing it now at Haney.

"Stop this!" Lizzy would have jumped off the porch, despite her condition, had Edmond not caught her shoulder.

"Sister, be weary."

Greer cast a withering glare at Lizzy. She shrunk back a step.

"What shall we put to rest this night?" Greer's voice boomed from the porch. "Dear Haney, or this vile rumor?"

A tear streamed down Haney's cheek. No one moved.

"I see," Greer scowled. "Perhaps I should call in my troops to restore order then?"

Miss Rachel gasped at this. All eyes turned to her and in the cold sneer of her master she saw the awful truth laid bare: none of them meant any more to her than the shambling troops she'd raised out of the grave on his behalf. Live or dead, they were all meat to his man, who would not shed a tear for one of them.

"Please, friends, no more of this," Robbe descended to the lawn, looking at Travis with pleading eyes. "If you would be so kind, sir."

Greer nodded. Travis lowered his pistol.

"Let us dispense with this farce now and return to honest work, yes?" Robbe looked over the gathered slaves.

There passed a moment, where anything might happen. But the tension broke like a summer storm passing.

The slaves turned and retreated back to their work, murmuring disbelief and consternation as they went.

Andre wrapped Haney in a hug.

Travis raised the pistol and fired into the air.

Everyone jumped. But he'd made his point, as clearly and far more succinctly than had the General.

Greer turned to Miss Rachel. "Do you have anything to say?"

"Yes'r," she handed Greer the crumpled and much creased letter. "One of the maids found this and brought it to my attention. I thought it best you see it, and had hoped to deliver it to you before the rumors took off like the proverbial headless chickens."

She cast a withering glare at the gathered servants.

Greer snatched the letter from Miss Rachel and read it quickly, noting the scribbled signature on the last page. He crumpled it in his fist and starred hard at Lizzy.

For a moment, she feared he might take the pistol from Travis and end her then and there. Later, she would wish he had.

"I am disappointed in you, Miss Lizzy. I had thought that you and I had reached an understanding. But I see now you aim to test my patience."Greer turned away form her. " Miss Rachel, escort our Mrs. Shonka to the silent room."

"Thy will," Miss Rachel said.

"What is this silent room?" Edmond asked.

Miss Rachel led Lizzy into the house, and up the stairs. Edmond followed along, jabbering all the while.

"What is this silent room?" Edmond caught up with them on the grand staircase. "Is it... Miss Rachel, is this really necessary? I do not abide corporal punishment!"

"What you and I can abide is of no concern here," Miss Rachel stopped on the second floor landing and appraised Edmond. "I thought by now you would have realized this."

"Still," Edmond tried to find something to say, some bit of wisdom but found his storehouse pilfered by the night's events. "Perhaps if I have a talk with the General, we can come to some other... arrangement?"

"You may of course talk with the General at your leisure, Reverend," Miss Rachel said. "And then perhaps you will learn that once he makes up his mind, there is no changing it, come Hell or high water."

They left Edmond standing at the top of the stairs.

He made to step forward but a glance from Miss Rachel told him his company was no longer required. So he stayed there.

"I will pray for you Lizzy!" Edmond called after them. "I will pray for your quick deliverance! You have my word!"

Rachel led Lizzy down the hallway, past her door. The silent room lay behind that locked door at the end of the hall.

"You don't have to do as Greer demands," Lizzy whispered. "You are free. You can do as your heart dictates!"

Miss Rachel fished a ring of iron keys from her apron and took what felt like a full day to select the right one.

"I wish that were so," she said.

The key scraped in the lock and the door swung wide.

Lizzy craned her neck to peek into the room. It was lit by an oil lamp turned down low, and smelled like rosewater, dust, and dry linens, clean and crisply folded.

Miss Rachel led her inside.

It took a moment for Lizzy's eyes to adjust to the dim light of the room's interior. She was at first startled to find that it wasn't the light of an oil lamp that lit the room in such gloomy shades, but dozens of glass jars filled with fireflies. Their lights blinked and dimmed in an eerie wave that rippled in a drowsy light across every surface.

Lizzy next took in her chamber mates. They sat at a table in demure repose, dressed in fine frills and silks, and stared at her with empty eye sockets.

There were three of them. Dressed in their bridal veils and gowns, they had been left in this silent room for who knew how long, unattended. Judging by the dry skin pulled tight across their skulls, they'd been there a long time, waiting.

"I will leave you to your ends," Miss Rachel said.

As she headed for the door, Lizzy said, "Every word of that letter was true."

Miss Rachel stopped. She turned back to Lizzy and looked for a moment as if she might say something. Instead, she turned quickly away and left the room.

The door slammed shut.

The key rasped in the lock.

Heavy footfalls echoed down the hall and were gone.

"Well if this isn't wholly expected, I don't know what is," Lizzy sighed.

THE RIGHTEOUS AND THE REST

The three dead women turned to her as one, their dry throats rasping and said, "Join us…"

Lizzy saw the deck of cards sitting before her. "I'll deal first, if'n you don't mind."

Lizzy took an empty seat at the table and shuffled the deck. "Alright ladies, since I'm new here, why don't y'all fill me in on the particulars of this setup, hmm?"

15
The Firefly Path

Jim and the rest rode through the delirious night, under unfamiliar stars and an angry red moon, full and keening for blood. They rode as the hand pointed, turning this way and that, crossing lanes and diving through bracken and across open plains.

At one point it became too dark to see, as even the moon hid her light from them in that lost place. They were, every one of them, afraid they might wander the lanes between worlds forever more, but shortly before dawn, they spied the blinking trail of fireflies in the distance, lighting the edge of the wild wood.

They rode the path lit by fireflies until the fingers of dawn crept over the horizon and swept them away, back into the night.

And then they rode some more.

Dawn found them on the edge of a dense wood that marked the boundary of Blanchefleur. Jim and the others dismounted and led the horses through the trees, approaching the hulk of the ancient manse with caution. They tied up the horses inside the tree line and collected what few weapons they had. Then they gathered behind a hedge, to try and get a lay of the land.

"So this is Blankenflour, huh?" Jim said.

"Blanchefleur," Francis corrected. "Yes."

"Ain't that what I said?"

"In all my days, I never thought I'd see a living plantation again," Charlie said. Jim couldn't help but note a tone of sadness in his voice.

"This ain't right," Mercy hissed. "Not one bit!"

From their vantage point they could see the field slaves building an improvised stable in the east field, while the house slaves carried flowers and other decorations out to the front porch.

"Looks like they're preparing for high-toned and fancy to-do," Jim said.

"The conclave," Francis reminded him. "The one Fontleroy was so kind as to provide us his invite to."

"That means we're going to have a lot more company arriving soon," said Mercy.

"So we need to find Lizzy, kill General Greer, and skedaddle."

The rest looked at Jim sharply. Even Gordo swiveled his empty sockets his way.

"Ain't that why we're here?"

The others shared a look and then shrugged.

"So what's the plan?" Gordo asked.

Plans would have to wait though, as Jim shot up, and made to draw his saber. The rest looked at what had grabbed his attention: Edmond had come out onto the porch. He was dressed in a much repaired Confederate Uniform with chaplain's epaulets and a wide brimmed calvary hat.

"Jim, slow your roll!" Mercy grabbed him by the shirt and hauled him back behind the hedge. "I know you got yer blood up, but we have to play this cool."

From their hiding spot they could hear Edmond issuing orders in his assured yet ill-informed baritone.

"Now Sarah, let us move the bunting a bit further to the left, shall we?" and, "Delores, now those flowers should spray, like a grand fountain! Yes, like that, good…"

Edmond clomped down the steps, which was when Francis reached out from behind the hedge, cupped a hand over his mouth and dragged him into the foliage. He was so startled he forgot to yell. He did however look mighty perplexed, as was to be expected.

"Jim!" he gasped.

Francis covered his mouth again. Mercy held up a finger to her lips. Edmond nodded and Francis removed his hand.

"James, you have no idea how happy I am to see you alive. You are alive, yes?"

"I am. And you will remain likewise, if'n you help us. Where's Lizzy?"

"Lizzy is in the manse, under lock and key. I tried… I tried, Jim, you must know, to sway Travis but he… you know how he can be!"

"And Travis, where is he?" Mercy asked.

"He's around here somewhere," Edmond craned his neck and looked around as if expecting to find him in the shrubbery with them. "I last saw him with the General and the other officers, in the ballroom. I think they were pacing out the wedding ceremony."

"Wedding?" Jim and Francis both nearly shouted at the same time.

"Yes," Edmond sighed. "Things have taken a dire turn, I am afraid. The major point of contention seems to be over when the band should strike up a march. I had said that the most natural moment would be when the bride made her entrance, of course. But you know, no one ever listens to me…"

"Edmond, focus," Jim whispered. "Can you get us into where Lizzy's bein' held?"

"Would that I could, James, but my fate, alas, is sealed, as much as the poor wretches he keeps here in bonda—" Edmond sneezed. " Excuse me. What was I saying? Oh! I have become a wretch, a wretch I say! I… I am afraid all the time! The General is a madman and his army of revenants are… Jim I do not say this lightly, but he is a genuine devil, straight from the pits of Hell! And I have, alas, fallen under his sway."

"Edmond, ol boy," Jim smiled, trying to ease his brother's mind, or at least calm him somewhat. "We've come to free you—free everyone. Now can you help us?"

"I am sorry, James. You are right. I… I will do my best." Edmond stood, and they let him go. He straightened his gray uniform coat and marched out from behind the hedge, only to return a moment later. "What exactly am I doing?"

"Play along with Greer till we… till…" Jim looked at Mercy, who looked at Charlie.

"Till we give you the signal," suggested Francis.

"Right!" Jim said. "The signal. Then you make a run for it."

"With Lizzy," added Charlie.

"Right! Make sure you stick to Lizzy and keep her safe. That's your only job. Got it?"

Edmond swallowed hard. "I think so, brother. I will endeavor to do my best." He looked grave as he left the hedge and returned to the porch to survey the decor and issue more orders.

"Oh, heavens, Sarah, look at this bunting! We will have to redo the whole thing!" He glanced at Jim and gave him an ostentatious wink.

"Do you trust him?" Charlie asked.

"Eh," Jim waved his hand as if trying to balance a scale. "I think he wants to do good but he always ends up doing it badly."

"So that is a no, then?" Francis asked.

"Pretty much." Jim was struck by the notion that he didn't exactly trust anyone no more. He didn't like this realization. But mulling it over would have to wait for another time.

"Now what?" asked Gordo.

"We'll have to do this the old fashioned way," said Francis.

"Set the house on fire and shoot them confederates as they run for it?" Mercy suggested.

"Let's save that for plan B," said Jim.

"So what's Plan A then?" she asked.

"Me and Francis will sneak into the manse and find Lizzy. Mercy, you Charlie, and Gordo try to—"

"I ain't leaving these people enslaved," she said.

Jim caught the look in her eye. He had never seen her more serious before, and it would be a long time before she was ever so determined again.

"I understand, Mercy," Jim took her hand. It was warm in his. "You do what you need to. But while you're at it, find us all an exit. We'll take as many with us as we can."

"Everyone goes free," Mercy said. "Or none of us are."

Jim nodded. "Everyone goes free."

While Mercy, Gordo, and Charle went in search of mischief, Francis led Jim around the back of the house. With all the comings and goings, every pair of eyeballs was too busy on the work in front of them to notice two shadows creeping along the wall to the kitchen door. The door was unlocked of course, and they slipped into the servant's hall and down the only hallway, up a narrow flight of stairs, and exiting through a concealed door. They found themselves in the east parlor, and ducked behind a bookcase while they sorted out their next move.

"Edmond said Lizzy was under lock and key," Francis whispered. "That suggests a bedroom."

Jim nodded in agreement. "Which means we need to get to the second floor."

The sight of a road weary cowboy and an Osage warrior creeping up the mansion steps may have startled someone, had there been anyone close by to see. But Francis had a knack for subterfuge and they managed to find the back stairs and reach the second floor landing unobserved.

It was touch and go for a moment though when they had to duck into an empty bedroom to avoid a pair of officers passing by the back stairs. They paused to adjust their cravats and sabers in the hallway mirror before making their way downstairs. Once the officers passed by, they crept back onto the landing.

"We're doing great so far," Jim swatted at a fly buzzing about his ear.

"Except we have no idea where Lizzy is," Francis added.

"Yeah, that is a conundrum…" Jim swatted at the fly again, only this time it alighted on the back of his hand and began to glow.

"Huh. Firefly…" he said. The firefly fluttered down the hall in lazy circles.

Jim looked at Francis. He shrugged. They followed that wayward firefly down the hall and around two corners, arriving at the door to the billiards room as a young maid exited.

She came to an abrupt stop right in front of them. Jim was about to grab his sword but Francis stayed his hand.

"…Is your name Jim?" asked the maid.

Jim held up a finger to shush her. They stepped into the billiards room. It was unoccupied.

"It is you, and Mr. Francis!" Haney grinned. "I heard all about you both from Miss Lizzy!"

"You know where Lizzy is?" asked Francis.

"Yes'r," Haney bit her lip. "It's only… General Greer had her locked up in the Quiet Room. I don't know what's inside but… no one ever comes out of that place."

"Don't you worry about none of that," said Jim. "Lead the way."

Haney checked the hallway and seeing it was clear, motioned for Jim and Francis to follow.

"Oh, I am glad to see you and of course Miss Lizzy will be beside herself when she finds out you two is still alive! Miss Lizzy talked an awful lot about both of you. She talked a great deal about many things, most of which I didn't really understand all too good, but I know when I hear tales of true love and she sure do love you, Mr. Francis. She didn't know I was listening, but she'd pray to the Four Winds every night that you'd hear her somehow. Though we all thought youse were dead, but you're not obviously, because here you are!"

Haney led them down the hall and around the corner, to the silent room.

"She's in here," whispered Haney. "But only Miss Rachel—she's the housekeepe—she has the only key."

Jim and Francis regarded the heavy oak door a moment. Jim nodded to Francis. They both took three paces back until they were almost hanging over the banister, then ran at full speed towards that door.

The door busting open sounded like a crack of thunder.

Francis stood in the doorway, trying to make sense of the scene before him. Jim picked himself up off the floor and said, "Ho-lee…"

Haney peered around the door jam. "Oh my!"

The room was lit by dozens of jars filled with tiny twinkling lights, like fireflies. They stood on the table and piled in the chairs, hanging from hooks over the bed and lining the windowsill. The blinking of the firefly lights cast a diffuse glow around the room, sloshing shadows against the walls and ceilings as if the room were not in a house but on some ship on a storm tossed sea.

Lizzy sat at a card table. Situated around the table were three desiccated brides in their veils and all, each with a handful of cards. At the sound of the clatter from the door breaking, they turned their empty eye sockets to look at their new visitors. All except Lizzy. She kept dealing out the cards to the other women.

"Lizzy!" Francis called out. "It's me!"

Lizzy?" Jim asked.

No response.

Haney crept into the room and appraised the situation.

"I do believe she is stupefied," she said.

Francis leaned in close, whispering, "Elizabeth, my love, I'm here. Come back to me."

Lizzy dealt another card. The Queen of Hearts.

"That's it. You are the Queen of my heart," he kissed her gently.

Lizzy's eyes fluttered and she came to, as if waking from a deep sleep.

"Francis!" She nearly lept from her chair and embraced him. They kissed long and slow.

"Were you scared I wouldn't come?" Francis asked.

"Not for a moment," said Lizzy.

Jium cleared his throat.

"And Jim!" She hugged him tight. "When I saw you two back in town, I thought maybe I was dreamin'!"

"It's no dream," Francis said. "We're here, but we need to go. And quick."

Lizzy saw Haney stranding in the doorway and smiled.

"Haney my dear! You showed them the way!" She embraced the young woman. "Oh I'm glad you're well."

Lizzy sniffed away a tear and turned to survey the room. She hadn't really had time to give it a proper look before the soporific effects of the place overtook her. She had been so lost to the dreary perpetual twilight of the room, and the turn of the cards that she had no idea how much time had passed. Then she saw the three brides sitting at the table.

"I can't leave them," she said. "Nor the others. We have to do something. And Greer will send someone to fetch me to the wedding any moment now. He means to marry me for some esoteric show."

"We know," Jim said.

"But I won't let that happen," added Francis.

"I don't see how we can stop it," said Haney. "The guards will be here any time to escort Miss Lizzy to the chapel."

"The guards, you say?" asked Francis. "Not any of the servants, or the General himself?"

"No, I heard the General say it in his own words. He'd send two guards when they was ready. Miss Lizzy is to dress herself, on account of her poor behavior and such."

Lizzy's white dress was laid out on a bed covered in dried rose petals. This had given the room an acrid floral odor that made them all a bit drowsy.

"What are you thinking?" Jim asked.

Francis looked at the three brides, and the card game they were still playing in slow motion. The nearest bride, with a face stretched taught over her dry skull, turned over the seven of hearts. She tapped it. And looked at Lizzy.

"I think I have an idea," Francis said.

Mercy, Charlie, and Gordo, meanwhile, were having difficulty securing their exit plan. The woods that ringed the plantation looked like any other copse of trees, mostly oak, ash and elm, with a few juniper and enough sagebrush to tangle their ankles. But every time they tried to plot an exit route through the line of trees, they would get turned around and end up back on the edge of the plantation, though curiously, never quite the same place they entered.

"This is mighty confounding," said Charlie.

"These trees are maldito," added Gordo, and he would have spit, if he had a tongue still.

"Now, it's not the tree's fault," Charlie patted a nearby oak tree. "They do what trees have always done. But someone has put a mighty geas on this land, no doubt about that."

"So what do we do?" Mercy was getting exasperated.

She wanted to be as far away from this place as possible, and as quickly as Abraham Lincoln could run.

"Short of cuttin' off Greer's head, I mean."

"Not entirely sure that'd do it," Charlie said. "I have my doubts that Greer is the sorcerer who raised up the revenants. I suspect he's got no knack at all for anything but exploiting others."

"So who is the wizard we're looking for?" Mercy asked.

"Well I don't think it's a wizard, per se," Charlie said. "A sorcerer of sorts, perhaps a conjure or juju man."

"What's the difference?" Mercy asked.

"Well there's a considerable difference to be sure…"

And while Charlie gave Mercy a brief primer on the different schools of sorcery he'd encountered over his protracted life and wanderings, Gordo's attention began to wander. Which was a good thing, as he was the first to spot the patrol of revenants.

"Not to worry anyone," hissed Gordo, "but some of them Hijo de puta soldiers are coming this way!"

Mercy turned in time to see three lumbering revenants lurching down the lane towards them.

"Mierda…" she spat.

She and Charlie looked around for any sort to cover.

They were in the East field, below a small hillock, on the other side of which the field hands were building a temporary stable for the expectant gusts. Between them and the line of trees where the revenants were approaching stood the blacksmith's shack.

"This way!" Mercy grabbed her pistol and ran for the cover of the shack.

She and Charlie, carrying Gordo, ducked inside. The shack was cold this time of night, the hearth having burned down for the night. But it wasn't unoccupied.

Ben had been sitting in the dark, watching the last embers glow, drinking from a small jug of moonshine. So at first, when the dark skinned woman and Cherokee medicine man shuffled in carrying a human skull and huddled behind the anvil, he thought they might be whiskey phantoms.

Gordo saw him before the others did. "Hola Señor," he whispered.

Charlie and Mercy turned and eyed Ben suspiciously. Mercy put her hand on the but of her Navy Colt.

"No need for that," Ben said. "I ain't gonna hurt no one."

"What about them revenants?" Charlie asked. "Might you call them?"

"I might," Ben said. Then he grinned, drunkenly. "If I wanna get my fingers chewed off."

He took a long swig from his jug, then offered it. Mercy took a belt but Charlie declined.

"Oh, I wish I still had a throat…" Gordo said as Mercy handed the jug back to Ben.

"You the blacksmith?" Mercy asked.

"I ain't nothin', 'cept maybe a coward."

"I don't mean to put a damper on your self loathin' but we got us a situation. So If'n you're gonna call the guard, do it now so's I can put you out of your misery." She drew her pistol.

"Now Mercy, that's no way to talk," Charlie patted Ben's hand. "Can't you see this man's grievin'?"

"We're all gonna be grievin' real soon, 'less we get a way out of here for when Jim and Francis find Lizzy."

"You know Miss Lizzy?" Ben sobered in a second.

"We sure do," Charlie smiled. "In fact, we're here to rescue her. And you, if we can."

"Rescue… me?" Ben was incredulous. "You got some aspirations for a moonshine vision, I'll give you that!" he laughed and took another swig.

"I'm no vision," said Charlie. "But if you know a way to get out of here, that sure would be something."

"No way out," Ben shook his head. "I tried when I was a younger man, several times. But this place is all turned around on itself. A real laby-rinth, I heard it called."

"Oh, a labyrinth!" Charlie slapped his thigh. "Of course! I'm gettin' too old to see the nose on my own face!"

"I don't think that's how that sayin' goes…" said Gordo.

"So how's we supposta get ourselves out of this here labyrinth?" asked Mercy.

THE RIGHTEOUS AND THE REST

"There's but one way to exit a labyrinth," said Charlie. "And that's to go all the way through it to the end."

"You could take a shortcut, if you made a big enough whatchacallit..." Ben swayed on his stool a moment. "A uh..." he mimed something blowing up and made the noise to go with it.

"An explosion?" Charlie suggested.

"That's the thing!"

He and Mercy shared a mischievous grin.

"Say, Blacksmith—"

"Name's Ben."

"And a fine name it is," Mercy said. "With all these soldiers about, they must have a store of powder and ammunition and such like."

"Oh sure, the Magazine," Ben said.

"Right! The Magazine!" Charlie's smile widened.

"Where would this Magazine be located, exactly?" Mercy asked.

Ben caught their intent and his mouth split into a wide grin, the first he'd worn in a long time.

"Follow me, friends of Miss Lizzy. We're gonna make us a righteous mess!"

Jim found Mercy, Charlie and Gordo down by an unassuming shack adjacent to the stables. They had prised the padlock off the door and laid it open. Jim found them stacking crates and rearranging barrels in this store room. And helping them were several field hands, and an older feller with graying hair.

"What in the blazes..."

"That's the plan," siad Charlie. He flashed a childlike grin. He and Ben were stacking crates in a precarious pyramid.

"This here is Ben the blacksmith," Mercy and two stout field hands were drawing signs and circles in the dirt with black powder from a keg. When they ran out, they tossed it in the corner with half a dozen others they'd already emptied. "And this is Fred and Jefferson, I didn't catch their occupations."

Charlie and Ben heaved the last crate of guns into place. Charlie huffed and wiped his brow. "You and Francis find your sister?"

"Yes, as a matter of fact we did. What is this now?"

"We may need to beat a fast retreat, once things get hairy," said Ben. "This is what Miss Mercy here called insurance."

"Huh. I see Mercy's been plotting again," Jim smiled.

"Better safe than sorry," she said. "But this idea was all Ben's."

He smiled, proud of his handiwork.

"So where's Francis?" Mercy asked.

"Ah, about that…" Jim filled them in on the plan Francis had devised. "…But you and me are in need of disguises."

"May have an idea about that as well," Ben nodded at the stables across the way, where a line of coaches was lining up in the dark.

The guests arrived in their twos and threes, dressed to the nines. Ben and the field hands had gone to ready the rest of the plantation, lay a few more booby traps, and generally prepare for the worst or best, whatever came their way.

Mercy and Jim hid in an empty stall and waited.

By and by, a handsome coach trundled up the drive. But instead of continuing on to the Big House where the others were disembarking, a short chauffeur dressed in oversized livery stepped in and waved them off to the side.

The carriage came to a stop right in front of the stable. A portly gentleman in a top hat climbed down from the coach.

"Why are we stopping here?" he demanded of someone, anyone at all. His companion, a much younger woman with a painted face and ruffles for days, followed him out of the coach.

"What's the hold up, Roger?"

"Back in the carriage, Coquette," Roger said. "I'll handle this."

The hold up was their driver, who shouted and jumped down from the coach, running into the night. The thing he ran from came lumbering out of the gloom, eyeless sockets aglow and cackling like a buzzard.

Charlie, having pulled his borrowed coat over his head, lurched towards Roger and his coquettish friend. He held Gordo over the collar, right where his head should be and Gordo did the rest.

"Boo!" the skull cackled.

Mercy and Jim leapt from the nearby stable and knocked Roger on the head. Coquette saved her the trouble and fainted while Gordo laughed.

It took but a moment for Jim to pull off Roger's suit and dress himself. Mercy took a moment longer, as Coquette was a tad smaller than she was. Also, Mercy had never had the pleasure of managing a corset before, and had to enlist the aid of Charlie, who deftly trussed her up, good and tight.

"This ain't gonna work," Mercy grunted as Charlie tied the last stay. "I look afright."

"You look fine to me," Jim said. He couldn't help his smile at her dressed in a fancy frock.

Mercy rolled her eyes. "Men folk, I swear…"

Charlie examined his own handiwork. "There, now you look the part." He seemed pleased by it.

"I feel like a prize goose at christmas time," she sighed. Or gasped. It was hard to tell.

"How do you know how to rig this here contraption?" Jim asked.

Charlie smiled and waggled his eyebrows.

They left Roger and Coquette in their skivvies, tied up in the stable.

"Good luck," Charlie said. Then he and Gordo headed out to see what mischief they could get into.

Jim and Mercy headed back to the house. The number of coaches and carriages had increased tenfold. Greer's big to-do was about to begin.

16
The Last Hootenanny

The Manse was all lit up with lanterns and that cast a warm glow in every window, and on the front porch. There were garlands and streamers and the place looked fit to welcome the President himself, until one realized they were all in the colors of the Confederacy.

Flickering lanterns hung from the limbs of magnolia trees punctuated the perpetual twilight of the late summer night, as did the fireflies. White banners bearing the red bar and rebel cross—the so-called "Stainless Banner"—hung over the front door and from the second floor landing. Bunting in white and gold ran along every banister while the rebel cross decorated the walls and tables. A large chandelier hung over the ballroom, casting sparks all around, while the chapel was done up in white and gold with a Stainless Banner draped across the altar.

Jim and Mercy entered through the front door, which felt like the bravest, most foolhardy thing they'd ever done. Which was saying something as one of them had recently clawed his way out of a grave and the other had been to San Francisco, twice.

"This can't possibly work," Mercy tugged on the bodice of her dress. "Surely we'll be recognized, and then what?"

"Not to worry. Anyone who might recognize me thinks I'm dead and won't be looking for me. As for you," Jim admired her for a moment, feeling a flush reach his cheeks. "You'll have no problem fitting in. You look uh beautiful by the by."

"I highly doubt that," Mercy grimaced. "About fitting in, I mean. I know I look spectacular."

She forced a smile as they set about to mingle with the Confederados, Revanchists, Klansmen, Dixiecrats, Flaggers, Daughters of the Confederacy, Sons of Confederate Veterans, Skinheads, Roundheads, FlatFeet (or Flatfoots, as they styled themselves collectively), Muggers, Duggers, Humbuggers, and Republicans gathered there in the ballroom.

As they made a circuit around the room, Mercy noticed that more than one gentleman guest had as his escort a dark skinned beauty the likes she had not seen since that time in Kansas City.

She didn't like to think too closely on the subject, but did recognize that, for the grace of the Four Winds, she could have ended up in similar straits. There weren't many opportunities outside the Switch for folk like her. And there seemed to be a dwindling number of opportunities for her left inside of it.

"What do we say if someone doesn't recognize us? Do we have some identity that comes with these get-ups?" Mercy regarded her dress, which had a bustle and everything.

"Certainly. I am Colonel Malachi Deuteronomy, hero of the Battle of Big Sur. I own a million acres of nothin' in particular and you are my roundheal coquette, Annie, from Jamaica."

Mercy smiled wide and fake and held his arm tight. "And if that don't pass the sniff test, then what?"

"Well if that fails, we will have to dazzle them with our charm and wit."

They both grinned wide and nodded to the other guests, Mercy flicking her fan open and shut, while Jim puffed out his chest.

An older gentleman with a long beard, dressed in a flannel suit of Confederate Gray, saw Mercy's fan action and gave a wink and little wave with his fingers.

"Uh Oh," Mercy blanched. "Think I may have told that feller I'd meet him out back by the stables."

"Let's hope it don't resort to that," Jim shook his head. "I feel like a dang performin' ape in this suit."

"Now I ain't seen any ape—performin' or otherwise—as dapper as you in that there snood, Young James Hawkins. Sorry, Colonel Deuteronomy, sir."

She squeezed his arm and they shared a genuine smile.

And for a moment at least, they felt relieved in one another's mutual discomfort; that perhaps this entire escapade might come off without a hitch. But it was a fleeting thought, one that passed quickly as Mercy recalled another hurdle they must leap before they fled into the night.

"Where's Francis?" she asked. "You said he'd meet up with us here."

"That's what he said," Jim looked around. "But I don't see him."

What Jim did see however was Travis, dressed in a Confederate dress uniform complete with a red sash and sword. He was chuckling heartily with Archibald Fontleroy, who had exchanged his old uniform for a dapper pinstripe suit and golden circle pin on his lapel. He sported a new wooden hand and seemed no less for it.

"Well now, there's a familiar so-and-so," Jim stiffened.

Mercy felt the heat coming off his look and followed it across the room, locating Travis under his hateful gaze.

"Now, Jim, no flying off half cocked," she whispered. "We got us a plan. Rest assured, Travis will get his when the time comes."

"My mama always said there's no time like the present…"

But before Jim could stalk off and make a scene, Mercy gasped and grabbed his arm tight.

"We got us another problem," Mercy nodded.

Jim followed her gaze across the crowded room to find Captain Talbot Swann. He was dressed in a fresh uniform, with his hat under his left arm and a saber on his hip. In his right hand he held a tankard of ale. An eyepatch covered his injured eye while the other gleaned in the lamplight, freshly polished to an obsidian shine.

THE RIGHTEOUS AND THE REST

Swann laughed heartily with some ne'er do well and drained his tankard. As he wiped the foam from his mustache, he spotted Mercy and Jim and smiled wide.

"Well then, plan B it is," whispered Jim.

He and Mercy turned on their heels and headed for the door. But every time they took a pace forward, they were forced, either by the crush of people entering, or to avoid either Swann or Travis, to take two steps to the right or left.

After a full five minutes of shuffling about in this awkward dance, Jim and Mercy ended up right back in the middle of the room, the door as far away as ever. Travis had mercifully not spotted them, and Swann was lost in the crowd somewhere.

"We seem to be going nowhere fast!" Mercy hissed.

"Don't I know it," Jim sighed.

They were about to make a break for the front door, they were apprehended by the man Mercy had waved her fan at. He was lean and wiry, with the gleam of cold hate that haunted the corner of his mouth, like some venomous bite waiting to find the right victim.

"I couldn't help but notice you and your fetching concubine here," He looked Mercy up and down without a scintilla of shame then turned to Jim. "I detect a fellow Virginian, am I correct? Jubal Early, at your service."

He bowed and kissed Mercy's hand.

"Careful, you don't know where that hand's been," she smiled.

Early stood and regarded them with a raised eyebrow. "What did you say your name was?"

"Uh… Pollard," Jim stammered. "Edward Pollard… uh Jr."

"Ah! Of the Lynchburg Pollard's?"

"Indeed," Jim grinned.

"Well now ain't that something? I am a great admirer of your father's writings!" Early slapped Jim on the back. He leaned in close and whispered, "The girl, how is she? Confidentially speaking, of course."

"She's... well, you know," Jim giggled. He thought he'd been found out for sure but Early just tittered along with him.

"Say no more, friend!" Then, "so what's the price? I happen to have a silver dollar for the evening. Return her not too late. What do you say?"

Jim reached for his saber but was caught up short by the sound of a snare drum beating a battle march and a hundred feet pounding into the hall.

All conversations in the ballroom stopped.

Heads turned this way and that in search of the source of the sound. There came another volley of drum beats from the left, and a third straight ahead. Soon, the marshal call was coming at them from every direction of the compass. From the right, a battalion of soldiers entered. They filed in, armed for the field, carrying the Stainless Banner before them, and accompanied by a snare drum to keep the pace. Another battalion of soldiers, identical to the first, entered from the left, while a third converged from the front of the house, tromping up the steps and through the front door.

As the soldiers advanced into the hall and formed ranks along the walls, it became apparent what it was that set this army apart from all others: every soldier was already dead.

More than one woman in the gathered crowd swooned.

The final soldier entered from the front and there was a pause. The drummers held their stiff hands at the ready. Then a palanquin entered, bearing General Greer between four stout revenants. As his entourage made its way to the front of the room, he was joined by his officers, who fell in beside him. All except Travis.

Jim looked around but could not find him.

The drummers picked up their beat again, sounding the call to arms as General Greer, dressed in a fancy new uniform, with a scarlet cape clasped by a gold circle pinned to his chest, was carried into the chapel.

The revenants marched after Greer, leading the now curious

guests. Edmond waited for them at the altar, decked out in a white cossack and holding the Bible to his chest. The revenant litter bearers lowered the palanquin to the floor. Greer stood and took his place on a small dais at the front. From a servant's door concealed behind a curtain emerged Miss Rachel. She wore a spotless dress in blue with white ruffles at the neck and cuffs. She took her place beside Greer. He raised a hand and the room grew silent.

"Welcome one and all to Blanchefleur. I look upon the faces gathered here before me and I see greatness. But alas, it is a greatness that has been thwarted!"

Greer paused to let them grumble and retort.

"Yes, thwarted! And I count my own self among you. For lo, these last fifteen years, we've had to watch those blue bellies hold our defeat against us. While they plot and scheme, enacting reforms and advancements for every sort of curr and degenerate spawn of a subhuman they can find. Meanwhile, the anointed masters of the world have had to scrape and beg for forgiveness," He leveled his gaze at Fontleroy, "Or flee to the farthest shores to live in some pauper's fairytale of what could have been," he glanced at the contingent of Confederados, fresh off the boat from Brazil.

"But that is enough of that, I say. And while some of you mocked me and laughed at my plans, I alone kept the faith! But I will not hold it against you. What a man does when he's been kicked to the dirt and demeaned by his social inferiors is an indignity all to itself. One you all have suffered long enough! For I offer you now, in this dark hour, a chance of salvation!"

Greer made a sweeping gesture and all gathered there looked at his revenant army, breathless, smelling of dry leaves and the fetid puddles of autumn.

"What are you on about now, Greer?" Called out Fontleroy. "What is the meaning of this ghoulish display?"

"This, deer Fontleroy, is the future! Our future! I have at my command one thousand men who will not feel pain, who will not flee, only advance! Who will not cower or disobey an order, even one that may test one's fortitude! These revenant soldiers shall sweep the usurper government away and allow us to reclaim our birthright!"

"You must be joking," someone called out from the crowd.

Men and women laughed and jeered at the General's army. They stopped when the General waved his hand and the nearest squad of revenants grabbed the jeering gentleman who had laughed first. They dragged him down to the ground and proceeded to rip the flesh from his bones, splattering the nearby guests in blood and tattered clothing. The man's shrieks stifled all laughter. And when he stopped screaming the chapel fell silent once more.

Greer snapped his fingers. The revenant reformed ranks, leaving what was left of the man in a pile at their feet.

"I encourage the skeptics amongst us to observe this as an object lesson in social etiquette. Now where was I? Oh yes, the future!"

Greer smiled. "This new world we will create will of course need a firm hand to give it proper shape. And a king of such vision and persistence would be nothing without a queen at his side. To that end, I give you, Elizabeth Anne Hawkins, your future Empress of the Americas and my bride!"

The chapel doors opened.

The band struck up the wedding march and in came the bride, looking resplendent in a white gown with a veil across her face. She was escorted by her brother, Travis, who proudly marched beside her.

The guests watched in silent disbelief as she walked up the aisle and took her place on the diaz beside Greer. Edmond smiled weekly and opened his Bible to the bookmarked passages he'd selected.

In a shaky voice, he read, "Two are better than one, because they have a good return for their labor: If either of them falls down, one can help the other up…"

"What are we gonna do?" Jim whispered to Mercy. They'd crept as close to the front as they could, settling in the second row, off to the right, behind a couple of Dixiecrats whose portly dimensions offered them enough of a barrier to discovery as they could hope for.

"Wish I knew!" she whispered back.

"...And that is... that is why we should all head the, I mean follow—follow the example of the sons of Cleophus! And keep silent, and remain attentive. And so we are gathered here tonight, to mark the nuptial occasion of General Greer and Lizzy... I mean—Elizabeth Anne Hawkins."

Greer stepped forward and threw Lizzy's veil aside.

A wave of gasps and murmurs washed over the gathered audience. For it was not Lizzy dressed up in white, standing in front of that altar, but Francis.

Greer's smile deflated, replaced by a grimace of exasperation.

"Well, now Tezu, my old friend. I would say that this is an unexpected appearance, But well, that would make me a liar."

Greer stepped back. Swann and Travis stepped onto the dais, with four revenant soldiers, rifles at the ready.

"You treacherous so-and-so!" Jim hissed at Edmond. He grimaced and tried to hide under the nearest pew.

Revenant soldiers approached Jim and Mercy, and escorted them likewise to the dais, beside Francis.

"Let us be honest with one another, then Elkanah Greer!" Francis shouted. "You always knew this day would come."

From his bouquet, Francis pulled his hunting knife and lunged for Greer's throat.

Jim drew his saber and hacked at the nearest revenant. He took off two arms, but it wasn't clear if they belonged to the same soldier, or were separate appendages from two different revenants.

Mercy, meanwhile, drew her Navy Colt and shotgun from beneath her bustle and opened fire.

The crowd scattered, heading for the doors, as blood and bullets filled the air.

* * *

Haney led Lizzy down the back steps. This took some doing, as Lizzy's belly had grown considerably.

"I don't remember being this dang big before I went into that room…" she huffed as she took the steps one at a time. "How long was I in there?"

"A night and a day, Miss," Haney said. She held Lizzy's hand to stabilize her as they hurried the last three steps.

"This house is mighty weird, Haney," Lizzy huffed.

They shuffled down the hallway and into the kitchen, which they found to be curiously empty.

"I see what you mean, Miss Lizzy…" Haney paused. "Kitchen's never empty, even after everyone's retired for the night, but especially not now, during a to-do!"

"Where is everyone, do you think?" Lizzy asked.

She turned around in time to see a large salted ham walk out of the larder. On top of it balanced a wedge of cheese that weighed three pounds easily, a bowl full of boiled eggs, a roast chicken, and a jar of pickled cucumbers.

It took Haney and Lizzy both a full moment to realize the food wasn't levitating, nor had it grown legs. Charlie Snow Owl juggled the pile of food in his arms until he could see over the bowl of eggs.

"Well, Hawe! You must be Miss Lizzy," Charlie said. "Charlie Snow Owl. Sure am glad to meet you."

Charlie delivered the food to a servant's table, where Gordo sat atop a small keg of ale. There was already an assortment of other foods laid out there, including sausages, smoked salmon, and a brisket he'd already pulled from the smoker and laid out on a sheet of butcher paper. A dozen small jars of jellied fruit, ketchup, relish, mint, and mustard (yellow, brown, and spicy) lay open about the table as well. Charlie deposited his armful onto the table and flopped into a chair.

"Pull up a stool and help yourself!" he said.

"Is that a... skull?" Haney knelt down to peer at Gordo. She reached out a tentative finger and he snapped his teeth, nipping her finger.

"Eep!" Haney jumped.

"Now behave, Gordo," Charlie swatted the skull. "He's really quite pleasant, when he hasn't been at the ale."

"Hola, chica," Gordo said. "Sorry to startle."

Lizzy sank into a large wicker chair beside Charlie and nibbled a leg of cold chicken.

"Your brother and husband have been looking high and low for you," said Charlie.

"Yeah, I found 'em," Lizzy nibbled some cold chicken. "They filled me in on this dang fool plan. My understanding was, you were to rally the sla—" she sneezed.

"Bless," said Gordo.

"—The uh, the... servants! You were to rally the servants. We have to go now!"

"Oh, sure. That's where the kitchen staff set out to do, once I told them what was what." Charlie took a bite of ham. "Needs more pepper..."

He reached into his pouch and pulled out a few dried peppercorns. These he placed in Gordo's mouth and the skull proceeded to grind them up good and proper.

"Thank you," Charlie dusted the pepper flakes on top of the ham slices he'd already carved off with his hunting knife.

"What the devil and his crosseyed brother is going on here?"

They all looked up to find Miss Rachel and Mr. Robbe standing in the doorway to the kitchen.

Haney jumped up. "Miss Rachel! Mr. Robbe! I can explain!"

"You can?" Robbe looked at Haney.

"Well... no. But there is an explanation... I think?" She looked from Lizzy to Charlie to Gordo, back to Charlie.

"Who are you, little man?" Rachel demanded.

"Me? Nobody in particular," Charlie said. "But you strike me as a very important personage, to be sure."

Rachel stood still for a moment. She was baffled by the sudden appearance of this elderly Indian with a skull in her kitchen, and by the fact he had called her important. No one had ever done so, not in her forty some years in this world.

"What's to stop me from alerting the General?" Robbe asked.

"'Spect he's a might busy at the moment," Lizzy set down the chicken leg she'd stripped clean.

"Miss Lizzy!" Robbe was startled. "I don't think this a terribly wise course of action after what the General had to say about your last little act of rebellion…"

"Hush, Robbe," Rachel turned back to Charlie. "Who sent you?"

"The Four Winds, ma'am, as always."

"And who is that?" she ran a finger across Gordo's ocular ridge. He cooed.

"This here is Gordo, Ma'am. Your handiwork, I believe."

"He's… one of the revenants?" Robbe asked.

"Ci," said Gordo. "You might say I retired."

"You'll have to excuse him," Charlie belched. "He's become a bit eccentric, ever since he died and was revived in service to your General. By you, weren't it?"

"I… I have a necromancer's knack, yes," Rachel said.

"Rachel," Robbe hissed. "Say nothing more to this… this interloper! He's here with them! Trying to undermine our ways, lead us to the doors of perdition!"

"Necromancer? Nah," Charlie chuckled. "I've met my share of necromancers, sorcerers, and the like. And they only dream of having the healer's knack you have."

"I'm no healer!" Rachel spat back. "And what makes you think I won't call the guards and have you conscripted?"

"Because that's not your way, is it? You don't like what the General has done to you, how he's twisted your knack for his own purposes. But that's what powerful men do, ain't it?"

"You aren't telling me anything useful, Charlie," Rachel said. "Perhaps I should call the guards now?"

"Good idea," Charlie yelled, "Guards! Guards!"

Guards! Woohoo!" Gordo yelled. "Guards, we're over here, empaca!"

Andre and another footman, William, came in just then.

"Mr. Robbe. Miss Rachel," Andre said. "What's the…?"

His question wandered off when he saw the sight: Charlie and Lizzy chowing down at the servant's table with Haney and a skull.

"Ruckus…?" Andre's words wandered off.

"We're all doomed!" Robbe slumped into a chair and dunked a slice of ham into the hot mustard.

"Oh, it's not so bad as all that," Charlie opened a small jar and set it before him. "Try the mint jelly. Freedom takes a bit of getting used to for sure, but I think you'll like it. No one tellin' you when to get up, what to do, when to do it…"

"No, you don't understand," Robbe mumbled around a mouthful of ham. "We'll never know a moment's freedom or joy ever again."

"What do you mean?" Andre asked.

"The General intends to conscript us all!" he sobbed into the mustard.

All eyes turned to Miss Rachel.

"He wouldn't… he won't!" she said.

"But the General, I heard him say with my own ears—"

Rachel cut Robbe off.

"I know what the General says! But listen to what I'm sayin'!" she looked at Lizzy. "You is free as the birds in the sky, if only you'd notice you had wings."

"That's the spirit!" Charlie grinned. He wiped his hands on his trousers. "So, shall we be about it then?"

"No, This won't do!" Robbe stood and straightened his jacket, he wiped a smear of mustard from his cuff and marched towards the door. "I'll inform the General and he'll see the reason for it, you'll see! I can talk to him, he'll spare us. At least, those of us who obey… Yes. That's what I'll do…"

Robbe barely took two steps before Andre nodded to Wiliam. They tackled Robbe and in a moment, had him trussed up like the cold chicken Charlie had been feeding to Lizzy. They stuffed him in the larder with the cheese, his muffled protests falling on deaf ears.

"Right," Charlie picked up Gordo. "Let's go save the day!"

Haney hoisted Lizzy to her feet and Miss Rachel led them through the kitchen and out the back door, into the night.

As they headed across the lawn back to the Manse, Charlie brought them all to a stop by holding up his hand. They gathered behind a hedge and peered over.

Hundreds of Revenant Soldiers had mustered outside the chapel. They were led by some of the officers, who had ranked them in regiments and surrounded the chapel entirely.

"What's that fool General up to now?" Charlie whispered, more to himself than anyone else.

"He's going to kill everyone inside," said Miss Rachel.

There came a moment's silent contemplation. Then,

"We gotta help them!" said Haney.

"Francis and Jim are in there!" Lizzy added. She was about to march in on her own, but for Charlie who took her hand.

"Mercy too, I reckon," said Charlie. "But we need us a plan of action."

Charlie looked at Gordo. "I think I got an idea. But I'm gonna need some help…"

17
Tell Old Pharaoh

The situation in the chapel had taken a dire turn. Jim's sword arm was giving out from all the hacking and slashing, and Mercy was almost out of ammunition. Francis was the only one of them who wasn't flagging, as spite had fueled him through their travels and he was now a burning bush of righteous fury. But every time he managed to corner Greer, one of the officers would arrive with a gang of revenants to stand between them.

Mercy and Jim had been backed into the nave. They heaved pews into an improvised barrier, but the revenants were advancing, climbing over top one another to reach them. Mercy picked off three with her shotgun, until she ran out of ammunition. Jim had picked up a rifle from one of the fallen soldiers but soon he too was out.

Several of the surviving Golden Circle members had taken refuge with them in their improvised hideout but there was little room and it was shrinking by the moment.

Jim heaved another pew onto the barricade. Skeletal hands in gray uniforms reached through every nook and cranny to grasp at him. He used the rifle as a club to fend them off long enough for Francis, whose wedding gown was now in tatters, to slide through the barricade.

He dragged Fontleroy in with him, for the man had been stupified by the events.

"...It's not proper..." Fontleroy mumbled to no one, to himself. "...not proper at all..."

Francis joined Jim and Mercy, who had hunkered below one of the tall stained glass windows, which depicted a gray-clad confederate delivering a group of slaves into bondage.

"I think it's going well." Francis scraped a wad of gore from his blade, cleaning it on the hem of the wedding dress.

"Oh, Tezu!" Swann called out in a sing-song voice that echoed throughout the chapel, "I'm comin' for ya!"

"We've gotten their attention, that's for certain," Jim said.

"Any ideas how we get out here?" Mercy asked. "Preferably live?"

A crash of breaking glass from above drew their attention as a large white stone flew through the upper window pane. Jim caught it and turned it around in his hands until he realized it wasn't a stone at all.

"Gordo! Am I glad to see you!"

"Hola," said the skull.

"That's not proper!" shrieked Fontleroy. He pointed his wooden hand at the skull.

"You ain't exactly proper yourself there, Jefe," Gordo chuckled.

"Any thoughts on how we make an exit?" Mercy asked.

"Si. Abe says to watch your head."

"Watch my—" Jim's question was cut short by a calamitous explosion of painted glass over their heads.

The same window Gordo had pierced exploded into shards as Abraham Lincoln thundered into the nave.

And just in time, too. A half dozen revenants had loosened the barricade of pews, pulling them out of the way.

Those slavering cadavers advanced on the cowering guests, only for the valiant horse to kick them away and scatter them like rag dolls. Packed on his saddle were rifles and cartridges of ammunition Charlie had pilfered from the armory, along with the spirit bow Francis had acquired from Doctor John.

"...'You can not fail in any laudable object, unless you allow your mind to be improperly directed...'," said Abraham Lincoln.

THE RIGHTEOUS AND THE REST 275

"Well, put Mr. President!" Mercy grabbed rifles and handed them around to anyone with enough wits, which wasn't many. She jumped onto the horse's back and pulled Jim up behind her.

He clutched Gordo in his left hand, while fending off revenants with the saber in his right, except for once, when he mixed up the two and brained an officer named Lieutenant Grimley with Gordo. This left Grimley unconscious on the floor and Gordo a bit dazed.

Francis put his knife between his teeth, hitched up his wedding gown, and followed Abraham Lincoln as the horse plowed through the revenants, towards the vestibule and the front door beyond.

Spirit bow in hand he pulled the string back and let fly with several invisible arrows, each finding their mark in a revenant's skull and two in the chest of confederados.

A revenant, badly scarred and missing an arm, lunged out of shadows at Francis as they neared the exit. Francis took his knife from his mouth and stabbed a revenant through the left eye.

"Come on, Fontleroy! we're leaving this party!"

"...It's not proper!" Fontleroy shouted.

Two other surviving Knights of the Golden Circle hoisted the catatonic feller to his feet and carried him towards the door.

Out in the yard, they found the rest of the soldiers, which was more than they'd counted on. Nearly nine hundred dead men filled the lawn around the manse, their breathless advance somehow sucking the light out of the air.

Mercy and Jim and the rest came up short under an old oak, the gaggle of fleeing guests huddling close to Abraham Lincoln's right flank.

Francis turned this way and that, trying to find a convenient target for his bow. But the ring of revenants, which was at least five men deep, closed ranks around them.

This sea of dead flesh parted, allowing General Greer to enter into the ring of firelight cast by a lantern from an overhead tree branch. He was accompanied by Travis, Edmond, and a contrite Miss Rachel, who kept her eyes downcast.

"Well, Tezu, it seems we have finally come to that place where all roads lead: the end," Greer smiled as he looked Francis up and down. "You look fetching, by the by."

"You will not win," Francis said. "Even if we fall, others will take our place. You will never succeed!"

"I care not for the pronouncements of indigent savages," Greer declared. "History will be my judge! History and God Almighty!"

Greer raised a hand.

But before he could give the command for the revenants to advance, there was a commotion at the back of the circle of soldiers.

The sound was low at first, like the hum made by a swarm of bees. But it quickly grew in intensity, until it was clearly many voices singing as one,

> Go down Moses
> Way down in Egypt land
> Tell old Pharaoh
> To let my people go!

"Where does that singing come from?!" Greer demanded.

All eyes turned to find the slaves marching out of the woods. Ben was at the lead, with Tom and Andre and Haney and all the rest following. They raised up their clubs and shovels and other implements they had picked up along the way and marched in time to the song,

> Oh when Israel was in Egypt land
> Let my people go!
> Oppressed so hard, they could not stand
> Let my people go!

"Enough!" Greer bellowed. "Kill them. Kill them all!"

At the command, the revenants turned and lunged for the slaves. But they were prepared and met them head on, swinging axes and clubs as the soldiers bared their blunted teeth.

The slaves hacked their way through the first two rows of revenants before they managed to get their footing. But the revenants used their superior numbers to isolate the slaves into twos and threes and pick off individuals.

Tom spied Tristan leading a contingent of revenants against them.

"You lot!" the Overseer ordered, "Your general told ya to kill these good-for-nothin' slaves!"

Tom shoved him onto the ground. Tristan heaved himself to his feet and pulled the whip from around his waist.

"No," Tom whispered. His voice trembled as he raised it to a shout. "No more!"

Tristan drew back the whip but Tom was faster. He grabbed the whip and pulled Trsitan towards him, knocking off his balance. Tom spun Tristan and wrapped the whip around the Overseer's neck. Tristan yelled and spat and choked as Tom pulled the leather whip tighter.

"I said, no more!" Tom yelled. He pulled on that whip until Tristan's choking and gasping and cussing stopped. Tom let the body of the Overseer slump to the ground, his purple tongue lolling from a red face.

Jim offered Tom a hand up.

"You must be Miss Lizzy's brother," Tom wiped the dirt from his hand and offered it to Jim.

"Yes'r, that's me."

All further pleasantries would have to wait however, as a gang of revenants lunged out of the trees.

Andre, along with Conner, Sarah, and several of the maids were cornered by a team of Revenants. The lead soldier held a rifle with bayonet affixed and was edging them back towards the manse. As they neared the burning barn, Andre recognized the lead revenant.

"Samuel? Is it you?" Andre looked into the dead man's eyes.

Though he bore the features Andre knew well, there was no spark there. No familiar grin, no wrinkled brow when he was concentrating, no gleam of pride from a joke well told. Nothing of his friend remained there. And yet, Andre stood firm.

He looked his dead friend in the eye and said, "I know this ain't your doing. But I can't let this go no further."

The revenant that had been Samuel raised his rifle and advanced.

Andre managed to wrestle the rifle from his hands and threw it to the ground. He then hugged his friend tight.

"I ain't letting go!"

But Samuel kept marching forward. Andre dug his feet into the dirt and this slowed him but a little.

Connor and Sarah took the moment of confusion to grab discarded weapons and rushed the other revenants, dispatching them. They held off the advancing soldiers that were slowly plodding towards them, giving Andre room to try and reach Samuel.

Tom and Jim and Francis stood back to back, fighting revenants with sabers and knives. When one dropped a rifle, Tom picked it up, fired off a shot, and then turned it into a club.

Mercy, meanwhile, drove Abraham Lincoln hard into the revenant ranks, crushing them under hoof while she unloaded her shotgun, taking off revenant faces. She'd managed to clear a small area and help a dozen or so slaves fall back to a defended position, when she noticed Swann.

That blaggard had been in and out of her view throughout the battle, but she saw him now, walking off towards the barn carrying Tandy over one shoulder and dragging Haney by the wrist.

The poor girl fought back as best she could, but Swann was

twice her size and even with a squirming child over his shoulder, Haney was no match for his strength.

Mercy dismounted.

"Help hold the line, Mr. President!" she said.

"The fight must go on. The cause of civil liberty must not be surrendered at the end of one, or even one hundred defeats'," said the horse. He then kicked a Confederado in the chest, sending him flying backwards.

Mercy found Jim, trying to wrench his saber free from a pile of headless corpses.

"Jim! Swann is up to somethin'!"

"When is he not?" He yanked his saber free.

They ran to the barn in time to find Swann closing the door. Judging by the muffled yells it sounded like he'd put every child on the plantation into the barn.

He grabbed a jug of lamp oil and splashed it onto the door and all around.

"Talbot Swann, you son of a bitch!" Mercy ran for him, but he caught her blow and sent her tumbling into an adjacent pile of hay. He picked up a torch he'd set beside the barn.

Jim raised his saber, only for Swann to block him with the flaming torch.

"When you left me to wallow in that quicksand, I had plenty of time to dream up ways to kill you!" Swann said.

"That's funny cus I ain't given you another thought since!" Jim turned and opened a long gash along Swann's arm. Red sawdust spilled out but it did not stop or even slow his fight. Swann landed a punch to Jim's jaw, sending him reeling into a sudden twilight.

Swann raised his torch, only for a sudden report from a gun to freeze him in his path. Mercy had drawn her Navy Colt and shot him dead center.

A great gush of sawdust spilled out of Swann's belly. He still had enough wherewithal to throw the torch: the barn burst into flames.

Swann grinned and ran into the dark, holding his gaping belly closed with one hand. He barely made it a dozen steps though before another sharp pain slid into his chest.

He'd ducked into the wooded stretch between two fields, Which is where Francis had seen him and sat waiting in the shadows. He pushed the bayonet in all the way, till the tip exited Swann's back. Sawdust spilled out of him until he resembled nothing so much as a half assembled scarecrow.

"It were always gonna be you, weren't it?" Swann smiled ruefully as the light vanished from his black glass eyes.

Francis let his body slump into the shadows.

He ran to the barn, which was now completely engulfed in flames. From inside, Haney and Tandy and the rest of the children called for their mothers, for help. For anyone. Jim, Francis, and Mercy looked around for anything that might help. Jim found an old wagon under an elm tree.

"Give me a hand!"

Francis and Mercy ran to his side and together they pushed the wagon up to speed, enough at least to bring down the flaming barn door.

Francis and Mercy leapt into the burning barn and handed out the small children to Jim. By then, the sight of the conflagration had alerted several of the slaves, many of them the mothers who had been searching for their children. They ran to the smaller ones and cradled them in their arms.

Francis led Haney out as the barn fell in on itself.

Together, they made their way across the lawn, now a bloody, muddy battlefield strewn with corpses. Out of the smoke limped a few tired and injured slaves, and another familiar face.

"There's Miss lizzy!" Haney yelled.

Francis took Lizzy in his arms and they kissed.

"There's little time," Francis said. He turned to Haney. "Get Lizzy to safety!"

"Yes, Mister Francis," Haney took Lizzy's hand.

Which is when Lizzy gasped and shook. Haney and Francis helped her to her feet, Francis pausing to lop off the head of a revenant that broke through the ranks and lunged for them.

Lizzy's breath was ragged now but her convulsion subsided. "I think I'm in labor!"

"Oh, Nelly!" Haney took Lizzy's hands in hers. "Okay, Miss, let's get you comfortable…"

The trio of washerwomen came and helped Haney guide Lizzy back to the slave quarters.

"We'll take care of her," said one of the washerwoman, name of Jenny.

Francis kissed Lizzy again. "I will return."

Then he and Jim drew their weapons and raced back to the manse.

The confederates had drawn a circle around the slaves and were slowly drawing it closed. By the time Jim and Francis arrived with a handful of reinforcements, they had fallen back to a couple of shacks adjacent to the stables. Revenants would lunge out, only to get a hand or head lopped off, but the fighters would fall back as two more moved in to take the place.

Francis picked off two or three revenants at a time with invisible arrows, but there were still dozens more.

"And where have you two been?" Mercy said. She fired into the advancing ring of flesh.

"Lollygaggin'," Jim slid his saber through the neck of a revenant, sending him into a heap on the ground. Three more trod over their fallen comrade, oblivious. "Where's Charlie?"

"Last I saw him, he was heading 'round back with Tandy," said Tom. He'd found a brace of pistols and was firing them into the oncoming crowd.

"Someone call my name?" Charlie appeared beside Mercy and

Jim. He grinned wide.

Tandy was with him, holding Gordo in his arms.

"Now, Mr Charlie?" Tandy asked, all smiles.

"Almost, Tandy. I'd say we need three Mississippis,"

Tandy nodded and yelled, "One Mississippi!"

The revenant army pressed forward.

"Two Mississippi!"

The Confederados yelled orders to, "kill on sight!"

"Three Mississippi!"

Charlie yelled, "Hit the dirt!"

Jim and Mercy huddle behind an overturned wagon. All the fighters likewise took shelter behind planks of wood or huddled together on the ground as the powder magazine blew. A wave of fire washed over them, followed by a sound like thunder, then a rain of dirt clods and debris.

Jim stuck his head out from behind the overturned wagon, which was now smoldering. Mercy peered around the side as well. One by one, Francis and Charlie and then Tom and Tandy and all the rest found their feet.

The revenants had been obliterated by the conflagration. The few who had not been blown to smithereens, limped aimlessly around the field, starting small fires as they fell onto the ground, or collapsed onto the few remaining confederate officers, or one another.

The former slaves of Blanchefleur made short work of the remaining revenants and officers alike, showing them no mercy. General Greer retreated onto the porch where he dispensed orders to his officers. But the officers hesitated. They shouted contradictory orders, yelling for this platoon to fall back and that one to advance.

The confusion only grew when the surviving members of the Knights of the Golden Circle managed to claw their way onto the porch.

Fontleroy had collected his wits and shook Greer half senseless, shouting at him, "This is your grand plan for a new era, is it Greer?"

"Unhand me, Fontleroy!" Greer shoved the irate mayor away. "You will show respect to your savior!"

Fontleroy cackled. "You have saved nothing, Greer! This ghoulish display will not win us the day! You cannot even command your own house! And you expect to lead a nation?! Hogwash!"

"I'll show you hogwash!" Greer lunged for his former friend, only to be brought up short by the sight of Abraham Lincoln, bearing Ben the blacksmith crashing through the last line of revenants. He was joined by Tom and Mis Coffie, who led the remaining slaves to the lawn, where they quickly surrounded the porch. Jim and Mercy and the others joined them.

Travis had managed to find Miss Rachel and secured her on the porch, and stood beside the General along with her, one hand on his pistol, in case she caught a notion. Edmond was there as well, though he was preoccupied watching the carnage and trying to keep his supper down.

"Ah, there you are, Miss Rachel," Greer said, acknowledging her though she had been there for some time. "When I give the signal, you know what to do."

"I…" Miss Rachel hesitated. Closed her eyes and sighed. "Thy will, General."

Jim and Francis and Mercy arrived.

"It's done, Greer," Francis called out. "Surrender and we will be merciful."

"Surrender?" Greer chuckled. It was a rueful wind-through-the-trees kind of laugh. "I will not surrender. I did not at Appomattox. And I shall not in my own house, and never to some mob of... savages!"

Greer turned to Miss Rachel and nodded.

She stepped forward but stood stone faced on the porch, as if she was but another column.

"Go on Rachel," Greer commanded. "Raise up the slaves, and count them among the ranks of the vengeful dead!"

Rachel turned to face Greer, tears streaking her cheek. "I will not."

"Mutiny!" Greer hissed. "Hawkins, your pistol at the ready!"

Travis drew his sidearm and cocked it.

"Dispatch this sorceress, so that we may get on with this!"

Travis did not move though. He stood regarding Greer with a quizzical look.

"Mr. Hawkins," Greer's smile faltered. "I gave you an order. Perhaps you didn't hear it?"

"I heard you." Travis aimed and pulled the trigger, shooting Greer in the belly. "I just got other ideas."

The General looked more startled than hurt, at least until he slid down the post to sit on the front porch.

There came a roar of cheers from the slaves. But it was a short-lived victory.

Greer took from his finger the ring with the small green shard of a crystal embedded in it. He prized the crystal from the setting with his teeth and swallowed it.

Greer's face twisted in pain. But he did not scream or cry out, only laugh low and hollow. His eyes glowed green as fungus, green as the swamp, and the laughter that gurgled form his throat turned into a hissing, as he rose up.

But he did not stand as a man would. Instead he rose as if he were a marionette on strings, maneuvered by some invisible puppet master. Greer's skin rippled as something inside him writhed and his throat bulged as that thing rose out of his gullet.

Through his distended mouth emerged the head of a great snake, stretching the flesh of Greer's face til his lips split, making room for two short horns. The Serpent shed Greer like an old suit of skin, leaving the man gasping, broken on the boards of the porch.

The Horned Serpent reared up, taller than Jim, scales glistening wet with blood. The crystal in its forehead was now a single unbroken piece, and it gleamed with a terrible light all its own.

Everyone took a step back and involuntarily gasped at the sight of the creature. Fully twenty feet long, the Horned Serpent whipped its tail and made to strike at Jim, baring fangs as long as bayonets.

"You cannot defeat me," hissed the Serpent. "I am eternal! I am your malice and your fear. I will swallow every one of you! I am your doom!"

The Horned Serpent lunged for Jim. He dove out of the way, stabbing at the serpent's throat but the scales were as thick as armor and hard as diamond.

Francis circled around the cleared area on the lawn, looking for an opening to draw on the creature.

Jim dodged as the Serpent lunged, all fangs and malice. But every time he slashed at the creature with his saber, the scales deflected it. He crouched, winded. Waiting as the creature slithered around him in the shadows cast by flickering torches.

Jim recalled then his vision in the cave (*a stab of pain between his ribs as he felt the saber pierce his flesh...*) and knew what he must do.

"Francis!" Jim called. "Be ready!"

"I hear you, brother!" Francis drew back on his bow. Everyone there would later swear they saw an arrow appear there, bright as a star.

Jim rolled into a crouch before the serpent. But instead of dodging or ducking or rising up to fight, Jim laid his saber down in front of the enormous snake.

"You're right. I cannot fight you," he said. "You're a part of me. Part of all of us. And one day you may prove too strong for us to deny. But not today. You no longer have any power here, serpent. Be gone!"

The horned serpent reared up. Francis saw his opening and let the arrow fly.

The spirit arrow was a flash of light in the dark. A kiss of clarity. It pierced the Horned Serpent's throat, just below its jaw. The Serpent writhed and howled and hissed as it shrank.

The fear that had fed it, the hate that had enlarged it so, was gone from Blanchefleur. It fled the moment the slaves disobeyed. Now it was only as big as a boa, weaving away from the porch, slithering under foot. By the time it reached the edge of the woods, it was little more than a worm, there and gone. For now.

Mercy and Charlie and all the former slaves rushed in, cheering, and picked up Francis and hugged Jim. A cloud had lifted from Blanchefleur, and the night, which had seemed dark and airless, was now bright and the sky full of infinite stars.

Jim ran to Francis and embraced his brother.

"I knew you could do it, James!" Francis hugged him tight.

A pitiful moaning came from the porch.

Greer's body was wrecked and he drooled blood from his ripped mouth. Still, he managed to and pushed himself up into a sitting position, using the porch rail for support.

"Rachel..." he moaned, "work your ways, do not... do not abandon me now..."

He reached out a blood-slick hand. But Rachel did not take it. She stepped back from him, tears streaking her face.

"Take my hand!" Greer slurred.

"No," she said in a quavering voice, shaking with rage. "No more!"

Rachel took a deep breath and called out in a voice loud enough to rattle the stars a single command:

"STOP!"

The revenants stopped. Every single one of them that could stand, halted as if frozen by a chill North Wind.

"Quiet, all of you!" Rachel whispered. The world was still enough that this was all it took. Every living person there listened.

The Revenants exhaled as if they'd been holding their breath this whole time.

"Wonder what will happen to us now?" Finch asked.

Hoots groaned in resignation.

"Yeah, that's what I thought."

They and every other revenant soldier slumped to the ground, now no longer the instrument of Greer's torment. They were the departed once more, already long gone from this world.

Andre caught Samuel's body and laid him down on the grass. He held his friend and wept till they came to find him.

Charlie sat on the edge of the porch and balanced Gordo's skull on his knee. "Farewell, Gordo, my friend. Till we meet again."

Gordo was silent for a moment. Then the glow that illuminated his empty eye sockets flared like two tiny candles. "Where do ya think I'm going, abuelito?"

"Gordo!" Charlie smiled. "You decided to stick around?"

"Guess so," said the skull. "Appears I still got business here. Besides, we all know I'm the real brains of this operation."

Francis and Mercy and Tom and Ben and the rest all gathered on the porch around the General. Greer regarded them without pity or malice as he bled onto the boards.

"I have been… beaten," he whispered. "This world… has ruined me… and so… I leave it… to you."

General Elkanah Greer doffed his hat, and bowed his head. Then he slumped to the porch. And moved no more.

Francis spat on the dead man's boot.

Jim ran onto the porch and faced his brothers.

"Travis. Let's end this now."

Travis dropped the gun and ran into the house.

"Travis! Wait for me!" Edmond sputtered, and followed after his brother.

Jim ran up the steps after them.

Travis took the stairs two at a time. Edmond, never so fleet of foot, huffed and puffed as he paused on the second floor landing.

"Travis…" Edmond gasped. "We need… to talk about this…"

"Talk later!" Travis yelled as he ran to this room. "Pack now!"

"Pack?" Edmond climbed the last flight of stairs and wandered down the hall. "Pack what?"

Edmond stood in the doorway to Travis's room and gawped. Laid out on the dresser was a large carpet bag full of knick knacks: gold plated candelabras, silverware, a couple bottles of wine, and a tintype portrait of General Greer standing with Robert E. Lee.

"What is all this?" Edmond demanded.

"Our ticket out of here," Travis grabbed a sack of bills and threw them into the carpet bag. Edmond took them out and flipped through them.

"This is Confederate money. It is worthless." He glared at his brother. "You killed the General and have endangered countless lives, all for trinkets? What of Lizzy?"

"Lizzy can go hang with the rest of them," Travis said matter of factly, as if he was speaking of nothing more than which steer to take to slaughter.

"Does that sentiment go for me as well?" Edmond stared at his brother.

"Course not. If'n you got the sense to come with me. Hand me that book there on the nightstand."

Edmond wandered over and picked up the book. He was about to hand it to Travis when he read the cover: Ordinance of Secession and the Constitution of the Confederate States. It was bound in leather.

Edmond opened his mouth as if to say something but couldn't find the words, and so stood there like a codfish.

"Oh don't give me that dumb look," Travis said. "Lizzy was already lost to us when she ran off with that... Indian! Why you worrying about her now?"

"Because she is my family, Travis! And I may not have approved of Francis but I never wanted the man dead for it!"

"Now that's a lie," Travis snatched the book from Edmond. "It was you who brung that ol' huntin' rifle of yours. Now you're gonna stand here and tell me that was for scaring up supper on the trail?"

"I may have acted rashly at the time..." Edmond conceded. "But that does not excuse this!" He grabbed the carpet bag and tried to yank it free from Travis's grasp. He managed to spill half the contents onto the floor.

Travis grabbed the bag and stooped to stuff everything Edmond had pulled out back in. "This may not look like much, but there are folk who will pay a pretty penny for these. Think of it as seed money!"

"Seed money? For what?"

They turned to find Jim standing in the doorway.

Travis smiled. "Well slap me nekid and hide my clothes, lookit you. Why, if you ain't the prodigal son!"

"Come on Travis, you've had your fun. Time to pay the piper."

"Well now here's my youngest brother, back from the dead to deliver me some ol' chestnuts of wisdom. You think I'm gonna walk down those steps and hand myselves over to some mob of slaves, let them have their way with me?"

"You will walk, or I will carry you," Jim drew his saber. "But you're goin'."

"Fat chance!" Travis threw aside the pillow from the bed. He lunged for Edmond's old hunting rifle, which he'd stashed there. Came up, chambered a round and aimed.

By the time he lifted it to fire, Jim had run the three paces across the room.

He slid that blade into his brother's belly.

Travis squeezed the trigger only to find that neither he nor Edmond had bothered to reload. The rifle clattered to the floor. Jim drove the sword all the way in, until he and Travis looked one another in the eye.

"I thought the world of you, brother," Jim whispered.

He withdrew the saber.

Travis opened his mouth to say something but all that came out was a trickle of blood. He slumped to the floor and lay still.

Jim leaned against the door jam, looking at the blood dripping from the end of his sword. Edmond blubbered over their brother's body. But Jim paid him no mind. He walked down the hall, bloody sword dripping as he went.

Jim didn't remember walking down the steps, or crossing the foyer. Next thing he did recall, there was Mercy standing before him. She took one look at the bloody saber in his hand and knew what had happened. She hugged him tightly to her. Jim dropped the sword and held her tight, shaking as he sobbed into her shoulder.

"It's over now, Jim," she whispered to him. "It's done now."

Once Jim had emptied himself of his feelings and wiped his face, he felt hollow, and brittle. Like he might blow away on a breeze.

Mercy held him at arm's length and smiled. "Come on. Lizzy needs you."

They ran to the slave quarters.

Lizzy lay on the dirt floor, propped up on a pile of old woven mats while Miss Rachel, Charlie Snow Owl, and the three washerwomen tended to her. Francis knelt to one side, holding her hand. Haney was on her other side, helping to mop her brow and singing sweet songs. Charlie chanted and rubbed his necklace of charms, offering prayers to the Four Winds.

The washerwomen came and went. They carried in hot water and rags and shewed out the lookie loos who retreated to the doorway of the longhouse.

Jim and Mercy stood with them, right at the front. Lizzy screamed and Rachel commanded her to, "push!" Lizzy screamed some more, until her screams were replaced by a baby's cry. Then Jim and Mercy and the rest rushed in to see the new child, wrapped in rags, handed to her mother.

Francis grinned like a fool as every man there slapped him on the shoulder. Jim hugged him and he hugged Jim back.

Lizzy waved him over, "Meet your niece, Zuma Jane."

Francis took the baby and held her while Jim looked on. She had a shock of dark hair and looked crabby and exhausted, like every baby ever born. And as beautiful.

"Zuma Jane," Jim grinned. "Welcome to the world. I promise to make it better for you."

Rachel took Zuma Jane and handed her to Lizzy. She waved Francis and Jim over.

"See to the brides," Lizzy said.

Charlie and Mercy followed Jim and Francis out of the slave house, and into the yard. There, they found Shadow and Abraham Lincoln, and Sebastian waiting patiently. Francis stroked their manes and smiled.

"Thank you, friends."

"'The best way to predict the future is to create it'," said Abraham Lincoln.

Mercy fetched the jug of spirits from Abraham Lincoln's saddle.

Together the four of them marched up to the manse. Francis took the jug and emptied its contents onto the porch. Charlie found a tinderbox in his pouch. He struck it true and the sparks sent the porch up in an instant. They backed away, along with the gathering crowd to watch as Blanchefleur burned.

It didn't take long for the house to be consumed by the flames. The old wood, dry from the heat and the spite of its owner, gave up quickly, collapsing in on itself.

Someone yelled, "Look!"

They all looked into the second floor window. There, three figures in their bridal veils stood. The curtains were already aflame around them, lighting them up in silhouette. Though their faces were obscured by shadow and smoke, Francis knew those faces. Jim did as well. He watched as they waved farewell as the flames took the house.

The roof caved in, exhaling a great sigh of smoke. Out of the smoke blinked first one then dozens, then hundreds of tiny fireflies. They drifted into the night sky and blinked out.

18
Where All Roads Lead

That night, they lit bonfires that burned like day, illuminating their new world. The slaves, now free, gathered the revenant corpses and burned them in great pyres, uniforms and all. The largest conflagration burned there on the lawn beside the smoldering husk of the manse, but there were more out in the fields, like beacons lighting the way towards freedom.

The realization of what had happened and what they had been denied swept over them in waves of grief and elation—for while there was much to celebrate, there was also much to mourn.

Miss Rachel and the others gathered their fallen dead and carried them by torchlight to the old graveyard. This place had been the last resting spot for the slaves of Blanchefleur for generations, and though they were now free souls, every one of them, there was nowhere else they wanted to bury their dead. Two of the footmen had perished, as had a maid, and half a dozen field hands. But the honored place at the head of the procession was the body of Samuel, the blacksmith's apprentice. The washerwomen had removed the accursed uniform he had been conscripted into and tossed it without reservation into the bonfire. Then they dressed him in finery procured from the General's own wardrobe.

They lowered him into the grave dressed in a silk cravat and dinner jacket, like the fallen prince they would all remember him as.

The ceremony was led by Miss Rachel and attended by all. She stood at the head of Samuel's grave as Ben and Andre and a couple of the field hands and the two surviving footmen lowered him into the grave.

"We lay our dead down to sleep forever more," Miss Rachel intoned. "In the hope of one day seeing them again when we all wake from this beautiful and tragic dream called life."

Andre next spoke.

"There ain't nothin' I can say to bring back my friend—my brother," he said, choking back the tears. "There's a hole left where he used to fill up with jokes and words that consoled me and made me want to be a better man. And I tell you now, Samuel, wherever yo is, that I'm gonna be that better man, so one day we'll see each other again."

Then they placed him beside the rest of their dead, to sleep forevermore.

When they were through, Charlie and Mercy joined the Hawkins siblings in the little churchyard. There, Edmond prayed over Travis's body, which had been pulled from the wreckage of the burning manse. They buried him in his snakeskin boots. No one said a word.

Afterwards, Lizzy and Jim escorted Edmond to the potting shed, where two stout field hands were set as guards. Edmond was ushered inside. Robbe was already seated there on one of the cots.

"Reverend Hawkins. I see you have come to take counsel with the sinners. Welcome."

"I do not see why I should be treated this poorly," Edmond whimpered. "After all, it was not I who masterminded your torments. If anything, I was as much a victim in all this."

"You truly believe that, don't you?" Lizzy met his eye. This was not easy in the flickering lamplight, which shifted as much as Edmond's gaze.

"I…"

A hard look from Jim rendered him silent. "Go on. Tell yourself more lies, as you tell them to us."

"I would never lie, James!" Edmond sniffed. "You know me."

"I know you too well, brother," Jim said. "And I know that while you may not have masterminded this affair, you were quick to follow Travis into this fool endeavor with Greer."

"I did it all to protect Lizzy," Edmond declared. "You must know this!"

"And what of me?" Jim roared. He grabbed Edmond by the lapels of his jacket and shook him. "What about your little brother? You did nothing as they tied a noose around my neck!"

Jim," Lizzy laid a hand on his shoulder. Jim let go of Edmond and walked away, only to pause and turn back.

"Some part of you may have known you were committing abominations. And maybe while you sit in here, you'll listen to that part of you that knew better and still turned yella."

Jim walked away then. Lizzy hugged Edmond and then left the potting shed. They shut the door and locked it.

"Obviously we can't leave him in that shed forever," Lizzy said as Jim helped her back to the old slave quarters, where the rest had gathered.

"Can't we?" he made a face and sighed. "Guess not."

But what to do, not just with Edmond and Robbe, but with themselves, that took some thought. Tom and Miss Rachel and the rest called a meeting in the old yard between the longhouses. Many summer nights had been spent here, looking at the stars as they ate their meager meals. Tonight, under those same stars, there was now a feast, which had been liberated from the ruins of the kitchen.

Tom stood at the head of the table and raised a mug half full of ale. It had already been refilled a few times, and he swayed more than a little.

"I want to take a moment—quiet now!" He laughed.

The talk about the tables quieted down.

"Now I ain't one for big speeches, but this is a special occasion, and I thought it best we marked it as such with a few words."

Tom held up his mug. Everyone raised a glass of their own.

"May the Four Winds guide us to our destinations, and let our own feet carry us there for we surely are free folk now. Free as the birds!"

The entire place burst into cheers.

"And we will remain free, so long as we see in each other's faces that hurt and fear we all used to know and seek to correct it," Miss Rachel added.

Tom drained his mug and everyone else did the same.

It wasn't long before what was intended to be a sober and solemn commemoration of the night's events turned into a swinging party. Though there were some important revelations that did come of it.

Of the forty souls who survived, about half intended to stay on the land, and build a new community. They'd do the hard work of living free right here. In that way, they could turn this palace of woe into a free, equitable, and just place, where all souls who were in want of a place to call their own could feel safe.

To this end, Tom and Miss Rachel were elected by show of hands (and unanimous hollerin') to the places of honor, elders leading this new community.

After a quick meeting of the minds between the new elders and the council of every other folk, Tom raised his tankard once more.

"We've been talkin', and we don't know if you got other plans, but if you were of a mind to, Miss Lizzy and Mr. Francis—"

"And baby Zuma Jane!" Interrupted Miss Coffie.

"—right, and baby Zuma Jane," Tom raised his mug to the babe in her mother's arms. "We wanted to offer you an invitation to stay here with us. It won't be easy work, but at the end of the day, you'll have a place of your own and all the stars above to call your home."

Lizzy and Francis shared a moment's look and that's all it took.

"We would be happy to help turn this place into our home," Lizzy said.

As for the others who wanted to get out and see the world, which included Ben and Andre, Mercy made the grand offer of leading them to Tulsa, where she had kin.

"They're buildin' a right noble little place there, where free folk and former slave alike can be happy. If'n ya'll want, and if'n young James Hawkins will help me wrangle you along the way, we could lead you there."

A wave of cheers swept the tables; Jim and Mercy looked at one another, quite sozzled both, and nodded.

"I'd be happy to join you, Mercy Nightingale, Ma'am," said Jim.

"There he goes, calling me ma'am again."

They toasted tankards amid a round of cheers.

Soon after, Francis built a tent on the edge of the bonfire where he and Lizzy and Zuma Jane could get comfortable for the night. The celebration would have to go on without them.

Charlie found an old drum and with Tom and some of the field hands, they found the rhythm of freedom in their blood, and set about making music.

Everyone took up partners and set to dancing. Even Andre cheered up when the former maid, Sarah came and took his hand. Haney and the Tandy and other children formed a ring and danced in circles.

Jim and Mercy found themselves dancing together and holding one another close, the electricity between them intolerable, until Mercy pulled Jim close and kissed him. They wandered off to find a quiet spot together. Everything after that was a blur of lips and skin and revelation.

In the morning, Jim woke to find a web of tree limbs holding up the bright blue roof of the morning sky overhead. It took him a moment to remember that he and Mercy had fallen asleep together in a hammock strung between two oak trees. The rest that passed between them he also recalled and it made him blush.

Jim disentangled himself from Mercy and the hammock as nimbly as he could, and made his way to the smoldering coals that was all that remained of last night's bonfire. There didn't appear to be any other soul awake yet, which suited Jim; he liked those quiet moments before the morning hubbub, when he could be alone with his thoughts.

After a trip to the outhouse, he performed his morning ablutions at a water pump. By then, the fire had been renewed and others were clearly up and about, as the smell of bacon cooking and coffee boiling filled the air.

In the pocket of his waistcoat, Jim found his watch, which he had forgotten about. It had wound down and stopped, now telling the time for a place Jim felt he would never see again.

"Jim, there you are!" It was Andre calling his name.

"Morning," Jim smiled. Then he clocked the severity of the look on Andre's face. "What is it?"

"Best you come see," Andre said.

Jim followed him to the potting shed. The two guards were there, along with Tom, standing in the doorway. Inside, Robbe sat on his cot. He looked like he had barely moved since the previous night. But Edmond was nowhere to be seen.

"...Now, Robbe, you gotta tell us all you know," Tom was saying as Jim walked up.

"I have said everything there is to say," Robbe muttered.

Jim stuck his head into the potting shed and surveyed the lack of his brother.

"What happened?"

"As I was telling Elder Tom here," Robbe straightened his cravat, "Reverend Hawkins absconded in the night."

"Absconded?" Jim sighed, "If a had a nickel for every time one of my siblings done that…"

From Robbe's account of the events, they were able to reconstruct Edmond's subterfuge. As prison escapes went, this one would not go down in the history books for innovation, guile, or bravado. He'd simply waited until the guards had fallen asleep before climbing out the narrow window, which was only secured by chicken wire nailed to the wooden window frame. This had all happened sometime before dawn.

"And I suppose you weren't invited?" Tom asked Robbe.

"I did not wish to impose myself upon him," Robbe said.

By the time they returned to the longhouse, everyone was awake, including Lizzy and Francis. Mercy and Charlie were there too, sitting around the table as the food was served. While they ate, they discussed the situation. Though in all honesty, there was little to discuss.

"We can't have him running back home and telling the authorities about the particulars of last night's events," Charlie surmised. "There'd be no end to the headaches that would soon follow."

Everyone mumbled in agreement.

What was also in agreement was who should be the one to do the thing though that was something they all were reluctant to put voice to, on account of the sadness wrapped up in it.

Eventually Jim said, "I will go after him. He's my brother. My responsibility."

Jim took a gulp of his coffee and then made ready to leave.

"You don't gotta do this," Lizzy said. She held baby Zuma Jane in her arms.

"If not me, then who? If he reaches home, or some town nearby and tells folk what happened here... You and Francis would never be safe. None of you would. The authorities would follow you 'round the world for the sin of bein' free. And I can't live with that."

"I will come with you," Francis said.

Lizzy nodded in agreement, though she looked pained at the

idea of separating from him again so soon.

"No," Jim shook his head. "Lizzy and the baby need you here."

Jim offered Francis a hand. He pulled Jim into a hug.

"And we need you," Lizzy said.

Mercy shook her head in agreement.

"I know. But it has to be me. And I have to go alone. I know where he's headed and I think I can find him the quickest. Sebastian knows these roads well and the horse will help speed my travels. Besides," Jim smiled at Lizzy. "You know I have to be the one. And don't you worry. I'll be back before she's even said her first word."

He hugged her. Then he stroked Zuma Jane's cheek. She was asleep and snorted a little, then smiled at his touch.

"Sounds like a vow you're making," said Mercy. "Now why would you go and do a dang fool thing like that?"

Jim smiled at her. "A man is only as good as his word, but words don't mean nothin' without the deeds to back them up. I swear on the Four Winds, I'll find that wayward brother of mine, and set things right."

He fetched his saddlebags and proceeded to stuff them full of what food might travel best—a few rolls, some hard cheese and skin of water. Jim packed all his gear onto Sebastian's saddle, including his saber.

Tom and the rest of the free folk of Blanchefleur came to see him off.

Charlie laid a hand on his shoulder. "May the Four Winds guide you to where you belong," he said.

"Thank you Charlie," Jim smiled at the old man. "You keep a count of those eggs, and I'll be back soon!"

Charlie held Gordo. Jim patted the skull like a puppy. "You keep an eye on these fools for me Gordo, yeah? Make sure nothin' goes too awry."

"¡No promises, muchacho!" Gordo said.

Jim looked at Mercy one last time. "I'm coming back."

"You're a bad liar, James Hawkins," Mercy said. She kissed him.

Once Jim had triple-checked his pack, he climbed into Sebastian's saddle and headed for the road.

Jim did glance back twice.

Once when all his friends and family were still within sight and he could see them wave to him, passing their luck on the wind.

The second time he looked, they were too far behind him, as he'd already set out onto the road.

Jim rode alone for days, with nothing but the rising and setting of the sun to mark him. He was his own clock, counting hours by the position and length of his shadow.

His whole world was scrub brush, mud, and his thoughts. Soon, even these became as empty as the wind blowing through the trees, which were now red and gold and brushed by autumn's cold breath.

When his horse, delirious and overworked, got turned around in the middle of the night sometime between the fifth and sixth day, and he'd lost all sense of direction, Jim found himself standing under a great starry sky, unsure which way to turn.

Jim had never had much use for religion and didn't know anymore if half of what he'd seen was truth or lies, but in this desperate hour, lost and in search of his brother, Jim Hawkins turned his face up to the heavens.

"Oh, Great Thunderbird, hear my prayer. Take pity on this lost soul and show him the way home."

A rumble of thunder swelled out of the clear night sky. From the West rolled in a cloud bank, big as the night and wide enough to blot out the moon. The cloud bank rolled on ahead of Jim, lightning striking in the distance, marking the path some giant might take, but heading East.

At that moment, Jim would later swear he saw the shape of a

giant bird in those thunderclouds. And the lightning and thunder led him on, straight and true.

A week later, when the trees looked like they were on fire and the autumn sun shone at that particular angle that says the seasons are turning for good and all, Jim staggered into a town that looked somewhat familiar. It wasn't until he saw the wooden sign that read: *Welcome to Pawhuska* that he realized he'd reached his destination.

Jim stabled his horse and headed out only to find Sheriff John Two Wolves there at the barn door to greet him.

"Hawé, James Hawkins. Long time," he said. He did not smile.

"Is he here?" Jim said in a voice whose timbre and hollowness startled him.

"He is," said the Sheriff.

Jim followed the Sheriff through the muddy streets of Pawhuska. The townsfolk went about their business like he wasn't even there. He'd become some phantom of the road, best ignored for fear of what ill omen might ride with him.

Jim found his brother at *Hattie's Saloon*. He sat at a table in the corner, looking for all the world like some wayward soul, searching for a quiet moment in the bottom of a mug. And perhaps that was the worst indignity of all, Jim would later decide.

"Edmond," Jim said. "Been looking for you."

"And you have found me, brother." Edmond finally looked up at his brother. He wrinkled his brow in astonishment. "James? You've certainly changed."

Jim rubbed the beard that had grown over the weeks of his wayward wandering and mad pursuit. "Guess I have."

Jim sat at the table across from him.

Sheriff Two Wolves nodded and retired to the bar, but kept a weather eye on them the rest of the evening.

"You come to take me back to that place?" Edmond asked after a while. He looked like he was about to cry at the idea. "Am I to stand frontier justice, then?"

"Far as anyone is concerned, you've paid your dues. But we can't have you making mischief neither, so I come to take you home."

"And why would I go back there?" Edmond looked at Jim. His eyes were glassy and distant. Lost didn't begin to describe his look. Untethered would be more precise; untethered and rushing down some river, bound who knew where.

"We got to tell Ma and Pa what happened. About Lizzy. And Travis."

Edmond laughed. It was a hollow sound, dry as the brown leaves rustling on the street. He emptied his mug.

"And tell them what? That our Lizzy married her savage prince? That they rode off to live in the wild world? That Travis... That their oldest son will not pass this way again? And for what? What was it all for anyway, James, do you know? Because I have been sitting here for a day now thinking, and I can not find a reason for any of it."

"It's an unlikely story, to be sure. But the truth of it will make it plain."

"Ah, the plain truth!" Edmond thumped the Bible which sat on the table, battered, dog-eared, and tattered. "I dedicated myself body and soul to the one and only Truth. But I saw so little of it on our journey that if the Truth stood before me now, I would not recognize it."

"Right. Well, that's enough feeling sorry for yourself, Edmond. You have a duty to perform and I aim to hold you to it. I know it doesn't seem like it now, but when we get closer to home and away from this place, you'll find your Truth again."

"Oh? And you are sure it will go like that, huh?" Edmond said. "Go home and all will be right, as the day follows the night?"

"Didn't say that. This whole experience has marked a change in us, to be sure. But it was bound to before we ever left. I told you as much when we were sitting in Mrs. Whatsername's dining room, over that ham, you remember? You and Travis were bound and determined to run off and kill a man. Now it turns out things didn't go as planned. But we set ourselves on this path. Weren't anyone else's doing but our own."

"I only did what was asked of me, James, you know that, do you not?" Edmond's voice was thin and shaking like it had come loose from whatever place normally kept it secured inside of him.

"I know, Edmond," Jim said. "And so will Pa."

They sat there for some time in silence. Jim ordered two plates of the special, and Aunt Mary brought them along by and by. Jim ate heartily, having had little to eat while on the Switch these last days. Edmond barely touched his food but drank another two mugs of ale.

Before long a show took to the tiny stage opposite the door of the saloon and the crowd grew loud and raucous. Jim thought perhaps the vibrant atmosphere would be good for Edmond, at least light that Puritan's fire in his belly, set him to a full head of steam about the lewd and lascivious ways of the world.

But Edmond sat there joyless and silent while the girls danced.

After the show ended and the girls all bowed and blew kisses and disappeared in a swirl of chintz and taffeta, the Sheriff returned to their table.

"James, it's getting late," he said.

"That it is, Sheriff."

Jim secured a room upstairs and with help from the Sheriff, they managed to lead Edmond up the steps and into bed.

"Think he'll be right again, Sheriff?" Jim asked.

"I've seen my share of morose drunkards before but he's got something else the matter with him," said John Two Wolves. "Seen it once or twice in those folk who go out into the Switch and come back again."

"Did they recover from it?" Jim asked.

Sheriff John Two Wolves was quiet for a moment. Then he

said, "The Switch changes a person, that's for sure. For good or ill, well that's not for me to say. A man's gotta stand up and take account of his actions, one way or the other."

Jim nodded. "Thank you, Sheriff. I'll take it from here."

The Sheriff shook Jim's hand and left. Jim pulled a chair over and sat it beside the bed. He stayed up all night by his brother's side.

Sometime before dawn, Lizzy came into the room quietly, like she had when Jim was a boy, coming to wake him for church on Sunday mornings. He smiled to see her here in the spare little room over the saloon in Pawhuska. But his smile faltered when she wiped a tear from her eye.

"See to Edmond," Lizzy kissed him on the forehead.

Jim woke to find himself alone. The room was filled with that somber blue light that creeps in slowly as the sun rises. Stiff from sleeping in the chair by the bedside, Jim took a moment to stretch his limbs. Out of the corner of his eye, he thought he saw someone through the window, in the street below—a dark figure on horseback racing away into the predawn gloom. But when he turned to look, there was nothing there.

Jim turned around to find that the bed Edmond had slept in was made up all tidy, with a note folded neatly on the pillow. Jim plucked the note from the pillow and read it:

Dear Father,
Please forgive me. I did what I thought was righteous and just, but it was not enough to save poor Lizzy, nor Travis. I hope you will remember me ~~with fondness~~ as the dutiful son who went to Hell in search of his siblings. Tell Jim and the rest that I forgive them.
Your son,
Edmond

There came a shout and a clatter of footsteps below.

Jim ran onto the landing. His heart thudded in his chest as he took the steps two at a time. But he knew what he would find, even before he reached the saloon.

Edmond had waited until Jim fell asleep. He'd waited until the last customer left the saloon, the gas lights were dimmed, and the proprietor retired for the night. Then he found some rope behind the small stage where the dancers had turned a burlesque the night before.

It seemed the whole town was there in that saloon by the time Jim arrived, though in truth it was the owner, the barkeep, and Sheriff Two Wolves. The Sheriff and the barkeep helped Jim lower Edmond's body from the chandelier. The Sheriff likewise helped Jim tie the body to a horse, using the same rope Edmond had tied for his noose.

He walked slowly beside Jim, who led the horses.

At the edge of town, Sheriff Two Wolves said, "I'm sorry for your loss, James Hawkins."

Jim nodded in thanks and mounted his horse.

"We were lost before we even began," he said.

Then James turned the horses towards Texarkana and set out at a slow, even pace.

The road was long and quiet and gave Jim time to reflect on matters. He realized that his time in the Switch had changed him, just as Mercy had said it would. Whether for the better or worse was not for him to say. The Four Winds knew and one day, perhaps so would he.

Acknowledgements

Along the way, several people indulged me in this feverish and silly endeavor, so in no particular order, here is who to blame: Jason Love, for reading an early version of this story when it was a script and suggesting it should be a book instead. My wife, Elvira, who was as surprised as I was to learn that jeans really are that old; this led to many an odd and fascinating historical fact being uncovered and the story is richer for it. To Jennifer Arnson, for reading an early draft and giving moral support. To Chris Braak and Jess Nevins, for many a socially mediated conversation about craft, genre, and all those other fine things that make us want to stare at a blank page until we begin to hallucinate. To my father, Edward, and Father-in-law, Ben, for always having old westerns on in the background. Years of listening to Clint Eastood and John Wayne being gruffly ignoble finally drove me round the bend, in a good way.

About The Author

Keith Edwards lives in Texas, where he works as a librarian. His love of the weird and the strange started at a young age, when he looked over the hedge in his backyard and saw fairyland instead of his neighbor's swimming pool. Ever since, he has been trying to rediscover the initial wonder at that glimpse of the beautiful and the tragic, the wild and the inexplicable.

Made in the USA
Coppell, TX
08 December 2025

64601228R00187